Maverick
M.D.

James W. Forsythe, M.D., H.M.D.

with Wayne Rollan Melton

Maverick MD

Copyright (c) 2016, By James W. Forsythe, M.D., H.M.D., and Wayne Rollan Melton

Forsythe, James W. M.D., H.M.D
Melton, Wayne Rollan

Book Design: Patty Atcheson Melton

1. Fiction 2. General

All rights reserved. No part of this book may be reproduced or transmitted in any form or by any means, electronic or mechanical, including photocopying, recording, email, text messaging or by any information storage or retrieval system, without permission in writing from the authors. Although loosely based in part on actual events, Maverick MD is a work of fiction and entirely the product of the authors' imaginations. The incidents and dialogues, including those involving living individuals, are not to be construed as real.
Any perceived similiarity to any person, living or dead, is strictly a coincidence.

ISBN:9781535242202

Dedication

To all my many patients, alive and dead, that I have treated during the last 50 years with both conventional and integrative medicine. I applaud their bravery in seeking alternative therapies, venturing beyond the boundaries of standard, Big Pharma-controlled medicine--in many instances despite criticism from relatives and friends. To my wife, family and friends for their support, and to Wayne Rollan Melton and Patty Melton for their talent and expertise in this venture.

Contents

One.....9

Two.....18

Three.....27

Four.....40

Five.....44

Six.....51

Seven.....68

Eight.....8

Nine.....89

Ten.....104

Eleven.....115

Twelve.....125

Thirteen.....137

Fourteen.....151

Fifteen.....175

Sixteen.....185

Seventeen.....205

Eighteen.....221

Nineteen.....236

Twenty.....259

Twenty-one.....277

Twenty-two.....301

Twenty-three.....312
Twenty-four....330
Twenty-five.....343
Twenty-six.....357
Twenty-seven.....361
Twenty-eight.....379
Twenty-nine.....389
Thirty.....406
Thirty-one.....417
Thirty-two.....432
Thirty-three.....440
Thirty-five.....444
Epilogue.....453
About The Authors.....456
Contact Information.....458

One

Tommy knelt beside the dark gray casket.

"Mommy, I'm mad at you for going away," this child thought, his hands clasped in a classic prayerful position. "Please never leave me ... Stay with us."

At that moment, the child felt a hand on his left shoulder.

The soft, gentle, loving touch from his father contrasted the boy's senses of darkness, despair and fear.

"Son, it's time for us to leave," Abe Davis said. "People are waiting for us at the church. Everyone is there to say goodbye to your mother."

The father and son were surrounded by 17 family members and close friends in the living room of the family's small home.

A cold, harsh and uncaring desert wind blew outside, its unwelcome whistling exactly 15 days after Polly Davis's final Christmas.

"No, dad," Tommy bristled, pushing his father's broad and strong hand away. "Mommy wants to stay here with us. There is no reason to say goodbye to her."

Through the large living room window, dozens of parked cars could be seen on Tranquility Avenue. Until that day, nine cars were the most Tommy had seen at any given moment on their isolated and rarely traveled residential street. Affectionately known by his friends as simply "Honest," without ever mentioning the word "Abe," the father then knelt beside his son.

"Tommy, remember, this is how your Mommy wanted today to be," the father whispered into his son's ear. "She wants us to take her to the church, so that everyone can say a final goodbye to her. And, she wants you to go with us."

The boy remained motionless.

Tears meandered down the child's cheeks, each droplet

plopping like a lonely raindrop onto the cherry wood floor--handcrafted 20 years earlier by his father.

"Please don't tell Mommy that I am crying," Tommy whispered back.

"Son, you are a good, strong young man and I am proud of you," Honest said, his voice still in a whisper. "It's OK to cry ... Your mother knows that you are brave."

*

At age 5, Tommy kept thinking that "I need to behave like a man, because that's the way Mommy told me to be on this day ... and for the rest of my life."

Instead of slouching as usual with his shoulders slumped forward, this time the boy sat at full attention. He tried to imitate his favorite Nutcrackers.

There in the back seat of the Davis family's 8-year-old white 1967 Pontiac station wagon, while en route to Saint John's Methodist Church, Tommy sat beside his two little sisters--one on each side of him.

Dressed in a fluffy yellow dress made the previous night by their Aunt Pamela, little 3-year-old Penelope dutifully sucked her thumb--as was her usual habit. Her left arm tightly clasped her favorite doll, which she called "Pee-pee."

*

On the other side of Tommy sat his 4-year-old sister Peggy, who had already gained a solid reputation as the town's boisterous tomboy.

Earlier that morning, little Peggy had screamed at the top of her lungs, from Tommy's perspective louder than a rambling train.

At the time--about a half-hour before breakfast, and one hour before their departure for the church--he had wanted to scream at her to "Shut up!" But to his great credit, the boy used every bit of willpower he could muster to refrain from doing so. A kindergartner, Tommy remained cognizant of the fact his mother would want him to behave like an angel on the day they would bury her.

"I do not want to wear a dress!" Peggy screamed at her two aunts, who collectively insisted that she wear a delightful red dress--sewn for her the previous night, just like tiny Penelope's had been. "I want my overalls!"

Thanks to a arduous non-stop effort that took 12 minutes, the determined ladies managed to put the new garment on little Peggy, despite her non-stop wailing and flailing.

For added measure, the women also hid her overalls in a cubby-hole inside a run-down shed in the backyard of the Davis family home.

"You are evil!" Peggy screamed, as Tommy's kindergarten teacher--Mrs. York--began setting the family's breakfast table--there to help.

"Where in the world did a cute, adorable little girl like you learn that word--'evil?' Aunt Paula asked, cradling an arm around little Peggy when the girl finally calmed down. "All of us love you, and we are here to take good care of you."

Peggy responded by scowling.

Her face reminded little Tommy of a wrinkled old prune.

As the boy stood beside the breakfast table, he resisted a strong temptation to mock Peggy for wearing what he considered a "stupid-looking red dress."

The boy knew that his newly-deceased mother would want him to remain on his best behavior--particularly on that morning. This marked a drastic change from when she was alive, his typical demeanor then usually rambunctious and downright obnoxious.

During the previous few years, Tommy had earned what most residents of that tiny high-desert town, Centralia, Nevada, considered a well-deserved reputation as a mischievous rabble rouser.

Even so, on this particular overcast morning, Tommy tried to behave as if a saint--fully aware that his mother lay in the casket--just 18 feet away in the living room.

*

Early on the day that she finally lost consciousness for the last time, Polly Davis had weakly whispered her dying wishes to her husband.

"Please keep..." she initially said, her voice fading.

"What do you mean, darling?" Honest gently hugged her on their bed--as the children lay fast asleep in their nearby bedrooms.

At precisely 85 pounds, mere bones and skin, Polly struggled to speak her final requests.

"Christmas..." she uttered, unable to speak clearly due to extreme frailty, her head bald from four months of extremely painful and useless chemo treatments.

From Honest's perspective, on that morning her once-glowing skin seemed as white as snow--void of any meaningful life.

"What about Christmas, honey?" He instinctively lifted her into a sitting position. She had lain on her back the entire morning until then. "Today is Christmas Eve."

Suddenly, as if a brief new life-giving energy had been deeply infused in her, Polly generated enough energy to speak; her next several sentences would become the final statements that she would make in her 32-year life.

"Honest, please listen carefully to my every word." Polly tightly squeezed her husband's hand as she spoke, sending proverbial lightning bolts of surprise into his entire body and psyche. She had been unable to lift even a spoon during the previous month, let alone eat.

In keeping with his usual habit, he spoke openly and respectfully--yet in this instance careful to hide his own nagging fears and worries: "My love, Polly, I am all ears--nothing but ears. Anything for you, even though you and I both know I have been far from the world's best listener since the day we married."

Polly motioned that she wished to lay flat on her back again. He immediately complied, although instinctively convinced that sitting would be the best position for her.

"Honest, do this for me. Keep the Christmas decorations

up, in place until my body leaves this house for the final time." She managed a wide, broad smile while Honest held back a flood of tears, convinced that his wife of 10 years was finally accepting her inevitable demise. "I want our house to be filled with love, joy and hope for as long as possible--even long after I'm gone from this earth."

"Please, you do not have to talk that way, Polly, about what is going to happen to ...."

As soon as Honest spoke these words, he realized that his own declaration had sounded somewhat odd--at least when considering the fact that during the previous few weeks he had gently tried to get his wife to acknowledge and accept her impending death.

And now, of all things, here he was putting himself into a sudden state of denial.

"Another thing, Honest," she said, just as vibrant as before, squeezing his hand even harder. "Please find peace in your heart. Find solitude. Find grace, and find love. Accept those things into your life ... And please ... Please ... Oh, please, let your anger fall by the wayside."

"Anger?" he said, gently kissing Polly's forehead--the touch of which made his lips feel as if his wife had finally dropped her fears. "I have no anger toward anyone. I have always been a loving, kind and forgiving man--you of all people should know that, my sweetness."

For the first time in many weeks, Polly had the strength, determination and gumption enough to look her husband eye-to-eye.

In her gaunt face, he saw forgiveness--a forgiveness toward the disease, a forgiveness toward her own faults, and perhaps most of all a forgiveness for his own imperfections as well--particularly his occasional ineptitude in helping to guide her through the treatment process.

"Honest, you need to release your anger toward my cancer doctor, the oncologist," she said, still smiling--so broad and loving that at least momentarily in Honest's eyes this dying lady looked once again like a healthy young woman in her late teens. "You need to forgive Doctor Robbins, and know that he did his very best, and..."

"But I hate what..."

"The time for hate is gone. All that should be left now is love and acceptance, the same lessons that we all must learn. ... The doctor has done the very best that he can do; he is highly professional, and no one could do better..."

"But he ... If I could only give him a piece of my mind, to tell him how angry..."

"Honest, you are better than that. You need to release your mind and your body of all hate. You are the strongest person I have ever known, the greatest wise man possible in your heart and in your instinctive wisdom--at least most of the time. Listen carefully to your soul, and you will learn that to forgive the doctor is the most noble and best thing. Our entire town needs Doctor Robbins, and everyone in this community needs you, too--most notably our children ..."

"Honey," he squeezed her hand. "You are losing your strength again. So, listen, I have to admit that I actually have hated that doctor--yet maybe you are right. Maybe I should forgive, release my anger, and..."

"Forgiveness is the only way, Honest, I love you--always."

The moment she finished speaking these words, Polly Davis closed her eyes for the last time--13 days before her death, which finally came mercifully and with ample solitude on January 6, 1975, the Epiphany.

*

From little Tommy's perspective, everyone in his extended family seemed to understand and respect his mama's final wish-- that all the Christmas ornaments remain on display in their house until her final day at home.

On January 9, the day that the casket containing Polly's body was finally removed from the living room, all the holiday knickknacks still remained in place there.

Besides the Christmas tree that Honest and his three children had cut in early December, the boy's favorite decorations were the eight 3-foot-tall Nutcrackers that Polly had purchased as a child, and an angel atop the tree that reminded him of his mother.

Although tattered, in this child's eyes that figurine featuring broad wings and a glowing wand could not possibly have been any more brilliant--something marvelous enough to generate envy and ample praise.

*

"I've got to throw up," Peggy said, still in the back seat of their Pontiac station wagon while en route to their church for her mother's funeral.

"Really?" Honest slowed the car to nearly a full stop, while briefly turning around to see his three children in the back seat.

Immediately up ahead of them, the hearse driver continued without letup, the driver apparently oblivious to the grieving family's plight.

Upon seeing his daughter's beet-red face, Honest stopped the Pontiac, and all the many vehicles behind them on Main Street also halted.

"Dad, I'm afraid she's not kidding," Tommy declared, while wiggling past his ailing sister in the back seat--before quickly opening the rear curb-side passenger door. "She is about to puke her guts out ... Get ready."

Honest shifted to park and then he got out and ran around the front of the vehicle. Meantime, almost as if a highly trained emergency medical technician--rather than a child--Tommy helped Peggy stumble out of the vehicle. Her usually energetic legs moved haphazardly, as if those of a old marionette.

Within mere seconds, the 4-year-old's incessant retching finally caught up with her; she threw up in the newly swept gutter.

Far more polite and gentlemanly than usual, Tommy resisted making fun of his favorite little enemy--primarily because he still instinctively knew that his mom would have wanted him to behave as if a Perfect Angel on this particular day--rather than his usual devilish self.

By the time their father reached them, Peggy's undigested breakfast from just a half hour earlier had already begun to slosh down the otherwise sparkly clean gutter. Always curious and intrigued by such things, Tommy paid particular attention to the remnants of fresh strawberries, fluffy pancakes, maple syrup and milk.

"Yaak! Aww!" poor little Peggy wailed and moaned as she continued puking, her brand new little red dress messed up by the unkind and uncaring splatter. "Oh, daddy. I'm sorry. ... I wanted to be good."

"That's OK, sweetness," Honest spoke in a loving voice, although from Tommy's perspective their father's face looked angry, confused and bewildered.

Tommy gazed up ahead down Main Street, realizing that the hearse carrying his mother's body had continued without letup, by this point having disappeared from view.

Luckily, at that moment their Aunt Paula and her husband, Hank, walked up to them beside the gutter; the couple had been in a yellow fast-back 1968 Mustang immediately behind Honest's station wagon.

"The poor little thing is literally burning up with fever," Paula said, the palm of her right hand across Peggy's forehead. "I'm afraid it's far more than merely nerves. This child is seriously ill."

By this point at least 15 other people crowded around, everyone from other cars that had been behind them in the funeral procession. At least 75 others waited in about 30 cars that had also been behind them in the procession from the Davis home. Even from his perspective as a young child, little Tommy sensed that most or all of these onlookers lacked any notion of what had just happened.

"We need to make a quick decision," Honest said.

Most people in their community usually looked to him

for guidance in making vital decisions in such critical situations. Yet now, for perhaps the first time ever as an adult, this newly widowed man realized he felt emotionally numb, lacking any notion of what to recommend in an emergency situation. "I think we should um... We should..."

"The poor little thing has passed out," Paula said. "Please hand this little angel over to me; she needs our immediate help, and..."

"But her mother's funeral, well," Honest's words disappeared, as he realized that he had fully lost his train of thought.

"Never worry," Hank said, putting a hand on his brother-in-law's shoulder. "We'll take the little one back to your house, and take good care of her. ... Hurry, Honest ... Catch up with the hearse and get to the church."

Two

Hand-in-hand with two of his children, little Tommy and tiny Penelope, the man everyone preferred to call Honest walked up the church steps.

The immediate family of the newly deceased mother and wife followed behind her casket, carried by eight strong pallbearers--all healthy young men. Most were from nearby small towns that dotted eastern and southern Nevada.

"Amazing grace, how sweet..."

Several feet from the front door, as the casket and pallbearers entered the church in front of them, Honest already heard the singing from inside.

"...thou art, that saved a wretch like me."

Immediately upon entering the building, Honest saw an unexpected spectacle that made his heart race faster than his favorite horse, the famed Triple Crown winner Secretariat. Hundreds of people packed the church, which has a congregation of just 47.

Just as stunning, seemingly unbelievable but true-- everyone already inside wore a Santa-style cap--each featuring the red with a furry white ball at the end.

Stunned and unsure how to feel, Honest clasped tighter at his children's hands as they walked together down the church's main aisle. Always a dutiful father, he briefly glanced down to tiny Penelope and little Tommy.

While still clasping Honest's hand with her right arm, his little girl used her left hand to clasp her favorite doll, Pee-Pee, and also to suck her thumb. Tommy continued assuming the posture and walk of a dutiful, obedient toy soldier--still a "good boy."

Honest momentarily noticed the absence of his other cherished child, the tomboyish Peggy who had become ill just 12 minutes earlier.

Every step of the way as they continued down the aisle toward the alter, Honest tried to maintain a stoic and kind demeanor. In a way that he deemed appropriate, while they continued following Polly's casket, this 42-year-old man glanced to the left and right to survey the mourners--eager to see what they looked like, the childlike expressions in their faces, and their curious reactions to this evolving ceremony.

"My lady would be proud," Honest thought, as he and his children reached the half-way point to the front of the congregation. "Polly would have wanted her funeral to be just this way ... So delightful, so festive, and so very positive."

Then unexpectedly to his right, as the mourners sang "twas Grace that taught my heart to fear," this newly widowed Vietnam veteran noticed amid the crowd the only man that had ever made him feel angry.

Doctor James Robbins' eyes met those of this grieving husband and father.

In that instant, for but a fleeting moment, Honest--praised by many for always remaining forthright, wise and thoughtful--suddenly felt angrier than a whistling teapot, threatening to boil over.

Far out of character for himself, many months of built-up instinct and rage made Honest want to bolt into the crowd and start choking the physician--right then and there for everyone to see.

"Someone needs to pay for my wife's death, and that man gave her poisons," Honest thought, inwardly feeling ashamed of himself for entertaining such devilish, inexcusable and deadly thoughts--the most sinful motivations imaginable.

There within the House of the Lord--miraculously, at least in this new widower's mind--the final words of his late wife raced into his head. ... Be forgiving ... The doctor did his best ... The physician is a good man, a consummate professional ... Live in peace.

*

Momentarily, while pallbearers gently placed Polly's casket at the center of the alter, a much different scene played out back at her family's small, modest home a mile away from the church.

Accompanied by another couple, Hank and Paula lay the still-unconscious tomboy named Peggy on an old green couch beside the Christmas tree in the living room.

"Honey, is this little angel still breathing?" Hank asked, as his wife put her ear against the 4-year-old girl's tiny chest.

For some strange reason, despite everyone's intense focus on poor Peggy, at that moment Hank noticed that needles from the Christmas tree had fallen atop the cherry wood floor and also an arm of the couch. He felt thankful that Mother Nature had waited until after the departure of Polly's casket for this tree to finally start showing signs of its own death--more than two weeks after the holiday.

"The poor thing," Paula frowned, her expression so severe and extreme that Hank realized that the little girl's health had reached a critical phase--far more severe than a mere cold or any nervous reaction to her mom's funeral. "She's barely breathing, her little heart is hardly pumping and her fever seems hotter than a raging fireplace."

Without hesitation Aunt Paula lifted the ailing child from the couch, before starting to carry the girl toward the bathroom.

"Hurry, Hank!" the woman hollered, while the other couple--Bill and Dorothy McCready--assisted as well. "Fill the bathtub with cold water. ... I need clean towels."

Hank had never heard his wife holler this way before, throughout their 12 years of childless marriage.

"I fear the worst, unless we can get this fever down." Paula began stripping Peggy of everything but her underwear. "I wish to the Lord that this town had its own hospital, a clinic or even its own doctor."

Hank dutifully did everything that logic commanded him to do, feeling almost as if he were back in the Navy--30 years earlier, near the end of World War II. Assisted by the McCready's every step of the way, he turned on the cold water full blast and then scurried like a determined mouse to the hall closet to fetch fresh towels.

The moment Hank returned with the couple to the bathroom he noticed a startled, reddish expression on his attractive wife's usually marvelous face--an aura and physical demeanor that impressed him as being both ominous and foreboding.

While gently cradling little Peggy in the bathtub, Aunt Paula barked out specific and to-the-point orders that reminded Hank of a Marine Corps drill sergeant. Hank and Bill McCready were to go immediately to the church to fetch Sheriff Jonathan Peters.

Just as important, they were to do this as deftly as possible, so as to avoid disturbing the funeral of Aunt Paula's sister, Polly. With equal urgency, the men also were to do their best to fetch any physician who might happen to be--miraculously--at the same service.

"Dorothy, please stay here with me," Aunt Paula said, gently cupping her hand into the cold bathwater before allowing the liquid to drip onto Peggy's forehead. "And if you do anything else, pray to Our Lord to spare the life of this innocent child. ... The last little girl I saw this sort of thing happen to--about six years ago--little Annie Edwards--died within one week of becoming ill ... Everyone blamed childhood leukemia. Please pray to heaven that our precious little Peggy avoids a similar fate."

*

The Reverend Martin Middleton stood at the podium just to the right of Polly's casket, spreading his muscular arms so wide that Honest briefly thought of how a super-powerful eagle appears just before taking flight.

"Just a few days ago, a brand new game show premiered on NBC--called the 'Wheel of Fortune.'" The Reverend's voice boomed so loudly that Honest felt convinced everyone outside from the overflow crowd could hear every word. "Now, why on earth would the Good Lord motivate me to mention a mere TV program at such a solemn and sacred moment such as this?"

This holy man lifted both his arms straight upward, seizing that moment to pause as if to emphasize the drama of his words that would follow--at least from the perspective of Honest. The newly widowed man always disliked this preacher's tendency toward melodrama, yet always wise enough to refrain from telling anyone of his many negative opinions about the reverend.

"Well, I'll tell you the answer--which I have no doubt will leave many of you somewhat surprised and even pleased, amazingly, at a mournful moment such as this."

Although he normally detested such hype-filled comments at church, Honest suddenly found himself filled with growing anticipation--eager to discover what this man of the cloth would say next.

"Just as life is for us all, just as Our Lord promises, life itself is a proverbial Wheel of Fortune--just as the blessed experience here on this earth has been for our departed dear friend Polly here, and for her grieving family as well. This is the promise we receive from the Bible, from the very Word of God."

From all that Honest had personally been through in many difficult struggles during the previous nine months, he felt as if every word from Reverend Middleton rang true and clear--despite his many private disagreements with this man.

Without hesitation, "Scout"--as he was affectionately known by many of his parishioners--left the podium and walked slowly toward Polly's coffin. Amid this process, Honest briefly glanced to the congregation all around them. The grieving father and husband realized that all eyes were fixated on the preacher, almost as if--he sensed--that everyone eagerly anticipated his every word.

Upon finally reaching the coffin, Scout gently placed a daisy atop the many others that family members and other mourners already had placed atop the casket.

"As just about every person here knows full well by now,

daisies were Polly's favorite flower--far and away her preferred pretty plant. Even today, all of these many years later, I still fondly remember at her wedding with Honest in this very church just 10 years ago--boy, how time flies--she certainly was a heavenly bride that day. She had insisted that daisies decorate every aisle, and each of her lucky bridesmaids carried similar flowers--symbolizing a love and an appreciation for life that permeates the atmosphere, even here on this very day of her funeral.

"Upon the births of each of her children, Penelope, Peggy and Tommy, at her request many of us here today sent daisies to that modest, tiny and unassuming Davis family home on Tranquility Lane--where each of those blessed souls were born unto this earth. ... Yes, through the example she gave us, and through her innocent, loving and kind desires, Polly showed each of us that--just as God has intended--life is indeed a Wheel of Fortune.

"Each of us can either spread hate, or we can spread nothing but boundless love. As each and every person here fully knows, Polly did nothing but show kindness to all her family members and to everyone in this community, and even--at times--to wandering strangers who had somehow stumbled into our small, little-known town. The daisies preferred by this woman were a mere reflection of the boundless love and the forgiveness that she had always showered upon others.

"Yet many of us might have been wondering why, in this non-stop, round-the-clock Wheel of Fortune of life here on earth, did this blessed woman prefer--of all things--mere daisies, as opposed to the many other types of flowers? ... Yes, our departed friend here easily could have chosen roses, carnations, daffodils, iris, lily, orchid, or hundreds of other species. Believe me, and I can personally testify to this as true, she was fully aware of those many other beautiful species.

"Well, struck by curiosity in this regard, as you might very well imagine, I asked Polly about this while visiting her family's home just one month ago--as she lay dying, slowly wasting away in bed. Amazingly, and I can fully testify to this, as many of you here already know, by that time her poor little body was already wasting away--and yet somehow, as if an added gift from God, she had a special glow about her, as if she were already spreading her wings--as if prepared to enter the Kingdom of Heaven at any moment. Then, although extremely frail--barely strong enough to talk--she answered me, uttering blessed and all-knowing words that I shall remember the rest of my life."

At this precise juncture, Reverend Middleton paused. Slowly, literally at what Honest considered a snail's pace, the preacher lifted his own right arm--until finally using his index finger to point straight upward. This was precisely the type of potentially over-the-top melodrama that typically made Honest cringe inside his own heart, without letting anyone know his secret, deep revulsion toward this preacher's propensity toward unnecessary drama. Yet deep down, this new widower--who made his living as a plumber--felt that he had to admit to himself that all the pieces of what Scout was saying fit together just right.

"Polly told me that to her, daisies represent an ideal mixture of both innocence and of love--the essential ingredients for each of us to thrive spiritually as ideal Children of God. During each of our brief times here on earth, she knew, we all have but one chance to live, and to behave and to worship as the Good Lord has intended. To her, daisies are among the shortest-living flowers, a cherished gift from Mother Nature--for only an extremely brief period of time. Like each of us, daisies are extremely frail while facing the possibility of death at any moment. Like each of us-- and this is an integral part of God's plan--daisies rise, blossom and disappear with each passing season or life cycle.

"This is why our departed Polly asked that daisies be here today--in abundance. Each of us here today is a proverbial daisy in the loving and forgiving eyes of Our Lord--in abundance. Together, as if individuals blossoming in a massive field of daisies, we mourn the loss of this woman. Her wish, I believe, is that each of us here can and should realize these things about ourselves--that each of us, specifically the life that we have, is a blessed gift from God. This is why, Polly had asked that Christmas be celebrated today--here at her funeral, although several weeks after the actual holiday. Forever devout, she knew that to each of us, Jesus Christ is represented by these daisies. And He is God's Gift of salvation to us, the hope for Eternal Life with him in Heaven."

Then, after an extended pause, while showing off a smile seemingly bigger than the moon--at least from Honest's perspective, the Reverend Middleton motioned for everyone present to stand: "Please rise, so that we may sing together the most blessed Christmas song that Polly had requested that we celebrate together here today."

As Honest started to stand, he unexpectedly realized that his legs felt unusually weak and wobbly. A small part of this widower wondered whether he would have enough strength to stand, his body, spirit and mind overcome by relentless grief. Instinct commanded that he refrain from showing weakness, while his heart felt gladdened by the unexpectedly strong grasp of his right hand by little Tommy. The boy looked directly up into his father's eyes. To Honest, the child's face appeared overwhelmed with grief, a sharp contrast to the boy's infectious smile at that moment--an obvious effort to display courage, strength and a much-too-early sign of manhood.

On the father's immediate left, he noticed that little Penelope had fallen fast asleep, sucking her thumb as usual and tightly clutching her cherished doll--Pee-Pee. Honest motioned to pick up his snoozing daughter, something he typically did every day with ease thanks to his somewhat legendary physical strength. To him, this tiny creature typically felt as light as a butterfly. Yet on this occasion, at this very moment, he felt as if lifting her was the equivalent of picking up a 900-pound bull with one hand.

Using every bit of physical might that he could muster, Honest pulled the 32-pound child into both of his arms--letting go of little Tommy's hand, while feeling as if a weightlifter struggling with all of his might during final rounds of televised Olympics competition. Once he reached an erect standing position, Honest felt a new burst of strength throughout his entire body--as if someone, somehow were there to help him through this steadily intensifying grief.

Then, he joined everyone in song without missing a beat: "Silent night, holy night, all is calm, all is bright..."

Three

Aunt Paula gently cupped the clammy hand of her niece, who remained unconscious as the funeral for the mother of this child reached its mid-way point a mile away.

"Thank God that this adorable girl's temperature has gone down somewhat," Aunt Paula told Dorothy McCready as the women stood watch at the child's bedside. The ladies took turns applying wet cloths to Peggy's forehead and using soaked towels to keep her body cool.

At age 60, Dorothy had the crusty, wrinkled and yet rock-solid appearance that Paula had often seen among people who had spent their entire lives in the desert.

From Paula's way of thinking, Dorothy looked as if about 90 or even 100 years old. The unforgiving dry high-desert air does that to a person, particularly anyone who lives in abject poverty for a entire lifetime--without ever visiting the ocean or even riding a boat.

Like almost all women who lived their entire lives in Eastern and Southern Nevada, merely "staying above ground" had always been a tough, relentless struggle.

The dreaded disease of cancer had exacerbated these challenges in recent years, killing many hundreds or even thousands of people throughout the region.

The pervasive problem got little mention in the news media. People unlucky enough to live in the region were often heard to say that the federal government and journalists behave as if "we never existed--as if we have never mattered at all."

Just about everyone throughout the region--from the poorest among them to the most prosperous families--agreed the culprit had been nuclear bombs, blasted above ground at the notorious Nevada Test Site from the early 1950s until the late 1960s.

The federal government had always assured these isolated communities downwind from the blasts that "everything is okay and there is no danger whatsoever." The public was always told that the typical, standard tests were harmless.

By many accounts, most people with at least some degree of common sense gradually started to believe otherwise. Public opinion throughout the region turned negative as reports of additional cancer deaths regularly riddled the obituary pages.

This led to a proverbial "clash of the titans." Steadily increasing numbers of residents claimed that the devilish government had known of the extreme danger to the public all along, while federal bureaucrats insisted otherwise.

"There has been no scientific evidence found whatsoever proving that such dangers have ever existed in these communities--all of them many miles away from the bombing tests," one official insisted, in an extremely rare interview on this hot-button topic. "Cancer deaths occur everywhere worldwide. We have no reason to believe that this area is any different, with instances of the disease at normal levels."

Such hard, matter-of-fact and cold comments gradually ignited intense anger among much of the populace.

Although officials insisted otherwise, lots of irritated residents suspected that the cancers emerged many years or even generations after the tests. From their way of thinking, deadly radiation poisoning often took several years or even decades to generate cancer--which finally managed to attack victims due to irreversible cellular damage.

Adding to these woes, at least from the view of some residents, the awful and invisible radiation sharply increased the likelihood that cancer would strike the future children of people who were youngsters and young adults when downwind from the above-ground nuclear bomb tests.

"Trust the government," federal authorities seemed to say collectively, in their brief and infrequent comments on the issue. "The probability of the disease passing from generation-to-generation is unlikely, if not impossible."

To the contrary, by the mid-1970s when Polly perished, at least judging from some accounts just about every family throughout the region had at least one member stricken by cancer. Many victims were the children born several years and even more than a decade after the tests.

Mirroring worldwide trends, within this particular region, some instances of the disease were far more severe than others. Amid the demise of the Nixon administration, people across Utah and Eastern Nevada steadily began to complain that the federal government had victimized them.

Like most of her surviving relatives, Aunt Paula felt a deep, intense and burning anger toward the government-- particularly politicians who refused to discuss the issue. Naturally, lots of people felt as if federal authorities considered these residents to be nothing more than mere insects.

"Paula, I'm so very sorry that you were unable to attend your sister's funeral," Dorothy said, while they each continued to apply wet towels and cloths to the ailing little Peggy--who still lay atop the same bed where her mother died three days earlier.

"Like this or not, we've got to do whatever necessary to help family," Aunt Paula said, briefly pausing to kiss her niece's forehead. "Besides, and I do not know whether you have been aware of this, but my sister and I never got along with each other anyway ... Most people lack any inkling of this, but Polly was far from being the angel that many people made her out to be. She was the complete opposite of being any kind of saint, as far as I'm concerned."

"Paula!" Dorothy accidentally dropped a towel, before immediately bending to the floor to retrieve it. "Heaven knows you should refrain from saying such a thing, particularly about your own recently departed sister. For the love of God, this child might hear every wretched word that you dare to utter about her dead mother."

"Fear not, my friend," Aunt Paula finally sat in the same

rocking chair beside the bed where Honest had spent many nights at his dying wife's bedside. "I suspect that this child has fallen into a deep coma. I fear that unless we take the appropriate measures, she could die within the hour."

"Really?"

Sitting motionless as she and Dorothy gazed at the child, Paula briefly thought about the emotional pain that her newly departed sister had caused her. This grieving aunt realized that most people lacked any inkling of Polly's selfish and uncaring behavior.

"I see you mommy, I'm coming to you," Peggy began to say this over and over, as she tossed and turned on the bed. "Mommy, I see you."

Dorothy immediately took her turn at checking the child's forehead.

"The poor thing," Dorothy frowned, her appearance making Paula think of how a bird looks upon discovering that one of its offspring has fallen out of a nest. "She's burning up, more than ever ... You say that you think she's in a coma? ... Do people actually talk and thrash about this way when in such a physical condition?"

Striving to remain as calm as possible, careful to avoid causing any undue alarm, Paula explained that several doctors had taught her in recent years that such symptoms occasionally occur amid comas.

"Mommy, I'm coming to see you," little Peggy said, still tossing and turning. "Wait for me ... Do not go away."

Aunt Paula felt sudden surprise upon discovering that tears had welled up in her own eyes. This happened upon realizing that about four and a half years earlier Peggy had been born in this same room. The emotional hurt intensified for Paula when also thinking of her own child, Harry, who had died from cancer a few years earlier at age two--from cancer.

"Let us get her back into the bathtub right away!" Paula jumped from the chair and picked up her niece from the bed. "Let us pray that we can get the fever down again. Although I despised and even hated my sister--bless her departed soul--with all my heart I love this child of hers. ... We need to get this fever down ... Lord, Jesus, help us all."

*

Pamela stepped behind the podium within a few moments after Reverend Middleton finished with his funeral sermon.

The youngest of the three sisters, Pamela slowly and methodically adjusted the microphone in order to accommodate her short physical stature.

Fighting a severe case of stage fright seemed the least of Pamela's most immediate worries. Her biggest concern became an urgent need to avoid saying anything wrong, primarily shocking revelations about her family's potentially scandalous secrets.

"Thank you for being here, everyone," Pamela said, adjusting the collar of her white blouse--accented by her long, curly, flowing blonde hair. She knew that her dark, healthy-looking suntan seemed a sharp contrast to just about everyone present, particularly because that winter had been extremely cloudy and bitterly cold throughout the entire region. She had just arrived in town the previous morning from Hawaii, where her husband Jeffrey served as a lieutenant at Hickman Air Force Base near Pearl Harbor.

"First off, I would like to let everyone know that I do not have any formal remarks prepared--primarily because I was not scheduled as the person designated to give today's eulogy for my cherished sister who lay before us here. ... The oldest of us three, Paula, had been designated to give the remarks. But sadly, as some of you might know by now, our niece--little Peggy--has suddenly become ill, and Paula took it upon herself to assist in every way possible over at the family home. ... I'm sure that if Paula were here, she would be telling many stories of her deep and eternal love for Polly. ... The two of them were so very close, almost inseparable--at least as far as I can tell."

Pamela paused and swallowed hard, literally lacking

any specific notion of what she would eventually say. Until this moment the only time that she had spoken before any group had been in the seventh grade, earning a "D" from the instructor for her sloppy presentation, disheveled appearance, and a bothersome propensity to slur her words--lazily failing to pronounce well enough for that classroom audience to understand. Unlike her beloved sisters, seemingly adored by everyone, Pamela had always been plagued by low self-esteem--at least until recently when people in the Aloha State began praising her keen intelligence--and an uncanny resemblance to TV star Farrah Fawcett, who during the previous year had just rocketed to fame thanks to recurring roles on "Harry O" and "The Six Million Dollar Man." The only significant physical differences were the undeniable facts that Pamela had slightly crooked teeth and a much larger, fuller and natural bosom than the increasingly famous media personality.

"Isn't the tremendous size of this gathering amazing--maybe 500 people strong, sensational when considering the fact that our little town here is the home to what some big-city people describe as a 'measly population of perhaps only around 700 souls?'" Pamela spread her arms wide in much the same way as Reverend Middleton had done shortly before; she felt well aware that her ultra-feminine aura provided a sharp contrast to the preacher's masculine demeanor. "The much-appreciated tremendous showing here tells all of us about our entire region possesses a strong sense of community, support and boundless love--a sharp contrast to today's confusing world that is sometimes heartless, cruel and uncaring."

Glad to realize her fears had suddenly disappeared for an unknown reason, Pamela realized that she was 'on a roll'--long after the harsh criticisms of her speaking abilities, made by her seventh grade teacher, Mrs. Portman. Like the preacher had done before her, Pamela also paused for affect--as a way to emphasize her message.

"Everyone, listen," she walked out from behind the podium, suddenly confident that her usually meek voice could be heard loud enough for everyone to understand. "For the next few moments, just look around this room. ... See in all these many faces your friends, neighbors, family members--and quite understandably many others whom you fail to recognize or individuals that you undoubtedly have never seen before."

Pausing for the crowd to do just as she suggested, from the altar Pamela carefully studied countless blank expressions, slight frowns and broad smiles amid the congregation. Biting cold air suddenly breezed inside through the church's wide-open front door, inspiring many to button or zip up their overcoats.

"There is a warm feeling here in this gathering that no one can take away from us, despite the biting cold outside that has formed long, snake-like icicles on the edge of every rooftop for many miles in every direction." Pamela realized the fluffy, chiffon-like pink dress that she wore seemed strangely out of place for these harsh weather conditions. "Despite today's finger-cracking cold, the undeniably warm feelings in our hearts for Polly, for her husband and for her children remind me of what she has meant to us all."

Once again pausing for effect, she took a few seconds to carefully survey the congregation. So many unforgettable faces--most familiar to her since childhood--intermixed with equal numbers of strangers. Pamela realized that her own face likely appeared calm at that precise juncture. This deceptively hid from everyone the fact that her heart had suddenly begun to race faster than an Olympian amid the peak of competition; this reaction struck Pamela as odd--since deep inside she actually lacked any hint of fear or trepidation.

"Since I have no remarks prepared, I can only speak from my heart--which provides a message that each of us needs to hear and to fully understand. It's a message about Polly's life, how she impacted each of us--whether or not we knew at the time that she was doing that. ... Lots of us who knew this woman well considered her a bit of a mystery. She always conveyed something profound to us, even though we failed to realize at the time what that message was all about.

"Let me give you a prime example here and now, although what I am about to say is likely to shock and stun the psyches of at least some of you ... To start off, I have got to admit that I have been very angry with my sister Polly for the past eight months--in fact I was downright mad at her as she lay dying. ... Yet why on earth would I have the audacity say something so shocking as this here and now, at a sacred time like this, a blessed moment where we have gathered to celebrate her life?

"Well, I have to confess here and now that I was angry at Polly, precisely due to the fact that she refused to become angry herself. ... I flew here from Hawaii four different times since last June, always to help in any way that I possibly could to do my share in caring for my sister, her children and her husband. ... Strangely, although she knew that she would soon die, Polly always spoke of how happy she was--delighted with the boundless courage and physical strength of her husband, Honest, and with each activity or comment made by her children.

"Finally, at Thanksgiving I broke down and cried, more profoundly than I have ever wept before--kneeling at poor Polly's bedside, pleading with her to be angry and to become mad at her situation ... I have to admit that my behavior that evening was childish, self-centered and immature, the complete opposite of this dying woman's demeanor at that moment ... There and then, with no one else in the room, I let my secret thoughts spring forth in a way that I should not have done--may God forgive me for my selfishness. ... But for the life of me, I just could not help it at the time; just about every angry thought that came to my head emerged from my mouth in the form of spoken words ... I told her that I was angry that the cancers that had taken the lives of our parents, Margaret and Frank Williams--who each died in their early 50s during the mid-1960s, each suffering from extensive and excruciating physical pain and heartache before they left us--each far too early.

"Yes, I was extremely selfish that night. Maybe I was

thinking more of my own emotions than hers ... But no matter how much I might have wanted to stop spilling my heart out, I just kept talking ... You see, I just couldn't take it any more--all of these wretched things that have kept happening to our entire community, far more than any one town or region should have to endure.
... Without any doubt whatsoever, I felt as if about to explode emotionally, while she still looked as calm as one of those daisies that Reverend Middleton has just told us about. Nonetheless, as if a dam that had just burst, streams of non-stop details flooded into that bedroom--all these scary facts, the wretched details that cascaded from my mouth, as if I had somehow become the proverbial know-it-all, the conveyor of disturbing details that I felt all of the world needed to hear.

"Without even giving poor Polly any time or opportunity to respond to my countless self-centered statements, I rattled off a lengthy list of beloved relatives, friends and acquaintances that had been cruelly taken from us by cancer--everyone from our town's humorous and always-fun baker, Mister Miller, to Mrs. Culbertson--the adorable old woman who always smiled despite her continual pain from bone-rattling arthritis--and eventually her cancer.

"Yes, at this very moment, I'm asking each of you here today to think of those whom you have known in our community--of our loved ones and friends who have died from cancer or suffered from that dreaded disease, particularly since the early 1950s when the federal government began exploding those horrible bombs--at the nearby Nevada Test Site. ... I'm asking you to take a full minute, starting right now--to think of these people, to remember each of them that you know, and to pray for their souls."

In keeping with her suggestion, Pamela began this period of silence. As everyone complied, some clasped their hands together in prayerful solitude, she checked the second hand on her Timex ladies' wrist watch. The crowd remained silent, virtually everyone gazing upon Pamela--while she walked up to the side of her sister's casket.

    From there, she saw tears welled up in the eyes of many onlookers throughout this expansive room. Every ten seconds or so, another person was heard to wail. About 30 seconds into this process, still from beside Polly's casket, Pamela started paying attention to her brother-in-law, Honest, and two of his three children. From her perspective, this man and his kids looked as if void of any expression--almost as though their loving hearts had somehow been plucked out of them, due to the many emotional hardships that they had recently endured.

    "Forgive me, please, if I have inspired sad memories for all of you," Pamela finally spoke, while gently picking up one of the daisies from Polly's casket. "But remember, I'm only speaking from the heart now, and my heart tells me to speak these words..."

    As she continued speaking without letup, from the alter Pamela could not help but notice that Sheriff Jonathan Peters and Bill McCready had entered through the church's front door. Instinct told her to generate an increasing degree of "fire and brimstone," as if a seasoned preacher herself at an under-the-tent gathering in the Old South--in order to distract this gathering from paying any attention to the lawman and his companion.

    "Look at me ... Everyone look at me now!" Pamela commanded, her voice rising in crescendo and pitch, far louder and more forceful than she had previously done. In doing so, she hoisted one of the daisies far above her head. "Take a close look at this daisy here, all of you, because this is super-important as we celebrate my sister's life."

    At precisely that moment, without signifying to the crowd what she saw, Pamela noticed the sheriff huddling with Doctor Robbins at the far end of the church. Realizing that in this very moment these men likely were giving the physician urgent news about her little niece, that tomboy--Pamela sensed an increasingly vital need for amazing, riveting and unavoidable drama on her own part. The desire to distract everyone from paying attention to the huddled men became paramount in her mind.

Yet she lacked any inkling of precisely what she was going to say.

"This flower ..." Pamela began stumbling her words for the first time, realizing an urgent need to get her commentary back on track. "This tiny little daisy here ... Look ... It represents..."

Thankfully, in that moment, out the corner of her right eye, Pamela spotted the doctor as he walked out the church front door with the sheriff.

"It represents life--not only Polly's life, but our lives as well. Here within this casket lay my sister, who epitomized the very essence of a loving and forgiving life--precisely the type of life that the Good Lord wants each of us to have. Beside Polly's tiny body--what remains--within this simple, modest casket is her favorite nutcracker from under the family Christmas tree--a strong, brightly painted wooden figure that she always called 'Hope." ... At her request, the family's four remaining nutcrackers have been reserved for the others, for us each to use--if we so choose--to be buried with in order to meet the Lord when their time comes.

"Whether I want to say this or not--it's true--and therefore I must speak these words. Maybe these nutcrackers actually do represent hope. This makes sense, because Polly always mysteriously represented hope in just about everything that she did ... She remained hopeful and optimistic when her husband, Honest, lost the lower part of his right ear during combat in Vietnam--a mere six months after they were married on a glorious spring day in this very church. ... She remained optimistic and hopeful three years later, in 1969, when after his release from the military, that same man--Honest--lost his left eye to cancer after he had moved back home to this town. We all know and adore Honest's somewhat famous eye patch--the image of which is embossed on the side of a modified milk truck, used for his plumbing business-- Honest Pirate Plumbing ... How about that!"

Rowdy cheers, applause and whistling erupted from the crowd.

Pamela had instinctively known that this declaration and an

ensuing celebration would help break up the mournful, solemnity of the moment--bringing a much-needed reprise from the many somber words spoken earlier.

"I know that Honest remains extremely popular, throughout Western and Southwest Nevada--as he travels from town-to-town, to bring his much-needed plumbing skills and superior service. ... I think that I can speak for my entire family in expressing our sincere appreciation to you for coming all the way here today--lots of you undoubtedly are among Honest's many customers who live in the many isolated high-desert communities, most living many dozens or even hundreds of miles away from each other. ... Lots of you, I am sure, traveled well over 100 miles to reach this church, here in the dead of winter to show your support for Honest--in most instances although you had never met Polly in person. By now, I believe that most of you have probably heard colorful and unforgettable stories about this departed woman, and the recent hardships that her immediate family has recently overcome--thanks largely to this man, her husband, who showed nothing but courage, during a personal situation that would have thrown nothing but fear into most of our hearts.

"So, in closing I would like to end this phase of Polly's story by telling you another interesting revelation ... You see, way back on Thanksgiving, after I cried and spouted off about my desire for her to become angry--the poor thing still had enough energy to speak to me. She told me that there is no need to become angry at the cancer, at the government, at the medical industry, or at her overall gloomy situation.

"Instead, she told me, 'We all need to only show love and forgiveness--in every situation, no matter how difficult.' She also told me that after she was gone, she was sure that our community and family would show the same to her husband and to her children.

"Believe me, I know that there are those officials who insist that these cancers are not out of the ordinary--that there is no scientific evidence to suggest or to prove that those horrific bomb blasts from many years ago are still killing many of us.

"And so, despite my own anger at the situation, I have decided to do my best to show the exact kind of strong, unbending love that embossed my sister's every action.

"And, yeah, so maybe it's a coincidence, some type of a quirk of fate. In any event, we're only here to talk about Polly ... But I feel an unstoppable need, in this final closing, to say that sometimes in order to show true love--strong and enduring love--we must fight legally and morally for what is right. ... From my view, to love is to show our deep, steadfast and relentless courage in standing up against what the government has done to us--this wretched death, the horrible disease, this sadness.

"You see, although I might appear to you as the perfect picture of health--or so I have humbly often been told, just two days ago--after being informed of my sister's expected death--my doctors in Hawaii told me the news flat-out. ... They told me that I have advanced Stage 4 colon cancer--with less than three months to live.".

Loud gasps erupted from the crowd.

Some people briefly cried out--each sounding, from Pamela's perspective--as if squirrels that had just been mortally wounded by a slingshot

Mustering every bit of courage and gumption that she possibly could, Pamela managed to hold back any inkling of her own tears--displaying only courage.

"So, at least I have been told, the time for my own anger is gone. ... When my own demise comes, probably this spring, I want to be buried next to her--hopefully with the nutcracker that they have called 'Mister Love' nestled by my side."

Paula and Dorothy stood arm-in-arm in the front yard of the Davis home.

Together, they watched the sheriff's car speed out of sight on Tranquility Lane. Neither woman wore a coat, only the modest dresses that they had intended to wear to Polly's funeral. It wasn't until the vehicle disappeared from view that Dorothy realized the 1 inch of biting snow made her feet feel as if they had been cracked in half.

Sensing that Paula must have felt the same, Dorothy pulled her friend back toward the front door. Once inside the living room, both women headed straight toward the kitchen, where they collectively started making a pot of hot coffee.

Neither lady spoke a word.

The previous 10 minutes had been a whirlwind from Dorothy's perspective. With the doctor and Hank, the sheriff had bolted into the home. Within 2 minutes of their arrival, the physician had pronounced what the women had already known--that Peggy was in critical condition, needing to be rushed to a hospital right away.

During the ensuing few minutes, the ladies crammed several of the girl's belongings into a large pillow case. Besides Peggy's favorite marbles and her cherished slingshot, the women even rushed to retrieve her overalls from the back-yard shed.

This area of East-Central Nevada lacked an ambulance service, a hospital or a single doctor. The only way to travel the entire 275 miles to Reno where Doctor Robbins lived was by private car--since Greyhound bus service had been canceled 15 years earlier.

In keeping with local custom, Sheriff Peters would escort the doctor all the way to the county line--as both a courtesy and a safety measure. All the way to their intended destination, Hank would drive the doctor and Peggy--still unconscious upon their departure--in his yellow fastback 1968 Mustang.

For many years, a handful of Centralia residents had predicted that someday soon officials would start using helicopters for such emergency transports. Others insisted that such efforts were a fruitless pipe dream, "since those worthless politicians never give a hoot about those of us who live in what they call--'the sticks,' those hooligans."

By this point alone together in the Davis home, Paula and Dorothy sat at the same round oak table where the children had just eaten breakfast a few hours earlier.

"I can imagine you must be sad that you missed your sister's funeral," Dorothy said, eventually deciding after a several-minute pause that a perfect time had come to talk. She made this attempt, although well aware that Paula rarely liked to chat.

"I didn't miss going there at all." Paula firmly placed her coffee cup on the table. "Can't we just keep quiet for awhile?"

Stunned, perplexed and nearly at a loss for words, since hardly anyone ever spoke to her in such harsh tones, Dorothy became increasingly determined to keep the peace.

"Forgive me, Paula, I was just trying to be kind and helpful."

"No offense to you, but I'm sick and tired of people trying to be just that--'kind and helpful.' And, I'm just as exhausted from everyone speaking about Paula as if she was some sort of saint--that woman was far from an angel as far as I'm concerned, in fact--the complete opposite."

Already physically and mentally exhausted this early in the morning and eager to avoid personal conflict, Dorothy stood and placed her still-filled coffee cup in the sink: "Well, I'm going to go. I can see from your anger that I'm not needed here any more."

Paula remained in her chair, while Dorothy retrieved her own gray coat from a modest closet at the edge of the dining room.

"Goodbye and good luck," Dorothy said, while putting on

her coat and retrieving her shiny black plastic purse from a table in the living room. "All my thoughts and prayers are with you and with your family--wishing you nothing but the very best."

Still planted in her chair, and making no attempt to look at the departing woman, Paula kept quiet--staring down at her coffee cup.

Dorothy opened the front door, enabling a crisp wind to send another blast of biting cold into the home. The swirling air pushed the angel from atop the Christmas tree. The figurine landed with a loud thud atop the nutcrackers, knocking them all down.

Without saying a word or even bothering to apologize, Dorothy stepped outside and gently closed the door behind herself. That second, while alone on the front porch as heavy snow began to fall, she heard an ear-cracking scream and cries from inside the home. Dorothy knew these were Paula's screams of fear, of helplessness and loneliness.

A deep inner instinct told Dorothy that the woman inside the residence desperately yearned for someone to talk with--to reveal her secrets, to get her own heartache off her chest and--perhaps most most important--to forget her own sense of being terribly alone.

In that very second, while still standing on the front porch, Dorothy realized that she needed to make a critical and increasingly critical choice.

She could go ahead with what she had just intended, walking the three blocks to her own home--despite lacking adequate footwear, something she had been fully willing to do in order to escape this awful conflict. Or, she could go back inside, showing persistence, fortitude, strength and boundless love, in order to help someone in need.

"Awa-hh," Paula's cries echoed from the home, from Dorothy's perspective as if the wails of a yodeler high in the Alps in the dead of winter. "Awww-awwww!"

Although uneager to face conflict head-on, Dorothy decided to do what she considered the "one, true and loving thing."

She made an immediate about-face and re-entered the home.

Without hesitation, this 60-year-old woman marched like a soldier across the living room, put the nutcrackers back up into standing positions in their rightful places and retrieved the fallen angel. Momentarily, Dorothy carried the figurine into the dining room where Paula continued weeping.

Strangely feeling far more powerful and loving than she had in many years, Dorothy gently placed her left hand on Paula's right shoulder--while using her other hand to hold the angel. Paula immediately stood, as her own wailing started to subside.

The women embraced, hugging tightly.

After a few moments, Dorothy took one step back.

Then, she held the angel out toward Paula, as if giving the winged object as a gift--which this grieving aunt promptly accepted.

Her own face reddened and still streaked, Paula smiled broadly and accepted the offering--which she promptly kissed in the face, as if the angel had been a long-lost friend.

"Love is the only answer." Dorothy spoke in a soft, soothing voice. "I'm afraid all of us are going to need that more than ever--it's the only thing that we have that really has any meaningful value ... Love."

Five

Silver dollar-size snowflakes delivered by the harsh wind whipped into the faces of everyone present, as pallbearers carried Polly's casket into Centralia City Cemetery.

A half century-old chain-link fence surrounds the two-acre site, nestled on a steep hillside just outside the north edge of town.

The many lilies blew from atop the coffin, the flowers immediately buried in the new-fallen snow. Lucky for everyone present, the deep grave already had been dug four hours earlier, before this latest band of storm clouds arrived.

As everyone trudged through the snow toward the gravesite, Pamela gripped as tightly as she could on the right hand of her brother-in-law. The angry weather became so harsh that the whiteness covered Honest's black eye patch--at least temporarily obscuring his usual appearance as that of a pirate.

At this precise moment, from Pamela's view he took on the appearance of the notorious Abominable Snowman. Thankfully, unlike that legendary character, from her way of thinking this 6-foot-5-inch-tall widower possessed the demeanor of Frosty the Snowman--always kind and friendly--even amid the continual prospect of death.

These are the kind of bitter and potentially deadly weather conditions in the isolated deserts of the American West that many big-city folks never know about.

Dangerous storms hit with sudden and unforgiving force, about five or six times each winter--some years many more, and some seasons not at all.

By the end of that morning, this would emerge as the region's most severe winter storm from the previous half century. Most snowstorms in Centralia bring only a dusting or a few inches at most. At this moment only a half inch had accumulated, a tiny portion of the 3 feet that would follow during the next 24 hours.

At Honest's instance, the children had remained in the Pontiac station wagon parked with the many other vehicles along nearby Cemetery Road. Family friend Bill McCready had volunteered to stay in the vehicle to watch and care for the youngsters. The tiny Penelope remained fast asleep, while little Tommy remained seated beside her--his soldier-like posture unwavering--having been told five minutes earlier by his father "that your mother would want you to remain on your best behavior now. She wants you safe, and to look after your little sister here."

The 12 chairs that had been set up near the gravesite for immediate family and close friends already were caked in snow-- looking to Pamela almost as if white vanilla frosting atop gigantic cupcakes made for a summer backyard party. The bothersome weather conditions obscured every word on the granite headstones of the three adult sisters' parents, Jay and Audrey. The gothic lettering and precise craftsmanship had been commissioned by Honest, who needed five years to fully pay off the debt--a combined total of $1,200 for each, a whopping sum considering his modest earnings. The plumber's somewhat legendary can-do attitude had enabled him to steadily pay off the loan, privately telling Polly one day that "this is the only heavenly thing I could ever do for them, considering the fact that the cancer put each of them through such hell."

Her mind captured by grief and fear as this snowy day's graveside services began, Pamela failed to understand or to assimilate a single word of what Reverend Middleton said there at the graveside. As far as she knew, this guy often affectionately referred to as "Scout" was speaking about how the Lord was eager to accept Polly's kind and loving soul into the Kingdom of Heaven. Or, maybe the good reverend was simply reciting the 23rd Psalm. Whatever was spoken, Pamela failed to understand the details.

All she knew for sure in these challenging conditions was that the preacher had a nose shaped like a giant fish hook, and that very soon--perhaps a few months at most--this community would be digging a deep hole for her own body, right here next to poor Polly's fresh grave.

"Will that day be as cold and as snowy as this?" Pamela thought as a few more family members lay a few lilies atop the casket--each flower immediately covered by snow. "Do you feel cold when you die? Will it be cold for me there underground, beside my sister and my parents forever? ... Will anyone here even bother to attend?"

Although mired in such gloomy thoughts, she started feeling warm touches. "Perhaps this service is over," she thought, as continual flashes of soothing warmth engulfed her body, each time as another person hugged her tightly there in the graveyard. The hugs from her neighbors and from people she had always known helped push away Pamela's dreadful thoughts.

There as the 50 people who had trekked to the graveyard began marching back toward their vehicles, Pamela once again felt what she considered the soothing, warm and all-encompassing touch of Honest's hand clasping hers.

"Pamela, dear," the tall man whispered. "You live on a tropical island that some people call 'paradise on earth,' the complete opposite from the conditions we have here. ... You must know by now that I love you like a little sister ... And, I will help care for you."

Suddenly and unexpectedly Pamela felt somewhat happy for the first time that day, at least temporarily forgetting the inescapable fact that she would soon suffer an extremely painful, excruciating and inescapable death.

When Pamela and this sturdy man reached about 15 feet from the station wagon, she heard the distinctive wail of a siren. Just about everyone in Centralia knew that the only vehicle in town with such a device was only used by Sheriff Peters--only about once every year during the community's extremely rare dire emergencies.

"I hope this doesn't have something to do with our little

Peggy--one of my precious babies." After letting go of Pamela's hand, Honest bolted around the station wagon toward the driver's side. Each of his flat-footed steps signified to her that this was his effort to avoid slipping and falling hard onto the snow-covered pavement. "We need to forget about the wake in the church hall--at least for now--and get home as fast as possible. ... I will do anything possible to keep that doctor away from my children--the same guy who poisoned my wife."

*

As that day's bothersome snowfall intensified, the windshield wipers of Hank's fastback Mustang kept making a "clop-clop" sound--which bothered him to no end.

By this point they were just 10 miles outside of Centralia, headed toward U.S. Highway 50. This stretch of east-west road traversing clear across Nevada had famously been dubbed by "Life" magazine as "America's Loneliest Highway."

Doctor Robbins sat in the back seat, attending to little Peggy as their speed approached 45 miles per hour--considered a snail's pace on this isolated stretch of roadway, where most drivers liked the fact that virtually no speed limit was posted.

This was among the many things that Hank cherished about the Silver State, the region's rebellious and independent nature. The big-city folks from God-awful places like New York and Chicago misunderstood this mindset, ensconced in their own warped metropolitan way of thinking.

"Hey, doc, I hope everything is warm enough for you back there." Hank adjusted the rear-view mirror, in hopes of getting a clear view of the doctor and his miniature patient. "I've got the heater up as high as possible."

Rather than getting a verbal response, Hank heard a low-pitched grumbling noise. To him, this sounded more like the ramblings of a grizzly bear, unexpectedly awakened by an unwanted intruder during the middle of a long hibernation.

"Uh-umm," the doctor grumbled. "What was that you said?"

"The heat ... Doctor, is the heater working well enough for you?"

Getting no response, Hank checked the rear-view mirror and momentarily watched the physician apply a wet cloth to the child's forehead.

"Fine ... Fine," the doctor said.

By this point, following several months of knowing this man, Hank fully realized that this physician rarely spoke much-- truly a person of few words.

Directly ahead of them, through the windshield and amid the heavy snowfall, Hank could still see the flashing red light of the sheriff's car. This official escort made the driver feel at least somewhat at ease, considering their mutual predicament.

Although this was a rebellious land, where almost every man in the wilderness strives to live a righteous life--behaving any way that he personally "sees fit"--there are certain rules that every lawman must adhere to. In this instance, bureaucratic regulations prohibited the sheriff from venturing into another county--while working in his official capacity as a sworn official who vowed to protect and to serve the public.

This meant, Hank knew, that in another 15 miles or so, that he, the doctor and this ailing child would need to continue traveling on their own. Many dozens--and occasionally hundreds- -of miles from the nearest towns, this notorious stretch of road tested the independence and gumption of weary travelers.

To fail, to be unprepared, sometimes meant their own demise from a lack of food or water. Those who foolishly dared to travel these parts without adequate gasoline supplies or engine- fixing skills sometimes learned the hard way--via their own excruciating deaths.

For his part, Hank had plenty of his own worries on that day, namely the fact that he and his wife Paula--the sister of Pamela and Polly--had not cordially spoken to each other for at least the previous three months. To him, it was as if his wife had suddenly and mysteriously turned into a proverbial statue of ice--

appearing to him as if a long-dead blues singer.

Worsening matters multi-fold, at least from Hank's perspective, their brother-in-law, Honest, had developed an illogical and irrational hate toward the same doctor who sat in the back seat at that very moment--striving to save the plumber's child.

"Lord only knows how Honest will react, once he discovers this morning that one of his beloved girls has been taken away by this physician," Hank thought, strumming his fingers on the steering wheel. "I can only imagine the rage."

Momentarily, up ahead of them Hank noticed that the right-turn signal on the sheriff's car had been activated. Then the law enforcement vehicle pulled slowly to the side of the highway. Common sense motivated Hank to slowly pull to a stop in the middle of the road, directly beside the glowing red cherry top.

While still in the driver's seat, Hank reached across and unrolled the Mustang's front passenger window. A sudden rush of snow blasted into the vehicle, taking him by surprise; stunned, this man realized right away that he should have known better.

"Hank, the emergency radio system has gone down!" The sheriff hollered from his own driver's seat. "This blasted storm is far more severe than forecasters realized. They had called for a wimpy storm and now we've got a giant."

Without warning, the doctor surprised Hank by leaning far from the back seat and poking his own head into the space of the open front passenger window. Snow suddenly accumulated on the physician's head, giving him a bold appearance that made Hank think of what a mountain lion must look like during the height of winter.

"Thank you, sheriff." The doctor yelled, far more words than Hank had heard him utter in a single sentence for several months.

"I have been unable to contact the ambulance crew by radio!" The sheriff used his left arm to motion for them to proceed forthwith. "I'm afraid you all are on your own. ... May God be with you on your travels."

"One last thing." Doctor Robbins seemed to speak--at least from Hank's perspective--as if he were in a cozy, warm doctor's office, rather than amid the height of a life-threatening storm. "This child's life is virtually in danger. ... We have no choice other than to push forward in every way possible. Please feel free to tell her father that, if you should happen to see him."

"You need to face reality," the sheriff said. "You need to get real ... You know how that man feels about you, doctor, the intense anger and the unstoppable rage, and.."

"I'm well aware of all those things, sir ... So there's no need for you to lecture me at an urgent time like this ... With any luck, we will enable this difficult situation will work itself out, when the time emerges. Until then, all we can try to do is move forward, and do the best that we can as fast as humanly possible."

Six

Just three minutes after leaving his wife's graveside services, Honest raced the station wagon along Tranquility Street. The vehicle swerved, skidded and slid in several positions--primarily because he drove much too fast for the snowy conditions.

Pamela lacked even a hint of fear, at least in that moment, knowing full well that within just a few months she would be dead anyway.

Nonetheless, while in the passenger-side front seat, she remained concerned for the welfare of everyone else--rather than worrying about herself. Honest's instant decision to avoid Polly's wake at the church hall had come as an automatic reaction.

As far as Pamela could tell, her brother-in-law's extremely dangerous behavior seemed oddly rational--considering the fact that family friend Bill McCready had spilled the news right when she and Honest got back in the vehicle back at the cemetery.

"Honest, I wanted to wait until now to let you know," Bill had said, while he sat beside Penelope and Tommy in the back seat. "The sheriff rushed Doctor Robbins and Hank from the church to your house ... Poor little Peggy has become critically ill."

Hearing this, Honest immediately shifted to "drive," and sped from the graveyard in a manner that reminded Pamela of those TV sports programs where speed-track competitors floor their accelerators as soon as a green light finally flashes.

Instead of smoke and burning rubber shooting from the rear of the station wagon, streams of mud-caked snow had sprayed onto the few onlookers behind them.

As the station wagon slipped along Main Street, little Tommy--still sitting like a dutiful soldier in the back seat--blurted out: "Dad, is mom in a hole in the ground now?"

Rather than respond, Honest made the sharp turn from Main Street onto Tranquility--sending them into a tailspin. At this juncture, Pamela recalled a plea from her now-dead sister, made just two months earlier a few weeks before Thanksgiving.

Polly had urged the suntanned Hawaii resident to always do whatever reasonable to keep Honest as far away as possible from her physician. While bedridden, the ailing woman told of her persistent worries that a deadly disaster might ensue.

Lucky for all of them, Honest somehow managed to straighten out the vehicle moments after they reached Tranquility.

"Honest, please try to keep a level head about this emergency situation." Bill McCready cradled the children in each of his arms, holding them in the back seat. "I'm sure that the doctor is doing his very best to to save Peggy ... We all need to keep our wits about us."

As the windshield wipers clapped full force, Pamela began to worry about everyone with her--rather than herself. She realized that the family likely would have to endure even more hardship after her own demise, which likely would be very soon.

The widower accelerated to 55 miles per hour, as visibility decreased to only about 250 feet. Pamela realized that they could crash into just about anything without having adequate time to stop--another vehicle, a pedestrian, or even a deer.

"Dad, I asked you, please--is mother in the ground now." Tommy's pleas for an answer struck Pamela as far more urgent and desperate than just a minute earlier.

"No, Tommy." Pamela decided to answer, aware that Honest had another pressing issue on his mind. "Your mother is not deep inside a hole ... Right now, she is up in heaven with God, who loves each and every one of us."

*

Amid near white-out conditions, with visibility a mere 100 feet, Hank drove along America's Loneliest Highway at what he considered a sensible snail's pace.

The Mustang speedometer indicated they were going only 20 miles per hour, although he guessed they actually went maybe 15 at most.

The doctor had remained quieter than a field mouse, since they had parted ways from the sheriff just 10 minutes earlier.

By Hank's calculation, at this rate the trek to Reno would take well over a full day, many times longer than the typical drive time of five hours. Complicating matters multi-fold, they had only half of a tank. The danger of running out of fuel remained a potentially deadly possibility, far from civilization.

As if these worries were not already enough to make Hank tremble, adding to the danger--as far as he knew--they had hurriedly left without bothering to gather food or beverages. Many people had perished in the Nevada desert for making lesser mistakes.

"Would you care for a sandwich?" From the back seat, the doctor displayed an 8-inch, fresh-looking turkey-on-wheat--which Hank, both surprised and delighted, could clearly see in the rear-view mirror. "Eating would be good for us at a time like this."

"Mister, you are a life-saver!" Hank made no effort to hold back his own smile. "You must be some kind of a miracle worker. ... You think of everything, don't you?"

While carefully concentrating on his urgent driving chores, Hank took just enough time to also notice that the doctor continued to care for the ailing child.

"I'm just a regular guy." The doctor reached over and placed the sandwich into Hank's right hand.

Unexpectedly getting this meal suddenly made Hank realize just how extremely hungry he had been. This entire morning had been hectic and stressful, accented by the fact that his wife, Paula, had refused to speak a single word to him in many days.

Oblivious from such concerns, at least for the moment, Hank used his right hand to manage the sandwich--while his left handled driving chores.

On the back seat, he saw, the physician take a slow, purposeful and tiny bite of a much smaller sandwich--which appeared to be a swiss cheese and salami on rye.

"I guess it pays to be prepared--doesn't it, doc?"

"Yes, I suppose. That's what my late mother always told me, bless her soul."

Glad to lighten the mood somewhat, despite the nagging and constant "klop-klop" of the tired windshield wipers, Hank decided to engage in a much lighter conversation, if at all humanly possible. From his view, their mutual situation had become far too exasperating to concentrate only on gloom and doom.

Well aware that Peggy remained unconscious, the driver decided to pose this question: "Doctor, how would you like to hear a bit more about your little patient here--her personality, her typical behavior, and what she means to our town?"

"By all means, fire away." The doctor unexpectedly displayed a newly opened bottle of soda. "Care for a beverage? ... I'm all ears."

Without bothering to say "thank you," Hank placed his sandwich on the otherwise empty front passenger seat and promptly accepted the beverage.

Just then, in an instinctive reaction, he suddenly slowed the vehicle to just 10 miles per hour--having spotted, through the expansive whiteness, what appeared to him as if a barely discernible dark image way up ahead.

While careful to observe the fuzzy-looking dark object, Hank started telling the doctor that in recent months Peggy had become somewhat of a local celebrity in their town. This 4-year-old full of boundless energy personally hand-drew more than 150 thank-you cards, delivered by mail carriers to residents throughout the community.

Despite her tender age, this child thought of unique ways to personalize each note of appreciation. This emerged as her way of showing the Davis family's sincere gratitude for the town's help in meeting their urgent needs, particularly during those last few months when Polly's fatal illness progressed into its final stages.

Hank commented that these behaviors by the girl seemed as if an "odd, mysterious and somehow magical" mixture of childlike innocence--along with a maturity far beyond her tender years. Because Peggy was still too young to read and write, each note had been addressed by Hank's wife--the child's Aunt Paula.

Overall public interest in these notes had intensified by the day Polly died, because Peggy had managed to draw and color unique and one-of-a-kind images for each thank-you letter recipient. The most noteworthy of these, judging by public comments, had been images of cookies and cupcakes for the baker, an image of Jesus Christ for the preacher, and a perfectly formed five-star police badge for Sheriff Peters.

"Pretty cool, huh?" Hank said, at this point slowing to about 5 miles per hour because the blurry dark object up ahead--barely visible through this intense snowfall--seemed much bigger than just a short while before.

While still applying a cloth to Peggy's forehead in the Mustang's back seat, the doctor responded by saying, "Sounds to me like this child has plenty of talent, and lots of love to give to the whole world ... For her sake, we need to get to the hospital in Reno as soon as we can ... I'm not trying to pressure you ... What was your name again, sir?"

"Oh, that's OK ... Everyone calls me Hank, although my actual name is Henry," he said, while turning the car's heater up a notch. "As soon as this storm eases up a bit, with any luck we'll be able to zip along like a race car."

Sensing a need to talk, rather than merely creeping forward in total silence, Hank said that the pictures drawn and colored by Peggy had all looked feminine in every regard--"totally girly, each one of them, if I must say so." This impressed town residents as particularly curious or at least somewhat interesting, because this child's demeanor had always been 100-percent masculine--from the forceful ways that she threw baseballs to her ultra-rowdy wrestling style, often eager to pick a fight with just about every boy her size. Even her older brother, Tommy, had long since learned to avoid engaging in such antics with Peggy--forgetting the fact that the boy always acted tougher than a hammer, obviously quite capable of whipping her had he wanted.

Adding to the town's sense of mystique, Peggy always chattered in a rather low-pitched, unusually masculine voice--seemingly out of place for such a dainty looking little girl. Conversely, although no one ever seemed to make any big deal of it, Tommy had a rather high-pitched voice laced with distinctly feminine tones.

"Isn't it quirky, doctor, how close relatives turn out so different from one another? ... In my day, I have come across several situations that ..."

"You better stop!" the doctor hollered, pointing straight ahead toward the blurry, indiscernible dark object straight ahead.

Hank applied the brakes hard, sending the vehicle into a slight skid--although they had only been going 5 miles per hour.

Momentarily, the car came to a complete stop.

The windshield wipers kept making a "clop-clop" sound, while both men sat in silence for about 10 seconds.

The snowfall suddenly began subsiding somewhat, to the point where Hank could fully see the object--motionless about 5 feet in from the front bumper.

"Look, doctor!" Hank made no effort to censor his own excitement, always exhilarated when coming upon such an unexpected sight. "It's a horse!"

During Hank's entire 35 years living in the Nevada wilderness, he had never seen such a stupendous natural sight up this close. Big-city folks unfamiliar with the expansive, wide-open Silver State sometimes became startled by such unexpected sights.

"Wow!" The doctor made no effort to censor his own deep-felt reaction, the first time Hank had seen the physician display any sort of intense emotion. "This is perhaps the most spectacular natural sight that I have ever seen."

The wonders of these seemingly endless deserts had never ceased to amaze Hank, and this particular instance emerged as no different. Around almost every bend in these lonely high-desert Nevada roads, or upon reaching the crests of new horizons, surprising new wonders often generated heart-pumping scenes such as this--so wondrous and spectacular that only the world's best photographers could capture such images, with any necessary degree of appropriate pristine elegance.

"Take a look all around us, doctor," Hank smiled broadly, feeling joyful for the first time in many weeks.

Like the driver, the physician gazed all around them--peering out each window of the vehicle, proclaiming, "such an amazing sight, during an emergency situation such as this ... These animals all seem spookily calm, almost as if unconcerned about whether or how they might survive these harrowing conditions."

The snowfall suddenly disappeared--enabling the men to carefully inspect these many wayward travelers.

Left speechless by the sight, Hank began to guess that his car was surrounded by from 50 to 70 horses. Some animals were extremely dark, almost to the point of being black, while others seemed a light-tan--a distinctive brown typical in worn-out cowboy boots.

Hank marveled at the diversity. Many looked to him as if emaciated, literally on the verge of starving--the shrunken rib cages offering stark glimpses of their taught skin and nearly exposed bones. Others among them appeared to Hank as if super-muscular, strong and exceedingly vigorous--almost as if, at least from his view, none of these particular individuals would ever submit themselves to being tamed.

"Doctor, if you haven't guessed by now, I'll let you know--these are wild mustangs, considered by some people as God's gift--his blessed message to us--that life can endure and live free, even here in desolate, little-known places such as this, amid the continual threat of extreme hardship and sudden death."

"Hank, I have to agree with you--but we need to realize

that these creatures have us locked in to an extremely precarious situation."

Right away, unexpectedly in the rear-view mirror, Hank saw a sight that left him startled and somewhat perplexed.

Little Peggy suddenly sat up straight on the physician's lap.

"Where are we?" she said, while rubbing both of her eyes. "Are you the doctor?"

"Yes," he said, smiling so broadly that Hank knew that this medical professional surely felt delight at this unexpected event.

She stretched her arms in opposite directions.

"Did you know that my dad wants to kill you, to send you to hell--and that my mommy is in heaven now?"

*

Pamela lacked any inkling of what she should do, or how to react to her brother-in-law's unpredictable behavior. Until that morning, she had never seen Honest behave in any way that seemed ridiculous or even unduly dangerous.

Yet this incident emerged as a significant exception.

The moment that this man parked the station wagon, he hopped out of the car and raced to the Davis family home's front door--painted yellow in the precise way that his late wife had wanted, her idea of "perfect curb appeal" in such a dull-looking town.

The moment that Honest disappeared from view, Pamela started helping Bill McCready take Tommy and Little Penelope from the vehicle.

The bothersome chill from the snow falling on Pamela's face irritated her, yet not quite as much as the boy when he inquired: "Is dad angry because I misbehaved? ... I was trying to be good. That's what mom wanted me to do, and..."

Unable to think of an ideal response, Pamela held tightly onto the boy's hand as they trudged across the front yard--her mind already focused on the much-anticipated warmth that hopefully would greet them once inside. Bill followed close behind, the "crunch-crunch" of his footsteps sounding to her as if those of a vibrant youth in his mid-teens--rather than those of a 72-year-old man--a full decade after doctors had declared him legally disabled, due to some weird muscular disease.

    Just as Pamela had hoped, a sense of warmth engulfed her body the moment they walked into the living room. Yet her hands and feet still trembled, trying to shake off that pesky sense of cold from outside. Pleasant and heavenly thoughts of Hawaii quickly entered her mind, although at this point--three years after moving to the islands with her husband, Jeffrey--the novelty of living in a tropical paradise had long since warn off.

    "Where is Honest?" Pamela asked her sister Paula, and Dorothy--as the women took her coat, and those of the children. Bill did his part in helping, promptly hanging the garments in a closet near the front door.

    "As soon as Honest rushed in here, he said something about needing to get his guns right away." Paula frowned, her demeanor unusually gloomy--at least from Pamela's perspective, even when considering the fact that this sister had seemed unusually depressed in recent weeks. "He said something about leaving right away, and a need to protect poor little Peggy on her trip to Reno."

    A second later, Honest stood with all of them in the living room.

    Pamela felt stunned and awe-struck, particularly at the unexpected sight of him pointing a shotgun toward the ceiling--while carrying a .357-caliber Magnum in his other, that weapon pointed toward the same cheery wood floor that he had personally built.

    "I've got enough ammo to get the job done," Honest proclaimed, the sharp tinge in his raspy voice making Pamela at least temporarily think of him as if an actual pirate. This made perfect sense to her because--after all--his rugged outfit conveyed only one thing--piracy. His well-worn leather trench coat, burly dark boots and curly, unkempt hair made him a perfect candidate to play Captain Hook in a big-budget movie--at least from her point of view.

Momentarily mesmerized by the situation, Pamela lacked any notion of what to say or how to react, because--after all--she would soon die from cancer. At least that's what the Aloha State doctors had told her would happen.

"Dad, are you going hunting now?" Little Tommy stood at attention near the nutcrackers. "If you are going out to shoot a deer, can I go with you? ... Have I been a good boy, like you and mommy wanted?"

Bill, Dorothy and Paula each started blurting out statements of protest, as if collectively and individually trying to convince Honest to stay put--urging him to avoid doing anything irrational that he might otherwise regret. None of them got any definitive words out edge-wise in this regard, although Pamela felt certain of their motivations.

Honest promptly held his right arm outward, level to the floor, using his hand to form the universal signal for "stop." He held both weapons in his other hand, each barrel pointed toward the floor.

"Tommy, you have been the best son that your mother and I could ever possibly have hoped for--in our wildest dreams." Honest smiled broadly, his bright white and perfectly aligned teeth looking perfectly healthy to Pamela, and--strangely--somewhat sinister as well. "No matter what happens in the coming hours and days, my boy, nothing can ever change the love that all of us feel for you."

Tiny Penelope briefly belted out a whelping noise, and then promptly scurried into her bedroom, while sucking her thumb and carrying her beloved Pee-Pee.

"Abe, I hope that you are not planning to hurt anyone!" Dorothy spoke in an unusually harsh voice. Using his actual name--Abe--Dorothy had conveyed to Pamela that this woman considered this situation as serious. People rarely used his real name, except perhaps when ensconced in dire situations.

"Have I ever even hurt a fly?" Honest grinned, but only on the right side of his mouth--the other side had been permanently numbed by the same Viet Cong bullet that had obliterated his ear, just eight years earlier. He spoke while twirling the tumblers in the Magnum, as if to ensure that the weapon remained fully loaded. "My lady, have you ever known me to even step on an insect?"

Pamela sensed Honest's declaration had a ring of truth, excluding the inescapable fact that he had been awarded four military medals for slaughtering at least 23 enemy troops during some of the most intense battles of the Vietnam War.

In a sudden move, Paula grasped her brother-in-law's right sleeve, falling to her knees while begging him: "Honest, whatever you have in your mind is wrong--dead wrong. ... Stay here, please, with your children--where you belong."

Rather than answer, this man--who had what many people claimed was an uncanny resemblance to a young Abraham Lincoln--took a giant step back from her, pulling away.

Watching this, Pamela stood still, transfixed as if a statue. Her large blue eyes locked onto her only remaining sister, still kneeling on the floor. More than ever, Pamela realized that she and Paula were physically complete opposites. Although stricken with deadly cancer, the Hawaii resident remained as alluring and enticing as ever from the viewpoint of a typical adult American male--blonde, and perfectly curvy in "all the right and perfect places," her feminine voice enticing and mysterious.

In sharp contrast, nine years older at age 34, Paula was slightly chunky, her dark complexion and black hair almost as if those of a full-blooded Indian--the term used back then for indigenous people, later called "Native Americans." From Pamela's view, her only living sister was perhaps one of only a handful of women capable of potentially battling Honest, in a fair fight--neither using weapons. While this man possessed obvious physical superiority, Pamela knew that Paula possessed a much more crafty and unpredictable degree of "cunning and street smarts"--ideal mental characteristics necessary to surprise, overwhelm and potentially obliterate an adversary.

"Calm down, please, everyone." While standing still, honest jammed the Magnum into a holster on his right hip--just as fast as he secured the shotgun onto a leather strap around his left shoulder. "Like any sensible Nevadan traveling on the open road, I need these with me at all times for protection."

"Traveling, dad?" Tommy marched without hesitation to his father's side. "Does this mean that you're going hunting?"

"Well, in a sense, son." Honest gently patted the top of the boy's head, while Bill and Dorothy McCready seized this opportunity to sit side-by-side on the green living room couch--holding each other's hands in the shadow of the Christmas tree, far more fallen needles on the floor than just a few hours earlier. "I need to rush to the side of your little sister--she is ill, you know? ... Everyone needs you to stay here and help out in every sensible way possible ... Can you do that for me?"

The boy stared straight down, his mouth closed tight.

This marked the first time that Pamela had ever seen Tommy speechless.

"Yes, dad, I can do that," he finally spoke after about eight seconds. "I'm upset. I really do want to go with you, and..."

Honest quietly lifted his son, before promptly carrying the boy to the couch--setting him down beside the McCreadys. All along, Paula remained in the same place on the floor, by this point sitting rather than kneeling.

"Peggy desperately needs me now--just as any helpless, ailing child would crave her only living parent in such a situation." Honest adjusted his belt buckle, so fastidious in this chore that Pamela briefly wondered whether some pirates try to look sharp or at least somewhat presentable--at least in their own strange way.

"Tommy, your father is right." Paula looked toward the child, her smile looking to Pamela as if forced and strained. "You need to stay here and help us, in just the way that you promised your father. We all need you to be good, more than ever."

Honest then took three long, purposeful strides toward the

Christmas tree.

The sight of him there impressed Pamela as somehow uncanny. A giant man decked out in rebellious garb--his demeanor and crusty voice like that of a wayward seaman--seemed far out of place beside such a tree, a universal symbol of peace.

Slowly, methodically and with his eyes fixated beneath the tree, Honest knelt in a arduous effort to find something there. Finally, after what seemed like an eternity to Pamela, he pulled up one of the nutcrackers.

"This is the one--the soldier--that you called love?" Honest held the wood figurine up, while looking toward Pamela for an answer. "This is the same nutcracker that you said during the eulogy this morning, the decoration that you want to be buried with in just a few short months--after you die from cancer?"

Mesmerized and left speechless, Pamela stood motionless in the middle of the living room. She stared at her newly widowed brother-in-law's face, his eyes as kind as a saint from her perspective--although he was literally dressed to kill. Until this moment, Pamela had spent that morning mentally fixated on the wishes and needs of others--having already accepted her own impending doom.

"Yes," she said softly, striving to keep her voice calm, without breaking out into tears--which Pamela worried would only complicate matters for everyone. "This is the one--please bury me with it, right beside your sweet Polly. ... My doctors say it will probably be in just a few months, probably March or April."

Paula suddenly bolted to a stand, up from the floor in a flash that reminded Pamela of a jack-in-the box toy that they had played with as little girls. This time the older, less attractive dark-haired sister rushed across the room and summarily locked a mighty bear hug around the adorable one.

"No! Please tell me that this isn't so!" Paula trembled and wailed. "This is not true! ... Tell me that I'm only dreaming now, having a nightmare."

From behind, Honest gently placed his hand on Paula's

right shoulder, instantly making Pamela feel grateful that he remained there for them.

"It's true, I'm sorry to say." Pamela delicately broke away from the sisterly hug, taking two steps backward--eager to avoid feeling as if physically and emotionally smothered. "We all need to accept my fate, and move forward."

Bill and Dorothy McCready remained on the couch beside little Tommy, all eyes locked on the unfolding scene.

Unlike during the eulogy less than one hour earlier, this time Pamela failed to feel any sensation that her heart was racing. Instead, she felt that continual, persistent, strange and odd ache in her torso that had nagged at her gut the previous five months. Rather than a sharp pain, this always seemed a barely noticeable yet bothersome hassle. Going to the bathroom in a natural, easy way had become something from the past.

"Listen, everyone," Honest held both of his hands high, as if a seasoned warrior giving a peace sign--at least from Pamela's view. Throughout her entire life she had always disliked being the focus of attention. In fact, she had always protested or argued whenever relatives wanted to host birthday parties for her. And now this open discussion regarding her own health became the worst of all. Here, in a sense, she had felt as if an adorably cute and enticingly beautiful princess who desperately wanted to hide her face. "We are all running short of time, in the sense that we all feel a burning need to save the lives of two people that we adore-- Peggy and our adorable Pamela here."

Finally this Aloha State resident caved in to her own burning desire to intervene.

"I appreciate what you are saying, Honest." Pamela instinctively sat beside Tommy. "There is no need to make me the focus of attention, and ..."

"Please be quiet for a moment." Honest put a forefinger to his mouth, giving the "shush" motion for her to stop talking. "Believe me, I'm being as gentle, kind and loving as humanly possible at this moment--especially considering this urgent situation. ... Young woman, you are not giving up ... You are not giving up on yourself ... You are not going to resign to death ... We are fighters, and we always will be fighters ... Because of that, I refuse--and we all refuse, each of us--to allow you to sit around and wait for what otherwise would be the inevitable--your painful demise, and..."

"But I can't..." Pamela wanted to burst into tears. She wanted to protest. She yearned to escape this situation.

Paula suddenly sat beside her and briefly interrupted, saying, "Listen to this man, you know what he says is always right."

"Well, thanks for saying that, Paula" Honest briefly changed the subject. "Just like everyone else here, I know that you and I don't always get along with each other--as different from each other as the moon and the sun ... Anyway, what I'm saying here Pamela is that you're coming with me now--willingly and eagerly, because we're going to catch up to that doctor, and ..."

"Dad!" Little Tommy unexpectedly interrupted. "Are you talking about the doctor that you told mother that you hate--the man that you want to kill?"

"No worries there, son ... Believe me, I'm going to take mighty good care of that guy ... No one could possibly do a better job in handling that weasely looking doctor than I am ... Well ... With just as much urgency, Pamela, we're going to get you and Peggy to Reno as fast as humanly possible ... If my girl, God bless her little soul, has cancer as well--each of you is going to receive the best treatment imaginable ... Young woman, you are not a quitter ... You are going to fight, aren't you? ... You are going to battle in every way imaginable, doing everything possible to help save your own life ... Can you do that, please? ... Pamela, can you tell me that you are willing to fight, to get medical treatment?"

Pamela suddenly realized that all eyes in this living room were fixated upon her. Just as important, she understood that the doctors in Honolulu had told her that any attempt at treatment would be useless--exceedingly painful, and without alleviating her discomfort or doing anything to keep her alive.

"To hell with those stupid doctors!" Pamela blurted this without giving her words any thought beforehand. She surprised herself in doing so; her accommodating personality before that morning had always prevented her from speaking forcefully. "Yes, Honest, take me to Reno--please--as soon as you can ... Suddenly, I realize--thanks to you--that I truly want to fight--for my own life. ... For heaven's sake, let's get out of here and on our way as fast as possible!"

Cheers erupted all around as Pamela jumped from the couch and hopped into the accepting arms of her tall, sturdy and irreplaceable brother-in-law. Now, for the first time in her life, she knew what a woman feels like, the sensation when swept willingly into the arms of a pirate--not in a romantic or passionate sense--but rather as if accepted by lovable scoundrel, a unique guy blessed with a devil-may-care attitude. Other than him, she supposed, only an angel like the one atop the Christmas tree could possibly have inspired such boundless hope and positive possibilities.

Within what seemed to her as if few fleeting minutes, Pamela sat buckled into the front passenger seat of his Honest Pirate Plumbing truck. This modified Nevada Dairy milk delivery vehicle served their needs just fine, at least as far as she was concerned.

With only the two of them on board, this rebellious plumber--always considered a wise man--soon shifted into a higher gear. Barely able to see their relatives and friends through the heavy snowfall, the two of them waved goodbye to Paula, Tommy and the McCreadys--who all responded by hoisting their arms high into the cool air.

"Do you really think there is hope?" Pamela asked as they they zipped along Tranquility Street, the road ahead barely visible.

Rather than answer right away, Honest let out a long and loud yawn, stretching his right arm forward toward the windshield. His salty behavior impressed her as unusually relaxed, the true mark of a maverick who refused to be tied down in any one place for very long. From the worn-out expression in his only visible eye, Pamela guessed that he had not slept in many days--although for the most part he always acted refreshed and energized. Santa Claus never looked as mischievous as this man, at least from her view--although in her mind at least, the rebellious plumber had just as big of a heart.

"Don't you worry at all about the doctor." Honest issued one of his typically broad grins, as always only able to use one side of his mouth. "Once I finish taking good care of that guy, we're going to get you the best medical treatment imaginable."

Wanting with all her heart to envision a positive outcome, yet fearing otherwise, Pamela briefly glanced at the many firearms that Honest had haphazardly placed atop the dashboard. To her, these many powerful weapons seemed strangely out of place with the smattering of daisies there as well, obviously remnants from the many flowers that he had recently purchased for his wife's funeral.

Forgetting such details, still in the front passenger seat, Pamela tightly hugged the nutcracker that her nieces and nephew had nicknamed "Love." This woman knew that with any luck, very soon she and Honest would catch up with the doctor and the adorable Peggy--somewhere out on the lonely, isolated, and snowy highway.

Seven

Typical for the Silver State's wide-open ranges and expansive wilderness, the storm clouds above the wild mustangs began breaking up within a matter of minutes.

"Look, horses!" Peggy squirmed in the back seat of Hank's vehicle, sitting beside the doctor as she pointed out the rear driver's-side window.

To Hank, from his perspective via the rear-view mirror, the child looked just as healthy as any average youngster her age. He considered the doctor's expression as somewhat worry-free; the physician sat beside the girl, looking out another window.

"The wild horse population has doubled statewide during the past four years." Hank felt as though a tour guide while making these comments, realizing that his voice probably sounded corny to the man in the back seat. "I'm only mentioning this, doctor, because you seem mighty interested."

As the snowfall rapidly subsided, Hank edged his Ford Mustang forward just a few inches, before stopping again. Any unnecessary sound or sudden movement might frighten the many horses immediately ahead on this isolated two-lane highway-- possibly sparking a stampede.

Hank decided to avoid taking any unnecessary risks, with around 50 of these untamed and unpredictable animals all around them, each in close proximity.

He knew from many years of close-up, first-hand experience that wild mustangs have enough power to kick hard enough to destroy any car--particularly when the animals get startled by human activity. Much more easily spooked than domestic horses or even typical jackasses, these untamed creatures deserve a heightened level of respect. Well aware of this, the last thing Hank wanted were mustang limbs smashing through the windows.

"So, doctor, can we say this little young-un here is out of the woods?" Hank turned off the windshield wipers, the snow flurries having disappeared. "Peggy looks as healthy as a feisty newborn colt."

"Let's avoid getting too optimistic." The doctor adjusted his own tie, a move that Hank considered odd--particularly considering the fact that they were at least 100 miles from civilization. As far as this trucker was concerned, having a dapper and clean-cut appearance made no sense whatsoever, particularly so far out in this desolate rangeland. Yet maybe, Hank figured, such odd behavior can be forgiven or overlooked. Perhaps this doctor was just a typical creature of habit, about as typical as a lazy black bear scratching its back on pine tree or a greedy raccoon stealing eggs from a robin's nest. "Severe symptoms like hers can quickly disappear and then reappear, just as mysterious as these storm clouds ... Using 'caution' as our guide, we need to get to Reno as soon as possible to perform urgent tests."

"Whatever you say, doctor." Hank edged the vehicle forward, with just a bit more conviction than a short while earlier. Several horses ahead of them darted off the highway. "Looks like our good friends here are beginning to get the message."

Hank continued forward, rapidly increasing speed--first at 5 miles per hour, and then after several seconds doubling that rate.

His persistence soon paid off in dividends. The last of the mustangs on the road headed toward the south, soon increasing to a full gallop. All the other animals promptly joined their companions.

Although there was no need to do so, Hank stopped the vehicle once again, mainly because he knew this would emerge as a glorious sight for him and for his passengers.

Within a mere 10 seconds these wandering champions of the wilderness--individually and collectively--began running away toward the south at full speed. To Hank, they looked far more powerful and glorious than those snooty, high-fallutin' race horses that often appear in racing competitions on television.

Unlike those well-groomed, top-notch and expensive stallions that grow up in manmade stalls and that eat lush, tall and un-mowed grass, the animals here depended on their own wits for survival. Rather than being horse-whipped and ordered where to go like their big-city cousins, these rugged, untamed and unpredictable animals stole the show--at least in Hank's opinion.

To his way of thinking, the metropolitan breeds are sissies and worthless, always taught where to go, appropriate ways to behave and specific grains to eat--each meal dished out in pre-measured portions.

Those high-falluting, big-city breeds, surrounded by the trappings of excessive human wealth, cannot possibly compare to the swirling power and natural grace of these mustangs--born into this desolation, where they continually must fend for themselves in order to survive.

A sharp contrast to their big-city cousins, these untamed creatures--some mighty powerful and others weak--always set their own direction. Instinct and an innate desire for survival, coupled with a continual desire to roam free, makes each of their days unpredictable and packed full of boundless energy. This emerges as a big difference from their metropolitan and domesticated cousins, which typically get transported like captured circus animals in livestock vehicles and trained to sleep and wake on pre-specified schedules.

"Wow!" Little Peggy smiled broadly in the back seat, pointing toward the mustangs as the animals continued running away. "Pretty! ... Pretty!"

Hank felt mesmerized, literally speechless as he watched this unfolding scene from behind the steering wheel, the vehicle still stopped.

His eyes beheld this all-encompassing scene, to him by the far the best scene that he had ever witnessed, eye-catching and glorious creatures in the great outdoors. As the clouds continued dissipating and moving in various directions, a blue sky served as a sensational background canvas for the eyes. This contrasted with the whiteness of the snow-covered ground, the curves and elevation differences of the distant hills barely discernible.

Among these bright objects, the blue sky and the white ground, moved the darkness of these animals. Even at this steadily increasing distance, each of their muscles and movements seemed to Doctor Robbins as if blessed symbols sent from heaven. They sped across the horizon, so far away that nary a sound could be heard. The resounding power of these horses' hooves whipped the powdery snow sky-high, the puffs seeming to him as if the comforting breaths of a distant arctic giant--accents for the human eye, sent by Mother Nature.

"I swear to God." The doctor spoke in a voice that seemed unusually firm to Hank, as if the physician were revealing a previously hidden aspect of his personality. "In all my life, I have never seen anything so spectacular ... I will never forget this ... Ever."

Hank refrained from responding. He knew that as corny as this might seem, silence was indeed golden--particularly at a blessed time like this. The most powerful message that this trucker could possibly make was simply to allow the unfolding scene to essentially "speak for itself." Delighted to see the wide-open road up ahead, he accelerated to 45 miles per hour--the fastest that he deemed reasonable and safe for the current driving conditions.

"I feel sick." Peggy slumped back in the rear driver's-side passenger seat. "Where are we going? ... Where is my daddy?"

"We are taking you to a hospital, to make you all better." Doctor Robbins took off his gray sports coat, before promptly placing the garment across her torso. "The best thing for you now, Little One, would be to get some much-needed sleep."

The child began complaining that she could hardly move, her legs and arms feeling what she described as "way too heavy." At the point when Peggy's voice became barely discernible to Hank, he sensed that her affliction was far worse than a mere common cold.

Within five minutes, from behind the wheel he started to

hear her snore, a delicate sound that reminded him of a healthy and happy kitten's purrs. At this point accelerating to 60 miles per hour--the road wet and slushy by then--in the rear-view mirror he noticed a stark and rather perplexing expression on the doctor's face--a look that Hank deciphered as sign of serious concern.

"Doctor, you can count on me. ... I'm going to get us there faster than even a bald eagle can imagine."

Rather than answer, the physician held Peggy's hand, taking her pulse--while also looking at his watch. Momentarily, the medical professional's eyebrows lifted. Hank wanted to take this as a sign that the girl's condition had improved, but felt otherwise due to what he considered a super-serious expression on the doctor's face.

"Hey, doc, would you care for a drink?" Hank moved his right hand toward the glove box, while using his left to drive. "I always take along plenty of necessities, just in case of emergencies."

"No, thanks. ... I never imbibe while working."

The moment that Hank pulled open the glove box, several small whiskey bottles tumbled onto the floor of the front passenger side--along with three guns, each a loaded .38-caliber Smith and Wesson.

"Sorry about this sudden mess." Hank quickly slowed the vehicle to under 20 miles per hour, while slumping down behind the wheel and using his right hand to fumble through these wayward objects. Within a few seconds he hoisted up a Wild Turkey bottle, refocused on the road ahead and accelerated to 70 miles per hour. "As you have most likely seen, I travel with plenty of firepower ... I've got three loaded shotguns in the trunk, and at least 14 handguns there as well ... If you haven't already learned this by now, people need this type of gear for self-protection, out here on the open road in the middle of the Nevada desert. You never know when somebody is going to rush you from behind, or from almost any direction. ... Just like way back, more than 100 years ago, when there were plenty of Indians in these parts, protecting their homeland, you never know for sure when some bandit or any other type of enemy is going to suddenly swoop down upon you."

Without making any effort to slow down, Hank used his teeth to unscrew the bottle--before summarily guzzling down a mouthful.

To him, there was no better taste than fine whiskey on such a glorious day as this, or at any other time for that matter.

Still focused on the road, his head unwavering, Hank blindly moved his right arm backward toward the physician.

"Doctor, come on now ... Are you sure that you wouldn't like to enjoy a healthy swig? ... This amazing concoction is by far the world's best medicine, did you know?"

"For heaven's sake, just drive--and not like a devil ... You concentrate on getting us there safely, in one piece ... While I work to save this little angel."

*

Pamela gently picked a daisy from the dashboard of Honest's plumbing truck, one of the flowers that had been nestled among his many firearms.

While her brother-in-law drove them onto America's Loneliest Highway, she gracefully sniffed the pedals. The sweet, calming and smooth aroma filled Pamela's spirit with a calmness that had been absent from her psyche during the previous several months.

Still in the front passenger seat, she momentarily glanced to her left toward Honest, who had always looked to her as if at least a decade younger than his actual age.

At least in her eyes, he appeared to have the muscular body and laser sharp gaze of a guy in his early 20s, rather than a 42-year-old Vietnam veteran who by almost every account should have a broken-down body.

From her perspective, just about every aspect of this man seemed like a confusing dichotomy. Ever since Pamela had first met him a decade earlier in the mid-1960s, she had viewed his entire life as if a giant and confusing puzzle.

As far as she could tell, all the many pieces from this proverbial maze had seemed as if broken, or as though the man's entire life could easily implode at any moment.

Striving to remain as quiet and relaxed as possible, Pamela began to think about such things as the snowfall subsided. As clouds floated away, she opened the front passenger window just a crack to get some much-needed fresh air.

With any luck, Pamela knew, she and Honest would soon catch Hank's Mustang, somewhere on this isolated highway. She refrained from worrying about what would happen when that moment finally came.

Instead, for now she concentrated on this new-found inspiration, her sudden decision to fight for her own life--to beat this devilish cancer.

At this precise juncture, while fully focused on that objective, Pamela felt grateful that she and Honest remained silent. Neither said a word.

As far as she could tell, her late sister Polly's husband had always been just this sort of guy, the extremely rare type of fellows who usually "never speak, unless spoken to." This characteristic had always struck her as among Honest's best attributes; such behavior counteracted some of his many flaws or quirky personality traits--which she suspected were far more numerous than many people realized.

For the first time, there in the solitude of his Honest Pirate Plumbing truck, Pamela began to ponder what her battle against cancer would be like.

During her four excursions home to Nevada to help care for Polly, the first trip late in the previous spring, Pamela had witnessed the destructive side effects of that era's modern cancer treatment. The continual puking and gut-bending nausea often emerge as equally disturbing to the loss of hair and the extensive decrease in body weight.

Mental confusion that often afflicted such patients, coupled with extreme physical pain from the cancer itself, failed to fill Pamela with fear.

"I am 'brave,' although the pure essence of that word seems difficult to understand, or to fully comprehend," she thought. "Everything in my soul and within my heart wants to be afraid, to literally become scared out of my mind--and yet I know that I need to feel otherwise."

Tears filled Pamela's eyes as she glanced toward Honest again. An inescapable thought had suddenly struck this woman, the reality that this man was the only adult who truly knew her, the only adult in her family who would be at her side when treatments began. Surely this drop-dead gorgeous woman who was dying of cancer realized that she could not depend on her own husband in that regard.

Back home in Honolulu, shortly after returning to the Aloha State from her latest excursion to the Silver State, she had broken the news of her own illness to her husband--Lieutenant Jeffrey Tremblay, a highly decorated Navy pilot. To her, this military man had seemed cold, uncaring and even unemotional upon receiving this tragic news--although he tried to come off as warm, caring and eager to help.

Both Pamela's broken heart and her uncanny intuition revealed these truths to her. Quite regrettably, she had married a rather robotic, military oriented man who lacked the ability to do anything significant whatsoever--at least in matters that involved getting emotionally attached with loved ones and truly caring for them in ways that mattered.

Never once had Jeffrey suggested, or even hinted in a slight way, that she seek treatment for the disease--to fight in every way possible for her own life. Instead, he fully accepted and never even questioned the Honolulu physicians' prognosis--their conclusion that Pamela's cancer was fatal, irreversible and that absolutely nothing could be done to save her.

Taking a 180-degree different course and strategy was this giant, focused and highly determined man now behind the wheel. Unlike her regimented husband who embraced a personal philosophy dictating that "I will always do everything in life in the right and perfect way," Honest had always impressed her as a warm-blooded rebel, always eager to take a rebellious course in life, whenever he deemed necessary.

First and foremost in this regard, Pamela knew just as much as anyone that--although an outcast of sorts or at least a man willing to stand up to mindless decisions by people in authority--Honest always made family his top priority.

As she lay dying the previous autumn, Polly's every need and comfort became Honest's paramount focus, along with caring for their children.

Honest had scoured Eastern Nevada during that entire period, driving non-stop from town-to-town, looking for much-needed work. His efforts became somewhat legendary, if only on a regional basis. By many accounts, most men in his position would have given up after about a week or two, since the vast majority of potential plumbing customers said, "No."

Yet thanks to Honest's never-say-die and can-do attitude, he had proven just about everyone wrong. He always somehow managed to get work and necessary income just in the nick of time, often confounding even his most ardent supporters. This never surprised Pamela or her sisters, because for many years they had seen what he was made of--the distinctive and irreplaceable marks of integrity that many people overlooked or refused to acknowledge.

"Hey, look!" Honest exclaimed from behind the wheel, interrupting Pamela's train of thought--as he pointed about 75 yards up ahead of them on the highway. "Jackrabbits! ... Holy cow ... Many hundreds of those little critters!"

Pamela needed a few seconds to focus her eyes on this unfolding scene, but sure enough she soon observed the full perspective of the entire skyline.

Far too numerous to count, these wild, energetic and mysterious rabbits enraptured the human senses. As if an 18-inch-tall fright train--the equivalent of a few football fields in length--at least from her perspective--the rabbits scurried en masse across the new-fallen snow.

To her, these flighty creatures seemed to zip at about 100 miles per hour, although she realized that their actual speed was probably only half of that at most.

"Beautiful," Pamela said, choosing only a single word to emphasize the obvious. Without telling these details to Honest, she began thinking that perhaps this site was some sort of clear, distinct and inescapable message from God.

This vision of the scurrying hares, collectively sending billows of snow into the crisp morning air, made her think that life is all around us--almost everywhere on this earth that the eye can see. Indeed, as proven by this scene, life is boundless and limitless--embossed with many positive possibilities.

Oh, sure, she understood that many people in her position probably would have felt otherwise. They might think of these creatures as mere pests, bothersome animals that needed to be shot--their pelts sold to clothing factories.

Contrary to such negative attitudes, Pamela suddenly realized that there was a broad smile across her own face. Yes, in that moment, while hugging the nutcracker that everyone called "Love," she began considering her own life as a blessed gift, straight from the very hand of the Lord God.

More than ever at this juncture, she knew perhaps better than anyone that her life, her very survival would depend on two men--Honest, this unique fellow--and also on Doctor James Robbins--very likely at that moment in the Ford Mustang somewhere on this same highway--way out ahead, and still far from view.

From recent experience, the entire family knew that the physician was Nevada's only licensed oncologist--a doctor that specializes in treating cancer. Whether or not Honest hated the doctor, that man was the only medical professional capable of generating a cure for her--even if doing so meant administering what her brother-in-law always insisted on calling those "deadly poisons."

None of that would eventually become possible for Pamela, she knew, unless all of them survived this arduous cross-state journey.

For that to happen, she first needed to rely on Honest--who had left discarded Hostess pie wrappers across the floor of this vehicle. She realized that this man who always looked healthy from outward appearances had survived on cheap junk food for nearly a year--always making his dying wife and children the top priority. Inexpensive meals generated necessary savings.

Partly as a result, she accepted his profound flaw in the category of cleanliness, realizing that Honest tried to set his priorities in order of importance. Taking every bit of available time to look after the needs of his loved ones had become a much higher priority for him, far more important than merely scooping away some typical, everyday trash from his vehicle.

As far as Pamela could tell, he always spoke in gentle tones, even amid potentially explosive situations. His arms had proven exceedingly strong; he often performed arduous tasks that many people would never dream of attempting.

Perhaps above all, at least from her view, he often had an ominous, mega-powerful or even sinister appearance, a distinctive and unforgettable look that would have made him the ideal actor to cast as a super-villain. To the contrary, though, along with just about everyone else from Western Nevada, she viewed him as having a kind heart--a man who truly lived by The Golden Rule.

"How about this!" from behind he steering wheel, Honest had fished into the front pocket of his old, worn-out leather trench coat. Using his right hand, he promptly pulled out a giant wad of currency ranging in denomination from $100 to $1. "Donations! From just this morning!"

"What!?"

Pamela suddenly realized that her heart had begun to pump rapid-fire, starting immediately upon this unexpected sight. She had never seen anywhere near this much currency in a single place in all her life. For the next 15 seconds or so, all without saying another word, he kept fishing more and more cash out of his front pocket. He dropped each new wad of bills onto the floor, the currency intermixing with the many discarded pie wrappers.

"Honest, did you rob a bank! ... You devil! ... This is horrible!"

"No, my little sister." He said this in a manner that impressed her as lackadaisical, a downright signal of apathy toward Big Brother--the rich people. "Rather than some sort of heist or highway robbery, all of this has come upon us legally."

This woman stricken by one of the worst kinds of cancers made no effort to block her burgeoning delight, while Honest promptly told how he got the money. He explained that immediately after Pamela had given her sister's eulogy an hour earlier--and as pallbearers rolled the casket from the church--the many mourners had promptly taken up a collection for her. These funds were later handed to him by Bill McCready in clandestine fashion, at the precise point when Pamela had sat in the station wagon with the children--there beside the cemetery, amid the blinding snowfall.

Seeing this currency inside the plumbing truck, Pamela briefly burst into tears, stricken by the reality that she had been worried about "how to pay for this"--almost as much as anything else.

"I'm so very grateful," she said, pulling a few $100 bills from the floor.

"Well, look!" Honest interrupted her as he pointed out the windshield. "Well, there is a sight for the eyes to behold ... What in the world is..."

Honest stopped his truck in the middle of the lonely highway, the road by now covered in slush rather than snow. Next to them, right beside the roadway stood Hank.

Pamela noticed right away that both of Hank's eyes had been blackened. At his mud-caked feet were two shotguns, at least

10 handguns and a maze of unopened whiskey bottles. She also spotted swirling tire tracks behind him, off the road and in the snow.

"Hank, what in the world has happened!" Honest bolted from parked truck, and ran around the vehicle. "Where is your car? ... What happened to Peggy? Where is she!"

"It's that doctor." Hank spoke in a low voice, his words slurred. "The guy that you hate, and would love to kill. ... He has stolen my vehicle, and taken your precious daughter."

Instinctively, Pamela hopped from the truck and approached them: "Hank? Good Lord, are you drunk?"

#

The clouds drifted away from town within a half hour after Honest left the community with his ailing sister-in-law.

Dorothy and Paula walked arm-in-arm together under clear skies, turning from Tranquility onto Main. Outside the church three blocks up ahead, dozens of cars still lined the street. By this point the bone-snapping cold had already been replaced by what the older woman considered as a refreshing and enjoyable tinge of slight coolness.

To Dorothy, these were the perfect kind of days where everything seemed quiet and super-peaceful, unlike those blazing hot summers that drenched a person's body in puddles of sweat--so much that that their clothes appeared soaked throughout summer.

As the retired county clerk, Dorothy felt she deserved to live out the rest of her life in relatively comfortable relaxation--forgiving the fact that she and Bill had a meager retirement, leaving them with barely enough to survive.

"I love you as if you were one of my own," she told Paula as they ambled through slushy snow on the sidewalk. "The fact that you trust me enough to tell me your secrets this morning showed boundless courage. I admire you for this, largely because other women in your position likely would have cracked under the pressure."

With their intended destination--the church hall--just two blocks away, Paula responded by stopping momentarily and giving Dorothy a brief, warm and generous hug.

"Thank you, for your willingness to listen to me earlier this morning." Paula reached out to hold her friend's hand; this marked a drastic change since they had been antagonistic toward each other just a few hours earlier, nearly to the point of becoming enemies.

Together, they promptly resumed their trek, having left Dorothy's husband--Bill McCready--back at the Davis home to watch after little Tommy and his sister Penelope.

Heading to the church as soon as possible had struck both women as the right, proper and necessary thing to do--considering the fact that hundreds of people had gathered there for Polly's wake. Out of respect and gratitude, someone from the family needed to attend with at least a semblance of grace and dignity--especially after Honest and Pamela had just high-tailed it out of town without any prior notice.

At this juncture, Dorothy felt clear-headed, calm and in complete control of her mental faculties, the total opposite from just 90 minutes earlier when she felt unsure of precisely how to react to Paula's short-term tirades.

Dorothy used these few minutes for thought and reflection as she walked with Paula. The older woman came to the conclusion that their insightful conversation earlier that day had the possibility of reaping huge rewards. Dorothy realized that by telling someone, Paula had finally been able to share some weighty matters with another human being. Keeping important secrets can lead to undue stress, making the body, mind and heart prone to disease or even death.

"To become overly critical of Paula would fail to do any of us any good," Dorothy thought, as they walked across First Street. "Spending a lifetime holding such secrets deep inside can only lead to heartache and sorrow. From the very young to the extremely old, everyone needs a simple and effective way to relieve their stress."

By the time their feet simultaneously reached the curb, Dorothy decided that she could never judge or blame this woman at her side. Paula had never done anything wrong in her view, although realizing many people likely would have thought otherwise.

Perhaps more than anything else, Dorothy sensed that she would have gone to pieces--mentally and physically--if stuck in a situation similar to Paula's.

The fact that Paula's former "secret" fiance--Honest--married her late sister had been insult enough. But the fact that the now-dead woman had lied to make this happen had worsened the already-difficult situation.

Upon hearing Paula tell the story, Dorothy came to believe that just more than a decade earlier Polly had concocted a devious plan to snare the man that she loved.

In 1963, while he was an Army sergeant home on leave from Vietnam, Honest and Paula had been secretly engaged to each other. They swore their undying love and devotion, vowing to remain faithful.

At face value, Dorothy believed, theirs had been a typical and predictable American love story--boy meets girl, and boy intends to marry girl.

But a few years later everything went off kilter in early 1965.

That is when Honest--then known by his birth name of "Abe"--returned home on leave again, only to discover at that time that Paula--the dark-haired sister--was away attending Boise Business College in Idaho.

This part of the story was true, but a "terrible lie" got interjected that would change the course of all their lives. The deception occurred when Polly--the golden-haired sister--went out with Abe to a diner for a cup of coffee on Valentine's Day, February 14, 1965, the evening that this soldier had returned home on leave.

Polly had suggested this outing under the guise of an innocent get-together. Yet during this chit-chat the younger and cuter of the two sisters made a bold-faced lie.

"Paula has been engaged to a Boise businessman--Walt Hawkins." Polly had said this in a matter-of-fact way during that fateful get-together for coffee, as--in all likelihood--Abe must have frowned. "Paula told me all this, everything about her brand new love, while she was home for Christmas. She was ecstatic."

Abe supposedly seemed dumbstruck for the next few days, behaving as if suffering from a severe concussion suffered in battle. He and Polly promptly began a whirlwind courtship of their own.

"I know this sounds like the plot from a bad soap opera--but it actually happened to me," Paula had told Dorothy earlier on the morning of Polly's funeral. "By the time that I returned home from college that summer, my sister and he had already made their wedding plans. I went into mental shock upon hearing the news. You see, I never was in love with or engaged to a man named Hawkins--he was just a guy that I had met."

Adding insult to injury, that summer during the week immediately before he married Polly, Abe refused to talk with Paula or to even broach the issue; he had ignored Paula's pleas when she begged him to chat with her. The tall, muscular and smooth-voiced Army guy had been the love of Paula's life--the man that she had thought about from the moment she awakened each morning, until going to sleep every night--praying for his continued safety.

"The nerve of that woman!" Paula wailed, when telling these secrets to Dorothy earlier that morning--on the fateful day of Polly's burial. "My own sister was evil to the core. She stole that man from me, just like a hunter that traps a cheetah in a net--way out in the African outback, where there are no witnesses to tell what really happened."

Opening up to Dorothy with these details had become the equivalent of a dam that had unexpectedly burst. Streams of specific details--all laced with anger--had streamed forth in a non-stop flow. Uncensored and without any particular order, scurrilous details cascaded from Paula's brain, rushing forth with the power and might of Niagara Falls.

At the time, Dorothy felt that everything was "right and perfect" about these many revelations; she appreciated the fact that Paula had finally, and courageously, been able to release these proverbial floodgates.

The proof of all this had finally come in the form of a diary, and love letters between Abe and Polly. Quite unexpectedly Paula had discovered these documents inside an old shoebox on a top shelf of Polly and his bedroom closet. This find had occurred while searching for Polly's favorite sweater, on an unusually cool April day--during the previous year, 1974, this light-haired sister had started becoming deathly ill.

Of course, Polly had refrained from admitting in those letters that she had flat-out lied to Abe. Instead, in carefully reading them, Paula had essentially put "two and two together," gleaning info such as a letter that Polly had sent to Vietnam, telling him in one particularly sappy note that "I hope the Lord can forgive Paula for leaving you, just so she could marry that rat Walt Hawkins, the man that she intends to marry up in Boise ... What kind of woman would do that to a great man like you, Abe? ... I hate to admit this, but my older sister must be a witch--the worst kind imaginable."

As if feeling an urgent need to give proof, Paula showed Dorothy this damning letter--atop dozens of other handwritten notes that the heartbroken sister swore were just as terrible, just as deceitful.

Perhaps worst of all, as a direct result of these changes, Paula's life had evolved into a proverbial train wreck. Instead of attaining even a smidgen of happiness, she had married a guy who ended up being as useless as an unemployed clown--but even worse, a goofy, mindless and incompetent drunk.

Getting hitched to Hank had been only one of Paula's many ill-conceived life decisions, but--as far as she was concerned--getting linked up with him had been by far the worst, most destructive decision of all. Unlike Abe, who had earned a well-deserved reputation as a sensational family man and a devout husband, Hank turned out to be utterly worthless in almost every regard.

In their eight-year marriage to that point, Hank had held at least 23 jobs--at least by his wife's count, almost always invariably getting fired after just a few months or so. Her husband always somehow managed to come off as being a dapper, stone-cold sober business type--although he swam in puddles of alcohol almost every night.

At least once every year or so, Hank got hauled into jail for some sort of minor infraction--every instance involving booze. Worsening matters multi-fold, Paula had returned with him to her hometown, determined to be a devoted housewife--rather than return to her chosen profession as a court stenographer.

"Deep down, most of all--I have wanted to be near, to occasionally see--to even glimpse for only a moment or so--every now and then, the only man that I have every truly, fully and really loved--and that is Abe," she had told Dorothy. "You might have noticed that I never refer to him as Honest--or even Abe ... You might have realized that I've always called him Abraham, because if he really and truly is as wise as everyone says, he would have figured all this out--that his wife was perhaps the worst kind of woman.

"I hate saying this about my own late sister--oh, she died young, didn't she--but for the life of me, I cannot change the way that I feel. ... In a steady progression during the last year, I have become increasingly angry at everyone ... Angry at Abraham for his ignorance ... Angry at my husband for being a worthless buffoon ... Angry at myself, for getting walked all over--tromped on--and for allowing all of this to happen.

"Perhaps more than anyone, I have been the real idiot here--slaving night and day to help my dying sister and her family, who actually must have hated me ... Being near the man that I have always continued to love, yet realizing that he must hate me to this day ... Yes, he really thinks--he must think and somehow believe, even to this day, that I actually used him and dumped him for a blue-suited guy up in the Gem State, best known for its tasty potatoes ... I realize that the only person to blame for all this is myself.

"So, yes, I'm angry ... But most of all, besides being

enraged at our federal government, I'm burning with contempt for all the people in this town--and a festering anger for all the people across Eastern Nevada as well. ... I'm angry because we're all supposedly fighters, a rebellious lot--but we refuse to band together to collectively battle against those wretched bureaucrats in Washington, D.C.

"If it takes the very last breath that I have, every moment of energy, I'm going to help lead this battle toward the bitter end," Paula had kept speaking non-stop this way, while Dorothy decided to refrain from interrupting. The older woman became convinced that enabling Paula to speak her mind and get these burning issues off of her chest would perhaps be the best release and the healthiest remedy for her. "Yes, we are fighters--or at least we should be--and we need to stand up tall. ... Americans, by their very nature, are collectively winners, but we--those of us throughout this region, we're behaving like losers."

At this point more than 90 minutes after Paula had uttered these words in a relentless, non-stop cascade of commentary, she walked quietly hand-in-hand with her friend, Mrs. Dorothy McCready.

The retired county clerk admired her friend's determination.

Upon reaching the church, the women walked down a side alley toward the entrance to the building's gathering hall.

Once there, they expected to be greeted by at least a few hundred people, at this point exactly 43 minutes after the wake began.

Right when Paula opened the door and the two ladies entered the room, many people surrounded them. Throngs of mourners crowded all around, lots of them asking how Pamela was doing--and about whether any news had been received on poor little Peggy. As she and Paula did their best to handle these many questions, Dorothy began to appreciate the fact that the people throughout his region truly care--they all just collectively have their priorities in the wrong place.

After a minute, Dorothy noticed that one of the mourners was a famous person.

Dressed in a spiffy, well-pressed black suit and with a cigar dangling from his mouth, U.S. Senator Larry Spickler looked to Dorothy as if much shorter in person than the image from his campaign advertisements; those always portrayed him as tall and powerful.

In her eyes, particularly up this close, he looked more like a white-faced chimpanzee, a sharp contrast to the super-strong King Kong image portrayed in the mainstream news media.

With all eyes glued on them, this pleasantly plump politician gracefully took off his small black hat, and bowed toward the women.

"So sorry for your loss ... Please accept my sincere condolences."

"Mister, you should be ashamed!" Paula spoke at the top of her lungs, her voice so determined, direct and focused that Dorothy quickly filled with unexpected pride. "How dare you, mister, show your stinking face in a place like this--at a time like this. It's worthless, greedy skunks like you and your Washington bureaucrats that are killing us all. I'm not afraid to say this here and now, because everyone here must know--or needs to know--that what I say here is true. ... So, get your unworthy butt out of here, now!"

Nine

    Showing up for work at Sierra Crest Regional Hospital had always been a hassle as far as Anthony Dunn was concerned. This 57-year-old grandfather had to walk five miles clear through downtown Reno to reach his job as the facility's only day-shift security guard.
    On most work days, Anthony dreaded the trek, mostly along South Virginia Street, the primary north-south route through the center of town. His cranky right knee always made these two-hour journeys an exceedingly painful endeavor.
    Every step of the way, this widower always smiled and waved at just about every motorist or pedestrian--hiding from everyone his loneliness, his persistent grief at the loss of his wife Maureen, and the inescapable fact that he felt like a failure in life.
    Topping this off, the pesky pain and nagging discomfort always continued throughout Anthony's entire shift. His old wound suffered in World War II continually reminded him of those battles, particularly when sharp discomforts would awaken him in the middle of the night--usually on weekends.
    Anthony hated just about everything involving his job, but he truly felt a deep love and devotion to everyone he encountered in the process--particularly the facility's relatively new cancer physician, Doctor James Robbins.
    As far as this veteran was concerned, all of the other doctors treated him as if he were a roll of toilet paper. At least from Anthony's way of thinking, those high-falluting snobs behaved as if far better than he--as if most of them considered him a worthless loser.
    By contrast, starting from the day they first met 11 months earlier, the doctor captured Anthony's loyalty, merely by treating the security guard with utmost respect. This became increasingly

evident during their first week of knowing each other, when this new guy always started calling him "General"--not in a degrading way, but rather as if a brotherly sign of camaraderie.

"This guy is loaded with barrels of class, a quiet charisma that all of the other doctors lack--those creeps," Anthony began thinking during their first few months of knowing each other. "I would trade all of those baboons for just one fellow like this."

Within five months, by the mid-summer of 1974, Anthony had realized that many of the other staffers had similar positive opinions of this younger physician--generally far more vigorous, charismatic and well liked than most of the other doctors.

Like Anthony, Doctor Robbins walked to work every morning, because neither of them owned a car. Muscular, svelte and in his late 30s, this medical professional's walking style was far more vigorous, faster and focused than the security guard's cumbersome gate--at least from this World War II veteran's perspective.

Occasionally these two had briefly encountered each other amid their walks, both waving and smiling a brief greeting--right before Robbins immediately blasted far out ahead, as if--from Anthony's view--the doctor had been rushing to save another person.

On the morning of January 9, 1975, bitterly cold even for Reno, Anthony still vividly remembered the previous May--eight months earlier--when the cancer doctor unexpectedly handed him a $20 bill, saying: "General, take this dough, and use these funds for your cab ride home every day this week."

"No, doctor." Anthony scowled, desperately wanting to accept the gift--but letting his pride rule out such a generous gift. "Never consider me as a pity case. I do not deserve..."

"Sir, I respectfully refuse to take no for an answer." The doctor continued holding the cash, his arm stretched toward the security guard. "You are going to get a similar amount from me every week, for taking a cab home."

"But I don't accept charity ... I refuse to take gifts."

"This is not a gift, this is far from that." Doctor Robbins made this statement in such a matter-of-fact way that Anthony instantly thought this might somehow be true. "This is your pay, that you deserve for your service to our country."

"But why do you..."

"There is no need for you to argue, and there is no need for you to try to save face, kind sir--because I fully respect you. ... I truly consider these earnings of yours as my pay-back to the veterans of our country. Our government has failed us--so many citizens that have earned our respect and admiration--people--men--just like you sir."

For the next few moments, Anthony faced an extremely difficult choice. He could refuse this offer--this "pay"--and walk the five miles to home, only to see his health deteriorate further, perhaps to the point of needing an amputation or becoming bedridden. From Anthony's view, the other option would have been just as potentially treacherous, the danger of losing a public perception of him as a capable and independent person.

"Okay, doctor, but only because you put it that way, I guess that I have no choice other than to accept this--what do you call it--'pay.'"

The moment that Anthony had taken the bill, the physician had another thing to say--a direct and to-the-point statement that left him even more mesmerized: "Of course, general, we both realize that there is the matter of how you get to work each morning. For the time being, I guess, you're still going to have to walk to work--partly due to the disturbing fact that this community still lacks a public bus service."

Across the desk from the physician, Anthony stared at the bill while sitting in a velvet-covered chair, feeling far more comfortable to him than the cheap furniture in the offices of the other doctors--those cheap creeps.

"General, you're going to get your $20 pay every week without fail ... All I ask is that you never tell a soul ... This is our secret, just between the two of us, and I think that you would want it that way."

"You've nailed that on the head ... Perfect."

"Yet there is more that I should mention--at least briefly. By this time next year, we're going to have an acceptable solution, so that you never have to walk to work either. ... Does that sound like an acceptable plan, General?"

The men agreed that sometime within the following month Anthony would visit Doctor Robbins' residence for an evening barbecue. The mere notion of this made the World War II vet somewhat excited, a reaction completely opposite from how he would have felt if invited to the home of any of the other physicians.

While taking his first cab ride home that spring day, rather than hobbling all the way as usual, Anthony began wondering if the doctor were as lonely as he. Did the doctor also feel isolated, as if cut off and far flung from the rest of the world?

Finally, three weeks later, while walking to this physician's home for the first time, Anthony anticipated that there would be lots of fancy, expensive furniture--along with a massive view of downtown through an expansive front window. A huge yard loaded with roses and an expansive house with a stately design would have been quite predictable.

Instead, upon arriving at the Yori Avenue residence, Anthony realized that this was merely a simple, inexpensive home--the type of place that this region's longtime residents typically called "matchboxes." If a person passed gas in one of these homes, the neighbors in any adjoining residence very likely would hear or smell.

"Nice place you have here, doc," Anthony said, his comment sincere while being welcomed by Doctor Robbins into the house for the first time. This humble place, seemingly big enough for a flea, was a paradise from the perspective of this security guard--who lived in a cramped, smelly, dirty and low-rent apartment complex near Del Monte Lane--several miles south of downtown Reno.

Rather than typical furniture, the common type of middle-class couches and chairs common in such homes, the modest living room of the doctor's house had only five lawn chairs. Right away Anthony noticed that dinged-up TV set was a mid-1950s Motorola--obviously a black-and-white, a far cry from Zenith color televisions popular in the 1970s.

Seeing this modest living environment, Anthony thought: "This is truly stunning--I thought that all doctors lived high on the hog, like royalty ... Boy, was I wrong."

During the ensuing 90-second tour of the home, which Doctor Robbins gave rather comically--as if imitating a docent at the Metropolitan Museum of Art--Anthony briefly glanced at: a bathroom that was barely big enough to squeeze into; a pint-size bedroom that contained only a single mattress atop the floor--without a bed frame and topped off by only a single sheet; a garage with an oil stain on the concrete floor, as cracked and greasy as Anthony had ever seen; and a folding card table in the kitchen--serving as the home's make-shift dining table, also surrounded by lawn chairs.

Through a smudged kitchen window big enough for a robin to peek through, this guest spotted smoke wafting from a small kettle-style barbecue.

"Tonight's dining menu, General, is a true classic--the best that men in our position can obtain," Doctor Robbins said this while opening the rickety screen door leading to the back yard, before summarily lifting the lid and displaying at least six hot dogs.

To Anthony, the meal looked pathetic, while also paradoxically emitting a -super-fantastic aroma.

"Would you care for a cold beer, sir?" The physician cracked open a Coors. "I just grabbed a few six-packs on the way home this afternoon."

"Sure! ... Normally I would argue otherwise, but somehow this impresses me as being great--super-fantastic, actually."

From that moment forward, through the remainder of that

tranquil evening Anthony felt as if he were a multi-millionaire in a low-rent district--but he didn't mind a bit.

The only noise in the neighborhood, immediately before and long after sunset, were the distinctive, crisp sounds of children playing baseball in the middle of the street. As the two men chatted non-stop, one ball even landed in the middle of the back yard--right before a boy of about 11 jumped the fence, saying: "Sorry, doctor ... I'll get this fast."

That evening Doctor Robbins became the first close buddy that Anthony had in nearly three decades. In intricate detail, they shared plenty of their own war stories.

The security guard started off by inquiring about the only image that he had seen affixed to a wall in the home--a head shot of a brunette above the fireplace. At first glance, the photograph reminded Anthony of Ava Gardner--the drop-dead gorgeous starlet once married to crooner Frank Sinatra. Unlike that lady from the movies, who always had a mysterious, alluring look--to this guest the image in the doctor's front room conveyed an unlimited aura of intelligence, intermixed with a different brand of feminine passion.

"That photo from the living room ... Is it your wife, doctor?"

"Yes, that's Maureen ... My bride ... The love of my life ... She died in a plane crash a year ago, on a mountaintop in the Andes."

"I'm so-so very sorry ... I cannot hardly imagine."

"Rest assured, my friend, I'll tell you about that later ... But first, please, I would like to hear lots more about you."

Although usually private and protective of his own personal background, Anthony felt safe and somewhat carefree as he began recounting his pleasant childhood, growing up as the ninth of ten children--on a farm near Stockton, California. Unlike most other families from that region, which mostly grew wheat, Anthony's relatives specialized in strawberries. As a child, Anthony had earned the nickname of "Little Rascal," a carry over from popular movie characters of the time--mainly because he always got into some sort of trouble; his typical mischievous behavior had included slithering into the neighbors' henhouses and swiping milk buckets crammed with fresh eggs.

"Those were the funnest times of my life, just being a boy--things like swinging above a river, while dangling from a rope affixed to a tree branch--or swimming in a pond with my buddies, even though the adults always screamed "No!"

These delightful times seemed a hundred million miles away from those wretched Pacific islands like Iwo Jima, where Anthony fought alongside his buddies--most of whom got their heads blown off or their limbs obliterated.

"Even to this day, I can still hear their ear-bending screams, the desperate sounds of those unlucky enough to get killed in an instant."

The security guard then described meeting his late wife, Betty. They quickly eloped in Santa Clara, even though she had described herself as "unlovable" because her legs had been deformed by polio. Nevertheless, they managed to have three children--all daughters, Charlotte, Karen and Christine--who these days never call him at all or return his messages. At age 47 in 1965, Anthony's wife died in her sleep from a heart attack.

"Doctor, please never feel sorry for me ... Life happens ... I have eight grandchildren, all boys--and I have never laid eyes on any of them. ... Now, tell me all about you ... Where did you come from, and how in the world did you end up in--of all places--this tiny city, Reno, Nevada?"

In what Anthony considered a rapid-fire, only-the-details manner, within the course of the next half hour Doctor Robbins gave all the basics of his own life story. The physician's rapid-fire habit of spouting off intricate information was perhaps the only thing that irritated the security guard about the physician--but only somewhat.

As a veteran himself, the security guard figured that the vast majority of doctors probably spoke that way--due to intensive training and eventually out of habit. The physician's just-the-facts-ma'am style reminded Anthony of the ultra-professional way that cops spoke in Jack Webb's hit 1950s and 1960s radio and TV shows.

Without going into much detail on this particular aspect, James Robbins told of growing up in an orphanage in Detroit, Michigan. His father, Daniel Robbins, a milk truck driver, had been instantly killed in a highway crash shortly after the future doctor was born in the summer of 1938.

Left penniless, James' mother, Jane--a housewife--had no choice other than to put her son, an only child, into the overcrowded facility. The Detroit Orphaned Children's Home had been built by the Methodist Church in 1922 to accommodate a maximum of 228 youngsters. By 1942, the building's population had swollen to 537.

Jane re-assumed custody of James in 1943, shortly after she married Byron Pfalmer, a traveling Bible salesman from Fort Wayne, Indiana.

When recounting these details to Anthony, the doctor recalled that he remembered little from those times--other than when children from outside the orphanage threw rocks at him through a chain-link fence.

The misinformed attackers, all of them from about 8 to 11 years old, had kept yelling "Die, little Nazi!" This happened although James was of English and Irish descent. That evening, although suffering from nasty looking head wounds that soon healed, he had prayed for his attackers before bedtime in the orphanage because--he had been taught--"it was the Christian thing to do ... Always keep forgiveness and love in your heart, since this is what the Lord wants from all of his many children."

After nine non-stop months of traveling from town-to-town in Byron's run-down, dented 1935 Ford Eifel, Jane divorced him in Cleveland, Ohio--citing irreconcilable differences. James always remembered that while he was a young boy, his mother had been a quiet, reserved woman who rarely spoke. That changed during her relationship with Byron; during the couple's most heated battles, they always yelled at each other from the top of their lungs, at least from James' perspective.

Alone together with his mom to fend for themselves during the remainder of his childhood, the boy suddenly found himself needing to become the man of the family. They both continually worked odd jobs at various Midwestern towns, always seemingly on the verge of becoming homeless.

When James was 12 years old in late 1950, they packed up their rusty 1940 Chevy convertible coupe and moved straight to the Los Angeles area--where she hoped to land work as a film industry seamstress. She landed infrequent short-term jobs doing that, but always quit in frustration because of the rock-bottom pay.

Meantime, while attending junior high and then high school, James served as the breadwinner of the family--always earning good grades, while working streams of after-school and weekend jobs, and also finding enough time to excel at tennis-- which would remain his favorite sport.

Hearing these details left Anthony feeling somewhat stunned and even amazed, sensations that he had rarely felt before. A part of him wanted to feel a tad jealous at James' many accomplishments so early in life. Yet for a quirky reason the security guard started feeling pleasantly proud, almost as if this young doctor were his own son.

"Can I call you my 'son,' in a round-about way?" Anthony interjected, right at the point when James finished recounting his first intimate encounter with a girl--a strawberry blonde named Jennifer, a high school classmate. "You might not realize this, doctor, but your story is nothing less than amazing--although this might seem difficult to admit. ... To me, you're exactly like the son that I've always wanted, but never had."

"Sure thing, General." The physician smiled broadly as he and the World War II vet clanked their beer bottles together. "Society dictates that just about everyone should call me 'doctor,' but by all means, you can feel free to call me, son ... Yet we'll always be of a much different rank, you know?"

"Now that is a little bit of poppycock ... How is that, just because I'm a General and you're a ... What is it, son, that you said your rank was?"

Already one hour after sundown, still on the back porch of James' rented home, James took the next five minutes to recap the events of his life from the past 20 years. By this point in the conversation, each man had scarfed down at least three hot dogs--the meat nestled into cheap white-wheat buns and slathered in watery mustard. For a make-shift desert, they both used strung-out wire coathangers to brown marshmallows over the still-hot barbecue coals.

"Some people might consider the last 20 years of my life as boring or typical, while the few individuals that I have told my story to insist otherwise ... By age 17, already poised to graduate from high school a year earlier than scheduled, I had already written my first novel entitled 'Raising Jane,' based on the fact that I essentially had to serve as the father figure and provider for my own mom.

"Thanks to my superior grades, I landed a full-ride scholarship to the University of California in Berkeley. ... Many people are mortified to hear this now, but at the time in that university, young men wore ties to class, a drastic difference from just seven years later in the mid-1960s when the emerging hippie culture dictated that everyone wear casual garb.

"Following my usual habit of always working multiple jobs, even while attending college for my undergraduate degree in pre-med, I worked every free moment possible of a limousine driver. One of my best customers was Calvin Harding, founder, president and CEO of Omni Healthcare International--at the time the world's largest hospital chain.

"Although age 20 at the time, I must have looked around just 15 years old--you see, I've always had that blessing or curse, if you will--looking significantly younger than my actual age. Although a super-busy man with many responsibilities, Mister

Harding liked me enough that he often called me for no particular reason--other than to encourage me to pursue my studies. ... Lots of people, I've been told, disliked this man because he always behaved like a hard-driving, rather unforgiving son-of-a-gun--although I always considered him among the best guys I've ever met ... And I must say, here and now, General, that I put you in the same category as that business magnate."

"You do?" Anthony felt stunned and surprised upon hearing this, blurting out his brief inquiry here as if to signify this opinion.

"I'm not trying to brag here, General, by any stretch of the imagination ... Some people might think otherwise, but I've always been an excellent judge of character."

Upon hearing this, Anthony became fixated on the physician's every word. The World War II vet sensed that this evolving story would become locked within his own psyche for the remainder of his life. He already felt close to his new buddy, unusual for the Stockton native--because for him, developing such bonds usually took at least a full decade--or perhaps much longer. This personal quirk had begun during Anthony's Marine Corps service, when learning that just about every guy that you get close with, as a brotherly friend, eventually gets shot to pieces.

Nevertheless, glad to have this much-needed day off from his boring hospital job, listening to the doctor's story somehow made him feel as if 20 years younger. Perhaps youthful vigor and the distinctive manly zest for life is super-infectious, especially for a guy who--approaching 60--feels as if life had quickly passed him by long ago.

James briefly recounted his subsequent years attending San Francisco State University Medical School, across the bay from Berkeley. By that point, strapped for funds, he had joined the Army as an officer--taking advantage of the military's agreement to pay for his schooling.

While a medical intern, patients that he assisted included the internationally acclaimed U.S. Army General Douglas

MacArthur--who had once famously said, "Old soldiers never die, they just fade away." Such a can-do attitude helped motivate the budding young doctor to simultaneously work jobs at numerous hospitals throughout the San Francisco area, while still attending medical school.

Seemingly possessing a super-human amount of physical stamina and mental energy, while approaching age 30, he worked overnight shifts at various hospital emergency rooms--attending class during the day. The notion of "sleep" had become seemingly non-existent to him. Even doctors need to realize that getting adequate rest is essential to maintaining optimal physical and mental health.

Yet throughout that period, James felt that he had no option other than to over-achieve--namely because his very survival, professional advancements and reaching his many goals required excessive dedication and commitment.

During the subsequent five-year period from 1963 to 1968, he underwent many transitions, so many that Anthony considered them as "enough to boggle the mind of a typical person."

Besides meeting his future bride, Maureen, at a USO social in the Grand Ballroom of San Francisco's Universal Palisade Hotel--remembered by James as the most pivotal evening of his life--"Oh, God only knows how much I loved her"--his many significant personal events during that time included: handling medical care for stoned-out hippies in San Francisco's famed Haight-Ashbury district--as anti-war sentiment intensified among many in the younger generation; got slapped with a mild reprimand from military brass for breaking Army regulations, violating standard procedure by working extra medical industry jobs--outside of his assigned course of study; got ensnared in a traffic jam amid rioting while traveling on business in Washington, D.C., in the wake of the Memphis, Tennessee, assassination of the Rev. Dr. Martin Luther King Jr.; and completed his internships and training at military hospitals in Virginia and Honolulu.

"By far, the most exciting and emotionally exhilarating

event during that phase had been my marriage with Maureen. While most couples have their snips and snaps, we were always stuck on each other as if affixed by Super-Glue. ... We made love with each other, both physically and mentally--without fail--every single night, at least whenever we were in the same community throughout our marriage. ... Of course, we never had children; our plan was to have plenty of kids--little Robbins--popping into this world around this current phase of my life ... But that, of course, was not to be ... Just thinking about her, remembering her--and what could have been, it's too difficult to..."

Anthony saw tears well up in James' eyes, as they sat together--still each roasting marshmallows and taking occasional sips of beer--which by this point--at least to him--seemed to have lost that cool, crisp taste--replaced by an unwelcomed warmth that confused the taste buds.

Quickly changing the topic, the doctor then spoke of his decision to go to Vietnam for a one-year stint starting in January 1969. The military had agreed to release him from service within a year after that hitch. Otherwise, by declining to go into the war's most heated action zone, he would be required to stay in the military for at least five additional years. For him, going into a deadly situation became by far the most logical choice; he felt highly motivated to begin his professional medical career outside of the military.

His one-year stretch in Southeast Asia had emerged as somewhat extraordinary--at least from Anthony's perspective, although James described his duties as fairly typical for many other doctors of his rank and experience.

Among just some of the many catastrophes or life-changing transitions for James while there included: personally conducting autopsies on 128 Army soldiers, inside a make-shift military shed deep in a jungle 117 miles north of Saigon; having to ward off no less than four attractive nurses, who each openly said that they were attracted to him--wanting to spend "alone-time" with him in his personal quarters; personally installing metal reinforcements around his bed, hoped-for protection from shrapnel--particularly during a period when the enemy intermittently fired upon their camp; being stranded overnight with 17 other military personnel on a small island, after a helicopter they were riding in crash-landed in the South China Sea--75 yards from the beach; and having the military transport aircraft that he was riding in--upon completion of his tour--shot at by the enemy, but not hit--as he left Vietnam with 238 other U.S. Military personnel on board.

Immediately upon James' return to the mainland, he and Maureen promptly spent three straight weeks in Northern California's Napa Valley--at the time mostly unknown, yet an ideal romantic getaway, even for couples who rarely got along with each other. Unlike those people, as James vividly recalled, he and his bride remained inseparable. They made love with each other all night--every night without fail, sharing each others' bodies and minds, while chattering and admitting their mutual excitement--dreams for a vibrant, thriving and prosperous future.

Exactly five weeks after this excursion ended, the tragic news came on February 23, 1970, via telegram to Doctor Robbins that his wife had been instantly killed in a plane crash. On her 30th birthday, Maureen was among the nine passengers and crew near the 6,634-foot summit of Yerupaja Mountain in Peru, while en route in an expedition to excavate previously unstudied archaeological sites near the famous Machu Picchu--the ancient 15th Century Inca community--high on a ridge above the Sacred Valley.

"Devastated, both physically and mentally, I merely went through the motions of doing my job--my heart shattered into a million pieces, my mind as numb as if shot with an overdose of novocaine," the doctor's speaking slowed down markedly as he said this, far slower than the rapid-fire speaking rate that had previously irritated Anthony.

While finishing up his military duties and studies, wanting to make a positive mark in the world, James then decided to enter what at the time was the relatively new specialty--a "cancer doctor," technically called an "oncologist." The late 1960s and early 1970s marked a pivotal period in the medical industry when many new doctors began becoming specialists. Before that many U.S. physicians were general practitioners.

James' decision to move to Reno had come quite unexpectedly, while visiting the community with several former Army buddies. His unexpected job offer came from Doctor Gerald Simpson, a senior citizen who had a small private practice-- primarily specializing in people suffering from cancer. Doctor Simpson died of a sudden heart attack five months after Doctor Robbins joined the practice. The former resident of a little-known Detroit orphanage had assumed full responsibility for the business, just a few weeks before his new associate died.

During the 11 months immediately before the impromptu back-yard picnic for the "son" and his new buddy, the "General," Doctor Robbins had already started serving hundreds of patients--who flocked to his medical clinic from across Nevada. Besides working at his Ideal Wellness Clinic, he also practiced and treated his most critically ill patients at the region's primary hospital--Sierra Crest Medical Center.

"He has got it tough, and he's helping people who face potentially deadly challenges," Anthony thought later on the night of their hot dog dinner, while taking a taxi ride home. "I can only imagine how his life is going to evolve ... The man is like a son to me ... I cannot help but feel loyal to him ... I would do almost anything for the guy."

Ten

At mid-afternoon on the day of Polly's funeral, Anthony sat at his security guard station just inside Sierra Crest Hospital's front door.

Although typically jovial at this time of day--while the end of his shift, he felt stressed and increasingly anxious. Doctor Robbins had not called him all day, the first time the physician had failed to make such contact.

By noon each day or often much sooner, without fail the doctor always called the phone at Anthony's desk. This had been the case even during James' current out-of-town excursion for his first vacation since moving to Reno nearly a year earlier.

Adding to Anthony's worries, as a seasoned security expert and public safety professional, he considered the doctor's decision to travel via hitchhiking as overly eccentric, bizarre and unnecessarily risky. The physician always tried to avoid driving, a lifestyle choice that continually perplexed Anthony.

On the positive side, at least from the guard's perspective, so far this had been an unusually slow day at the hospital. To him, most afternoons continual streams of patients and their families made the place seem like a disorganized beehive.

Yet the placid calm and serenity of that afternoon ended in a flash, as soon as Anthony glanced out the front window and saw a yellow Mustang screech to a halt. The vehicle had been going so fast that the tires sent out smoke upon stopping.

Right away, the guard recognized the driver as the man he called "son." Anthony grabbed his walking cane and hobbled quick-step to lend assistance.

Doctor Robbins had already exited the vehicle and reached the front passenger door by the time Anthony got there.

"General, time is of the essence." The physician opened

the passenger door, pointing to a little girl on the back seat. "She's critically ill. ... Get emergency personnel here right away!"

Anthony used his walkie-talkie to call for orderlies. The medical personnel arrived within one minute, immediately placing the child on a stretcher.

Momentarily, as these attendants rolled little Peggy toward the building, the General and the Son stood beside the parked vehicle--the engine still running hot.

"Please listen, General." The doctor spoke much slower than usual, the only time that Anthony had seen this physician without his hair perfectly combed. "I only have time to tell you this once ... Please do exactly as I say ... Take this vehicle to my home right away ... Fully wipe the car of any and all fingerprints, inside and out ... Then bring this car back here, park it in the loading zone and then call the police ... Ask that they have the vehicle towed right away--preferably to that junk yard way out of town."

*

Exactly 43 seconds after the child arrived, Doctor Reginald Conners spotted Doctor Robbins bolting into the Emergency Room.

"Aren't you supposed to be away on vacation right now?" Conners briefly glanced toward his associate, whom he disliked with intensity. The ER doctor thought of this new cancer specialist as overly brash and far too reclusive, a paradoxical mix that might tend to unduly endanger patient's lives. "James, is this your patient?"

"Yes, at least for now." Doctor Robbins quickly put his overcoat on a hook and quickly donned a traditional white, knee-length medical smock. "The patient is four years old, and I suspect she may have sudden onset of childhood leukemia, and..."

"Stat! ... Hurry!" In his late 50s, yet barking orders as if a college quarterback at the line of scrimmage, Doctor Conners issued commands to three nurses. "Oxygen! ... This poor little thing has just stopped breathing!"

*

Dorothy felt her own heart race rapid-fire, as Paula stood face-to-face with politician Larry Spickler.

"Woman, I'm afraid that your grief has overcome you." The politician slowly put his black hat back on. "I can fully understand that you must be overly upset ... The deceased was your sister?"

Watching the two of them up close, as at least 100 people stood around them inside the church hall, Dorothy worried that the politician and Paula might immediately start wrestling each other at any given moment.

From what this retired county clerk had seen of Paula in the past, she had little doubt that the 32-year-old housewife could whip the stink out of this portly first-term U.S. senator. From Dorothy's perspective, witnessing such a fracas would be a spectacular sight, particularly if this jerk got his butt kicked.

"You, sir, are a murderer!" Her face reddened, Paula stood her ground without moving--except for holding her right fist tight, the arm held upward toward the politician. "How dare you deny these killings, these cancers ... Worthless scabs like you endanger all of us ... Killer!"

Rather than yell back, the politician responded in a tone that Dorothy considered low-key, humble and even somewhat graceful.

"Miss, I sympathize with your tremendous grief." Senator Spickler bowed again, this time while slowly walking backward--away from her. "If you will be so obliged, I will humbly excuse myself now from this premises ... I respect the time that you so desperately need to grieve, in the right and proper way."

"Stay here and face me, you miserable coward!" Paula instantly picked up a wood chair, which she held high as ready to throw the furniture at him. "Are you a strong man, or a typical wimp?"

Just then from behind her, Sheriff Jonathan Peters clasped Paula's arms--an unexpected and sudden move that not even Dorothy had expected.

"Once again, my heart goes out to you all." Senator Spickler stood just inside the exit, waving goodbye to everyone as he used his other hand to push open the door. "I'm so very sorry for your loss ... That is why I cared enough to show up here today."

"Coward!" Paula hollered at the top of her lungs, and more than ever before Dorothy felt a deep love for this woman--whom she had once failed to understand and despised.

Several people from amid the crowd emitted the sounds of "oooh" and "ahhh," reactions which Dorothy considered as signs that many from among the throng disapproved of Paula's behavior--while equal numbers supported or even encouraged her feisty behavior.

Before anyone had more time to react, Paula squirmed and wiggled away from the sheriff's grip. She then set the chair firmly on the floor, stood up on that same seat and faced the crowd--her arms spread wide. To Dorothy, she looked as majestic as a bald eagle about to take flight.

"Everyone, listen to every word that I am about to say." Paula slowly moved her head in various directions as she spoke, a display that impressed Dorothy as similar to that of a seasoned politician--making eye contact with each person there. "Until now, we have individually and collectively been hiding from this issue-- as if ostriches sticking our heads into the sand ... But now we need to band together and fight for a worthy cause ... Let me tell you why, and how we are going to do this."

*

"Her pulse rate is finally increasing, doctors." Nurse Hannah said, while adjusting an IV. "And this child's breathing rate has improved, but only a bit."

The 20 minutes of non-stop efforts to save Peggy had paid off, at least for the time being. As the Emergency Room's chief of staff, Doctor Conners knew that James was licensed to handle general medicine such as this--rather than just cancer treatment.

"Doctor Robbins, can I assume that the parents of this

child are right out here in the lobby, waiting for word on this little one's condition?"

"My guess is that the father is not here yet ... This girl's mother is deceased."

While taking off his medical gloves, Doctor Conners scowled, the expression hidden behind an anti-bacterial mask. Something about this cancer doctor irked him even more than usual, a suspicion that James "broke the rules" far more than advisable.

"Should you talk to the man, or should I?" Doctor Conners inquired, as he and the other physician walked together--away from the bed where little Peggy lay.

"No worries ... I'll handle this. ... But first we need to get a quick blood test, to determine what disease--if any--that this girl might have."

"Fine." Doctor Conners entered another emergency patient's treatment stall.

James quickly submitted a form, ordering the test. Using a phone affixed to an emergency room wall, he then called hospital security.

"General, anything to report?"

Anthony quickly explained that there were three people in the lobby--a gorgeous blonde, a tall muscular fellow who looked like a pirate, and a white guy with two blackened eyes.

"Son, the injured fellow keeps yelling that you stole his car and attacked him. And the other man--the pirate--insists that you poisoned his wife--that you murdered her. This might sound unbelievable, but it's really happening. ... The men keep trying to burst into the emergency room ... Thankfully, I have three other guards, each helping me to hold them back ... The woman--my God is she beautiful--she is remaining quiet for the most part, but says that she needs medical attention."

"General, here is what you need to do for me right away, without fail ... Make this happen ... I know you can ... Have the men arrested ... Call the police ... Get the guys charged with disorderly conduct and assault."

"Sure thing, son. ... Anything else?"

"As soon as those fellows get hauled away, please call me and then I'll come out and check on the woman ... Do you know her name, and who she is?"

"Pamela ... She's the little girl's aunt."

"I'm familiar with who she is ... Oh, real quick, and just one more thing, General ... Did you get the Mustang towed and wiped clean as planned?"

"Sure thing, young man. ... The vehicle is in a junk yard, 20 miles from town."

*

Already exhausted nearly one hour before noon, Sheriff Peters trudged through a slushy and muddy parking lot behind the church.

Aware that he was extremely out of shape for a man his age, this 35-year-old lawman always disliked the notion of meeting with Senator Larry Spickler.

The notion of political payback and glad-handing always repulsed this lifelong Centralia native. Nonetheless, he approached the politician's parked limousine, while sucking in his own sprawling stomach--as if doing so might fool everyone.

"This guy's brain is made of poop," the sheriff thought, while smiling broadly in an effort to mask his contempt for the senator. "For the life of me, I wish that I never had to talk to jerks like this."

As the sheriff made a final approach to the long black Lincoln Continental, he saw the rear passenger side window zip down.

The lawman caught a clear view of the politician's apple-shaped head, those blue eyes strangely seeming to him as if out of place on such a stormy day. The cheery demeanor of the politician's gaze counteracted this deadly cold.

"Larry, great to see you, sir!" Peters made every effort to hide his contempt for this man. "I was hoping that we would be able to meet like this today."

Rather than respond in kind, Senator Spickler frowned--his expression making the sheriff think of a spoiled schoolboy who fails to get his way. The senator still had on his black hat, but by this time also wore thick horn-rimmed glasses--never used in public.

"Sheriff, let's forego the niceties." the politician growled. "Dag-nab it, you fooled me today ... You told my staff that this funeral would be a piece of cake, a sure-fire way to gain popularity by showing sympathy ... But then I had to face that woman!"

"Do you mean Paula?"

"Is that her name, for heaven's sake? ... I have other words to describe her, and in this instance I'm not talking about 'sweet' or 'adorable.' ... Quite the opposite..."

As the sheriff kneeled and looked through the open limousine door, noticing the senator's chief of staff sitting on the other side of the back seat. Dick Cooper was a classic "Little Napoleon," as far as the lawman was concerned--a fellow of small physical stature who always behaved far more important and powerful than circumstances justified.

"Senator, that woman took me by surprise--just as much as she did you ... But I'm sure that you'll be pleased to learn that hardly anyone paid attention to her after you left the room ... Most folks left right away, everyone acting as if she had gone loco--as if she had become somewhat crazy, overcome with grief."

"Sheriff, listen to me, and listen to me good--because I'm not going to repeat this. ... You make sure that everyone in this town actually feels that way ... People need to know that she is a loony bird, a cuckoo bird for a grandfather clock ... Understand?"

"Understood." Sheriff Peters gave a casual, friendly-like salute. "As the old saying goes, 'Your wish is my command.'"

"Fine. Make it that way." The senator reached forward and tapped the chauffeur's shoulder. "Charles, let's make haste ... Got a flight to catch ... Oh, and sheriff, I know that I can count on you to come through for me on this."

The politician summarily rolled down the window, as the vehicle suddenly sped off--sending streams of slushy snow across the lawman's face and upper chest.

Sheriff Peters spent the next few minutes in a fruitless attempt to brush himself off, fully aware that political skulduggery is a grimy business--to be avoided at all costs.

*

Registered nurse Helen Portman always disliked giving messages to doctors, preferring instead to fully dedicate her professional time and to assist physicians in their duties, while also helping patients one-on-one. Directing the swing shift of 11 nurses filled up her working time.

As far as Helen was concerned such mundane duties as communications should be handled by lower-level personnel--such as Candy Stripers, teenage girls or young women who volunteered in order to get health care industry experience.

"Doctor Robbins, there is a woman named Pamela in the lobby, who insists on talking with you as soon as possible." Helen got right to the point, never one to waste words. "Insists that she is this little girl's aunt, and claims that her two male companions were just arrested by police ... I witnessed part of the confrontation. Boy, what a ruckus!"

"No worries, Helen." James momentarily looked up at the nurse, while sitting at Peggy's bedside. "This little one's vital signs have stabilized ... She is out of the woods, for now at least. ... I can only hope that her aunt has calmed down."

"Quite the opposite, I'm afraid, doctor."

Helen watched intently as James promptly walked quick-step toward the exit door.

Like just about every member of her staff, Helen had remained intrigued and mystified--even confounded and confused--by this new physician's appearance and demeanor since he first started practicing at the hospital nearly a year earlier.

Although his face bore similarities to actor Sean Connery,

who had portrayed James Bond in the movies, Doctor Robbins had a much gentler expression--a perplexing mix of both danger and compassion--at least as far as Helen and the other female staffers were concerned.

*

While walking with Paula back into the living room of the tiny Davis home, Dorothy felt both nagging disappointment and intense pride.

The retired county clerk had been surprised and pleased that her friend had urged the funeral mourners to fight against the incompetent federal government. Yet sadness, sorrow and regret emerged in equal force, when the vast majority of these people--who should have cared with all their hearts--chose to ignore Paula's pleas.

"Hello, Aunt Paula!" Tommy marched as if a soldier into the living room to greet the women, his behavior still obedient and regimental as far as Dorothy was concerned. "Something horrible has happened to my little sister."

"What!?" Paula's voice was soft from Dorothy's perspective, yet embossed with a desperate sense of urgency. "I hope the little thing has not become sick."

Right away, Dorothy's husband Bill McCready entered the living room, while cradling the 3-year-old Penelope in his arms.

"See this giant swelling in her right arm." McCready held the child near the women, so that they could inspect the illness up close. "As you can see, her right bicep is swollen--perhaps three times its normal size."

Dorothy's heart ached with sadness upon seeing this, sensing right away that Paula felt the same as well.

"Perhaps cancer?" Paula blurted. "Could this be a tumor?"

"That has been my worry," Bill McCready said, looking to his wife Dorothy as if he had aged at least a few years during the 90 minutes that the women were away.

This time without holding her doll or sucking her thumb, Penelope occasionally muttered "Ow!" or complained "Hurt!"

Before another word could be spoken, a soft knock came from the front door.

Hearing this, Dorothy thought that the last thing that they possibly needed at a crucial time like this were guests--people dropping by unexpectedly to pay their respects.

Before anyone else in the living room could react, Tommy rushed across the room and opened the door.

Along with the others, Dorothy saw Sheriff Peters standing alone on the front porch. She felt perplexed and dismayed by the mud all across the lawman's face and upper torso, unusual for a man who prided himself in always looking spiffy and dapper.

"Hi, Sheriff ... We think that my little sister might have cancer!"

Dorothy cringed upon hearing this, convinced that the child had blurted out the wrong thing--a detail that should remain private within the family.

"Oh, I'm sure that Little Penelope doesn't have cancer." The sheriff used both his hands wipe at his face and chest. "Do you all mind if I just come in for a moment, and to have a quick word with you ... To give my condolences once again, and to give you an update--urgent details on what has become of Honest and Peggy? ... These are critical details that each of you will want to know right away."

*

As Senator Spickler's Chief-of-Staff, Dick Cooper took pride in the graceful and easy way in which he handled challenging, difficult and highly detailed situations.

He considered this unexpected non-violent brush-up with the uneducated, low-class housewife from rural Nevada as the perfect foil for the senator's ambitions.

"Dick, that mouthy woman has raised an issue that I had hoped was dead and buried several years ago." The senator paused to take a long sip of bourbon on the rocks, as they rode in the limousine back seat. "How do we dig ourselves out of this pit?"

A lifelong teetotaler, Dick took an equally long sip of his

orange juice, and then smiled--knowing that his demeanor was quite the opposite of his boss.

"Well, senator, the answer should be obvious to us both." the administrator put his glass into a cup holder, and summarily scooped a handful of peanuts. "Instead of trying to escape this pit--this political crevasse, if you will--we simply dig the hole deeper."

"What in the world do you mean by that? ... We dig ourselves into a bigger hole, rather than deny that nuclear fallout is still killing people."

Dick immediately popped a single peanut into his own mouth, and summarily gave his analysis while chewing: "We pretend that we care ... We go through the motions of trying to be helpful to the people ... Senator, you're going to be holding public hearings on this issue, in these God-awful desert towns all across Eastern Nevada ... As if you're caring, and actually trying to get at the truth ... Hell, we'll even have Department of Defense officials there to give false testimony--telling everyone that there is absolutely no reason for them to be concerned."

"Bravo!" The senator raised his glass, proposing a toast. "I'll come off as a true hero, although you and I both realize the disturbing truth."

The chief-of-staff responded by clanking his orange glass against the senator's bourbon container. Dick felt particular pride at keeping clandestine secrets such as these. Both he and his boss had previously read the top-secret, eyes-only government reports, intricate details on the sharp rise in cancer rates across the region--a direct result of excessive exposure to nuclear fallout. Authorities had known all along that this would occur, particularly the sharp increase in cancer rates. Their collective mission would be to always deny the truth, continually proclaiming that there simply was not enough scientific evidence to prove such scurrilous allegations as those made by that "insane" woman just a few hours earlier.

Eleven

Pamela sat alone in the main waiting room of Sierra Crest Hospital, her usually vibrant psyche now emotionally numbed and dazed from the many challenging events throughout the day of her sister Polly's funeral.

"I refuse to die." She tried to remain positive while waiting for Doctor Robbins to appear. "My brother-in-law is right ... I am a fighter."

By this point several hours after sundown, she pulled a compact mirror from her tan leather purse and checked her make-up--determined to appear as if a vision of perfect health, rather than a woman slowly dying of colon cancer.

Pamela's eyes popped up from the mirror the moment that Doctor Robbins opened the Emergency Room door and walked toward her in the waiting room.

Along with Polly and several of their relatives--including Honest--Pamela had seen this physician many times during the previous eight months. In all of these visits, Doctor Robbins and she had never talked to each other one-on-one; those conversations had been handled by her brother-in-law, while she and the ailing Polly remained quiet.

This time, as the physician approached her, Pamela remained somewhat mystified and feeling at a loss for words. The Hawaii resident knew this was a change of character for herself; she usually spoke directly about critical issues.

"Pamela, so good to see you." Doctor Robbins sat beside her. "Sorry this isn't under much better circumstances."

To her, his friendly tone just then seemed rather odd, considering that they never had spoken directly to each other before. Yet at least he behaved as if truly kind and caring, a sharp contrast from her husband Jeff back in Honolulu.

"Yes, I wish these were much more pleasant circumstances." She pushed the compact into her purse, still intrigued that this doctor had remembered her name. "Without beating around the bush, let's get straight to the point. How is my niece doing?"

While looking at a medical chart, he explained that upon arriving in the hospital Peggy had been in critical condition--in a coma with her vital signs at dangerous levels. On the positive side, the girl's condition had been upgraded to "fair," and that she had awakened--although still somewhat groggy.

"What is her illness, doctor? ... Cancer!"

"As to the nature of her illness, that's still too early to say ... I have ordered blood tests, and we soon..."

"But you suspect cancer, don't you?"

"Such a diagnosis cannot be given at this point. I need more data."

Determined to avoid wasting time on idle, unnecessary chit-chat, Pamela got straight to the point on this and other important issues. While stressing the need for immediate positive action on each problem, she explained that: each of her brothers-in-law had been unjustly hauled off to jail from this very room, and that they needed to be bailed out right away; that in Hawaii she had recently been diagnosed with advanced colon cancer--that on this very day she had finally decided to fight for her own life, despite the proclamation by Hawaiian physicians that she would die anyway; and that her primary concern was saving Peggy--especially if the child's diagnosis ended up being cancer.

"Pamela, it sounds to me like you are carrying the weight of the entire world on your shoulders." Doctor Robbins spoke in a soft, slow voice--sounding self-assured and truly caring to her; she sensed an inquisitive and perplexed expression in his eyes.

To her, at least for the moment, the doctor seemed to have an odd and somewhat perplexing personality. Pamela had always prided herself in quickly and accurately detecting just about any individual's personal characteristics and motivations.

Yet especially up this close and personal, right beside him, from her view he had a stare cold enough to freeze water--out of place with the rest of his caring and thoughtful expression, which to her seemed warm and genuine enough to make almost any person feel at ease.

Assured that she had his full attention, Pamela promptly opened a leather tool bag from Honest's plumbing truck.

Doctor Robbins' gaze immediately focused his eyes toward the mound of cash, mostly bills ranging from $1 to $20s--intermixed with several century notes.

He reached over, zipped the bag back up, and promptly placed the container on her lap, her hands trembling slightly by this point.

"You are a bright woman, I would imagine much smarter than even you probably know. So, Pamela, you need to realize that this isn't just about money. This is about you, and your entire family. ... I'm here to help in any way that I possibly can. I truly care."

The moment the physician finished saying this, Pamela spotted the outside entrance door open.

Bill McCready held tiny Penelope, while walking beside his wife Dorothy--who carried the child's doll, Pee-Pee. The unexpected sight of them briefly warmed Pamela's heart, although she instantly sensed that some sort of major problem was well underway.

"Doctor, we have another emergency for you, whether you want this or not." Dorothy focused her gaze on the physician, while also rushing over to hug Pamela. "We're praying to God that you'll be able to tell us that 'This is definitely not another cancer,' and that everything is going to be OK for this little one."

*

Nearly 45 minutes after sundown that day, Reverend Martin Middleton started driving to the Tranquility Lane home of the Davis family--responding to the phone pleas of Paula, who insisted that she urgently needed his spiritual assistance right away.

Paula had refused to go into specifics during the call, saying only that the "Lord wants you to help me and my family ... If you care about us at all, you will get over here as soon as you can, Scout."

Throughout that brief chat, the reverend had tried every tactic that he knew to delay or hold off Paula's in-person meeting. He tried using his own family obligations as an excuse, and his wife Janelle's insistence that he remain home for dinner. For added spice, he briefly mentioned feeling bushed and utterly exhausted from the day's many events.

Upon hearing this, Paula had drawn an even stronger playing card, specifically using his admiration and devotion to God. The reverend knew, or at least he sensed, that many people who attended his church knew that this was his biggest weakness--although there were plenty of other flaws that they lacked any inkling about.

"For heaven's sake, Paula, can't you just tell me over the phone?"

She insisted that these details were far too personal, so sensitive that the information could only be given face-to-face in private.

When getting within a block of the Davis home, from behind the wheel of his orange 1972 Ford Pinto, the pastor started to think that he and Paula were similar in several ways. Scout realized that he wanted with all his heart to dislike the woman, but he simply could not even approach doing that--perhaps because he realized they had so many similarities.

Like this man of the cloth--at least from his perspective--Paula always preferred to communicate using a high sense of drama. Like him, she often paused for several seconds at mid-sentence, just for emphasis to get the listener to think. Unlike him, though, she never spoke in flowery terms while intentionally over-exaggerating details.

"Scout, it's about time you finally showed." Paula gazed directly into his eyes when opening the door. "I was afraid that while you were on your way over here, you might have been captured and eaten by the Abominable Snowman."

"My lady, not even the biggest monster could keep me from my duties in serving the Will of the Lord." The preacher promptly took off his hat, which he placed on one of eight hooks affixed to the living room wall next to the front door.

"Feel free, kind sir, to sit in that chair ... Because I'm about to tell you some mighty freaky things that I just learned about. ... Would you care for a hot chocolate or a cup of coffee to warm you up? It's still as cold as the North Pole outside, although--thank God--lots of people around here still have warm hearts on a wretched day like this."

At this precise point, the preacher resisted his own burning desire to cringe, this up-close and personal sight of Paula's high drama making his stomach turn. Scout felt the turkey and pumpkin pie from his own family's dinner from earlier that evening churning in his gut--uncomfortable now, although he considered such "comfort-food" meals as perfect for the region's bitterly cold winter.

"Thanks, but no thanks." Scout patted his belly while sitting in a dark-leather recliner beside the green couch. "I feel as stuffed as a Thanksgiving bird, but grateful that the holidays are finally behind us."

"Reverend, I feel the same, but even more-so."

Striving to maintain his patience rather than telling her to "please get to the point," he took a deep breath while watching Paula start to box up the Christmas decorations.

One by one, she placed the five remaining nutcrackers into a battered old cardboard box. She moved as fast as a vibrant teenager as far as he could tell, a sharp contrast to her drawn and expressionless face--which reminded him of a 100-year-old nursing home resident.

Paula quickly explained that Tommy, whom she described as being "unusually well behaved" on that day, had already gone to bed--fast asleep by 8 o'clock.

"What about Peggy?" The Preacher yearned to get these details, thinking that perhaps the child's health would emerge as the focus of this impromptu session.

"No word, yet, but I'm sorry to tell you that things have gotten even worse."

The preacher's mind swelled with both grief and shock upon Paula's additional revelation regarding tiny Penelope's sudden arm pain.

"But that's not the worst of it. Just six hours ago, reverend, there was a heated argument right here in this very room--by the worst and most contentious shouting match of my entire life."

"An argument? ... But with who? ... Why?"

"Scout, you probably have a much better answer to the 'why' than I do ... All I can say is that incompetent, lazy and good-for-nothing sheriff poked his nose into our personal lives ... That creep has no business trying to..."

"Paula, for heaven's sake, please slow down. You're getting yourself all worked up. Learn to control your emotions, because otherwise you might have a heart attack or a stroke--God forbid ... Please, take a deep breath and get control of your emotions."

Rather than respond, Paula stopped talking.

This time the reverend sensed that she was truly angry and frustrated. He felt as if this pause in the conversation had not been merely one of her usual lame attempts to create an over-the-top sense of drama.

Still firmly ensconced to the chair, he reached this conclusion while watching the feisty way that Paula yanked these ornaments off the Christmas tree, plus her stormy, turbulent and threatening manner when slamming these objects into the various boxes.

From Scout's perspective, this marked a sharp reversal from her usual behavior, which until then he had always considered as delicate and ultra-feminine.

"Paula, I'm praying for you ... I can only imagine what

you're going through. Throughout life, the Lord tests each of us in mysterious ways--puzzling situations that we find baffling and perplexing--situations that we fail to fully understand at the time."

"That, sir, is nothing but a worthless bunch of hogwash." Upon saying this, she slammed the angel from atop the tree into a box perfectly sized for the figurine.

"Calm down, please, Paula. The Lord knows everything that we do, and he will forgive us if..."

"Well, reverend, can he forgive you, too?" She slowly pulled down the tree until it lay flat on the floor; dried-out and fallen needles scattered throughout the room. "Can God forgive you, reverend, for what you failed to do today?"

"Forgive me? What are you talking about? What did you fail to do, and..."

"You don't have a single clue, do you, Scout?" While still talking, she yanked open the front door. A swirl of moist, cold air blasted into the living room as Paula picked up the tree and hoisted the entire thing onto the snowy front yard--before she immediately slammed the door shut. "Until this very day, I've always been kind and sweet, but those days are over. From this moment forward, you're going to see me angry at an appropriate level, until an adequate resolution emerges for our overall situation."

At this point, Paula started cramming discarded Christmas wrapping paper into a large plastic garbage can. To him, she looked as burly and weather-worn as a seasoned garbage collector, betraying the fact that the red plaid dress she wore looked ultra clean, feminine and pristine enough for a fairy tale princess.

"Scout, whether you want to hear this or not, you should be ashamed of yourself for refusing to stand up for me--when I tried to get people to listen at the church hall. You must know, perhaps better than anyone, of the death, heartache and disease that the demonic nuclear fallout has caused. ... And, yet you refused--or failed--to help people see the light ... The Lord would want us to stand together, and fight against what is wrong."

"Paula, those things are unfair of you to say!" The reverend jumped to a standing position. He had always considered himself as willing and able to accept criticism, other than reckless and bogus allegations such as hers. Desperate to stand tall for his own pride, he considered storming out the door and leaving Paula to fester all alone in her growing anger. Yet a compassionate, caring and loving part of this man demanded that he stay. "I have a mind to leave you here and now, young woman--but the Lord is ordering me to remain here for your own good. Can't you see that you need guidance and assistance?"

As he spoke, Paula began removing strings of multi-colored holiday lights from the interior of the living room's front window.

"You and the Lord were not here to help, when that good-for-nothing sheriff bolted in here, insisting that Penelope does not suffer from cancer--like her mother did ... And you and the Lord were not here to help when Mister and Mrs. McCready--bless their hearts--they stood their ground like no one else ever has to help us. The aging couple volunteered to drive the tiny one to Reno, despite the sheriff's objections that doing so would not be necessary ... What medical experience does that loon have anyway? ... What gives him the right?"

"Paula, we can talk about these things." The reverend slowly walked across the room and promptly started helping Paula take down the holiday lights. "What you are saying--the fact that you are telling me these things--is good. The Lord wants you to fully express yourself, to open up your heart. Only that way can we seek and receive the eternal blessing of His guidance and understanding."

"Well, if that's true--there is plenty more--lots more that you need to hear about." While holding several strings of lights, she walked across the living room and took out three large boxes that had been positioned behind the couch. "As if all these problems were not already enough, I got even more disturbing information--just before calling you at your home this evening."

"No worries. I'm here to listen. Fire away." He started pulling more strings of holiday lights from a smaller window at the side of the living room.

"Scout, I got a call from the Police Department in Reno. ... Bad news ... Just about the worst thing that..."

"A highway accident? ... Involving Pamela, Honest and your husband?"

"Oh, the men were arrested for disorderly conduct. But that's not the worst of it."

The reverend carried an armful of holiday lights toward Paula, before summarily helping her stuff them into the same box where the others had been placed.

For the first time in that moment Scout felt that he had a much better understanding of her precarious personal situation. Besides feeling as if Paula carried the burdens of their entire region and community, from his view she also seemed to carry the weight of persistent illness and death all around them. Any additional urgent problems would only serve to increase the already-heavy load upon her back, or at least he felt that way.

"Paula, you're telling me that there are even worse details?"

"Yes, I admit my feelings of being mortified. ... The police told me that besides disorderly conduct, that stupid husband of mine has been charged with running a car-theft ring based in Las Vegas ... Communicating with Reno investigators, the Southern Nevada lawmen have confirmed finding Hank's fingerprints in dozens of stolen vehicles that were recovered from a warehouse-- called a 'chop-shop.' ... A judge has refused to set bail for him, and if convicted--as they say they will--Hank faces a 40-year prison sentence. Until now, I had believed that my husband was nothing but a typical, common, worthless drunk."

"My Lord, I think that..."

"That's precisely it. How is the Lord going to help me now?"

Just then, the reverend spotted Tommy. The child stood in

a doorway, leading from the living room toward the bedroom area. The boy wore tattered old blue pajamas, briefly reminding Scout of one of those nutcrackers that had just been packed away.

"Why is everyone always arguing here?" The boy scratched at his own head, by this point his blond hair mussed up, rather than perfectly combed. "Can't we have any peace around here? ... That's what mommy would want."

Twelve

While still en route back to Washington, D.C., later on the day of Polly's funeral, Senator Larry Spickler and his chief of staff, Dick Cooper, sat together in a private VIP room for Pan American Airlines passengers at Salt Lake City International Airport.

The senator had always insisted on traveling via Western Airlines--for image purposes--whenever traveling. But 14 of that carrier's essential connector flights had been been canceled due to the massive storm socking much of the American West.

Cooper motioned toward a flight attendant in the Pan Am Red Carpet Club, signaling for her to come over to him and the politician--who for the moment had his head glued to the front page of the "Salt Lake Tribune." Cooper liked the fact that the senator had always been an ardent news junkie, with only one thing of greater interest to him--tons of beautiful young women. The more, the merrier.

"Senator, get a load of this hot gal." Dick said, smiling broadly--always proud of himself when introducing his boss to another worthy-looking female prospect.

Despite the nasty weather outside, the young woman--whom Dick judged to be about 23 years old at most--wore her airline issued outfit: A mini-skirt up so high that it threatened to reveal her scanty pink panties; a pink-lined neckline low enough to inspire the imagination; and a smart cap that made the political crony think of playtime.

"Miss, may I politely say--speaking as a gentleman--that you have legs fantastic enough to launch ships." Dick winked, grinned and motioned his left hand toward the politician. "So I can assume that your name is 'Misty,' as I see from your name badge?"

"I would never jest the likes of you, sir." She bent over far toward the men, placing pink napkins on the table--while affording Dick what he considered an exceptional view of her generous cleavage. He knew from experience that his boss certainly would appreciate this spectacular sight just as much.

"Well then, Misty, may I please introduce you to one of the most respected and famous leaders in the history of our national government. This gent right beside me here deserves all of our praise and thanks, United States Senator Larry Spickler."

Glancing away from the newspaper, the politician looked up toward the woman--a posture and reaction that Dick knew from much experience was the senator's expected and typical behavior when first meeting a prospective female "victim."

"Might I say..." The senator spoke in a slow drawl, which Dick always considered a strange mixture of Italian and old-style Western English; the politician always spoke this way when interacting with young "babes," a term that these men preferred calling such women--but only in private. "that the honor and pleasure of meeting you is mine."

Dick realized that sophisticated, big-city women of any upper-class heritage typically balked or at least scowled at the senator's sappy behavior. These men had previously concluded that poorly educated lower-class "hick-city" gals like Misty were stupid enough to get captured by power, money and fame.

Sure, these fellows had learned together from first-hand experience during the previous several years that the super-wealthy, Fifth Avenue, Manhattan chicks also got chatty, nervous and over-excited when in the presence of such unstoppable might. Yet by this point Dick knew that wealthy breeds of chicks from upper-class high society were far too needy, vengeful and always eventually hateful--at least as far as the senator was concerned. By contrast, air-headed gals from the sticks such as Misty were much easier to use, discard and forget about--similar to disposable razors that had started to gain popularity in recent years.

"Sorry, sir." Misty stood straight, no longer bending

low enough for Dick to get a healthy view of her bosom. She refrained from extending her hand toward the senator, although the politician kept his arm outward toward her. "Airline regulations prohibit me from becoming overly familiar with our customers. I'm sure that you can understand why--that you can envision the possibilities of what might happen between us. ... May I please take your order?"

"The senator will have a Harvey Wallbanger, and I'll take a tequila sunrise." Dick took pride in ordering their meals and drinks--thereby, hopefully, putting Larry in a perceived position of power. "Misty, the faster you get back, the bigger your tip."

"Sure thing." She smiled, before promptly heading toward the bar.

Dick took pride in knowing that his boss never bedded down with his delicious looking "targets," always faithful to his wife of 14 years, nicknamed "Lady Cat." Modeling himself to the public has a moral pillar of strength in the Congress, unlike some other senators of that era he never actually made love with his many conquests. Instead, in keeping with his consistent plan, the senator always laughed at these women as soon as they took their clothes off in front of him--before he promptly left the room.

Perhaps most of all, Dick admired what he considered the senator's mischievous and cruel behavior. As far as this chief of staff knew, the politician always kept his vow never to get caught in the type of sex scandals that had brought down numerous other congressional representatives during the previous century.

The recent political downfall of Arkansas congressman Wilbur Mills, chairman of the powerful House Ways and Means Committee, had served as a lesson for them all. Just two months earlier in November 1974, Mills was allegedly inebriated when attending a press conference, an instantly scandalous appearance inside Argentinian stripper Fanne Foxe's dressing room at the Pilgrim Theater in Boston. The previous month, Foxe had notoriously jumped into the Washington, D.C., Tidal Basin, in the wake of a scuffle with Mills. Rocked by scandal, Mills left the committee's chairmanship, publicly acknowledged his alcoholism and checked himself into a Florida institute for rehabilitation.

Shortly after Misty went to get their drinks, Senator Spickler and Dick winked at each other, a sign of their mutual prediction that the Nevada politician soon would be able to see her fully naked--while laughing his head off.

Dick always got an emotional kick out of this process, never telling the boss of his opinion that the senator was a "wimp" for always failing to carry out "the deed." In fact, the chief of staff secretly thought of this as an odd, paradoxical situation--a guy who portrayed himself publicly as manly and vibrant, yet perhaps somewhat emotionally weak and incapable of performing his duties--whatever those chores might be.

Finally down to business, with Misty away at the bar, Dick opened a briefcase and promptly showed the senator Top Secret documents from the Department of Defense. These charts--never to be seen by, or revealed to, the public--showed that severe illness and deaths from cancer in Eastern Nevada and Southwest Utah were expected to surge drastically during the next 30 years.

"The public is never to know these details, under any circumstance," the first line of the report said. "Our scientists have confirmed that the onset of the disease in those areas is the direct result of above-ground nuclear bomb tests at the Nevada Test Site. At least 17,000 additional Americans within this fallout zone will die as a result, in addition to the 9,000 that have already perished. Under no circumstances is the public ever to know these details, as our various federal agencies always contend that there is 'no statistical evidence whatsoever' to prove such allegations. Perhaps most important from our government's perspective, to reveal these truths--specifics on what caused the deaths--would be a violation of national security. No nation is ever to realize or confirm the fact that we have--the U.S. government--intentionally sacrificed many of our own people, all in the name of scientific research."

Shocking, startling and even momentarily scaring Dick, the senator slammed the binder atop the airline waiting room's

Red Carpet Club table.

"Hogwash!" the senator bellowed.

Dick knew right away that the senator was pissed, only uttering this word about every year or so--his favorite, and only-- swear word.

"My watch?" the senator spoke in a much softer voice in a few moments, his tone now at a whisper so low that only Dick could hear. "This is happening on my watch? For the love of God, you know that I'm up for re-election in just another year."

"Forgive me, sir, but I told you about this earlier today and..."

"You never said it was this bad."

"Like I said earlier, all we need to do is hold hearings--in a bogus effort to fool the public into believing that there is absolutely no scientific evidence, and..."

"Dick, I almost always respect your opinion. But you need to realize that--and I truly believe this--people are not that stupid."

The chief of staff slowly reached across the table and scooped up a handful of peanuts and promptly hoisted them all into his own mouth.

"To the contrary, senator ... Most people are stupider than rocks. Think about it," Dick smiled broadly, swallowed the peanuts en masse and gently patted the senator's back. "The people were stupid enough to vote for you, weren't they?"

At first, to Dick, the senator's eyes looked about as focused as those of a lion on the verge of attacking its prey. Then, within a few moments, this crony saw a sudden twinkle in this politician's gaze, as if he had suddenly been struck by an unexpected revelation.

In unison, the two men broke out together in uproarious laughter, each saying things like "yeah, they are stupid enough to vote for you," and "I've got to admit, people really are stupider than rocks."

Dick always enjoyed these encounters most, as if he and his boss were merely mischievous little brothers--rather than among the world's most powerful people, perhaps even capable enough to convince the highest authorities to start a nuclear war.

Senator Spickler suddenly quieted down, grinning while whispering into his confidante's familiar ear: "But what about what happened to Richard Nixon, resigning just five months ago? Scandal? Cover-up? ... Things like Watergate?"

"No need for worries in this regard, senator. Remember, this is 'top secret,' the public will never know the truth. Also, keep in mind that the entire government is behind us on this. ... All that we need to do is hold those phony hearings, and you're in the clear--a virtual hero in the public's eyes, for courageously trying to ferret out the truth."

Just then, Misty returned with their drinks.

"Gentlemen, I can see that you're having an important discussion ... About taxes? The economy maybe? ... If you fellows don't mind, I'll just leave you right away, for..."

"Miss, feel free to stay here and join us," Dick said, while trying to reach out for Misty's hand and winking--his sign to the senator that playtime seemed possible.

"Sorry," she took one step backward. "I've got to go ... Otherwise I'll be late for my class, at the University of Utah School of Medicine."

"Oh, you're going to be an entry-level nurse?" The senator piped in, his purry voice as cool as that of a tomcat--at least from Dick's perspective. "You can give me a check-up, if you would like. Did you bring your stethoscope with you?"

"Far from it." She poured more peanuts in the men's table tray, before stepping back again. "I'm on the verge of becoming a psychiatrist. ... You might say I'm interested in what makes people tick."

Misty promptly did an about-face; the men watched her every step as she slowly ambled back toward the bar.

"Well, doctor!" the senator called out. "If you're interested in what makes people tick, you can check mine out at any time."

She kept walking away without responding. The men

promptly huddled together again, Dick intently listening as the senator whispered: "A woman? Becoming a doctor? A head shrink? ... What on earth is the world coming to? Remind me later this week to check into the Senate appropriations for her school ... If she won't check out my ticker, I'm sure going to check out hers."

The moment Misty got to the bar, she commented matter-of-factly to her friend, Maurice the bartender: "See those guys over at table 18? ... Politicians ... Big-time losers ... The world's worst."

*

At precisely 8:27 in the morning, on the day after Polly's funeral, Doctor Robbins entered the back door of his Silver State Cancer Clinic on South Wells Avenue, three blocks from Sierra Crest Medical Center.

Because he still lacked a car of his own, the physician had just jogged there from the hospital. Robbins had stayed there overnight to care for and to observe the ailing sisters Peggy and Penelope, plus four of his patients.

From a work station in the facility's lobby, the receptionist--Richard--had heard the familiar sound of clattery footsteps and the clang of the rear door closing in the doctor's office.

Most days Richard eagerly anticipated Doctor Robbins' arrival, when a handful of about two or three patients--or prospective patients--usually sat in the waiting area.

Yet on this morning the receptionist already felt sure that this would emerge as far from an average day--perhaps with heated arguments and door slamming.

"If you'll excuse me, I'll be back in just a few minutes," Richard told the four adults on this particular day, before promptly going down a short hallway and entering Doctor Robbins' office.

Eager to get right to the point, Richard spoke in a to-the-point manner, which he knew that this physician preferred: "I have bad news and then more bad news--and I'm sorry to say there is nothing good to report at this point."

"Well, Richard, let's start with the lesser of the bad news." Doctor Robbins leaned far back in the chair behind his desk, his feet propped on the table.

Richard explained that Grace, the secretary to Sierra Crest Hospital President Gregory Crowley, had called first thing that morning. The woman had explained that her boss had discovered what she described as an "extremely serious problem," and that Doctor Robbins would be expected to report to that office as soon as possible.

"Did she give any indication of what this supposed issue is about?"

"I only got a sense that you better show up there fast."

"When I can squeeze in a moment. My patients take the highest priority. ... And the other so-called 'bad news,' please; I'm eager to listen."

"That pirate guy is in the lobby ... He has fire in his eyes, worse than I have seen ... I thought you previously had told me that we would never see him again, after his wife died ... He has three other people with him, an old man, and two women."

"Sounds fine to me."

The doctor's devil-may-care attitude, his supreme confidence always mystified Richard, a 20-year-old geology student at the University of Nevada, Reno--working part time at the clinic to earn tuition money.

"Oh, doctor, and there's just one more thing." Richard paused briefly while leaving the physician's private office, turning around to address his boss.

"Yes?"

"I cannot swear to this. It's just a guess on my part. I'm not sure, but I notice what appears like the outline of a 3-foot-long object under that pirate guy's knee-length coat. Do you think that he might be carrying a rifle?"

"I don't know. I guess that I will just have to find out." The physician yawned for a few moments, before summarily taking a gulp of coffee--from a cup that Richard always pre-filled for him each morning. "By all means, send them right in ... I'm eager to discover all of the latest details."

*

As the wife of the only preacher in Centralia, Janelle Middleton took pride in the positive reputation that her husband had steadily earned over the years. Since 1969, she had realized that people from their congregation often joked about their offbeat appearance, strangely laced with a modern and exciting All-American demeanor as well.

"The two of them--when together--seem sort of like the crusty, stern-looking guy with the pitchfork," people often said about the Reverend and Mrs. Middleton, when discussing the couple, particularly during conversations with the community's new residents. "You know, that world-famous painting by Grant Wood, called 'American Gothic House.'"

Only when chatting with friends, Janelle sometimes privately admitted the many eerie similarities. Indeed, like the stern-looking wife from that world-famous painting, she always kept her hair pulled back in a tight bun. On occasion, she also fessed up to the fact that--like the female subject in the painting--she appeared as if a person who rarely smiled.

Contrary to that famous artwork, however, Janelle was about 6-foot-2, a willowy woman who towered over her chunky--yet strapping and muscular--5-foot-10 husband. The other essential difference from the painting's forlorn and gloomy image was the fact that Janelle had always been blessed with an uproarious sense of humor.

All along, she also occasionally admitted that in real-life situations, her husband--the preacher that the townspeople affectionately called "Scout"--was a strict and firm looking guy who also seemed to have an uncompromising demeanor.

Every six months or so, as people left the church services, she heard people casually mention that if the couple had been a comic act--Janelle would serve as the obvious jokester, with Scout fitting the perfect part of a dour-looking straight-man.

Yet in a real-world sense, Janelle felt as if the two of them had switched roles, a half hour after sunrise on the morning after Polly's funeral.

Scout had kept nagging at Janelle, starting when he returned home from his impromptu trek to see Paula the previous night. Throughout that night in intermittent fits and spats, the preacher kept insisting to his wife that they should help play a key, vital and essential role in Paula's planned political battle against the federal government.

"That's nonsense, Scout!" Janelle had hollered at him, a feisty and contentious behavior that she knew was out of character for herself. "Your job and mission is that of a spiritual leader, not as a political advocate who helps lead a major public protest."

To the contrary, the preacher claimed, within his own mind he had heard from the Lord that helping Paula's effort was the justifiable, loving and correct course of action.

"Listen to me, Martin!" She felt far from comical or humorous that night. "Think of our position in the community. We need to remain neutral, for our own sake."

During the previous 15 years of their marriage, leading up to the night of this heated and increasingly intense conversation, Paula had taken pride in the fact that she and Scout had rarely spoken a cross word to one another.

From her way of thinking, though, on this particular night a proverbial volcano blew sky-high, creating an increasingly wide crevasse between them. She surprised herself by acting angry and head-strong, particularly considering the fact that until that night she had always been a dutiful, obedient and eternally faithful wife--never once questioning or protesting Scout's decisions.

"Mister, you go sleep on the couch!" Janelle pointed toward the living room, while standing in their adjoining kitchen. "I refuse to stay in the same room with you tonight, if you're going to behave this way--without considering my opinion."

A few minutes later, when alone inside her bedroom, she sat quietly on their well-made bed--while listening to him knock loudly on the other side of their locked bedroom door.

"Janelle, please!" he pleaded for several minutes, until he finally stopped. A short while later, she could hear him weeping in the living room. This wife made no effort to go out to him or to reconcile; Janelle felt as though she remained the only person in town with any inkling of his many weaknesses and imperfections.

As his weeping gradually faded in the living room, Janelle slowly fell into a deep sleep while alone on their bed. She began dreaming about herself--from way back--as a small child, frolicking in a meadow--smiling and laughing with a little boy. Scout and she had been that way, playmates and best friends since early childhood.

Her dreams of those early, much happier times from rural Missouri--from way back when they were children--continued throughout the night as she tossed and turned. She dreamed of the time when they chased ducks, each pretending to waddle and quack like those creatures--or of the day when Scout caught a live frog, proudly naming it "Mister Green Jeans"--and giving it to her for her sixth birthday.

Janelle's first thought when she finally awakened--feeling refreshed--a half hour before sunrise was simply this: "I love that man with all my heart. I always will."

She jumped from bed in a flash, and promptly marched to the living room, and looked at Scout--his stocky body stretched out on the couch.

"Get up, sleepy-head!" Janelle tried to make her voice sound cheery, while playfully tossing a light pillow toward his head.

"Am I forgiven?" The preacher rubbed his eyes, a display that she knew was merely his attempt at play-acting.

"You know--Mister Preacher Man--that there is nothing to forgive. ... Now, get your sorry butt up, because there is work for us to do."

Then, without saying a word, they each went to the kitchen and promptly made a sizable pile of scrambled eggs, bacon, wheat toast and coffee.

Without him having to say so, Janelle knew that he instinctively realized that she had decided to follow his recommended course of action. As she had been taught to do since early childhood, Janelle realized that her place in the home was to fulfill the wishes of her husband--even when she strongly disagreed with his behavior.

"Old habits die hard," she thought, while he scurried to the bathroom to brush his teeth and comb his hair.

Right away, with Scout still in the back of their house, Janelle heard a light knock at their front door, which she soon opened.

"Hello, Janelle!" Paula stood on the front porch, holding the hand of her nephew Tommy. "I hope that we're not too early ... Scout told me that this would be a good time."

"By all means, we have breakfast prepared already!" Janelle motioned toward the dining room table. "I'm eager to do my share, to work hard on this worthy political fight."

Momentarily, with the boy between them, the women sat at the table as Paula rattled off her ideas for a phone bank, a mailing list and a tour from town to town, encouraging people to join their dispute against the federal government.

"Can I have some orange juice?" Tommy interrupted. "Are we going to fight someone? ... This sounds like it's going to be fun!"

Scout entered the room, gracefully picked up an empty glass, and then said in a tone that unexpectedly made Janelle feel more proud of him than ever: "Your orange juice is coming right up, my little friend ... And, yes, you're about to witness first-hand the start of a political battle--a protracted fight that people are likely to remember for many generations to come."

Thirteen

By the time she became a Pan American Airlines cocktail waitress, Shira Levy had already worked five years for Israel's spy agency, an organization called Mossad.

She always preferred covert operations, particularly since her recent assignments in what the Jewish nation's commanders dubbed "Operation Wrath of God."

Three years before she served cocktails to Senator Larry Spickler and his lackey--while wearing the "Misty" name badge--Shira had infiltrated two Palestinian militant groups. Black September and the Palestine Liberation Organization, each had been blamed for participation in the Munich massacre of 1972--terrorist raids that killed 11 members of the Israeli Olympic Team.

Shira's successes had become legendary within Mossad, particularly her efficient performance in the assassinations of five key leaders of the terrorist organizations.

After using her physical beauty and sparkly personality as bait, she had strategically used a standard-issue and reliable .22-caliber Beretta 70 to expertly place bullets between the eyes of three terrorist ringleaders. She poisoned two others by working as a waitress, placing a deadly potion of strychnine in their meals.

Far more talented than merely a trained assassin, she also excelled in infiltrating private businesses and the bureaucracies of other governments. Each time she used her keen wit, and magnetic physical allure to collect critical information.

Shira's immediate superiors at Mossad had correctly sensed that such assignments had left her bored, perhaps due to her innate and intense desire to work primarily in extremely dangerous life-and-death situations. Since early childhood she had felt a burning desire to take revenge against the world's evildoers, her soul wounded by the wretched stories of how Nazis had exterminated her grandparents on September 3, 1942, at Auschwitz Concentration Camp in Poland.

As a three-year veteran of Mossad's core team in mid-1974, Shira had immediately seized the opportunity to take a coveted assignment within the United States. A trusted and proven member of the Israeli spy agency's core team, she worried that the heart of the USA's military and defense infrastructure should never be trusted--although America had remained her nation's closest ally and financial supporter.

Like several top politicians within Israel's government, Mossad's top brass worried that most members of the U.S. Congress were corrupt, immoral, and the likely targets of covert bribery that could result in the destruction of the Jewish homeland.

Par for the course, as soon as Senator Spickler and his crony left the Pan Am Red Carpet Club to catch their flight back to Washington, D.C., Shira scooped up a small tape recorder that she previously had affixed under the table where these men had sat.

Mossad's research team had designed the Salt Lake City airport as an ideal site for covert operations, primarily because U.S. politicians and top business leaders continually changed flights in the facility--a major travel hub in the middle of the American West.

Later that evening, alone in her cozy downtown Belvedere Hotel apartment, Shira listened to the tape-recorded conversation between the senator and his chief of staff. She felt no surprise whatsoever upon hearing their devilish secret about the U.S. government covertly killing many thousands of its own people. She lacked any sense of revulsion, fully suspecting--like many of her comrades--that the USA remained evil to the core.

Right on schedule, at precisely 5:15 Mountain Time on the morning after her encounter with the senator, under cover of darkness she jogged alone in downtown Salt Lake City's Liberty Park. After briefly surveying the site to ensure that no one else was nearby, she used a key to open a fist-sized latch on the side of a

12-foot-tall lamp post.

First, Shira took out a small package that had been placed there by her colleagues. Then she placed the tape recording of the senator, already packaged tightly, inside of the same compartment for one of her associates to retrieve within 24 hours.

From the park, she jogged straight back to her apartment--proud of herself for remaining in top shape at age 23. Soon afterward, while sitting alone at her kitchen table, she read the latest message from her bosses at Mossad, her first communication from them in six months: "Prepare for reassignment within three weeks. A new blast may be necessary. Watch your back."

Her eyes widened upon seeing the word "blast," her employer's code word for "assassination." And the term "watch your back" signified that someone might be onto her--aware of her actual identity. A potential attack against her life seemed imminent.

*

Glad to finally return to Spickler's headquarters in Washington's Russell Senate Office Building, Chief of Staff Dick Cooper went straight to his own office. Sitting at his desk, this bureaucrat looked warily at an 18-inch-tall pile of messages.

"Shirley!" Through his office door, Dick looked toward his secretary and gave a beckoning motion for her to walk inside. "Can we chat for a brief moment?"

"Sure thing, boss."

Momentarily, she sat across from Dick, who always appreciated her professionalism--forgiving the fact that she had what he considered as an irritating, high-pitched, chirpy voice. To him she sounded like a chattery parakeet, although as far as he was concerned her job performance was always worth its weight in gold--many times over.

"Shirley, can you be a time-saver for me? Which of these countless messages should have top priority? ... I lack the time to deal with the senseless junk."

"The Israeli Embassy--from my humble view, sir, their call

to the Senator was by far the most important."

"Why? ... Details, please?"

"Only a handful of senators are invited, along with President Ford."

The notion of this immediately struck Dick as somewhat odd, considering the fact that their boss was only a freshman senator, without serving on any substantial committees. Complicating matters, and adding to the confusion, the Republican president and Spickler were in opposing political parties.

"Why the Israelis would select a novice senator for such a coveted invitation is beyond me. I have no doubt that if the boss attends, that President Ford will snub him. You know that Larry has been highly critical of the new administration."

"Well, as we all realize, Dick, it's your decision to make along with the senator--not mine. ... Will that be all, sir?"

Dick summarily excused Shirley from the room, after confessing to her that he would ignore the vast majority of these messages--"most of them are pure nonsense."

Right after she left, closing the door behind herself, Dick rifled through his desk drawer, hunting for a file containing an 18-month-old press clipping. A news junkie, he had saved the "Washington Post" article on a hunch. Exceedingly ambitious and carrying aspirations of going much higher in politics, the senator hoped to someday become the Senate Majority Leader. Such an ascension would become increasingly possible thanks to significant alliances and campaign contributions from the U.S. Jewish community.

Dick finally found the file and immediately started reading the article. On July 1, 1973, a military attache to the United States who also served as an Israeli Air Force officer--Josef Placek--was assassinated by gunshot in the driveway of his Maryland home. The Czechoslovakia-born official who served in the Israel War of Independence, had been assigned in 1970 as the Naval attache at that Middle East country's embassy in Washington, D.C.

According to news reports, Placek's wife, Dvora, had witnessed the killing moments after the couple finished the half-hour drive home in their Ford Galaxie from a party honoring a departing embassy staffer. Shot five times by a foreign-made .38-caliber revolver, he died at 1:27 that morning after being rushed to a nearby hospital.

Dick recalled that the FBI apparently was continuing to investigate the murder, suspected of being carried out by members of Black September--terrorists who carried Lebanese or Cypriot passports.

At this juncture, the chief of staff sensed that in all likelihood those killings had absolutely nothing to do with U.S. domestic policies and activities.

So, he instinctively picked up the phone to return the call of Aviv Cohen, chief of staff at the Israeli Embassy, who had made the initial inquiry.

Just when Dick began to dial, Shirley entered the room and handed him a sturdy, large envelope.

"Sir, I thought that you would want this right away. The formal invitation from the Israeli Embassy has just arrived."

"Fine. Fine ... I'm calling them now, just to put a feeler out. The boss will want to know my opinion on this, before we formally accept or deny."

As the phone rang on the other end of the line, Dick hoped for the best--although instinctively struck by worries that perhaps extreme danger loomed.

"Only time will tell," he thought. "But I fear that we may be in for an unwelcomed surprise."

*

Worried about what might happen, Pamela had done her best to get Honest to calm down during the hour before their arrival at Doctor Robbins' Perfect Wellness Clinic. Along with Dorothy and Bill McCready, she had told Honest that violence would never enable the children to get adequate medical treatment that they desperately needed.

"I never talked about or threatened violence against the man," Honest said, while driving their other couple and Pamela from the Washoe County Jail--where they had just bailed him out. Hank remained incarcerated due to the additional car-theft charges against him. "That doctor will eventually get what the Lord intends for him; the universe always works that way. Like they say, what goes around, comes around."

Pamela had hurriedly swept away the discarded Hostess pie wrappers from across the entire floor of this former milk truck, before she picked up the McCreadys at Sierra Crest Hospital's main entrance in the middle of the night.

Pamela and the McCreadys left the hospital to bail out Honest and Hank. Before they left, Doctor Robbins had told her that he suspected that tiny Penelope suffered from a sarcoma in her left bicep. Yet he needed the results of more tests to determine such a diagnosis, plus his theory that Peggy suffered from childhood leukemia.

"I can take the pressure. The stress never bothers me." Honest shifted to second gear, when driving the final block to the clinic. "It's the fact that guys like these use deadly poison in an effort to cure cancer. Even an average baboon is smart enough to know that such attempts are ludicrous and insane--to the point of being murderous."

Honest also explained that he had taken his late wife to Doctor Robbins' clinic many times for her chemotherapy treatments many times during the previous summer and fall. He remembered that "each time she became sicker, throwing up and losing weight, all of her hair falling out as her stomach turned literally upside down ... I'm convinced that the poison killed her, an exceedingly slow and painful death.

"With the kind of deadly concoction that this doctor gives, eventual death seems like a 100-percent certainty." Honest turned into the clinic's front lot, before parking his large vehicle in two adjoining spaces. "And now, of all things, I'm supposed to consider allowing him to poison at least one--and possible more--members of my family? ... We are good, innocent and kind people. We don't deserve this."

"Honest, please, you're scaring me." Pamela tried to keep her voice calm. "That poison--that horrible concoction--I'm told that it's the only way to cure me."

"Sorry, little sister, if I unduly frightened you." He shifted to park, his face unshaven and his hair greasy--unlike the previous day--curly, fluffy and healthy looking.

While the four of them walked to the clinic's front door, Pamela noticed that Honest stumbled as he walked. She worried that he might be suffering from a serious knee or hip problem, not to mention the fact that his shoulders and head slumped slightly forward, a significant change from his usual muscular, strong and manly posture.

Honest yanked at the front door, unable to open it until the 75-year-old Bill McCready handled that chore with ease.

Soon afterward, while still in the clinic's front waiting room, she noticed Honest's head slumping forward onto his own chest. After a few minutes, while Richard the receptionist was away in a back room of the facility--presumably in Doctor Robbins' office--Pamela and Dorothy began voicing similar concerns.

The women kept making inquiries: "Honest, are you feeling all right?" and "Did you get enough sleep last night?" and "Is your body hurting somewhere?"

Before the plumber had time to answer, Richard returned to the reception room to announce: "Please follow me. Doctor Robbins is ready see all of you now."

Pamela tried to keep her nerves calm, because violence--and particularly gunplay--was the last thing she wanted. She felt as if her entire happiness hinged on getting adequate medical care for herself and for all of her relatives needing similar help. This made perfect sense to her, because Our Loving and Eternal God wants all of his many children to do their very best in maintaining and achieving optimal health.

She and Honest sat in separate chairs, each across from the doctor at the other side of his desk; the McCreadys sat on a couch behind the in-laws, holding each other's hands.

"I'm going to get right to the point." Doctor Robbins remained seated. "I know, Mister Davis, that you are extremely angry with me ... I understand that ... Yet each of us needs to realize the unbendable fact that the American Medical Association, and also the federal government for that matter, each mandate that only one type of treatment can be used for the most advanced cancers--and that, whether we want to admit this or not--involves the administering of chemo drugs, and that we..."

"OK, but what about my daughters? Let us please stop beating around the bush."

Worried that a sudden confrontation might erupt, Pamela noticed that Honest had both of his hands jammed into the front pockets of his leather trench coat.

The doctor's left hand remained free, moving about and expressive--while his right forearm stayed out of view, somewhere under the desk.

"The blood results just arrived, indicating that Peggy suffers from advanced-stage childhood leukemia. To give her any hope for a long and happy life, we're going to need to begin full treatment right away."

"How can God do this to us?" Honest's head slumped forward to his own chest, while the McCreadys simultaneously heaved a long, heavy sigh. Pamela gasped as well, concerned for the well-being of her nieces. "And little Penelope? What about her?"

"Mister Davis, we need to take a deep breath, because we can only do our best."

"Yes? ... Yes?"

"Biopsy results indicate that Penelope suffers from an advanced Sarcoma. ... Her hope hinges on a full amputation of her arm as soon as possible."

"Oh!" Honest's voice seemed almost too soft and mournful

for Pamela to hear.

"The kids are now resting," The doctor's face was rather expressionless from Pamela's perspective--except for what she perceived as a genuine appearance of concern in his eye and forehead. "Each child is now in her own separate patient room, under continual care from professional nurses."

"But what gave you the right?" Honest's voice had an angry tone from Pamela's perspective, although so weak that she almost failed to understand his words. "Doc, you brought Peggy here, clear across the state and started treating her, without first receiving my permission."

While still in his chair, the doctor used his left hand to hold a single piece of paper high, as if displaying it for all to see--at least from Pamela's perspective.

"Mister Davis, remember? ... You and your wife each signed this permission slip last summer at her insistence. Surely you recall Polly insisting that you each sign this as a precautionary measure--to be used in case of emergency ... She kept speaking of her worries that your children would suddenly get cancer, because of the supposed trend of the disease afflicting many people in your region?"

Without warning, Honest suddenly fell to the floor from his chair. His large, tall body sprawled across the center of the room, both of his eyes closed.

Doctor Robbins rushed around his desk, bent down and immediately unbuttoned the top few buttons of Honest's shirt.

As the McCreadys and Pamela crowded around these two men, the door to the physician's personal office opened. The receptionist stood at the entrance to the room.

"Richard, call an ambulance!"

*

Janelle felt a biting cold clear down to her bones

This preacher's wife sat in her husband Scout's office, watching him and Paula chat rapid-pace about their effort's urgent action plan.

Janelle decided to keep quiet while listening to them banter,; the topic focused on intricate details necessary for getting widespread publicity on the nuclear fallout issue.

Her opinion of Paula unexpectedly changed within the next few minutes. For many years until then, in Janelle's eyes Paula had always been a typical and barely noticeable housewife--although always demure, unassuming, meek and modest.

Such perceptions changed lightning fast during the course of that morning, thanks to Paula's determined and focused demeanor while talking with the preacher.

Janelle swelled with pride when watching her husband interact with this feisty woman. There were plenty of things that Janelle disliked about her spouse, namely his propensity to move his arms all about as he spoke and that nervous habit of his--occasionally using his left hand to flick his earlobes. Even so, his innate ability to listen intently to people and truly care about their problems always mystified her.

Forgiving Scout's continual propensity for over-the-top drama, as far as Janelle knew he truly cared about the community--while developing solutions for many problems. As if a community leader, rather than "just a spiritual adviser," his many successes through the years had included devising an economical and efficient strategy for replacing their town's run-down old sewer system, and sprucing up the weed-covered cemetery.

Despite Scout's numerous eccentric quirks, the preacher's wife adored and appreciated his sense of style, particularly the decor he had personally selected for this office. Besides the intricately woven 283-year-old Persian rug, her favorite trappings included: a Lincoln-era roll top oak desk with just enough scratch marks to give an aura of useful experience; a Victorian-era oil lamp, with just enough of a light cranberry color to emit a sense of comfort; and these walls covered with rustic wooden planks, a perfect accent to the room thanks to forests 138 miles to the east. The only thing out of place or that never seemed to fit into this decor, at least as far as Janelle was concerned, were his clanking electric shoe-polishing machine--on the floor at the side of his desk, a type of contraption that had surged in popularity during the mid-1970s.

With even more pride, Janelle adored the classy type of suit that Scout wore that morning, a tight-knit tweed that would have been perfectly suited for top-class Hollywood movie star James "Jimmy" Stewart. Janelle knew that most people in town appreciated her husband's casual--yet somehow elegant--clothing style. Little did they know, however, that she had persistently nagged him to start wearing such outfits before they moved to Nevada from Iowa; Scout's typical Hawkeye State garb had been overalls common in rural farmland, a sharp contrast to his natural mix of "spiffy" and "casual" in the Silver State. Janelle suspected that people in the West respected him far more than others had in the Midwest, primarily due to something as simple as this change in clothing style.

After 30 straight minutes listening to Paula and Scout's non-stop banter about their planned anti-government campaign, Janelle finally decided to interrupt. She felt that they had overlooked a critical strategy.

"What about radio?" Janelle interjected. "We could easily reach everyone with..."

"Sorry, but I'm afraid that radio is far too expensive." Paula turned in her chair to look directly at the preacher's wife. "We need to keep costs to a minimum, and..."

Rather than behave as if a dutiful lady resigned to keeping her mouth shut, Janelle told them about a relatively new radio broadcast--beamed nightly across the Western wilderness by a mysterious announcer known as Bobby Blair. Just like the famed Wolfman Jack had done several years earlier, Blair--nicknamed Coyote Pete--broadcast from just south of the border in Mexico. Unlike the Wolfman, who always howled on air amid cutting-edge and eclectic rock 'n' roll, Coyote specialized in a relatively new form of broadcast communication that a handful of people had labeled "talk-radio."

"I'm stunned that you both haven't heard of him." Janelle smiled, proud of herself for being the first among them to realize this unique transition. "Coyote Pete only broadcasts in the wee hours of the morning, from about 1 to around 4 ... His show and network are called 'Rip Roarin' Rebel Radio.'"

Scout and Paula sat in silence, each without saying a word--their mouths wide open. Janelle took pride in the fact that they both seemed at least somewhat stunned.

She quickly explained that Coyote's program always focused on the wild, roaming and free-spirited independence of rural westerners. Coyote had quickly become a heroic figure to many residents across the region; the announcer often declares his pride in their rebellious or renegade spirit--and admits his bursting anger at the persistent intrusions by the federal government.

"Coyote stands against the Washington bureaucracy, which claims ownership of public lands throughout the West." Janelle stood and pointed to an 1800s-style map affixed to the wood-covered wall, a valuable and historic image that she had bought for Scout's office three years earlier; at the time she had been determined to help give her husband an authentic aura, reminiscent of the original settlers of these lands. "Without letup, this announcer blasts the feds for endangering thousands of wild horses, while he courageously declares that those same mindless bureaucrats also cruelly and viciously keep pushing our independent ranchers from wilderness that they..."

"But what about the nuclear fallout issue?" Paula scowled while also emitting a tiny smile. This seemed like a puzzling expression from Janelle's perspective.

The preacher's wife admitted that as far as she knew Coyote Pete had never mentioned that burgeoning controversy; perhaps the increasingly popular announcer remained relatively unaware of the issue.

Even so, getting Coyote Pete to discuss this problem on air--and particularly recruiting the announcer as an ally--might help decrease the need to raise funds, to produce massive mailouts and to organize rallies in numerous Western Nevada towns.

"Brilliant!" Paula leaped to her feet and opened her arms wide toward the preacher's wife. "Your idea sounds like a winner!"

Janelle stood and reciprocated, hugging the woman super-tight, while saying: "We still need to figure out a way to contact Coyote Pete--to get him to join our cause."

Scout stood behind his desk, and motioned his arms wide toward these gals.

"Ladies, this idea sounds like something that could potentially lead to a pathway toward happiness for us all--the spread of vital details, plus a blessed chance to ferret out the truth about what the federal ..."

Just then, a light knock echoed from the closed office door.

"What is it?" Scout turned his attention toward this interruption.

"It's me, sir." An adult female voice emitted from the other side. "I'm so very sorry. Something very important has just occurred ... Can I please come in."

"By all means, Cate." The preacher turned toward the door, while Paula and Janelle did as well.

The preacher's personal secretary opened the door. A stout, strong-looking woman in her early 40s, with her dark hair tied up into a bun, Cate stood in the doorway.

The secretary held little Tommy's left hand. The boy stood stationary, looking from Janelle's perspective as if a small, dutiful and obedient soldier--typical for him.

"Scout, I don't know any other way to say this." Cate's giant dark eyebrows lifted high, appearing to Janelle as if a cat that had been shocked by an electric wire. "I just got a message about an emergency ... Sir, can I tell you the details right now, or should I wait until a more private time?"

"All of us need the truth now." Scout sat in his chair, while Tommy bolted from the secretary--who had been waiting with this child in the office reception room. The boy promptly hugged his

Aunt Paula.

"Reverend, you are being summoned by the hospital in Reno." Her head hung low, Cate gazed down toward the old Persian rug, rather than look her boss in the eye. "You are being summoned to Reno, to give the last rites to poor Penelope, Peggy- -and also to their father Honest as well. ... May the Good Lord have mercy on each of their souls."

Fourteen

Always ready to kill if necessary on behalf of her Israeli homeland, Shira entered the front entrance to the classic Belvedere Hotel after completing her daily morning jog.

She disliked and felt repulsed by the assassination process, yet her superiors always labeled her as by far "the best" in that regard.

Her favorite duties by far involved the collection of raw and essential data, such as the tape recording made the previous day of Senator Spickler and his crony.

As sweat beads glistened on Shira's forehead, she yanked open her mailbox in the building lobby--upset with herself for forgetting to check its contents the day before.

Without looking at the contents, she grabbed a handful of envelopes from the box and hopped the stairway steps 2-by-2 to her second floor apartment. Once inside, she closed the door behind herself, plopped the unopened mail atop a desk beside the living room couch, and went to fetch a healthy drink from the kitchen.

Refreshed after her first gulp of tomato juice mixed with herbs, she stood alone at the edge of her living room. Proud of herself for remaining in tip-top shape, her breathing and pulse rates had already returned to normal--a few minutes after her daily workout.

In keeping with her usual custom, she gazed lovingly toward a framed 36-inch by 24-inch black-and-white photo displayed above the fireplace of her late grandparents, Abraham and Ayala Levy, the couple slaughtered in 1942 by Nazis at the Auschwitz concentration camp.

Shira always felt a strong bond with these ancestors, whom she had never met; they died nine years before she was born in

Haifa--the largest city in northeast Israel. The 3,000-year-old settlement on the Slopes of Mount Carmel had become the favorite gathering place of her European relatives who had survived or escaped the Holocaust.

During Shira's early childhood and teens, her parents Rivka and Guy Levy had struggled to minimize her rugged and rebellious spirit. She had continually gotten into trouble while attending the Hebrew Reali School, Israel's largest K-12 institution, and later the University of Haifa--where she had majored in law enforcement.

Shira's parents and their many adult friends often described her as the most alluring and physically attractive girl and young adult that they ever laid eyes on. Yet she also had earned what many people insisted was a well deserved reputation as rambunctious and rowdy, just as mischievous as any boy that they had ever known.

Although well aware of how other people felt about her, by Shira's late teens she considered herself as primarily a sweet, loving and ultra-feminine person--willing to do just about anything to protect her homeland. Always on the lookout for young adult female citizens with these attributes, the Mossad spy agency discovered and recruited her at age 18 upon her entrance to the university.

Even more than her nine confirmed kills of enemy spies during a three-year period before her Salt Lake City assignment, at age 24 Shira was most proud of the fact that she remained a virgin--determined to "save herself" for the man of her dreams.

Forgiving the fact that Shira had not yet come across the type of strong--yet sensitive--and ambitious Jewish man that she craved, she considered herself as the "right person, the ideal individual at the right-and-perfect time to serve and protect my homeland."

With a tomato juice in hand, she sat on the couch and plopped the mail on her lap. She first zipped open a monthly Utah Power and Light bill. Unbeknownst to that company, Mossad had infiltrated the utility with a low-level informant. This served as an ideal way to temporarily and effectively send messages to operatives in the heart of the American West--before they subsequently moved on to other assignments.

Shira inspected this invoice, a bill for $38.73, the payment due in full by January 25, just more than a few weeks away. Her greatest interest was one of those confusing lines of data across the bottom of the page, the type of line that most people ignore--such as account numbers and data on wattage and natural gas usage.

Right away she spotted the clandestine details intended for her, information that she had eagerly anticipated during the previous six months. On this slip, the term "DC PRO URG," was her signal to immediately drop her Salt Lake City assignment and travel to Washington, D.C., to await further instructions.

This delighted Shira and she smiled broadly while sitting alone, by this point bored with Utah and feeling isolated. The notion of America's capital enticed her, the heart of the USA's government filled with many people and boundless possibilities. From experience, she knew of the urgent need to leave for Washington within 24 hours--dropping everything in order to await further instructions.

Her mind fully focused on this transition, Shira suddenly got taken by surprise while sitting on her couch.

Without any warning whatsoever, in a typical "flash-and-awe" surprise, a man wearing black clothing jumped into her living room; he smashed through her window overlooking South State Street near the heart of downtown Salt Lake City.

Well trained to defend herself against such attacks, she instantly realized that this interloper had swung by a rope--likely attached to the building's roof.

Within two seconds after his sudden arrival, the man had stepped up to Shira--who remained seated.

He placed the barrel of a gun at the middle of her forehead. She felt the cold steel on her skin, unafraid and already thinking of many possible ways to escape.

"I am about to kill you." He cocked the weapon, looking

her straight in the eyes.

"Well, mister. I guess you have to do whatever you have to do."

Shira had trained several years for a moment precisely like this. She realized that showing fear was precisely what adversaries like this wanted from her. Instead of becoming terrified, she concentrated on her many options.

Her ears perked up the moment that she heard him cock the weapon.

Looking him straight in the eyes, she realized that this guy was likely an amateur, in all probability on his first hit job. Within a millisecond, she decided to do her best to take advantage of his obvious inexperience.

To her the big tip-off signaling this muscular fellow's apparent ineptitude came in the form of his black hood and mask. Only an unskilled and poorly trained provocateur would try to cover up his identity in broad daylight like this.

Contrary to this creep's sleazy style, highly trained operatives showed their faces--primarily because they already had getaways planned well in advance. The best assassins realized that even without masks, any unwitting witnesses would be terrified out of their minds--far too shocked to recall minuscule details.

Within the course of a mere second, Shira already felt proud of herself for realizing these things. Rather than fear for her own life--a reaction that she knew very likely would emerge as fatal to herself. This moron now pointing a gun to her head had drawn undue attention to their situation.

She knew that if this imbecile had any kind of class whatsoever, he would have abducted her during her job--or ever more efficiently, blown her head off with a high-powered rifle at a significant distance, Lee Harvey Oswald-style.

"I am about to kill you." He spoke matter-of-factly.

She felt pissed off at this, not so much the fact that the guy had just announced his devilish intentions. Of course, killing was an accepted and expected part of this profession. What angered her most was the disturbing fact that someone would send such a moron as this to whack her. If "the end" of Shira's life would have come this way, she would have expected a top-notch professional, rather than a bumbling klutz.

"Before I pull the trigger and blow your ever-loving brains out, lady, I need you to to tell me--honestly--what you have discovered here. ... Can you please do that for me?"

"Sure, mister. ... It's time to spill some guts."

Boom!

The sound of the weapon going off hurt Shira's ears.

The pain reverberated through her head, as if an echo that wouldn't go away.

She immediately stood and looked down at this interloper.

The man lay on his back, sprawled across the rug.

In Shira's right hand was the 22.-caliber Beretta 70 that she had just fired. Blood spurted from her assailant's groin, puddles already forming at the base of her coffee table.

The injured would-be assassin began to flail and moan, but only just as much as his horrific wounds could accommodate. More than anything, she felt grateful that she had escaped any wounds. The man's gun lay at his side.

As this guy looked up straight, still on his back, she stood directly above him.

Shira planted both her feet on each side of his head.

Thankfully, at least from her perspective, this man remained wide awake--although he obviously suffered excruciating pain.

"Sir, how dare you force me to make this God-awful mess in my living room." She poured what remained of her tomato juice right on top of his face. Some of the cool fluid splashed on Shira's bare legs, sending a cool sensation up her spine.

An overwhelming sense of pride filled her, a realization that her intense training had paid off big-time. Surely her instructors at Mossad would have given her an A+ for this, that sudden shot--so effective that at this point Shira finally realized that one of this man's errant, worthless and unworthy testicles had blown clear into the fireplace.

Still standing above the man, Shira bent down and ripped off his mask.

"You are so ugly, sir, that you have to hide your face with a cheap mask?" She threw it into the fireplace, the material landing right next to the man's balls. Shira pointed her gun between the man's eyes and cocked the weapon.

"Lady, please kill me. ... The pain. ... Shoot ... Me ... Now."

"I would be happy to oblige, but first you need to tell me who you work for."

"C..."

"C? ... What? ... I'm willing to help you by killing you, but first you need to tell me what I need to know ... Otherwise, you will suffer for several hours."

"C ... I..."

"What are you saying? ... Do you mean the CIA?"

"Yes."

"You people are incompetent ... Stupid amateurs!"

Pitifully, she continued to look at this man's ugly face, finally feeling at least a tiny bit sorry for the guy. Besides the fact that he had chosen to work for such a monstrous employer, in her eyes he looked unlovable.

"Lady, please kill me."

"Would you like us to say a long prayer together first, so that you can ask God for forgiveness?"

The sad way that he looked straight up at Shira made her think of a strange mixture of discarded trash and a person who was about to get rightfully executed for inexcusable crimes against humanity.

"Kill ... me ... now."

"OK, kind sir ... Have it your way."

Boom!

The guy's inept brains sprayed all across the room in every direction. This failed to bother Shira at all, primarily because she had not planned to bother tidying up the place anyway--before her sudden planned departure for Washington, D.C.

Acting on pure instinct, in perfect sync with her intensive spy-school training, she yanked the photograph of her late grandparents off the wall--before tossing it into the fireplace, frame and all. A healthy dose of lighter fluid then helped do the trick, topped off by a thrown match that landed on the guy's balls--which lay next to the image of them, each grandparent smiling--their heads nestled together during much happier times.

With luck, Shira hoped, these wonderful flames would obliterate any evidence of her true identity--other than her fingerprints.

She grabbed her purse, stuffed her trustworthy Beretta inside, and promptly shimmed down the rope all the way to the sidewalk on South State Street.

Hearing sirens from a distance, she looked all around in every direction, overjoyed upon the realization that no one apparently had seen her to this point.

Wearing only her blood-stained exercise outfit, she headed straight toward her 1969 yellow Camaro in the nearby parking lot.

Within 45 seconds, as police cars and fire engines started parking in front of the Belvedere Hotel, she eased into traffic and stayed at the speed limit--so as to avoid attracting any undue attention.

Par for the course, in keeping with the Mossad's standard procedure, she had already developed an efficient escape plan--intended for use at a moment's notice should the need unexpectedly arise.

With the driver's side window wide open, she inhaled plenty of fresh air and felt thankful to God that she remained healthy and alive. Although briefly feeling a bit sorry for the job that she had just performed, Shira already felt a sensational blood rush, just thinking about her new-assigned location.

She had never yet been to Washington, D.C., but had always dreamed of going there--mesmerized by the mere thought of enjoying that city's many famous tourist magnets. Besides the Lincoln Memorial, the National Museum of Art and the Smithsonian, she yearned to tour the U.S. Capitol Building.

In her mind, an ideal assignment would be to work as an operative in Congress, perhaps as a low-level or personal assistant to a congressman or senator.

*

As chief of staff to freshman Nevada Senator Larry Spickler, Dick Cooper took pride in knowing that he rarely argued with his boss. He realized that the politician relied heavily on his advice as a 25-year Washington "insider."

Passing along his predictions to the Silver State native, during the previous year Dick had correctly forecast: President Richard Nixon's downfall and resignation; that one month after Nixon resigned, the new president--Gerald Ford--would grant his predecessor a full pardon from potential prosecution; and that Ford would testify to Congress about the issue.

Dick Cooper never shied away from the fact that many of his contemporaries on Capitol Hill knew of his keen knowledge of the interworkings of congressional politics.

Like the previous president, who earned the nickname "Tricky Dick," the Nevada senator's right-hand man got similar-sounding label, "Slippery Dick." Yet Mister Cooper knew that there were major differences between himself and Richard Nixon.

As president, Tricky Dick got clandestine insider information via illegal or immoral skulduggery, such as the notorious burglary at the Democratic National Headquarters at the Watergate Hotel. By contrast, Slipper Dick from Senator Spickler's office got his urgent political information "the old-fashioned way," primarily by establishing highly informed contacts from deep within the halls of government.

For this reason, "Slippery Dick" Cooper realized that Spickler had scored a proverbial grand slam in recruiting him to the office of a "mere" freshman senator. Upon accepting the job, this political expert made clear to his new boss that "my only reason for doing so is to help make you the most powerful senate majority leader in U.S. history."

Slippery Dick realized that nothing could possibly make either of them more happy than to eventually seize such power. Both of them knew full well that doing so would require getting Spickler re-elected to several more six-year terms.

They also realized that a necessary first step in that process would be to carry out their plan to hold the "bogus" public meetings throughout Eastern Nevada. To successfully pull this off, Spickler would need to fool everyone into believing that he truly cared about the public's welfare, while aggressively trying to ferret out the "truth."

Early in the afternoon on the day of their arrival back in Washington, Slippery Dick lightly tapped on the large wood door of Spickler's personal office. This seasoned crony ambled inside without bothering to wait for permission to enter.

"Sorry, Dick. ... Not now." Senator Spickler leaned back in his office chair, smoking a huge cigar. "Can't this wait? I've got a ton of phone messages to return ... Greasin' the wheels."

"Super-critical stuff here." Dick plopped a file on Spickler's desk, and promptly sat in a chair opposite from his boss. "This needs your immediate review ... It'll only take a second. Urgent."

Dick knew this would grab the senator's attention; the chief of staff only used that word--"urgent"--about every six months, and only in "vital" situations.

During the ensuing minute and a half, the crony waited while Spickler wrapped up his current phone call--the politician rattling off the usual niceties like "how's your gorgeous wife" and "you mean to tell me that you're already a grandpa? No way!"

Spickler took a long puff of his cigar and winked across the table toward Dick as he said this, heard by this crony as a sign that his boss was doing his best to quickly get rid of whoever was on the other end of the line. While eagerly waiting for the call to end, Dick gazed all around the senator's office, taking a careful assessment of all the usual trappings: three mounted heads of trophy kills, Nevada's state animal--a mountain bighorn sheep--at the center in a place of honor; a few dozen award plaques, most notably signs of appreciation from 27 all-star Little League teams, from Las Vegas to Reno; and autographed black-and-white photos of the late presidents FDR and Truman, on opposite sides of the room. From Dick's point of view, all of these accouterments were downright predictable and even somewhat bland--except for one notable exception. In the highest place of honor, the most visible to any visitor, was a giant blown-up color photograph of Senator Spickler standing with two men--the famed "King of Rock 'n' Roll," Elvis Presley in full showroom white-costumed regalia on his left, and "Ol' Blue Eyes," crooner Frank Sinatra on his right. The image captured each of the three smiling broadly, the entertainers hoisting their arms around the senator's shoulders.

Dick had personally selected the photo for this wall, an aura and conveyed popularity, acceptance, camaraderie and--most important of all--extreme power.

"Real quick, boss." Dick spoke immediately after his boss hung up. "For your review, here is an initial draft of our office's press release, on the public meetings that we are going to hold on regarding the nuclear fallout and cancer issue."

"Ha-ha!" Spickler reached across and snatched up the file. "We're going to get them all hooked. Nothing less than brilliant, I must say. ... Is this all?"

Dick realized that on sporadic and intermittent days the senator lacked any motivation to sit around for long "shooting the breeze" about a wide range of issues. Yet at other times, the politician spent many hours in this very room--chewing the proverbial fat on a wide range of inter-woven issues and strategies.

This time Dick sensed that the boss was in no mood whatsoever for idle chat.

So, the crony got right to the point, explaining that the senator and his wife, Maureen, had just received a coveted invitation to a Israeli Embassy party the following months. Guests at the prestigious, classic, old Embassy Row Hotel were to honor the new president, Republican Gerald Ford and his wife, Betty.

"No!" The senator suddenly sat straight, no longer leaning back. "There is no way on God's green earth what I will ever associate with--let alone celebrate the leader--of the other political party ... Those guys..."

"Calm down, senator." Dick put his own right hand up toward his boss in a classic "stop" symbol. The chief of staff explained that by being one of only a handful of Democrats present, Spickler actually would be displaying his own willingness to reach across the political aisle--actually a symbol of his own risk-taking, bravado and power. With equal importance, Dick explained, if all went well the senator could use the event to generate powerful alliances with people of the Jewish faith--potentially garnering significant campaign donations in the process.

To sweeten his argument, Dick also mentioned that congressional Democrats had made significant gains in the mid-term elections just two months earlier--retribution from U.S. voters eager to punish Republicans for the Watergate scandal.

"But, Dick, I smell a giant rat in here somewhere. ... Do you think that this is just a ploy to suck me in, before they try to take me down?"

"That goes with the territory, sir; that's the nature of politics. ... As you know, perhaps just as much as anyone else, virtually everyone serving today on Capitol Hill is some sort of target. ... With that understood, I have little doubt that at this very moment you are directly in the cross-hairs of someone ... Exactly who that is, or how they will attack you politically, I cannot say for sure. ... We can only hope that this Israeli Embassy gala will help you and strengthen you, rather than cause you great harm."

"Okay, Dick. ... If you insist. I am in no way trying to threaten you here--you know that I would never do that, my friend. But you have to know that both of our butts are on the line on this one. We can only hope that we avoid getting burned, or having a few dozen holes shot clean through our political careers."

*

As a seasoned and highly acclaimed physician himself, Sierra Crest President Gregory Crowley disliked the notion of disciplining or reprimanding other doctors.

While sitting in his office just before noon on the day after Polly's funeral, Crowley reached into his desk for the personnel file of Doctor James Robbins.

Crowley reviewed the documents, glad to see that the records reflected the Vietnam veteran had earned high marks from his Reno peers and patients since being allowed to practice in the hospital--as Northern Nevada's only licensed oncologist.

The last thing in the world that Crowley wanted to do that day was to unduly upset this cancer specialist. At this juncture such doctors were considered as "relatively rare birds," which--if lost--could take a year or more to replace during the mid-1970s, particularly in relatively isolated high-desert regions such as Reno.

Doctor Crowley answered a buzz on his office intercom: "Yes, Grace?"

"Doctor Robbins has arrived, as you requested. Sir, are you ready to see him?"

"Send him right in."

Until that morning, Crowley had only met face-to-face three times with the oncologist: in this same office 10 months earlier, during a required initial interview; four months after that at the July summer barbecue for all hospital employees in Reno's Idlewild Park; and unexpectedly at an election night Republican rally in the convention room of downtown's Harrah's Hotel and Casino.

At each of these sessions Doctor Robbins had impressed Crowley as being cordial, far more gentlemanly than most other physicians, and a sharp, rather dapper dresser. The biggest surprise had been bumping into the oncologist at the GOP gathering, primarily because he had heard rumblings that Robbins was strapped for funds--contrary to the standard image of most voters who support the conservative cause.

By this point just more than two months later, Crowley still vividly recalled Doctor Robbins saying that "as far as I know, Senator Spickler might be a good guy--at least as a human being, but his politics stink--almost as if he actually hates people."

Such words by Doctor Robbins had rung as a blessed melody in Crowley's ears, since--as the hospital's chief administrator--he felt precisely the same about the freshman senator. Another thing sparking the hospital president's admiration for Doctor Robbins came when--at the same political rally--the oncologist briefly blurted out that he served one weekend a month in the Nevada Army National Guard. The only negative about this in Crowley's mind was the "Army" branch of military; the hospital president favored Air Force, having served in that branch as a Korean War surgeon--proud of himself for saving the lives of many U.S. servicemen.

Within seconds after getting the go-ahead from her boss, Grace opened his office door and signaled for Doctor Robbins to take a seat opposite from Crowley.

"I have no idea what this is about." Robbins firmly shook Crowley's hand while moving to sit. "I'm glad that you called me up here anyway, because I urgently need to talk with you this morning anyway."

"Fine." Crowley sat in his own seat, before briefly shuffling papers on his desktop. "We're both super-busy, so let's get straight to business ... I'm afraid that you are not going to like what needs to be said now, but it's something that you need to hear."

"Like almost any doctor in my position, as you very well know, I engage in life-and-death conversations every day ... So, feel free ... Fire away."

Crowley held up the front page of that morning's "Reno Globe-Herald" newspaper, pointing to the police booking mug shots of two men. One photo featured a guy wearing a pirate patch over his right eye; the other fellow was shown with two bruised eyes.

"Doctor Robbins, please understand that we need to talk about this urgent situation." Crowley tried to keep his own expression blank, determined to avoid any unnecessary conflict with this oncologist. "As you may have heard, both of these men were arrested yesterday evening right here in the hospital lobby, for disturbing the peace. The police tell me that both of these men kept yelling that they were angry at you. ... The pirate here claims that you poisoned his wife and also that someone named Hank kidnapped his 4-year-old daughter, supposedly with your assistance. ... As if that wasn't already enough of a problem, the other guy also complained that you beat him to a pulp--as if you are a championship prize fighter--and that you stole his car after abandoning him in the middle of the Nevada desert. ... The newspaper reported these allegations, without even bothering to first get a response from my office--and I imagine the reporter never tried to contact you as well to get your version ... Naturally, as you can very well imagine, Doctor Robbins, I need some answers from you."

"Yes, indeed ... I'll have to admit that these are extremely serious matters."

"So?"

"Well, Doctor Crowley, there is a far more serious issue that I need to talk with you about, other than the behavior of these two characters."

"Rest assured that we'll get to chat about whatever problem has arisen, but first we need to tackle this particular situation head-on." Crowley gently tossed the newspaper, which landed on his desktop directly in front of Robbins. "This hospital needs to maintain its solid reputation ... I'm sure that there is no need whatsoever to lecture you about that. ... And, before you start giving me any sort of explanation, as far as I'm concerned this scurrilous article was written to a certified nincompoop. ... Duane Shelton, the guy whose byline you will see atop this offensive, defamatory and scandalous article is merely a college student, an intern working part-time at the 'Globe-Herald' to earn class credits ... Worsening matters, as far as I'm concerned he's a spoiled daddy's boy. ... He is only 19 years old, can you believe that? Adding to this problem, Duane's father is the top executive--the primary shareholder--of this rag and dozens of other papers nationwide ... My fear is that this controversy might get out of hand ... Anyway, Doctor Robbins, you can very well imagine the importance of the explanation that you're about to give me."

During a lengthy pause that ensued, Crowley watched intently as Doctor Robbins calmly picked up the newspaper and began reading the article. While watching this oncologist scour the story, the hospital president began wondering about the persistent rumors that at least a dozen nurses had strong crushes on this man. Every few weeks during the previous several months, Grace had privately peppered Crowley with details about women who dreamed of walking down a church aisle arm-in-arm with Doctor Robbins. Grace always insisted that women easily became intrigued by the Vietnam War veteran, who possessed a unique sense of mystery--intermixed with a quiet sense of charisma, embossed with the distinctive aura of manliness. Many times Grace had told Crowley that "no one can figure out Doctor Robbins, his demeanor always seeming courageous--and yet simultaneously kind and truly caring about his patients. ... When he isn't around, everyone--all the nurses anyway--refer to him as a Maverick. So many women wish that he would sweep them into his arms, before taking them to his home. Yet he is always a perfect gentleman, at least as far as I know." Crowley would always gently scoff at such statements, telling Grace in each instance that "we all need privacy" and that "as long as he keeps doing his job well, everything will be OK." Secretly, however, without telling anyone he felt this way, Crowley admired Doctor Robbins' supreme ability to enrapture the hearts of women, apparently without ever trying to do so.

"Doctor Crowley, you deserve straight answers." Doctor

Robbins put the newspaper back on the executive's desk. "So, here is the truth as far as I know."

The oncologist promptly explained that the "Pirate" has temporarily lost all sense of logic--angry, depressed and grieving the recent death of his wife. The man widely known as Honest is a good, decent, hard-working guy who just happened to become raging angry. ... At present, the Pirate is downstairs in Intensive Care, having suffered from complete exhaustion--both mentally and physically. ... The other guy, Hank, the fellow who had blackened eyes, is nothing but a common criminal--a suspected car thief and the Pirate's brother-in-law--described by Doctor Robbins as a dangerous, real-life "Captain Blood." Currently unable to get bail because "virtually no one seems to like or love him--even his poor wife," this known alcoholic had drunk himself into a rage while behind the wheel of a stolen car--with Robbins and the head Pirate's critically ill 4-year-old daughter stuck in the back seat. ... Naturally, clicking into survival mode, the oncologist went into action--using his superior hand-to-hand combat skills learned before his tour in Vietnam ... In an effort to ensure the safety of himself and the child, the oncologist had quickly taken control of the situation. The oncologist admitted to hurling himself into the front seat, subduing this drunken Captain Blood guy--fiercely struggling for control of the fast-back yellow Mustang as the vehicle hurled down the slushy high-desert highway at 90 miles per hour. Soon victorious, and miraculously managing to prevent the vehicle from spinning out of control, "I disarmed this perpetrator, administered those beautiful and glorious black eyes that you see here for good measure, and summarily left him out in the middle of nowhere--where he belonged. As you can imagine, my top priority was then--and it still remains--to save that innocent child's life."

Caught up in Doctor Robbins' story, the Korean War veteran struggled to refrain from grinning from ear to ear. The notion that one of the most talented doctors at Sierra Crest Hospital was actually a "tough guy" made him proud, not to mention the stupendous fact that all this sounded like a real-life plot fit for a "super-spy" movie. Nonetheless, Crowley tried to maintain a stern and unemotional expression.

"Sounds to me, Doctor Robbins, like you did what you thought was right. ... You need to know that I am fully on your side, at least on this particular matter, although you might have suffered from a few lapses in judgment ... Who am I to say what you should have done in such a deadly situation? ... My suggestion is that you avoid the police and the press; never answer any of their questions ... Let me handle those queries ... We just need you to do your job. ... As far as I am concerned, you can head back downstairs and tend to your patients."

"Before I can do that, there's another urgent matter that I need..."

"What can be more important than these goofy pirates?" Crowley reached across, grabbed the newspaper and plopped it into a trashcan; he refrained from saying that Grace had purchased 14 additional copies for hospital records.

"I'm not trying to behave in an overly dramatic fashion here, Doctor Crowley. But several of my patients will die very soon, unless this hospital's pharmacy gets its act together--fast."

"Problems? ... With our pharmacy?"

Doctor Robbins explained that at least 10 times during the previous three weeks he had ordered or prescribed specific chemotherapy drugs; these pharmaceuticals were necessary for the treatment of cancer patients suffering from severe levels of the disease. Yet he explained that, "in all due respect, Doctor Crowley, I'm increasingly frustrated by the disturbing fact that none of these drugs ever arrive." Patients who desperately need treatment--but who soon will die without the chemo--include the Pirate's 4-year-old daughter, who suffers from advanced childhood leukemia; that child's 24-year-old aunt, who has advanced colon cancer; and four patients from other Reno-area families. Compounding these problems, the girl's 3-year-old sister will need an arm amputated due to carcinoma, followed--quite possibly--by her own round of chemo.

"Three weeks with no chemo drugs!" Crowley became unexpectedly angry, breaking his strategy of keeping an unemotional face throughout this session. "In this hospital? ... Doctor Robbins, I realize this is no fault of yours whatsoever ... But believe me, I'm going to get this problem solved as fast as humanly possible. ... By all means, you're excused to go now ... I respect the fact that those patients of yours need as much of your professional care, especially at a critical time like this."

Momentarily, Doctor Robbins turned the door knob to go, while facing the executive and saying--while briefly bowing his head--"I would like to thank you for your valuable time."

Just then Crowley realized that he had forgotten to tell the oncologist an essential detail, a type of update that hospital administrators considered a housekeeping matter. The executive stood at his desk and smiled broadly toward the departing doctor.

"Oh, just one more quick thing ... I almost forgot to tell you that our front lobby security guard ... Anthony Dunn ... I understand that you are a friend of his ... Calling him 'General.' ... He refuses to give us any details about what happened during the commotion last night ... Anthony won't even tell us what happened to Captain Blood's Mustang ... We had no choice this morning, other than to place the guard on unpaid administrative leave ... You and I can talk about that in a few days, if you would like, Doctor Robbins, but right now I don't have time--as you might very well imagine."

*

One week after her sister Polly's funeral, Paula felt angrier than ever at the federal government and particularly at her husband--who remained jailed in Reno.

Although highly concerned, Paula had refrained from traveling there to see her ailing and hospitalized relatives. Instead, she remained the entire time in Centralia to care for her nephew Tommy and to work on launching their community's anti-government campaign.

"This entire week seemed to flash by, seemingly faster

than a single second," Paula thought while fetching that morning's January 16 edition of the "Centralia Independent Journal" from the front porch of her own home. With Tommy, she had returned there the previous day, after spending the past several months living at the home of Polly and Honest; Paula had dedicated her every waking moment to their family.

Common sense had told Paula to avoid visiting Honest, fearing that she would break down and tell the ailing plumber of her enduring love for him. The possibility of also revealing his late wife's treachery also would unnecessarily complicate matters further.

And, as far as Hank, Paula hoped to avoid seeing him for the rest of her life. From her view, this man had hoodwinked her-- playing her for a fool, double-crossing her good nature, while once doing everything possible to wreck their lives.

While refusing to accept Hank's daily "collect" phone calls from jail during the previous week, she had called Reno attorney Christopher Frederickson several times to make arrangements for a divorce. Paula hoped that with any luck her worthless spouse would get served with the appropriate documents within the next several days, hopefully while sitting in his cell.

Paula had forgiven Hank perhaps three dozen times during the previous several years, yet from her perspective this latest infraction had become the "final straw."

At least on the positive side, the message from a week earlier had been confirmed as "bogus," the incorrect report that Honest and his youngest two children were on "death's doorstep," and needed last rites.

Paula's brief phone chat with Doctor Robbins had confirmed that Pamela, Peggy and Penelope each remained in stable condition--all of them seriously ill, yet much better than critical stages. From her view, another good sign came from the fact that Dorothy and Bill McCready had volunteered to continually stay at each of their bedsides--giving much-needed moral and spiritual support. Thanks to the McCreadys' meager but sustainable retirement incomes, they had enough steady funds to pay for their own food and lodging--even for an extended multi-month stay if necessary.

On the downside, efforts to raise funds for a letter-writing campaign and a phone-bank to call residents throughout Eastern Nevada had fallen flat. Contacting these prospects by phone had become impractical, due to over-the-moon long distance phone charges imposed by AT&T--then widely known as "Ma Bell" due to the company's nationwide monopoly.

This seemingly insurmountable stumbling block made Paula feel almost as if her blood had begun to boil over--but not quite. Like her deceased sister Polly and her ailing sibling, Pamela, she had learned from their late father Jay Williams that "persistence is the key; never give up under any circumstances." The three sisters each were born in the wake of World War II; Jay had served as a tail gunner on a B-24 bomber, surviving 35 missions over enemy territory.

Several years before they were born, Jay had joined the service as a teetotaler from Idaho, but returned home to the mainland as a hopeless drunk. Within a few months after Jay's honorable discharge, while in Las Vegas--then a little known desert town with a population of only a few thousand--he had met their future mother. Audrey was a native of Angel's Camp, California, a descendant of the Golden State's original Gold Rush settlers.

Even all these many years later, at the onset of 1975 Paula still remembered her early childhood when Jay drove them from town-to-town throughout the West--always looking for work as an auto body repairman. Their entire immediate family literally lived in the front seat of this man's pickup truck. Shortly after entering each new town, while penniless, Jay would drive along residential streets looking for dinged-up vehicles. Finding such wrecks almost always seemed easy, primarily because the federal government had prohibited the use of steel for basic auto repairs during wartime.

"I have three hungry kids and my wife outside there in my truck." Jay would invariably say, while chatting on somebody's front porch "Hire me to repair your vehicle, and you'll be glad that you did. I'll have your car looking like it's brand new, within a flash. I charge much less than any auto body repair shop, and I do a better job, too."

Somehow, Jay always landed work in the nick of time, earning barely enough income to ensure his immediate family's short-term survival. Many nights he would walk away alone or leave run-down motels where his small family stayed; each time this happened, he invariably returned to his young wife and children in a drunken and potentially violent condition. Shortly before Paula's sixth birthday, her mother Audrey put her proverbial foot down--telling Jay in no uncertain terms that "I cannot take this any more. This is no way to raise children. There is going to be a divorce, unless we settle down--and Centralia is a centralized location, as good as any for you to continue your craft."

Jay quickly caved in to this threat, later telling his daughters during a Thanksgiving dinner in 1955 that "your mother was right." At this point, thinking back on those times, Paula realized perhaps more than ever before that her father had been seriously flawed: a drunk, never hiding his contempt for wealthy people; although considered handsome enough to model for a Marlboro cigarette magazine ad, his attire always reflected that of a man who cared little about his appearance; and although one of the West's premiere automobile experts, he actually could care less about cars.

On the positive side, however, far outshining anything else within Jay's own flawed character--at least from Paula's view, and she sensed that her sisters felt the same as well--he instilled in his daughters a can-do, never-give-up attitude. He always fought peacefully, yet respectfully, against the so-called "powers that be," huge corporations or local government bureaucrats that "tried to screw the little guy."

Deep within her own heart, Paula realized that this is why she loved Honest--her late sister's husband--virtually with every fiber of her being. Like her late father, the man with the birth name of Abraham Davis, courageously traveled from town-to-town, always looking for just enough work to feed and clothe his family. Yet Paula also realized that the late auto repairman and the plumber were much different from each other--at least in one important regard. ... From her view, Jay had married the "right and perfect" woman for himself, while Honest had wed a lady who never deserved him.

  Fully cognizant of these details, Paula glanced at the main headline in the "Independent Journal" that she had just fetched from the porch: "Senator Spickler to Hold Public Hearings on Nuclear Fallout." Right away Paula's eyes raced through the article, which detailed the politician's plans to hold sessions for residents in 12 relatively small towns. Chief-of-staff, Dick Cooper, was quoted as saying that "Senator Spickler is extremely concerned about the safety, health and welfare of all Nevadans. For this reason, he is determined to get to the truth of the matter."

  "That's a bunch of poop!" Paula hurled the newspaper onto the floor.

  Just then, she heard a knock at the front door.

  She opened it, to find Janelle--the preacher's wife--right on schedule at their pre-arranged time.

  "Paula, did you see that front-page article?"

  "That's just a bunch of manure, and we know it, don't we?"

  The women briefly hugged, before Janelle carried her own suitcase into the living room. Paula already had separate bags packed and placed there, one each for herself and for Tommy. The boy scurried from the hallway into the living room, no longer walking and behaving as if a dutiful, mindless soldier.

  "Are you really going to take me to Mexico?"

  "You bet we are." Paula briefly patted the top of her nephew's head. "Now, young man, quickly--go brush your teeth and comb your hair."

  As soon as the child disappeared from view, Janelle blurted

out the fact that her husband--Scout, the preacher--remained angry about these women's decision to drive south alone. Going to Nogales, Mexico, just south of the U.S. border at Arizona's southern edge, seemed to Paula and Janelle as if the only possible way to directly contact the increasingly famous rebel radio announcer, Coyote Pete. From their view, the mysterious and elusive DJ was their only hope in getting the truth to the public about nuclear fallout.

"Janelle, you don't believe any of that junk from the newspaper, do you?"

"Not for a single second."

The preacher's wife then explained that her husband had become increasingly angry at the notion of her leaving him for this planned two-week excursion. Janelle and Scout had never once been apart during their decade-long marriage. This marked the first time that Janelle had ever broken free, taking her own course in life--rather than merely serving him as a dutiful wife.

"Paula, I stood up for myself ... You would be proud of me ... And to think that just a week ago, Scout had been the person who convinced me to join this political battle. I know without any doubt whatsoever that this effort is that important."

Delighted at having Janelle as a devoted ally, Paula suddenly felt more thrilled than she had been in many weeks--or perhaps even years.

Within five minutes, along with Tommy, they loaded the luggage into a dark green 1968 Volkswagen van--parked at the rear of Paula and Hank's home. As far as she knew, he had legally purchased this vehicle, which seemed to have an appropriate, up-to-date registration. Excluding the many hippie-style swirls and decals covering the vehicle's outer body, the van seemed perfect to Paula.

As planned, the women and Tommy would travel cheap. The only money that they needed was for gasoline and for food--most of which had already been packed--and also perhaps for a brief motel stay. A camper stove would serve just fine for cooking, and the women could sleep in the vehicle's rear with the boy.

Exactly 10 minutes after Janelle's arrival, Paula drove them in the van away from the residence. The women agreed that their chances for success seemed good, and Tommy kept blurting out that he loved this adventure--"like the Old West."

A few minutes after they started heading south on U.S. Highway 93, in the rear-view mirror Paula saw flashing police lights. Always dutiful in obeying the law, she pulled to the right side of the highway.

"Janelle, it's him--Sheriff Peters." In the driver's door mirror, Paula looked at the lawman walking toward them after parking his car. She cranked down the window.

"Good morning, ladies." The sheriff tipped his hat, while leaning toward the open driver's side window. "What a fine day, huh? ... You didn't think that you were going to go to Mexico, did you?"

Fifteen

Six days after fleeing Salt Lake City, Shira remained in hiding at the Midwife Hotel, an old run-down complex two miles from Interstate 70 in Little Rock, Arkansas.

In perfect sync with her extensive training, on the day after the Utah attack, she had used a Molotov cocktail to destroy her yellow 1969 Camaro. The vehicle erupted in a fireball that shot straight up 30 feet, attracting hundreds of onlookers in Frederick, Colorado, a small town near Denver.

Well aware that she had become the target of an intense nationwide dragnet, Shira had dyed her hair blood red and purchased tattered hippy-style clothes. She paid with cash at Morton's Consignment Store on Humphrey Boulevard.

From there, she hitchhiked 987 miles to her current location, stopping only once while en route for food at the Pop-n-Shop Diner off Interstate 135 in Wichita, Kansas.

All along the way, Shira never once worried seriously about getting captured, since failure had never been part of her mindset. Instead, this agent thought primarily of living in Washington, D.C., which--as far as she knew--remained her next assignment.

Following her training step-for-step, she decided to stay at the little-known, isolated Arkansas motel for a minimum of at least 45 days. The tried-and-true strategy of "shelter in place" sharply increased her chances of escaping detection.

Shira also refrained from wondering who her attacker had been, back at the historic Belvedere Hotel in Salt Lake City. She knew that her comrades would do everything in their power to get that information, before passing those details to her as soon as possible. With equal importance, she knew the vital importance of refraining from any effort to contact the Mossad spy agency or her comrades.

The mere thought of buying junk food repulsed her, but she did so anyway. Healthy meals might serve as a tip-off to her whereabouts. By this point authorities, most likely the FBI, had established a reliable profile on her as an exercise and nutrition aficionado--her personality fixated on maintaining good health.

Also breaking the mold for herself, at the Winn-Dixie store near the motel she also bought five magazines. Back in Utah Shira had always purchased business and financial publications; this time this woman broke the mold again, buying what she considered "throw-away" periodicals like "TV Guide" and "Playgirl" magazine.

When alone in her Arkansas motel room on her first full day there, Shira already felt much lonelier than she had in her entire life. Although technically a "loner" herself without any close friends--unless being attacked or assassinating someone--she always got along well with people. She had always credited this to her stunning appearance and cheery personality with generating these positive interactions. Yet deep inside she felt a burning desire to spend lots of quality, intimate time with a handsome man.

Still a virgin by choice, determined to save herself for marriage someday--hopefully in the near future--to a suitable Jewish man, she tossed and turned in frustration on her motel room bed. The idea of needing to spend an entire month alone until the "heat blew over" already started to fill her with apprehension.

Sweat beaded across Shira's entire body, still fully clothed while on her back. Right when she began flipping slowly through the "Playgirl" magazine--gazing at vibrant photos of semi-nude men--burgeoning storm clouds outside erupted into a cascade of thunder and heavy rain. Failing to get any relief from the unseasonable heat, she began to wonder what it would be like to spend quality time with a handsome, kind and powerful physician. Since her late teens, Shira had begun fantasizing about spending her life with just such a man; she became well aware of the fact that handsome, charismatic and muscular men with a superior expertise in medicine turned her on--big time.

Just as Shira's mind began to swirl and spin with the mere idea of such boundless possibilities--a potential eruption of life-changing magnitude--the phone began to ring on a nightstand beside her motel room bed.

"Should I answer?" She thought, while dropping the magazine's centerfold onto her sweaty stomach. "No one is supposed to know that I am here."

The ringing continued for a half minute, seeming like a lifetime to her.

"Hello?" She finally picked up, uncharacteristically caving in to her curiosity.

"Melody?"

Upon hearing this, Shira remained quiet for a few moments before remembering that "Melody" had been the phony name that she checked in under.

"Yes?"

"This is Matthew at the front desk. About one hour ago, a little girl dropped off a package here for you ... Would you like to come and get it now?"

"I'll be right there."

The Israeli spy hung up, wondering what she should do. Would the package blow up? Was it a communication from her superiors? Who had sent this delivery?

*

As Israel's ambassador to the United States, Amos Berkovich always required that his staff avoid wasting his time. When appointed to the post 15 months earlier in October 1973, he had announced to all personnel "the key to our success--to the survival and prosperity of our homeland--is relentless efficiency from each of us. We should expect nothing less of each other, and of ourselves."

Still keeping this directive paramount in his mind, the ambassador's chief assistant--Elijah Horowitz--carried an updated file folder when entering his boss's embassy office at precisely

10:31 in the morning Eastern Time on January 15, 1975, a date and time that later would be verified by their nation's top investigators.

"Sir, here is the list of those who have confirmed that they will attend our invitation-only gala next month--honoring President Ford at the Embassy Row Hotel."

Without wasting time, Berkovich scoured the list. Horowitz had always admired the ambassador's keen attention to detail, his ability to make good but quick decisions, and his insistence on exhibiting formal behavior at all times. One of only a few things that this assistant disliked about his superior was that persistent twitch in his right eye--caused by nerve damage from wounds suffered in the 1948 war for independence.

"Excellent!" Berkovich bellowed, a positive and heart-felt type of emotional display that Horowitz rarely witnessed from his superior. "That fool--the freshman senator from Nevada, Spickler--he has decided to attend. Right into our trap!"

"I knew that you would be extremely pleased. Getting that jerk into our Web is just what we need ... Another thing, sir ... I have an urgent updated report for you, the latest on our agent Shira Levy. I'm confident that you will find this mighty interesting."

Striving to appear as efficient, Horowitz placed a second folder on the desk in front of his boss. They both knew that 83 Mossad agents worked from coast-to-coast in the United States, each busy ferreting out vital information on federal activities. Although Israel and the USA remained strong allies, each continually spied on each other--supposedly as a precautionary measure. Any loss of agent Shira Levy would be a significant blow to the Jewish nation's clandestine operations; the possibility that her cover might have been blown--leading to the failed attempt on her life--had heightened concerns throughout the spy agency's hierarchy. Horowitz knew that Mossad listed her as among its top three agents--vastly superior to their contemporaries.

"Another good report." Berkovich inspected the folder on Shira. "But any word yet on who the guy was--the person who tried to whack our favorite angel?"

"Sir, those details are not in the document that you're reading for security reasons ... I'm afraid to tell you here that our initial indications reveal that the would-be assassin was from Israel. From all the evidence that we have been able to pin down, we have been betrayed by one of our own."

"Get me more details as soon as possible. It looks like we're in for a blood-bath, perhaps within the next few weeks ... Make sure our top three assassins prepare for the worst, and may the God of Abraham save us all."

*

Abraham Davis--commonly known as "Honest"--squinted in an effort to open his only remaining eye. He moved both hands toward his face, while laying on his back.

"Where am I?" He kept mumbling. "Am I still alive?"

"Yes, you are alive."

"Who are you?" Honest struggled to think straight, his thought process convoluted and garbled. "I can hardly see. ... What happened?"

"I am Doctor Robbins. ... You are in Sierra Crest Hospital ... You are having difficulty seeing, because you have been asleep for nearly a week."

"A week!" Startled by this unexpected revelation, Honest suddenly got some of his wits about him. He quickly tried to sit, but two nurses gently held him down--one on each side of the bed. "I'm suddenly starting to see ... You're right; I'm in a hospital."

"That is correct." Doctor Robbins held a clipboard, which he kept inspecting.

"Doctor, didn't you hear what I asked? What happened to me?"

"Exhaustion ... You are suffering from complete, total exhaustion--on a physical level, and I expect emotionally as well."

"Are you saying that I'm not a strong man? Why, I can whip anyone who..."

"Please calm down, Mister Davis."

"Calm down? How can you say something like that?

Where are my children? Are they OK? And my sister-in-law, Pamela? Are you poisoning all of them, the same way that you killed Polly?"

"Sir, everyone here is working diligently, in the best interest of your entire family." Robbins motioned to another man standing beside the bed. "This is Doctor Conners, your personal physician."

"Why don't you tell me about my daughters! Are they alive!"

"Pamela and Peggy are each undergoing care, in separate patient rooms."

"But what about the tiny one--my baby--little Penelope?"

"Sir, your youngest remains a patient here as well ... In fact, we have her right out here in the hallway, ready to see you-- we thought that seeing her might raise your spirits."

"Certainly, bring her in." Honest felt at least some degree of happiness for the first time in several weeks. "But may I please sit up straight before she gets in here; I refuse to allow my little baby to see me in a weak condition."

"By all means." Doctor Robbins motioned toward each of the two nurses. The women promptly helped Honest put his head up a tiny bit--too early amid this stage of recovery to have him sit straight. "But Mister Davis, before we let her in here, I need to explain to you that there has been a significant change in her appearance."

"I don't care what she looks like. I will always love each..."

Suddenly Penelope scurried into the room, followed closely by Dorothy and Bill McCready.

"So sorry, everyone." Dorothy piped in. "This adorable little thing got away from us, before we could catch her."

Penelope summarily hopped onto her ailing father's hospital bed. They promptly hugged each other tight for a few moments. The sudden realization of what had happened left Honest feeling mortified, dumbstruck and emotionally numb.

"My good Lord in Heaven." Honest hugged his daughter tighter, never wanting to let her go ever again. "You guys have chopped her right arm clean off of her body. How in the name of God could you have done that?"

"Papa! Papa!" The 3-year-old Penelope kept planting kisses on her daddy's cheeks. "Love! Papa! Love!"

*

The Volkswagen van reached Nogales on Arizona's southern border two hours after sundown, with Janelle feeling bone-tired after their long day of travel. She sensed that Paula and Tommy felt equally exhausted.

Despite their confrontation earlier with Sheriff Peters, their 12-hour trek from Centralia, Nevada, had seemed relatively uneventful from Janelle's perspective.

She appreciated the bold way that Paula had told the lawman to "mind your own business," and "we have a right to go wherever we want, young man."

Janelle had unexpectedly surprised herself by telling the official, "we need to say a lot of prayers for you, mister--because you're being a stupid jerk."

This marked the first time in Janelle's life that she had openly defied authority.

"You women are making a mistake, you just need to know that," Sheriff Peters had said, when giving Paula her driver's license back. "Mexico is no place for two beautiful American women without a man."

"Hey, I'm a man!" Tommy hollered from the back seat, while taking out a toy cap-gun from his holster. "My mom always told me that I'm brave and good."

"I agree that your mother was very wise and loving." The sheriff took one step back from the driver's door. "Okay, you guys can go on your merry way to Mexico. But never forget that I warned you about the need to take actual firearms."

Janelle felt an unexpected sense of surprise and glee when Paula suddenly floored the accelerator, the vehicle's wheels sending clouds of dirt into the started lawman's face.

For the next 45 miles while zipping southbound on the isolated highway, Paula kept chatting about her distrust for the lawman. She kept referring to him as a "brown-noser" whenever politicians were around, particularly Senator Spickler.

"Aunt Paula, what is a brown-noser?" Tommy sat in the back, peering out the windows toward the rolling high-desert.

"That term just refers to a person who fails to respect himself, without doing the 'right thing' for his friends and neighbors." Paula slowed the van to 35 miles per hour, interrupted by a farm tractor in front of them on the two-lane highway. She then moved into the opposite lane, accelerated to 75 miles per hour and zipped on the open road.

Tommy remained quiet for the next five hours, taking occasional brief naps until they stopped for a two-hour lunch break in Mesa--about 30 minutes south of Phoenix. The women chatted non-stop about their anger toward the government during the first leg of the excursion.

Paula kept insisting that creeps like Senator Spickler should be impeached or booted out of office by voters if evidence emerged that the government knowing endangered rural residents with nuclear bomb fallout. Feeling much more accommodating--yet equally feisty--Janelle said that "we need to forgive them, as the Lord would want us to do--before working together for a viable solution."

Their banter about this issue ceased from Mesa onward, after Paula proclaimed--as they entered the diner--that there "can be no solution, because many more people likely are going to die--due to the radiation exposure from many years ago."

By the time they reached Nogales on the U.S. side of the border, Janelle began to worry that perhaps the Sheriff had been right. How would two unarmed women be able to protect themselves and a little boy in a rough-and-tumble country without a man's help?

From Janelle's view, Paula seemed oblivious to such

potential dangers while driving them to the border check-point called Nogales-Grand Avenue Port of Entry. Rebuilt just nine years earlier, the border crossing connects U.S. Interstate 19 with Mexican Federal Highway 15.

"Are' you afraid at all, Paula?" Janelle said, after a border guard with a name badge saying "Gonzales" inspected their driver's licenses and signaled them through.

"If I were afraid, I wouldn't be here." Paula immediately started cruising the Mexican town's residential streets. "Can you tell where we are?"

Janelle squinted while striving to decipher a crude hand-drawn street map that her husband--the reverend--had hurriedly made before their departure. Scout had visited this Mexican town many years earlier, and recently heard via word of mouth shortly before Polly's funeral that Coyote Pete's clandestine radio station was on Enrique Avenue.

"I cannot see a thing--too dark."

"For heaven's sake." Paula reached up to a control panel above the driver's seat. "All we need to do is click on these interior lights."

"We're going the wrong way!" Janelle felt almost as though heading in their current direction would lead to tragedy. "You need to turn around."

"This is an adventure!" Tommy started popping off his toy gun in the back seat. "Are there any Indians down here?"

"No, honey. These are Mexican people." Paula stopped momentarily while making a U-turn, briefly patting the boy's head.

After flicking off the van's interior light, Janelle unexpectedly began worrying--far more horrified than she had expected. Besides knowing hardly a word of Spanish, she wondered whether her husband's many warnings had been right on the mark. Scout had insisted that the Mexican side of this town was riddled with criminals, perhaps some of them deviants eager to prey upon helpless American women traveling alone without men. Rumors had continued to swirl that every few months the bodies of savagely attacked U.S. women had been found dumped as if trash on this town's dirt-covered streets--where Janelle saw packs of wild dogs on about every other street corner.

Momentarily, Janelle spotted a flashing red light in the sky, about two miles up ahead, at a height that she calculated was about 150 feet above ground level.

"Look! Straight ahead." Paula pointed in that direction, proud of herself for finding this potential clue. "Could that be the radio tower?"

As they continued at an average 12 miles per hour, the van rocked intermittently from side to side, the noisy tires traversing deep ruts in the crude-smelling dirt.

"Do you guys see something in the road up ahead?" Paula frowned, her expression interpreted by Janelle as a negative sign. "Are those men standing there?"

"Bandits!" Tommy shouted. "I'll fire my pop-gun at them."

Janelle's worries reached a reality stage, when Paula stopped--three men visible at the end of the headlight beams. Each guy stood in the middle of the road; two carried handguns and one held a shotgun seemingly big enough to use as a cannon.

One of them men aimed his revolver toward the van's windshield.

Paula suddenly bent and whipped out a 38-caliber revolver from under the driver's seat. Janelle promptly heard her friend cock the weapon.

"Aunt Paula?" Tommy slumped down in the back seat. "Are those men going to kill us? ... Are you going to kill them?"

"Get ready, you two." Paula reached down and pulled out a second gun. "Some things are worth fighting for, and this looks like it's one of them."

Sixteen

Unusually exhausted this early in the day, Dick Cooper went through the cafeteria line with his boss in the dining room of the Dirkson Senate Office Building. At exactly 11:37 on the morning after they had accepted the invitation to the Israeli Embassy party, Dick felt much better--physically and mentally--than he had in several weeks.

In keeping with his predictable habit, the senator piled his tray with two buttery American cheese wheat sandwiches, two bowls of chocolate pudding, two pint-sized milk cartons, deep-fried onion rings and a cup overflowing with pistachios. Always preferring a much different type of meal--far more in a healthy mode than his boss--Dick choose a fluffy salad laced with chicken strips and a hint of vinaigrette dressing, a sliced apple, half of an avocado, and iced water.

Dick thought of his own lifestyle as far more vibrant and vigorous than these politicians, whom he considered as if they lacked any respect for their own bodies. To him, the cliche of smoke-filled back rooms became the worst of all. The mere notion of spending even a second in this dining room made his eyes twitch, particularly on moments such as this when Senator Spickler lit a huge cigar as soon as they sat across from each other.

At least four other senators sitting at nearby tables began smoking as well, except that three of them preferred cigarettes--and another beside the wall, a guy with eyebrows big enough to use as eagle wings, sucked on a pipe. As usual, he resisted the strong temptation to cough. The mere possibility of smoking repulsed Dick, whose late parents had been cigarette hounds--each dying of lung cancer in their mid-50s, back in the early 1960s.

"Fantastic news today, boss." Dick put a closed fist to the front of his mouth, while clearing his throat. "The Israeli Embassy was so thrilled to receive your positive RSVP that they sent an offer this morning, wanting to pick you up in their limousine to take you to the event."

"I still don't trust them." The senator hoisted a heaping spoonful of pudding into his mouth, a smattering of the food still on his right cheek. "I don't care how powerful those people think they are; inviting me makes no sense whatsoever."

"Sir, you've got a smudge on your..."

"To invite a freshman senator--even if it's me--shows that they either disrespect me, or they're up to something--or both." Spickler took another generous bite of the pudding, this time errantly depositing some of the concoction onto his left cheek. "Maybe we made a serious mistake in accepting."

"Sir, the smudge is on both of your..."

The senator snatched the cigar from an ashtray, before summarily taking another long puff. As he suckled the tobacco--as if a baby sucking on its mother's breast, at least from Dick's view--a smidgen of pudding transferred from the right cheek onto one side of the senator's cigar.

"Dick, this better work like you predict, more donations and..."

"Sir, your cheeks..."

Just then, Republican Senator Kevin Downing of Idaho stood near the Nevadans, beaming broadly down toward the pair.

"Well, I'll be--Senator Spickler!" The Gem State politician looked almost like a spitting image of the dwarf mayor from over the rainbow in the classic 1939 film "The Wizard of Oz," at least from Dick's perspective. The only difference that he could see was the fact that this rotund guy stood a few taller than a typical dwarf. "I understand that you're the only person from your side of the aisle, invited to the Israeli hoe-down."

Spickler shook the other senator's hand. This marked the first time Dick saw his boss interact this way with someone from the opposite side of the political aisle.

Much of the time senators of opposite philosophies

shunned each other by avoiding contact or "snubbed one another" by briefly interacting before walking away. Dick felt he knew better than just about anyone else on Capitol Hill that the nation's leaders generally behave like selfish and overly competitive school children.

Sure enough, right after shaking hands with Spickler, the Idaho senator immediately started to leave--before suddenly stopping, turning around and facing Dick's boss. Downing's expression reminded the chief of staff of an enraged chipmunk whose pine nuts had been stolen by a devious squirrel.

"Pudding?" Kevin Downing snatched a napkin from the Nevadans' dining table and began wiping the goo away from his own palms. "You had the nerve to put this on me? ... Well, look in the mirror, and see that food smeared all across your cheeks."

Seizing the moment right away, Downing immediately motioned toward four other Republican senators sitting at a nearby table--politicians from Arizona, New Mexico, Wyoming and Kentucky.

"Hey, look everyone!" Downing motioned for them all to look toward Senator Spickler. "Take a good look at this Nevadan! ... This is the kind of respect that he chooses to give to our esteemed institution!"

The adversaries' table erupted into uproarious laughter. Two of the conservatives pointed toward Spickler, chuckling so hard that tears welled up in their eyes.

"Dick, let's get out of here!" Spickler hurriedly used a napkin to wipe the food from his face. He stood, grabbed his cigar from an ashtray and began stomping away.

The chief of staff summarily followed, hurrying fast enough to remain close behind his boss. Soon they walked quick-pace, side-by-side down a hallway toward the Senate chamber.

"Fool!" Spickler carried a thick pile of papers, while sucking the cigar--which dangled from in his mouth. "Why didn't you tell me about this mess?"

"Please calm down, sir. We have important matters to

review."

Determined to remain focused on what he considered the most vital issues, the freshman senator's crony began rattling about their essential short-term objectives. First, Dick said, the public hearing had been quickly rescheduled for the following day in Centralia. This is "our genius strategy," snatching time away from potential political opponents who want to argue that the nuclear fallout still causes widespread cancer. Second, that bumbling Sheriff Peters had telephoned Dick early that morning. The lawman reported that Paula had blasted out of town, to an unknown destination--possibly Mexico--in an apparent effort to build opposition to the senator's scheme.

"Mexico?" Spickler stopped in the hallway, resting his back against a wall near a portrait of President Andrew Johnson from the late 1860s. "Why on earth would she go there? ... Common sense says that..."

"The answer remains unclear. We don't even know precisely where she went."

"Find out!" Spickler casually dropped his cigar to the hallway floor, crushing it with the heel of his left shoe. Several senators then brushed past them, including two of the politicians who had just broke into laughter a minute earlier.

While walking past Dick and Spickler, one of these Republican senators called out: "From now on, we can call you The Chocolate Pudding Senator."

"Funny." Spickler responded to them, in a soft voice that Dick sensed was laced with boundless rage. "Ha-ha."

"Senator." Dick accepted the pile of papers from his boss, well aware that the politicians' staffers were prohibited from entering the Senate chambers. "Always remain calm, strong and hold your head high."

"Stop lecturing me about the basics. Find out where that woman has gone, and what she is up to. ... Tell that bumbling sheriff that he needs to earn his pay, or else his law enforcement career goes out the window. ... And, to protect our rear flank, you need to learn a hell of a lot more about what is going on over at the Israeli embassy. ... I can smell a dirty rat, but I'm unsure where or when our worst adversary will emerge."

*

As the Israeli Embassy's executive administrator, Elijah Horowitz knew that his current mission was imperative to his nation's security.

At age 37, a graduate of Tel Aviv University with a bachelor's degree in social sciences and a similar certificate in pre-med studies, on this particular morning Horowitz tried to behave and to perform precisely the way that his boss would have wanted.

Right on schedule at precisely 10:17 in the morning, Horowitz entered the Noah Hebrew Cafe on K Street--a major thoroughfare in the U.S. capital, hailed as a center for advocacy groups, lobbyists and political think tanks.

Horowitz felt much more confident and fashionable than usual, decked out in a yellow and ivory necktie popular among Jewish businessmen in the 1970s--and a distinctive black brimless cap called a kippah.

Immediately upon entering through the front door, escaping the cool and brisk breeze, he spotted a woman sitting alone at the rear of the establishment. Even from nearly 45 feet away he noticed her bold, dark and piercing eyes.

"Melissa?" he said, after reaching her table, using the Israeli government's code name for agent Shira Levy.

"Benjamin?" she responded, using the Mossad spy agency's listed and required term when referring to Elijah Horowitz in public places.

Rarely required to personally contact or even interact with his nation's spies, Horowitz felt both repulsed and intrigued when handling such dangerous duties. He always became energized by the "cloak-and-dagger" aspect, but invariably became horrified at the realization that sudden violence could erupt when interacting with agents--particularly individuals of Shira Levy's top-notch caliber.

Confident that they had confirmed each other's identities, while moving to sit across from Shira he handed her a copy of that day's "New York Times." Each of them realized that on Page F-17, the period symbol at the end of that page's final sentence contained a micro-dot with her instructions--plus a detailed update on the man who tried to kill her in Salt Lake City.

"Pleased to meet you, miss." Horowitz said, instantly aroused by the mere presence of her. He had always been faithful to his wife of six years, Bracha, but for the moment his spouse remained the furthest thing from his mind.

For the previous three years, Horowitz had been fully aware of Shira, her reputation increasingly positive in the back hallways of high-level Israeli government operations. Like his male contemporaries, Horowitz had often heard of her mysterious allure--an inescapable magnetism that enraptured men, while also keeping them at an arm's length.

Finally in her presence for the first time, Horowitz's logical brain and his enraptured heart confirmed to him that all those rumors were right on target.

From his perspective, while sitting across from her, she seemed like a woman who tried to do absolutely nothing to look and behave sexy. She wore no make-up, made no attempt to flirt, and wore bland-looking clothes. Yet just as many other guys had previously told him that everything about Shira seemed to exude femininity, from the delicate sparkle in her eyes to the gentle way her tongue briefly moved across the back of her teeth.

When the waiter appeared at their table, Horowitz promptly ordered for them both--well aware of Shira's preferred Jewish drink: "We will each have a kliuk vennyi." Known under various names, the cranberry beverage is sweetened with honey and pureed fruits.

"I'm looking forward to a peaceful spring--particularly here in this sensational town." She spoke in a hushed yet merry tone, sounding to him as if they had known each other all their lives. Her words conveyed to him Shira's apparent hope that her next assignment would be less dangerous. "Believe me, I'm tired of the nasty weather."

That word "nasty" impressed him as being perhaps a double en tendre, a revelation that perhaps she had been through far more challenging conditions than her comrades might realize--while also perhaps that she had enjoyed the extreme danger, if only a bit.

"From what I hear, miss, the weather around here should remain pleasant for quite some time to come." Horowitz felt sure that Shira would realize that this was his signal to this agent that her next assignment was planned as fairly long-term, several years at least, right here in Washington. As the Israeli Embassy's executive administrator, he also knew that--like him--Shira fully understood that visiting that facility would never be an option for her. Going to the building would blow her cover, since U.S. authorities and likely other nations as well, kept the Israeli headquarters under continual surveillance.

"Benjamin, I suppose this means that we will never see each other again." Shira emitted a faint smile, the first display of apparent emotion that he had seen from her so far--glad that he had used his code name.

"Well, Melissa, although it was certainly my pleasure to meet you here, of course, as far as I can tell, there will never be any need for that."

"A pity." She smiled again, this time much broader than before. Then, just as the waiter arrived with their fruit beverages, she stood, tucked the newspaper under her arm, and winked at him. "Just one quick thing before I leave. ... Benjamin, I realize that we'll never see each other again, but I just want you to know--and this is true--you are by far the most handsome, intriguing and enticing man that I have ever met."

Immediately upon hearing this, Horowitz felt glad that she had received the package in Arkansas, instructing her to show up for this rendezvous. Unlike their American counterparts, the Israelis had easily tracked her down in that region--aptly nicknamed "The Natural State."

"Sure." He stood at the table, bowing his head momentarily--making no attempt to shake her hand or to give a brief hug. "However you feel, young woman, that is perfectly fine with me."

Horowitz tried to avoid thinking about the compliment that she had just given him. Instead, striving to remain professional and calm, he sat back down--carefully watching Shira's every move as she walked from the establishment.

While sipping the juice and sitting alone, he felt little doubt that she would soon feel somewhat dismayed and even perhaps overjoyed when soon reading the microdot--hidden for her within the newspaper. Along with his boss, Ambassador Amos Berkovich, the executive administrator was among only a handful of Israeli officials who knew what the document contained. Most important, Shira's next assignment would be to infiltrate the U.S. Food and Drug Administration's Washington, D.C., headquarters. The Israelis suspected that the U.S. government was recklessly endangering tens of millions of its own citizens--not just with its nuclear bomb tests--but by also allowing the legalized distribution of extremely dangerous pharmaceuticals likely to generate addictions and potentially fatal medical complications.

Just as horrifying, at least from Horowitz' perspective, Israeli intelligence had tentatively identified Shira's Utah assailant as a Russian operative--who had managed to infiltrate the U.S. CIA. The Jewish state remained unsure why or how this had happened, but suspected that Vladimir Ivanovich wanted to eliminate Shira; perhaps the Russian agent viewed her as a threat to the communist nation's efforts to infiltrate America's nuclear testing and development efforts. Precisely how Ivanovich determined Shira's identity and whereabouts remained unknown.

"Shira might realize this." Horowitz thought as he left the Noah Hebrew Cafe, nine minutes after her departure. "That woman is perhaps our nation's very best, but I fear that very soon she will have a target on her back--because not only is the

U.S. government corrupt to the core, but also due to the fact that America's medical and drug industries are equally devilish ... May our God look out for her, and protect her."

*

One week after administrators suspended Anthony Dunn from his security guard job at Sierra Crest Hospital, he sat alone in his run-down south Reno apartment.

Within the span of just seven days, Anthony already felt substantially older than he had during the holidays several weeks earlier. On this evening one hour after sundown, he sat on an old milk create in the middle of his living room.

He sipped from a can of Coors beer, which had gotten warm from sitting on the kitchen counter for several days. The landlord refused to repair or replace the broken-down 1957 refrigerator until Anthony paid his rent--now four days overdue.

Although most of his neighbors enjoyed Zenith-brand color TVs, the World War II veteran's meager pay prevented him from upgrading. The 1957 black-and-white Admiral suited him just fine, although the ancient tubes kept blowing and needing replacements.

Nagging worries bothered Anthony as he quietly watched the "CBS Evening News with Walter Cronkite." He yawned loudly while viewing a report on a jury's decision that forced the District of Columbia government to pay $12 million to anti-war protesters who had been illegally arrested during a 1971 protest at the U.S. Capitol.

"To heck with hippies," Anthony thought, amid the report. "I fight for my country, and lose my family and my job--about to become homeless. Those protesters get rich for hating our country, while I'm about to start living on the streets for loving our nation."

Increasingly angry, a part of Anthony wanted to toss the half-empty can at the TV. Yet common sense and a solid judgment prevented him from doing so; he preferred living in quiet dignity, rather than behaving recklessly like typical war protesters.

The former security guard heard a knock on his apartment

door, set his half-finished beer can on an adjoining coffee table and began to stand.

"Ow!" Anthony grimaced at sudden pain, which shot through his right hip and knee. Walking had become almost impossible for him in recent days. "Who is it?"

"General, it's me!"

Still alone in his living room, Anthony smiled for the first time in days. He lacked a single friend in the whole world, except for this Vietnam veteran--the doctor.

"Come right in, son! ... The door is unlocked."

Momentarily, Doctor James Robbins stood in the living room, while Anthony sat back down on the milk crate. The older man stuck out his hand, offering a shake to his pal.

The physician reciprocated, giving a sturdy and manly handshake, before saying apologetically: "General, please forgive me for dropping by unannounced. ... Every time I call your home phone, all I can get is a busy signal."

While motioning for his guest to sit on another milk crate nearby, Anthony explained that Nevada Bell had shut off his line for non-payment.

"General, I didn't realize that things had gotten that bad." The doctor sat on the other crate, while motioning toward a few unopened beers on the floor. "Mind if I crack one open for myself?"

"By all means." Anthony picked up a can, before tossing it to his friend.

"You are probably wondering why I finally showed up, being as I have never been here before." The doctor immediately took a sip. "Pretty good. Strangely, this almost seems like it's cool, although warm."

"Yeah, life is that way sometimes, isn't it?" Anthony finally realized that his friend still wore his doctor's smock. "Things never seem to work out exactly in a predictable way ... How did you get here? ... I know you don't have a car."

"Cab."

"You took a taxi all the way out here, just to see me? ... What an honor ... Son, you didn't have to ..."

"In a round-a-bout way, you're like the only father that I have ever had."

"You wouldn't want a poor guy like me for a dad."

"Oh, wouldn't I? ... I don't know if you've figured this out yet, but I'm loyal to those who are loyal to me--particularly people that I respect ... And, believe me, I do respect you, sir, to the utmost."

"The feeling is mutual, although neither of us is perfect-- I'm sure." Anthony raised his beer can in offering a toast, and the doctor immediately clanked their cans together. "To buddies! ... Hey, I've been wondering. I know that it's none of my business, but whatever happened to that family--those people from Centralia who all became sick."

In a slow, meticulous and "regular-guy" fashion, at least from Anthony's perspective, Doctor Robbins began to give details about the Davis family's tragic situation.

Peggy had taken a sudden turn for the worse three days earlier, shortly after an aggressive sarcoma gave doctors no option other than to amputate her younger sister Penelope's right arm. Worsening matters multi-fold, following a one-week wait the hospital's pharmacy still had failed to deliver chemo drugs--the only known pharmaceuticals capable of curing Peggy and her ailing Aunt Pamela, who suffered from advanced-stage colon cancer.

Aggravating the overall situation even more, the children's father--affectionately called Honest by almost everyone who knew him--had transformed into "some sort of madman," a few days after awakening from treatment for complete exhaustion. Twice in recent days, the grieving man had run up and down the hospital's third-floor hallways--flailing his arms and screaming: "They're poisoning my family!"

Doctor Robbins admitted that two of the hospital's psychiatrists reached separate--yet similar--conclusions. Each concluded that Honest was a good, decent and kind man who suffered the equivalent of "shell-shock," primarily because everyone in his immediate family--except his son, Tommy--had started suffering from fatal or near-fatal levels of cancer. Both mental health experts, Doctor Lincoln Fowler and Doctor Anton Schwartz, concluded that Honest's health problems were temporary--but only correctable if provided with an expert capable of listening to, empathizing with and understanding his fears--real or imagined.

As if these issues were not already enough to worry about, in Doctor Robbins' professional opinion, Peggy likely had "just one month to live, at most, particularly if the hospital continues failing to deliver the necessary chemotherapy drugs." Nonetheless, the physician believed that she would have a fighting chance, but only if the pharmaceuticals arrived soon.

And, as for Hank, the man whose yellow 1968 fastback Mustang the General helped dispose of--that man remained in jail, where just about everyone feels he belongs because, "at least according to them, he is nothing but a greedy car thief."

Adding further to the Centralia family's woes, the husband of Pamela--Honest's ailing sister-in-law--an Air Force officer and pilot, had not bothered to visit Reno to see her, or even to call his ailing wife. She remained bedridden in a patient room, looking as beautiful as ever, although in increasing discomfort.

Lacking help or personal assistants to aid in his many tasks, Doctor Robbins had remained in the hospital for five straight days--leaving that facility only a few times briefly to treat or consult with other cancer patients. All along, the Vietnam veteran kept butting heads with the Hospital's President and CEO, Gregory Crowley.

"We have engaged in about two hours daily for about the past week." Doctor Robbins finished his beer, and moved his arms toward several unopened containers, in requesting another drink. Mesmerized by this story, Anthony quickly popped open one of the cans before handing it to his buddy. "I have got to admit that some of my words are not repeatable here. I've never been the type of person to use salty language. But you need to know that I've really been letting 'em have it. ... Whether he hates me or not for telling him so, I need to speak the truth. People will die, and there will be no hope of their survival--whatsoever--without the chemo drugs that they desperately need. ... What is our world coming to, when people fail to receive basic medical attention? ... My patients deserve much more than this, and I'm determined to give them the very best."

"Son, do you mean to tell me that you've worked for five straight days, without sleep ... If that's the case, this is certainly a super-hero situation."

"In all respect, sir--General--I'm just a regular guy, just trying to do my job to the very best of my ability ... I have been..."

"Do you mean to tell me that you're not sleeping at all?"

"Maybe one or two hours per night ... I have no other choice than to do my very best for each of my patients ... That means staying at their bedsides, around the clock, doing my utmost to keep them alive and as healthy as possible."

"Are you telling me, son, that you have worked for five straight days--and then you came straight from the hospital to here? ... My leg is beginning to fail me, and I'll probably become homeless any day now--but those people need all of the attention that you're willing and able to give to them--not me."

"To the contrary, my friend, General ... I need you, and they do, too."

"I cannot even begin to understand what..."

Doctor Robbins interrupted, the first time that Anthony ever remembered him doing that in such a bold, blunt and direct way. The physician explained that the receptionist and assistant at his clinic, Richard, had unexpectedly quit--no longer needing the job thanks to a full-ride university scholarship.

"General, I'm here not only as your friend to visit you and to find out how you have been doing, but to offer you a fair-paying job as my clinic's receptionist."

"You know, son, I desperately need a job ... But I'm an aging cripple, and I have absolutely no medical or office experience whatsoever."

"You will learn in less than a day ... And, as for your health situation, let me do the worrying about that ... With my help, I'm sure, your medical condition will improve."

Anthony pondered this for the next 15 seconds. He could decline the offer and soon become homeless, or he could accept the job and work at a superior level of efficiency--while realizing that doing so might prove extremely difficult.

"If you insist, son, I'm on board--100-percent ... You really are a super-hero, aren't you--or at least someone exceptional in many ways?"

"Do not tell me that kind of nonsense. ... How many times do I have to say, General, 'I'm just a regular guy?'"

*

Paula's confrontation with the three gunmen in Nogales, Mexico, had gone well as far as Janelle was concerned. The two women and Tommy had escaped any violence without a single shot being fired.

The next morning, while in their room at the Saguaro Motel just north of the border in Arizona, Janelle sat in a chair next to the bed and pondered what had happened.

"We come here in peace and in the spirit of love," Paula had said while pointing her revolver to the ground. "We have traveled here in hopes of meeting and honoring our hero, Coyote Pete--the famous radio announcer."

At that moment, Janelle realized that Paula had taken a huge risk. The three gunmen could have instantly shot the three of them dead in a flash.

"Drop your weapon, lady, and then we can talk." The shortest of the men, a stocky guy of about 5 feet 3 inches tall spoke perfect English. His deep, husky, ultra-low voice reminded Janelle of her favorite male singing group, The Temptations.

"Mister, I want you to know that we are fighters, but as

a display of our faith I want you to know that we come with our hearts open." Paula dropped her weapon, while Janelle watched from their vehicle's front passenger side--eyes wide open.

With each of their weapons aimed toward Paula, the shortest man then ordered Janelle and Tommy to exit the vehicle. As Janelle started getting out of the van, she urged the boy to get out of the vehicle as well.

"But I want to shoot those guys with my pop gun." Tommy protested, still in the back seat.

By this point standing beside the van with the front passenger door open, Janelle whispered loud enough for the child to hear: "Tommy, drop your toy and get out. Do as these men say, or they will shoot your Aunt Paula right here and now."

The boy did as he was told, but upon exiting the van he immediately ran to his Aunt Paula and tightly hugged her. Momentarily, Janelle stood beside her traveling companions.

"You guys, we are not afraid of you at all." Tommy let go of his aunt and faced the three gunmen, who continued pointing their weapons at the three Americans. "My Aunt Paula is right--we are fighters, and we're here for a good reason."

Overcome by the child's feistiness and bravery, Janelle surprised herself by suddenly speaking--although she had intended to remain quiet: "Tommy, you're behaving like a man, rather than a boy, and I'm..."

Janelle stopped speaking when the tallest of the three men suddenly started walking toward them; his two companions held their positions. This fellow stood well over 6 feet tall, with a mustache that Janelle considered as almost big enough to use for her brush. His giant shoulders and biceps made her think of what a professional football player must look like when wearing shoulder pads underneath civilian clothes.

He wore tattered blue jeans and cowboy boots that looked to Janelle as if they had been worn for a few years. His black leather overcoat reminded her of something that Honest would have worn, except that from her view this man's garb looked far more burly and devilish than those of a mere pirate.

She wondered whether these men were bandits or perhaps typical perverts. Above all, Janelle realized that this dastardly looking trio easily could shoot the three of them on the spot--leaving their bodies to rot in the open air, or perhaps tossing them into shallow graves.

The huge man stopped about five feet in front of Paula and her companions. Under the faint moonlight, he glanced one-by-one directly into their eyes.

"Quermos paz, también." The tall man spoke Spanish. From Janelle's perspective, his voice seemed unusually high and somewhat squeaky--unusual for such a big and muscular fellow. She held back an instinctive impulse to laugh nervously, since to her his voice sounded as if cartoon-like--similar to a Saturday morning children's TV animation.

"Mister, you sound funny." Tommy interjected. "Can't you speak English?"

"Honey, please quiet down." Janelle gently patted the top of the boy's head. "Paula, do you speak Spanish? Do you know what this guy is saying."

"I think he said something about peace as well, but I'm unsure of that." Paula stood steady, her right hand around Tommy's shoulders.

Janelle felt grateful that this huge guy casually pointed his shotgun toward the ground, rather than at her and her friends.

Seconds later the two other fellows walked toward them as well, their legs moving so jerkily that Janelle suspected that they might have been drinking--to the point of inebriation. She had expected these fellows to smell awful, perhaps as bad as a sewer. Yet instead, their aroma reminded her of cologne--perhaps Old Spice. Just as startling, at least from her view, she had expected each of them to have a stubbly beard, appearing dirty and unkempt. Instead, up close, she could see that each was clean-shaven, and looked fairly well groomed. Perhaps, as far as she knew, they looked dapper enough to teach or attend any Ivy League school.

Their brownish skin signified apparent Hispanic descent. Yet to Janelle their overall demeanor seemed strangely American. To her, the only predictable thing was the mouth of the third, middle-sized guy. All of his front teeth were missing.

"Ladies, we can forgive the fact that you do not understand Spanish." The short guy with the deep voice said, as he and the toothless fellow stood beside the giant man. "Enrique here has just told you, 'We want peace, too.' I hope that all of you agree."

"I am glad that we are not going to have a gunfight." Tommy said, the broad smile on the child's face making Janelle feel unexpectedly delighted.

In unison, all of them--including the men and Paula--suddenly broke out in laughter, a response to the child's statement. Janelle sensed that this reaction had been a way for all of them to release pent-up nervous tension.

From that point the short fellow did all the talking for the three gunmen, who each holstered their weapons. As the conversation ensued, Janelle felt increasingly proud of Paula, whom she believed did the common-sense thing by being courageous enough to drop her gun, rather than shoot. Otherwise, Janelle believed, there truly could have been a bloodbath of tragic proportions.

"You women and this boy should never have come to a seedy and dangerous place like this, particularly at night." The short man impressed Janelle as being empathetic and caring. "Thieves prowling this community, men willing to shoot each of you for a mere peso. Life and death mean absolutely nothing to such bandits, while we are quite the opposite--men of Christ, God-fearing people who love our independence."

"That's great." Paula did all the talking for the Americans, which suited Janelle just fine. "Like I say, all we want to do, please, is have a meeting with Coyote Pete."

"Your request can be granted--possibly." The short man tipped his black cowboy hat, which looked to Janelle as if several sizes too big for him. "But first, we would need to know why ...

You must realize that Coyote is a very busy man."

"We respect that." Paula unbuttoned the top few buttons of her delicate, light brown blouse. "Please understand that we need to chat with him about a matter of life and death for people across the American West."

The short guy, who identified himself as "Paco," insisted on more detail. Yet Paula stood her ground, telling him that this was an intricate matter that required a direct conversation with the radio announcer. She described Coyote Pete as a hero to her and to her companions, and that they would never do anything to jeopardize him. Their primary goal was to save the lives of many people, and to reveal to the public the reckless actions of the U.S. government.

"What you say sounds intriguing." Paco said, adjusting his hat as if to make it fit better, at least from Janelle's perspective. "First, we need to get the three of you to safety, just north of the border. I suggest that you wait there until shortly after sunrise. Then, there is a possibility that you will be contacted about a possible meeting with Coyote--but you need to understand that there can be no guarantees whatsoever. ... Safety for the three of you--and safety for our radio industry friend--remain our top priority. Violence of any kind can never be tolerated, unless absolutely necessary. That is our mode of operation."

Within five minutes after Paula agreed to this strategy, she traveled with Janelle and Tommy in the van--in the middle of a caravan, northbound back toward the United States. The van followed a shiny blue pickup truck driven by Paco, while a second truck carrying the tall, muscular Enrique and the toothless man tailed the Volkswagen.

By 11:14 that night, Janelle, Paula and Tommy had checked in to the Saguaro Motel on the U.S. side of he border.

Shortly after sunrise the next morning, the boy rushed outside to play with his pop gun. Sitting in dark green metal chairs just outside their motel room door, Paula and Janelle watched him scurry about in the sagebrush.

Paula pointed toward several giant saguaros in the nearby wilderness. She told Janelle that specimens of these huge cactus have been known to live at least 150 years, some growing to at least 45 feet tall or perhaps much higher. Speaking almost as if a scientist, at least from Janelle's perspective, Paula explained that these cactus grow in only one region in the entire world--a swath of extreme Northwest Mexico, stretching through Arizona's Southwest region.

"In a sense, Janelle, I guess that I could say that these glorious plants are somewhat like human beings. Like people, each cactus has the magical gift of life. But there is a major difference ... Our federal government is working diligently to save this unique species, so that people for many generations can continue to enjoy this plant. ... By contrast, our reckless bureaucracies give people--the lives of human beings--far less respect than those federal agencies give to these plants. ... Although I consider myself a loving person, this makes me extremely angry. And I believe that many people will feel the same, once they learn the truth ... Do you agree?"

"Certainly. Normally I might argue, but this time you're right."

Just then, at 7:13 in the morning, Paco pulled up in front of their motel room, alone in his shiny pickup.

Following a brief discussion with this man, Paula agreed to go alone with him for what he promised would be a rendezvous with Coyote Pete. Janelle and Tommy were to stay behind at the motel, despite the boy's objections, telling them: "Aunt Paula, I want to go with you! ... Why can't I go?"

Soon afterward, Paula waved goodbye to Janelle and Tommy as she disappeared from view--with her driver in the pickup truck.

Intense fear suddenly engulfed Janelle, worries that Paula failed to know specifically who she was interacting with. The notion of those men possibly torturing or beating Paula--or perhaps even worse--petrified Janelle's psyche.

"Janelle, can you take me to breakfast?" Tommy plopped his pop gun into a trashcan outside near their motel room door. "I'm hungry enough to eat a horse."

"Tommy, did I just see what I think that I saw? ... You threw away your toy? ... Why would you want to do that?"

"After what happened last night, I decided that violence stinks."

Seventeen

Israel's ambassador to the United States, Amos Berkovich, sat alone in the living room of his family home in Alexandria, Virginia--an upper middle-class suburb of Washington, D.C.

On the day after his executive assistant Elijah Horowitz' rendezvous with Shira Levy, Berkovich seized a rare opportunity to take some of his most important work home. The ambassador's wife, Adi, along with their three children, had traveled to Hod HaSharon in central Israel to spend a month with relatives.

He set a glass of his favorite alcoholic beverage, Aviv 613 vodka, on a classic mid-century modern round table in the living room beside his favorite place to rest--a refinished beechwood Danish modern lounge chair with gray upholstered cushions.

Because her husband considered high-end furniture essential for a man of his stature, Adi had purchased the best available amenities for their classic four-story 1780 federal style, 4,721-square-foot brick home--featuring eight bedrooms, five bathrooms and a spacious back yard.

Berkovich cherished their home, except for the fact that as far as he was concerned, Adi seemed to consider the residence as a non-stop playland for their children, ages 3 through 7--plus as many of their neighbor kids as possible. He took pride in overseeing the embassy, demanding continual efficiency from all personnel--marked with a special attention to cleanliness.

A personal commitment to keeping everything in perfect order, in its pre-assigned place, had been a hallmark of Berkovich's personality since his own early childhood. By contrast, at least in his own opinion, Adi thrived on around-the-clock chaos, particularly as reflected by her scant attention to housekeeping; this lifestyle contrasted with the preference of many other Jewish women, who considered keeping a spotless home as a necessity for any good and descent housewife.

After driving Adi and their children earlier that day to Washington's Reagan International Airport, for their flight to Israel, Berkovich returned to their home to complete his office work in a much quieter environment than inside the embassy.

Toys remained scattered throughout the living room, dirty dishes overflowed from the kitchen sink, and crayon scribblings remained on several hallway walls. Berkovich considered their home an embarrassment for these reasons--a sharp contrast to the perspective of Adi, who always insisted that a home should look and feel "lived in."

Glad to have them gone for at least a while, Berkovich reclined in his favorite living room chair, and began reviewing in-depth reports by embassy personnel.

The first report concluded that Nevada's freshman senator, Larry Spickler, had quickly become perhaps the most corrupt congressional politician on Capitol Hill in perhaps nearly a century. Mossad agents confirmed that this native of the small town of Lighthouse at the base of Mount Charleston, 39 miles from Las Vegas, had amassed massive land holdings--sold to him for "pennies on the dollar" in sweetheart deals in the form of bribes. Now in his early 40s, Spickler had grown up in a mega-wealthy family, his Mormon father, Slate, an early pioneer in the Silver State's casino industry.

"There is not a person that Larry Spickler would refuse to stab in the back in a political sense, as long as doing so might line his own pockets," the embassy's Top Secret report concluded. "With little doubt, we can exploit these considerable weaknesses of his--plus his tendency toward over-the-top liberal policies--using them to our advantage. We can make Spickler's devilish and selfish greed as our formidable strength. The biggest question facing us in this regard is what we should offer him, to get the greatest bang for the buck."

Many possibilities swirled in Berkovich's mind, ideas that he considered excellent, while setting the file folder on the living room table--beside two Barbie dolls and a 5-inch-tall GI Joe tank, featuring all the latest weaponry for their son, Isaac.

Berkovich had recently become fully aware of Spickler's latest schemes, thanks to the clandestine tape recording that Shira covertly made of the Senator's conversation with his crony. The ambassador also realized that Spickler was willing to endanger the lives of tens of thousands of people--just to protect and to cover up the unspeakable corruption within the bowels of the United States government.

"We will snare that monster into our web, shortly after he attends our embassy gala next month, honoring President Ford," Berkovich thought, while sipping his vodka. "From that point forward, all we need to do is assassinate the senator or use him to our best advantage. The choice will be ours and ours alone, thanks to his weakness. If you ask me, I could care less one way or the other, as to whether that creep lives or dies."

*

Dick Cooper finally found a pay phone, while shopping in the Capital Plaza Mall in Washington, D.C..

He had been hunting for an appropriate present for his wife, Nicole, in celebration of their 15th wedding anniversary. Dick realized that his 34-year-old blonde wife, a graduate of Georgetown School of Law, always preferred home appliances such as refrigerators and vacuum cleaners--items that she always referred to as "useful things that we can benefit from."

Yet instead, Dick always embraced a philosophy taught to him by his late mother, Beatrice, who occasionally proclaimed: "Son, if you love a woman, you should never buy for her what she needs. Instead, to show your devotion, get her something that she doesn't need at all--things like jewelry or romantic getaways."

Sure enough, each time Dick gave Nicole such an "unnecessary gift," she initially feigned protest--before insisting that she loved him more than ever.

On this particularly morning, the moment that Dick spotted an appropriate diamond necklace at the Ardan jewelry store, he suddenly remembered the urgent need to telephone his office to check for any urgent messages.

"Shirley, real quick." Standing in a phone booth at the back of the mall, Dick grabbed a small notepad and pen from his sport coat breast pocket to take notes. "Any important messages this morning."

"Just one that I think you would consider urgent, sir. The Israeli Embassy called to let you know that inside the limo taking Senator Spickler to the gala will be none other than the Israeli Prime Minister Yitzhak Rabin."

"Holy cow! Israel's top elected official! ... That's fantastic for the senator."

"I'll have to agree with you, Mister Cooper, although I personally take these developments with a grain of salt. ... I'll leave it to you to deliver this news yourself to the senator ... As you know, he is not expected back into the office for a few more days."

"But why would they put our boss with their nation's top guy?"

"I'm not trying to be flippant at all in saying this, but your guess is as good as mine. ... Sometimes fate gets dealt out in mighty mysterious ways. ... Shirly, please call the National Security Agency and ask for Horace Plimpton. Set up a personal meeting for me with him. Refrain from giving them any details. We just need to have some street-smarts about this thing. ... Specifically, between you and me, we need to know exactly what we're getting into by attending this gala. ... I'm not trying to be over-dramatic, but the senator's career and even his life could be on the line."

*

Her mind in what some medical professionals call "a fog," Pamela tossed and turned on her bed--in a patient room at Reno's Sierra Crest Hospital.

Doctor Robbins carefully adjusted the IV line, in what Nurse Hannah realized was an attempt to regulate the at rate of morphine drips.

Earlier that day, the oncologist had consulted with Doctor Conners, the hospital's on-call general practitioner and Emergency Room physician. The men had agreed that this opiate in small, consistent doses would be the best and most effective way to regulate this young woman's ravaging pain--caused by the side effects of colon cancer.

"Jeffrey?" She moaned, her eyes remaining closed as she uttered her husband's name. "Jeffrey? Are you here, honey?"

Under specific instructions from Doctor Robbins, the nursing staff and other physicians refrained from giving details about Pamela's husband. The U.S. Air Force officer from Honolulu still had not bothered to return numerous phone messages left for him by hospital personnel and by Pamela's Nevada relatives.

Within a few minutes, Pamela gradually began to realize that she was in a hospital. She started hearing the distinctive and calming voice of Doctor Robbins.

Deep in this young woman's heart, she yearned for a relative here to love her, to care for her, and to root for her every step of the way in this struggle to survive.

"Pamela, I am here for you, little sister." She recognized this as the sturdy and protective voice of her brother-in-law, Honest. Despite Pamela's excruciating pain, she realized his presence here meant that he had recovered--after passing out in Doctor Robbins' office. How long ago had that occurred? She lacked any notion of the answer, without a mental grasp of time and space.

"Honest, is this really you?" Pamela opened her eyes fully, delighted at the sight of him. She realized this truly was her late sister's husband, thanks to that eye patch and the goofy looking ear. "How are the children doing? Are they OK?"

"Everyone is in good hands, including you." Honest tightened his grasp on her hand, and she reciprocated--delighted someone had arrived to bond with her.

"I think I'm in a hospital--is that right?"

"Wow! ... You really are waking up! My prayers are answered."

Pamela then told everyone that she could see Doctor Robbins in the room, plus Dorothy and Bill McCready; the couple were in seats near the patient room door.

"Where is Paula?" Pamela moved to sit up, but soon slumped back.

"She is back home, I'm sure, taking care of my son. ... Someone has to keep the home fires burning, you know."

"What is happening? ... Will I get better?"

Honest began talking non-stop, leading Pamela to believe that he was pouring his heart out to her for the first time. Until this moment, the two of them had never engaged in any in-depth, one-on-one conversation. The plumber told her that he realized any medical diagnosis and discussion regarding her treatment should be made by Doctor Robbins. Honest described the physician as a fantastic guy who had literally been working around-the-clock without letup for the past week--diligently trying to save the lives of her and several other cancer patients. With tears welling up in his eyes, Honest also revealed to Pamela that his opinion of the oncologist had drastically changed.

"Before, I was foolishly angry at the doctor, enraged because of my perception that he had been poisoning my wife." Honest gently kissed Pamela's forehead, a gesture that made her feel warm all over as he continued talking. "Yet now, my opinion of him has changed in the complete opposite direction. ... I know, dear, that you're far too weak to speak much, but I just need to tell you all of these wonderful things, so that you will know and realize that there is hope for you ... You have been in this bed for well over a week. For the first several days, I literally went nuts--somewhat crazy ... Along with your doctor, several of the other experts concluded that I had suffered from a severe case of exhaustion--both mentally and physically. ... Thanks to their patience and persistence, I have been able to recover. ... We're not here to talk about me, of course, you are the focus of all of our attention now. I am just telling you all of this to let you know that you are loved by everyone here. ... You need to know that we're on your side, and we're pulling for your recovery ... We are here for you."

"Bless you, Honest ... Thank you."

Pamela then felt the touches of Dorothy and Bill McCready, each holding her other hand. She looked at both of them and returned their soothing smiles.

"We are not going to talk much." Dorothy spoke softly. "You just need to know that we're on your side, and that we are going to let you rest ... We'll be back here in just one hour or so ... Right now, you need to talk alone with Doctor Robbins about your treatment ... Bill and I agree 100-percent with Honest, that your cancer doctor is truly one of the most amazing guys that we have ever met."

Dorothy then kissed Pamela's forehead, immediately followed by Bill and Honest, who each did the same.

"Goodbye." Pamela smiled broadly. "Thanks for loving me. I love you."

A few moments later, Dorothy stood in the Third Floor hallway with her husband and Honest. The retired county clerk's heart remained locked in grief, still in shock from the many events of the past few days.

By pre-arrangement, in full agreement with this course of action, none of them had mentioned to Pamela the many trying events all of them had been through.

They never mentioned tiny Penelope's amputation, the child now wearing a prosthetic arm with a metal hook for a hand; the little one now rested in a pediatric ward patient room on the Second Floor.

With equal conviction, they refrained from talking about the dozens of crayon drawings that had arrived by mail for Penelope and Peggy from Centralia and nine other isolated Eastern Nevada towns. The residents of those communities, both adults and children had sent these personalized drawings as get-well cards--reciprocating Peggy's efforts from a few months earlier, when she had distributed her own images in soliciting funds for her mother's medical care. The hundreds of people who had mailed their own drawings had included mailmen, bakers, electricians, electricians, housewives and school children from grades kindergarten through 12. The adults drew and colored just they way each of them had done many years before, when they were children themselves. The images they sent to Penelope and Peggy had included fields full of flowers, sunrises, horses, unicorns, teddy bears, houses with chimneys emitting smoke, birds of every color, giant blue lakes, and also schoolhouses.

Upon each new arrival, the nurses--and in some cases, even doctors--taped these innocent-looking drawings to the walls of the two Davis girls' separate patient rooms. The children each marveled at these images, occasionally pointing to them--saying, "tree." "house," "sun," "smile," and various other descriptions.

These images had cheered the girls so much, in fact, that three days before Honest, Dorothy and Bill greeted Pamela as she awakened, the children had run together up and down the Second Floor hallway. Peggy had unexpectedly bolted from her bed during the only brief pause of her negative symptoms.

By late that evening, Peggy had lost consciousness again.

From that point, the McCreadys and Honest spent most of the next three days in the pediatric ward's waiting room. The three of them lived mostly on luke-warm coffee and stale donuts, intermixed with brief excursions to the cafeteria.

Doctor Robbins had remained at Peggy's bedside during most of that time. He oversaw all activities of each crew of nurses; as their work shifts began, he updated the medical professionals on the latest details regarding her treatment.

"Peggy's vital signs are fading," the oncologist told Honest and his two friends in the waiting room, on the evening before Pamela awakened on another floor. "I have two other doctors who have agreed to assist."

"Will my little one die tonight, doctor?" Honest spoke in a

soft voice.

"I need to be direct with you--that is a possibility. We are doing everything in our power ... If you believe in prayer, now is the time."

For the next five hours straight the trio prayed, reading aloud from Bill McCready's family Bible.

Finally, at 1:17 the following morning, Doctor Robbins returned to the waiting room, telling them: "Organ failure has begun ... This is called sepsis ... Her blood has become toxic ... This condition is often considered irreversible."

"Can we see her now, doctor?" Honest spoke in a soft voice that Dorothy considered both kind and respectful toward the physician. "Is she going to die?"

"Very likely, she will pass away within the next few hours ... Yes, you can see her, but before doing so you need to realize what she will look like."

The physician explained that bacteria had infected little Peggy's bloodstream. The cancer had weakened her immune system. Doctors treated her with intravenous fluids and antibiotics. Yet negative symptoms progressed to a critical level. He told them at this point her entire body was severely bloated, to nearly twice its normal size. Her skin would look unnatural, at this point a bright yellow due to liver failure.

"If you enter the room, you will be shocked by what you see." Doctor Robbins gently rested one of his hands on Honest's right shoulder. "Each of you can choose not to go inside to see her. And if you do, you need to be mentally prepared."

Along with Honest, the McCreadys announced that they were ready.

Within moments, they each knelt in silence at Peggy's bedside. Dorothy kept thinking of the many challenges that Honest had recently endured. Looking at his face from the opposite side of the child's bed, the retired clerk admired his ability to bounce back from extreme exhaustion--before facing this new hurdle head-on.

For the next three hours, the three adults prayed aloud--while also weeping. Dorothy disliked the continual, raspy, and startling sound of Peggy's efforts to fight for her every breath. The noise sounded maddening to the 60-year-old, who had witnessed four of her own relatives pass away through the years. To her, none of those experiences had been nearly as bad as this--the pending death of an innocent child.

Doctor Robbins continued his non-stop efforts to save Peggy, administering intravenous fluids and monitoring antibiotic levels. Like Honest, Dorothy had started to greatly admire the oncologist. Gladness filled her heart in this regard, replacing her previous apprehension toward this physician.

Peggy's death came at 4:37 that morning. Her breathing stopped at the same time as her heart.

"My adorable princess." Honest kissed his daughter's right hand. "Go to your mommy in heaven now. She is waiting for you there, little angel."

Softly blowing her own nose and wiping tears from her eyes, Dorothy decided that much later she would break important news to Honest--details that he very likely had not yet heard about. From her view, Paula had launched a clever way to battle the insensitive federal bureaucracy--which showed no regard whatsoever for human life.

*

While en route to her planned rendezvous with the rebellious and legendary radio announcer, Paula kept thinking about the plight of her family and many hundreds or thousands of others across Nevada, Utah and Arizona.

Concentrating on what she would eventually say when finally meeting Coyote Jack, she sat in the front passenger seat of the pickup truck--driven by the short man who had identified himself only as "Paco."

The vehicle's radio played a hit song that flew up the "Billboard Magazine" music charts that final week of January in 1975. This marked the first time that Paula had heard the tune,

"Mandy" by singing star Barry Manilow.

"I never usually listen to this type of hit music stuff, most of it is pure junk as far as I'm concerned." Paula rolled down the front passenger side window, while trying to make small talk with this driver. "But I've got to admit, this is cool."

"Yep." Paco turned up the volume, speaking in what she still considered a characteristically low and manly voice; to her, this deep voice seemed as if in sharp contrast to his small physical stature. "Whenever I'm not working with the boss--alone in my truck--I play this kind of music."

While briefly smiling to acknowledge what this driver had just said, she tried to avoid pondering the warnings that Janelle had given her about traveling with this stranger. The preacher's wife had mentioned the possibility of rape, kidnapping or even murder. Paula had immediately scoffed at the suggestion, insisting that a legendary announcer like Coyote Pete never would threaten or harm anyone. Any such violent shenanigans surely would incur the wrath of authorities.

"Please tell me a little bit about Coyote, before I meet him. What kind of man is he?" Just when Paula finished asking this question, she deeply inhaled the cool and refreshing desert air. Her eyes marveled at dozens of saguaros that dotted the hillsides along this windy dirt road, the huge branches or off-shutes of the plants reminding her of a person's arms--except that these were dark green. Although stationary and faceless, these cacti made her think of human-like qualities, although she wasn't sure why.

"Miss Paula, you ask me, 'What kind of man is Coyote?' ... Can I be blunt in answering?"

"By all means, because I'm all ears."

"He is a man who deserves mountains of respect, although he never gets any from the U.S. federal government. ... Coyote believes in freedom, specifically without unnecessary federal intrusion."

"I kind of suspected that." Paula looked at the road up ahead, noticing a few lizards zip across the dirt--their feet briefly sending up a small whiff of smoke-like soil into the air behind them. "But what really makes him tick?"

"Within a few minutes, lady, you'll be able to see for yourself. But I probably should let you know that when first meeting Coyote most people seem to think of him as stupid. ... Even he laughs at such observations sometime, admitting that he probably looks dumber than a rock. His voice when broadcast over the radio, of course, comes in loud and clear--booming. But when you're just talking with him one-on-one, his voice will seem almost at a whisper--and his choice of words and western accent might make it seem like he has nothing more than a second-grade education. ... But I can testify--at least in a sense--that he has a master's degree in psychology--pretty amazing when you finally realize that he never even graduated from high school--dropped out in the 10th grade ... No, instead, his education about how the human mind operates came from something called 'good, old-fashioned street smarts.' ... What he has taught me--and many others as well--is that we should never under-estimate anyone. ... Even uneducated people can give themselves tremendous power--physically, financially and emotionally ... Sure, lots of folks these days disagree with such can-do, positive and goal-oriented philosophy, while all of these interesting attributes--by the way--are hallmarks of Coyote's unique personality ... Most of all, I suppose, he insists that much of the time, the only thing getting in the way of our quest for happiness is the dastardly government."

"Paco, I have kind of figured this to be true, but your description--what you just said--puts everything in a succinct way that I've never heard before ... Anything else, please, that you think I should know when talking with him? ... And how are you connected with Coyote? ... Are you a bodyguard?"

Instead of answering, Paco unexpectedly and gradually stopped the pickup truck.

He pointed to four wild coyotes that stood in the middle of this same dirt road, about 25 yards up ahead of them. A desert hawk soared high overhead.

The four-legged animals stood still, each turning its head toward Paula and Paco.

To her, their large black eyes seemed strangely all-knowing, and yet somehow also paradoxically exempt from any need to learn anything other than their own intense and instinctive desire to "let nature take its course." Although these animals obliviously were wild and free of the constraints of city life, form her perspective they seemed: almost as if kind, despite their reputation for gnawing wildly at their innocent victims; almost as if wanting to help these intrusive humans in any way possible, although their collective situation made it obvious that these creatures would soon bolt away; and almost as docile as typical household pets, excluding the fact that two of them had the gizzards of dead mice hanging from their drooling mouths.

"Take a good look at them." Paco pointed toward the animals. "All these fellows that you see here are exactly like Coyote Pete ... See the way that they're behaving ... These animals might look stupid to us, but they're smarter than us mere humans in many ways because--unlike us--they behave the way that Mother Nature commands of them. ... Just as important, any wild coyote like these will always strive to avoid close contact with humans, especially people who attack them ... Well, this is spot-on and 100-percent true, Coyote Pete is the same way ... He will avoid direct confrontation in any way possible, when provoked and pushed way too far--this man, he will fight back--in a legal way, through Freedom of Speech ... He is normally soft-spoken ... But when unfairly agitated and harassed, his message literally bites harder than the diamond-back rattle snakes that usually hide out here in the shade, during the light of day."

"Mighty interesting." Paula watched the animals bolt away in a flash, their feet moving so fast that her eyes barely discerned what had happened until they disappeared. "But you haven't answered my other question ... What is your association with Coyote Pete, and do you work for him in some way?"

"You're mighty nosy, lady, but I guess it's okay for me to

answer you honestly, considering the fact that Coyote has agreed to meet with you." Paco accelerated back up to 20 miles per hour, and allowed his right hand to move across the rim of his cowboy hat--this one pure white, a sharp contrast to his coal black head covering from the previous night. "Like about four other guys who also are loyal to Coyote, I help him with a variety of duties--everything from security, to getting and preparing food, and lots of other things like shuttling people around--as you can imagine, streams of folks want to talk face-to-face with him. ... In just the past few months, he has become so tremendously popular among the general public across the American West that the crowds streaming down here have swollen to difficult-to-manage levels. ... That's why, I suppose, we're going to need other people very soon, on our committed team--doing whatever we reasonably can to assist his effort."

"Sounds like a major challenge." Paula streamed the fingers of her right hand through her medium-length dark hair, instinctively realizing that upon their eventual meeting--Coyote would think better of her, if she looked clean and natural, while also behaving as if an open-minded free spirit. "But why, if Coyote is in such tremendous demand, do you think that he has agreed to see me?"

"You probably won't believe this, but he's following my recommendation--also the suggestions of the other two guys that you first met me with last night." Paulo turned the radio louder as another top hit from that week began to play, "Please, Mister Postman," by the Carpenters. "Like Coyote and the animals that you just saw, those of us who help him, we all listen and think with our hearts. ... Paula, our instincts collectively tell us that you have some sort of powerful and essential message to bring to him--most likely something about personal freedom, personal safety and the personal need for all of us to empower ourselves against the treacherous U.S. government."

"Thanks for your faith, mister ... Don't take this the wrong way, but I feel a need to say honestly that you look like the type of guy who could care less what a woman thinks--but your actions are telling me quite the opposite."

Momentarily, Paula spotted a small wooden structure near the crest of a hill, about 150 yards off the side of the dirt road up ahead. The soil underneath was reddish, a distinctive tinge that helps make the Arizona wildlands and desert world-famous.

"See." Paco pointed. "That tiny house, about big enough to fit into a donkey's rear end ... That's where the boss lives--we respectfully refer to this place as The Coyote's Lair. Free. ... Wild ... Rugged ... That's the way he likes to live life, and that's exactly the way all of us who support him feel, too ... So, while we're on the subject lady, I suppose you should know that in the past four years--you are without a doubt the first person who we have allowed to visit here, that is--specifically--someone who has not already been a member of our core group for quite awhile. ... I'm just saying this here now, so that you'll know how important is is for you to be here."

Paco slowed down and turned the pickup onto another dirt road, this one leading uphill toward the isolated wooden structure.

"I feel honored." Paula flipped down the visor in front of her, and began gazing at her reflection in the mirror. Even more than a few minutes earlier, she felt an instinctive and burning desire to look her best upon her first meeting with Coyote Pete.

"It is us who should feel honored. Like I say, among those of us who assist Coyote, we instinctively feel that you have the right and perfect message to bring to him." Paco parked the pickup in a circular dirt driveway at the front of the structure. He then pointed toward the front porch. "Oh, there he is now."

The man from the front porch walked to the front passenger side of the truck, and he promptly opened the door for Paula.

"Welcome to my lair." Coyote Pete smiled broadly.

The sight of this radio announcer's muscular body and his magnetic face mesmerized Paula--leaving her unexpectedly stunned and speechless.

Void of any thought, she let him softly take her extended hand--which he bowed toward and briefly kissed. As her senses gradually returned, this--she thought--was a man, a "real man"--a sturdy, tall and unbendable specimen of pure masculinity. Far more impressive than merely an average drop-dead-handsome Marlboro Man--typical of images during that era, advertisements promoting cigarettes--to her this guy was "the real thing, the real deal." Until that point at age 34, she had never yet laid eyes on any Western outdoorsman as independent and feisty looking as this.

Pure.

Rugged.

Sturdy.

"Could this be the man of my dreams--the savior of our cause?" She thought, her heart racing faster than she had ever thought possible. "Could this gentleman at my side help lead the way in our fight against the federal government--and helping to get adequate medical care for the increasing numbers of people with cancer? ... What should I say?"

Looking at him once again, Paula lost her train of thought--except for one overwhelming and electrifying sensation.

For the first time in her life in the minutes and hours that followed she felt beautiful in almost every blessed way imaginable. From that point forward, gone were the days when every man that she felt attracted eventually made her feel ugly, both inside and out.

To the contrary, this time while held tightly in Coyote Pete's warm arms she felt as if a flower at sunrise. Sure enough, Paula opened up her heart, mind, body and soul in creative ways that energized the very essence of her being.

"More!" Paula thought, eager to enjoy the relentless emotional rapture that she had desperately sought for her entire life. "Despite what some people might think of me, I'm truly beautiful, and in this moment I desperately need and desire all the many good and fantastic things that this man has to offer."

Eighteen

Mossad agent Shira Levy passed the standard security clearance at the U.S. Food and Drug Administration within one week after her arrival in Washington, D.C.

"These fools are bumbling idiots," she thought, upon getting an official government letter by mail, informing her that she had been accepted by the agency. "Their background check process is nothing less than a joke."

Thanks to forged documentation supplied by her Israeli counterparts, the agency's officials immediately believed that she had earned a undergraduate degree in biology at Boston College--before entering Boston University School of Medicine.

Yet after only one year of getting excellent grades there, according to the phony documentation, she had been forced to drop out due the deaths of her parents in an auto accident--which also had left her two teenage siblings disabled.

Financial considerations then supposedly had forced her to get a consulting and laboratory analytics job at the Israel-based Gliopax Pharmaceutical Company.

Thanks to this sparkling--but bogus--resume, a Mossad insider at the FDA rubber-stamped her job application as approved. This step became easy after she scored high in four separate interviews with mid-level agency administrators.

The FDA's hiring process normally took from three to five months. Yet Shira's insider connections enabled her to get a position in less than three weeks.

Now that official word had finally come that she would start work in another week, she already set in motion a strategy to infiltrate the agency's vital "eyes-only" reports on how and why certain drugs receive federal approval.

Getting this critical information would prove vital in the

Israeli government's intensified efforts to verify what its operatives considered the corrupt and inept American oversight into the medical and hospital industries.

"This might emerge as by far the best assignment that I've ever had," Shira thought, amid her morning run in Washington, D.C.'s National Mall. "Wouldn't it be wonderful if I became the first person to dig up the truth, about how the U.S. pharmaceutical industry is endangering the lives of millions of people? ... Imagine what such revelations could do to drastically help improve cancer treatment, especially the lives of those many innocent people--the poor souls that the wicked Nevada senator is trying to trick ... If it takes the rest of my life, my hope is to reveal his treachery. When that happens, only God will be able to save him from the deepest fires of hell."

*

Chief of Staff Dick Cooper and his boss had been arguing all day about whether the senator should proceed with plans to attend the Israeli Embassy gala two weeks later.

The men exchanged frequent barbs throughout the afternoon, although their disagreement never intensified to the level of a shouting match.

Nonetheless, in keeping with their usual habit, the pair ended that work day by walking together to the bus stop nearest to Capitol Hill, on Pennsylvania Avenue. A new Washington Metro subway was currently under construction, slated to open the following year in 1976.

Each of them avowed penny-pinchers, the men took pride in refusing to buy personal cars for themselves. The mere idea of purchasing and maintaining a vehicle in this bustling city struck these men as ludicrous--even Senator Spickler, who hailed from a mega-wealthy family.

Their verbal banter continued when sitting beside each other, while waiting for the bus to Foggy Bottom--an upper-class neighborhood near the infamous Watergate Hotel. Coincidentally, they each lived with their wives in separate condominiums in the same community.

Eight minutes before their bus's scheduled arrival, the men made their conflicting opinions clear. Each remained careful to refrain from mentioning specifics, in case someone nearby happened to be listening.

Dick kept insisting that the senator should withdraw his previously submitted notice that he would attend the Israeli gala. As the politician's top adviser, he insisted on a need for caution, based on insider intelligence reports supplied by the National Security Agency. Recent data collected by U.S. spies indicated that an unknown number of Israeli agents had recently begun to infiltrate the American mainland. Dick warned that the Jewish nation's unscrupulous tactics might divulge damaging information about the senator.

"I could care less, Dick." The senator lighted a cigar, as the crony saw two people nearby curl their noses in apparent disgust. "Those connections might be far too lucrative to pass up. Remember, you were the one who talked me into this in the first place."

Dick let the issue drop, deciding to wait a few days before pressing the matter. For now, he decided to change the topic.

"The good news, sir, is that we're on tap to hold our first public hearing this weekend in Centralia." The adviser dug in his right front pant's pocket for a stick of Wrigley's spearmint chewing gum--which he promptly put into his mouth. "There should be lots of concerned people there, eager for detail on the nuclear fallout issue."

"Excellent." Senator Spickler exhaled a giant cloud of cigar smoke, as the same two people who previously curled their noses turned their backs on them. "So, I can assume that you've got that bumbling sheriff back in line, and that we've also got plenty of federal bureaucrats ready to testify there--to support our story about safety?"

"I'm afraid that Sheriff Peters remains an unpredictable, misguided missile, although our government officials all have their stories as straight as an arrow."

"Dick, if there's one super-important thing that I tell you today, it's that you need to get that bumbling lawman to do his job right. ... Otherwise, all of our political careers could sink together, as if those pour souls on the Titanic."

*

Following the pattern already set from his first two weeks on the job, Anthony Dunn was the first to arrive on that late-January morning at the Perfect Wellness Clinic owned by his new boss--Doctor James Robbins.

For the previous several days, Anthony had enjoyed having a new lively step. His vibrant new walking pace reflected what he considered an unexpected--yet much welcomed--cheery disposition.

Cortisone that Anthony's new employer injected into his right knee had done the trick. The nagging, mind-numbing pain had disappeared, soon replaced by full use of the knee without any need for intense and ongoing physical therapy.

Sierra Crest Hospital's human resources department had tracked Anthony down the previous day, to notify him that his suspension had been lifted following an internal investigation--and that he was welcomed to return to his security guard job.

"Thanks, but no thanks." Anthony had told Charlie Vargas, the hospital employment division's public liaison. "Suspending me was wrong. Most guys in my position would be angry, but I hold no ill feelings--primarily because I'm the forgiving sort."

Anthony felt more energized than he had in years on this particular morning. Instead of that boring security job where he mindless walked from one check-point to another, here at the clinic he was able to interact with people. He empathized with each cancer patient, particularly the children or people with the disease who had youngsters.

Anthony greeted the day's first two cancer patients, who each arrived on schedule shortly after the clinic's 9 o'clock opening time. Bartholomew Eyre, a 78-year-old retired taxi driver, had prostate cancer, and 28-year-old Kathleen Culverson, a fourth-grade teacher, had advanced breast cancer. Both lived in Reno.

Par for the course, in a pattern that Anthony already had learned was typical, Doctor Robbins had failed to show up before the day's first appointment. Nonetheless, Anthony poured a huge cup of coffee, which he brought to the physician's back-room office. There, in recent days, during his few minutes of daily free time, the doctor had put framed black-and-white photos of wild Nevada mustangs on the walls. The office's previous bland amenities and unadorned walls had been replaced by an aura of natural wonder and mystique, at least as far as Anthony was concerned.

A few days earlier, the doctor had told Anthony that during the past month he had a new-found appreciation for the Silver State's expansive outdoors--particularly these wild and untamed animals, free spirits sent by Mother Nature for people to enjoy watching. The doctor's favorites were those who ran with such speed, fury and vigor that the photographs captured images with all four of their legs simultaneously off the ground.

"General, these glorious creatures are like us." the doctor had said, while hanging the largest photograph across from his desk. "We are untamed mavericks, we follow our own unchartered course in life--hopefully for the betterment of other people."

"Son, I'm sure that many patients would fail to understand what we're talking about, but I admit that I agree with you 100-percent on this."

With that conversation still embossed on his mind, Anthony watched the clinic's back door open as Doctor Robbins promptly entered the building. The physician's normally well-combed hair was drenched and scattered in every conceivable direction. The oncologist folded his small black umbrella while closing the door, the harsh wind and cold rain briefly blasting inside.

"This should warm you up, I hope." Anthony placed the coffee cup on the desk in front of Doctor Robbins' chair. "Did you get any sleep at all last night?"

"Not a wink, I'm afraid." The physician took his first sip of the brew. "Too many people hospitalized with cancer. Lord knows that somebody with my skill needs to care for them, using the best treatments that modern medicine can provide."

Taking pride in his new job as the clinic's chief assistant, Anthony mentioned that a few patients already were in the waiting room. He asked the doctor if, before seeing them, he would give a quick update on what had become of the Davis family.

The doctor said that since little Peggy's death 10 days earlier, Honest Davis, 3-year-old one-armed daughter, Penelope, and Mister and Mrs. McCready had moved into the Merry Wink Motel eight miles south of Reno.

They had returned briefly to Centralia for Peggy's funeral. Several hundred mourners attended, just like they had done for her mother. The child was buried with a nutcracker that the family had nicknamed "Love" inside her casket--interred next to her mother. Doctor Robbins had been unable to attend, but he soon heard that lots of people who went had become increasingly angry at the federal government.

Upon their return to the Reno motel, Honest and the other three regularly visited the patient room bedside of Pamela--whose overall condition had briefly improved.

During that interlude, Doctor Robbins started giving Pamela a chemotherapy regimen--shortly after other physicians had performed surgery to remove as much cancer as possible from her colon. The chemo sessions began after three days of recovery from the operation. Since then she had predictably begun to vomit several times daily.

Within several weeks her once flowing, curly and shimmery blonde hair had fallen out. On the day that she became fully bald, Pamela's estranged husband--Jeffrey--had divorce papers delivered to the Sierra Crest nurse's station.

"You say, doctor, that her spouse is in the Air Force?" Anthony interjected, angered by what had occurred. "That devil is not worthy of wearing a U.S. military uniform."

"General, I fully agree. But I would suggest much stronger punishment for him, any guy who would treat such a delicate flower so cruelly ... As far as I'm concerned, he should be court martialed and then summarily shot."

"Son, I know you're only just kidding--saying that in jest."

"Maybe ... All I can say for sure is that sometimes the best, most wonderful people get cancer--while some of the world's biggest jerks live healthy, care-free lives."

"Will Pamela die?"

"Her odds of living are minuscule at best ... Yet I always tell my patients, and I honestly believe this, that 'You should never give up hope. ... Always remain as positive as possible.' ... Once people in Pamela's condition give up, their days are numbered."

The doctor then quickly explained that his interactions with Doctor Crowley, the hospital's president, had become increasingly testy. The key issue remained chemo drug delivery problems at the Hospital's pharmacy. Worsening matters, at least from Doctor Robbins' view, the hospital had failed to do enough to interact with the Western Winds Nursing School at the Silver State University in Reno. The Vietnam veteran had complained to Crowley that largely as a result of this blatant oversight, the Reno area still lacked a certified cancer care nurse. Treatment protocol established by the American Medical Association dictated that only medical professionals certified in cancer medicines were authorized to administer chemotherapy treatments.

As a result, besides being the only registered oncologist in all of Northern Nevada, Doctor Robbins got saddled with the additional duties of personally administering chemo to each of his cancer patients. These were duties that normally would be done by a highly trained nurse; these were responsibilities that such trained experts already were doing on an increasingly wide-scale basis--primarily in other communities, such as major high-populated metropolitan areas.

Such factors, in turn, coupled with Doctor Crowley's

apparent failure to aggressively integrate such teachings into the local university, often forced Doctor Robbins to work at least 20 hours daily; the oncologist needed to continually monitor his patients and personally administer their cancer drugs.

Tragically, at least from the view of Anthony's new boss, the overall health care process remained sub-standard throughout the Reno area. This physician's frustrations intensified with each passing day, knowing that not a single nurse already employed at Sierra Crest Hospital could legally administer chemo.

"Son, you're an amazing person--far and above the rest." Anthony stood and walked toward the doctor's office door leading to the clinic's main hallway. "Sounds to me like you're doing the work of at least five people ... Can I send in your first patient of the day, to examination room Number One?"

"By all means, you should not even have to ask ... It's time for us to get started ... And, no, General, I do not want to have to keep telling you, 'I'm just a regular guy, trying to do my very best to do my job well.'"

A sudden thought struck Anthony just as he began opening the door. He hesitated and turned toward his new boss to say: "Oh, and sorry ... I almost forgot ... There is a reporter that just arrived from the Reno newspaper ... Says his name is Duane Shelton ... Asks if he can interview you about the potential for cancer caused from nuclear fallout, and about the public hearings that are soon to begin on that issue in Eastern Nevada."

"Tell him to go fly a kite ... Do you realize, General, that Shelton is the same snot-nosed reporter whose inaccurate and sensationalized stories indirectly resulted in your suspension from the hospital?"

"He's the guy? ... That nincompoop."

"You get the drift ... The man has earned himself a solid reputation as an incompetent daddy's boy ... Please send him on his merry way, while I spend my valuable time doing everything humanly possible to save lives--particularly sweet and loving souls like that wonderful woman from Hawaii."

*

    Paula's heart kept pounding with steadily increasing excitement and anticipation, beginning as soon as she entered Coyote Pete's small wood home in the Arizona desert.

    Her senses of touch, smell, sight and even taste got triggered into overdrive, the moment that she stepped through the front door beside this reclusive and increasingly popular radio announcer. A brief and unintentional touch of his hand sent shivers down her spine. Her entire body soon became equally invigorated by the inviting feel of the cool brown leather upholstery that covered rustic furniture throughout the living room.

    From there, a huge window from wall-to-wall and all the way up to the ceiling afforded an excellent view of at least 120 giant saguaros. Seeming to Paula almost as if huge green humanoid figures that somehow had been frozen in space, the sight of them made her feel more vitalized and invigorated than she had been since childhood.

    With equal fervor, in those first several seconds in his home, she looked at a wood ceiling high above them--crafted from the region's unique and highly coveted blue palo verde trees. To Paula's mind, these solid formations throughout the structure emitted an innocent--yet bold--aura that galvanized an instinctive human desire for both solitude and protection. Above all, she supposed, the entire layout and craftsmanship gave a paradoxical sense of both safety and boundless freedom--far away from the creepy and spirit-crunching hubbub of living in cities and towns.

    The many intermixing smells added restorative sensations, soothing her nerves and even her anger toward the federal government--if only somewhat. Along a wall of the living room, opposite from the massive stone-lined fireplace, were numerous potted native Arizona plants--many of which Coyote Pete briefly pointed out to her. Admittedly not a flower lover until he reached age 40, his favorites by far--almost as if members of his family--included: the 18-inch-tall desert agave, 10 inches in diameter with bright yellow flowers; an appropriately named "butterfly mist" of equal height, famed throughout the desert southwest for its magnetic ability to attract butterflies; a 6-foot-tall fishhook barrel cactus, which soon mystified Paula due to its reddish orange flowers; and her favorite by far, a 2-foot-high hedgehog cactus with magenta flowers. As soon as Paula bent slightly to smell this species, the aroma sent all of her senses into overdrive.

    Without even taking a single bite, she could almost taste the foods laid out on a board on the kitchen counter--the sight of which made her feel both vitalized and exhilarated. The mere glance at this fresh salami, pine nuts and cheeses of many kinds normally would have made Paula's mouth water in anticipation. Yet for the moment at least, Paula felt what many people call "cotton mouth," while realizing that her own heart and breathing rate remained somewhat elevated.

    "May I call you by your name, 'Paula'--would you care for something cool to drink?"

    "Yes, call me Paula ... And, yes, a tall, cool glass of water, if you don't mind--I might look cool, but I feel increasingly warm inside."

    "Sure. By the way, when we eventually chat about whatever you traveled here to discuss--would you like to go riding together?" He poured water from a sizable container into a yellow-tinted glass. "You look like you probably have never been on a horse, but I just thought that I would ask anyway."

    "Mister, you bet I would like to go riding bareback." She spoke instinctively, without taking any time to ponder her answer. "Something like 14 years ago while in my late teens, I won the Helldorado Rodeo Queen crown in Las Vegas."

    "Well, I'll be darned." Coyote Pete walked toward a back door and promptly signaled for Paula to follow him. "I can show you a perfect secluded trail."

    Within two minutes they were each on the back of stallions, his pure white and hers a tan animal smaller than his. As she and Coyote Pete initially rode side-by-side, neither speaking a word, she stole quick glances at his generous round shoulders and biceps as thick as ham hocks.

Before that morning, she had envisioned that this man would be somewhat chubby or even overweight, at least judging from his slow and methodical voice on the radio. Instead, this fellow appeared to have the body and vigor of a much younger man, behaving as if a guy in his early 20s--rather than what Paula knew must be his actual age, probably in his early 40s at the very least. This estimate seemed logical to her, since she knew that Coyote Pete had steadily increased in fame during the previous few decades.

Marveling at the cottony clouds and dark blue skies, Paula kept up with him as their galloping pace steadily increased.

She soon felt unexpectedly free and unincumbered, lacking any significant worry in the world--because finally she had someone powerful, a man who eagerly and fully listened to her every word. About eight minutes after the two of them had departed from his house, Paula started letting her heart out as they arrived at a generous watering hole.

While the horses drank, this man and Paula sat on separate huge boulders--their nearby surroundings dotted with giant saguaros.

Without any hesitation whatsoever, she spoke non-stop about the many cancers and the nuclear fallout, and the tragic illnesses that had befallen her family. She told of her distrust of Senator Spickler, of the scheduled public hearings--which she remained convinced were "phony set-ups," and of her intense anger toward the federal government.

Paula spoke without letup for at least 15 minutes, or maybe even much more. She realized that this man was careful to listen to her every word.

Coyote Pete's expression convinced her that he empathized with everything that she communicated. When she eventually calmed down, she realized that this man had not spoken a single word since their horse ride began.

"Coyote, this is amazing. You're actually listening to me."
"You bet I am ... Every word ... Did you have any doubt?"

Speaking purely from the heart, making no attempt whatsoever to conceal her feelings, Paula confessed that no one else seemed to actually care. From her view, she said, just about everyone seemed to accept the government propaganda--the federal bureaucracy's claim that nuclear fallout never endangered or harmed the public.

"Mister, I am sure that your wife or girlfriend sure must be a mighty lucky woman. To have a man that listens is an extremely rare find for a gal."

"Oh, I am not married--and I don't have a steady girl. My wife passed away in a car wreck about ten years ago."

"I am so sorry that..." Paula suddenly became speechless, after having just spoken without letup for a considerable time. Often unable to keep gazing at his marvelous face, which magnetized her eyes, she started looking downward toward the reddish earth. A warm feeling rushed across Paula's entire body, and she realized then and there that she must have been blushing. Upon realizing this, she felt an odd mixture of embarrassment and also pure excitement. Her husband, Hank, who remained jailed in Nevada, remained the furthest thing from her mind.

"Paula, you look like you are going to cry. ... If you want, I can..."

"That's not it ... I'm okay, believe me ... It's just that I finally have someone listening to what I have to say." Paula unexpectedly began shaking uncontrollably as she did this, and to her surprise she began to cry fully and wonderfully--with her head bent slightly downward, her tears cascaded to the soil below--each bit of moisture as if a raindrop that sent up tiny puffs of dirt upon hitting earth.

Momentarily, she realized that Coyote's generous and comforting arms curled across her shoulders. He sat beside her.

This unadulterated flow of tears made Paula's heart, spirit and mind feel much better than she had been in a long time. His soothing and kind embrace added to her feelings of escape, her sense that she had finally found much-needed relief.

Without hesitation, Paula made the first move.

She put no thought into the effort.

She pulled his head toward hers.

Coyote made no attempt to fight off or move away from her advancements.

Within seconds, they kissed, warmly, wetly and tightly. Paula suddenly forgot her sadness or her anger. All she could think about was this kiss, the touch of which made her heart pound with ever-increasing intensity and anticipation.

Paula wrapped her arms around him as tightly as possible, never wanting this powerful man to leave her side. Every fiber of her being wanted him to be a "bad boy," for she desperately needed Coyote and also the many fantastic things, which instinct told her that he could efficiently provide.

To her regret, the radio announcer gently pulled away from Paula, and suddenly he stood--while she remained seated on the boulder.

"Mister, I apologize to you." She felt flustered, grasping for just the right words--that all seemed difficult or even impossible to find. "Please forgive me ... I didn't mean to do that to you ... You need to know that I am not that kind of a woman."

"No apologies needed." He took off his white cowboy hat and briefly whacked it against his thighs, as if to slap away some dirt.

Coyote then grinned, an expression that impressed her as being an interesting mix of both mischievousness and cordiality. Then and there, she scowled, feeling extreme frustration--upon realizing that she had wanted him to be a bad boy. She realized that she had wanted him to take more of her, all of her--everything that she had to give.

Paula's intense passions flowed, engulfing her entire aura. In all her life until that morning, she had never felt such a burning desire for any man--even her husband Hank way back on their wedding night.

Just when Coyote held out his hand toward Paula,

signaling his desire to help her stand, she felt increasingly frustrated. She kept thinking over and over again, "I wish that this guy was not such a gentleman ... Slow down, Paula ... You are going to scare him away ... I need to keep my mouth shut ... Too much is happening in my heart and mind, too fast for me to assimilate."

Within a minute, they were each back on separate horses, which they leisurely rode on various dirt roads and isolated back-country pathways for the next three straight hours. Throughout that entire time, they spoke very little--primarily commenting only on certain plants or animals.

Close to 1 o'clock in the afternoon, as they continued riding--stopping briefly to enjoy beef jerky and plenty of water from a canteen--he suggested that she appear as a surprise guest on his radio show, broadcast live across the vast American west.

She felt a sense of relief while heading back to Coyote's house, each discussing how they should develop a perfect strategy and timing for her on-air appearance.

The remainder of that day went by fast from Paula's perspective.

By 3 o'clock that afternoon as they arrived via horseback at Coyote's home, she felt more optimistic than ever about the possibility of exposing the government's plan.

Exactly how and when Coyote Pete and Paula would accomplish this remained a topic for future discussion. Her optimism solidified when they agreed to meet several more times during the coming week.

At 3:45 that afternoon, Paco picked her up at Coyote's rustic home, to drive her back to the Saguaro Motel in Nogales. Along the way, Paula kept thinking that although she had been somewhat pessimistic beforehand about how that day would transpire, in her mind it had ended up being perhaps one of the most glorious periods of her life.

"Hi, Janelle!" Paula felt happier than she had been in a long time as she hopped out of the pickup, as soon as Paco parked the vehicle in the motel parking lot. "How is everything going? ... Have you and Tommy been okay while waiting for me all day."

"Paula, you need to sit down on this chair." Janelle pointed toward the furniture outside their motel room door. "There is going to be no easy way for me to tell you. ... I phoned Scout a few hours ago, and he gave me some disturbing news about what has happened to Peggy, and Penelope and Pamela--and even to Honest."

Ninteen

Along with 14 federal bureaucrats and several of his primary staffers, U.S. Senator Larry Spickler entered an old school bus.

These travelers converged into the vehicle, parked beside the runway at the small Elko Municipal Airport in Northeast Nevada. The group had just arrived via jet from Washington, D.C., during which the aircraft had brief stops in Denver and Salt Lake City.

Their landing back in the Silver State culminated two weeks of intense non-stop advance work by Dick Cooper and others from Spickler's Capitol Hill Office.

As scheduled, the Elko County High School Band played numerous patriotic tunes written by the famed late composer and conductor John Phillip Sousa.

The internationally famous "Stars and Stripes Forever" melody filled the cool mid-afternoon air as Spickler stood at the bus door--shortly before he addressed the crowd--mostly local Democrats that local party leaders had encouraged to attend.

The senator's chief of staff felt enormous pride, particularly as the politician started giving a fiery 5-minute speech. To Dick's ears, these pre-scripted remarks rang with a natural cadence, thanks to Spickler's charismatic speaking skill--one of this politician's few redeeming qualities.

Raising his arms in continually fluid motions, while also always moving his gaze throughout the crowd, the senator assured everyone that he was eager to ferret out the truth about what impact nuclear fallout had made on the region--if any.

"Thank the Lord that Nevada has a champion like me, someone willing to look out for your needs and concerns!" Spickler's voice reached a particularly high pitch, while the crowd cheered--in precisely the way that many of them had been instructed to do.

Only one TV camera was there, a decade-old device operated by one of only two television stations in the entire region at the time. Dick felt confident that this would suffice, since that station's manager--Maurice Petre--had privately agreed to beam the footage to its sister outlets and to the main CBS News headquarters in Washington.

The crony issued a broad grin, thinking as the senator concluded his remarks that "people are stupid. ... The average person will believe just about anything that we say, especially if the remarks are made with some degree of eloquence."

Right on cue, the band started playing another famous Sousa composition, "The Washington Post," as Spickler concluded his remarks, waved goodbye to the crowd and the bus doors closed behind him.

While inside the bus with the many bureaucrats, Dick cringed upon hearing this off-key rendition of this world-famous tune--so badly played that he began grinding his teeth. To him, this sounded like the attempt of a second-grade band, rather than the nearly perfect rendition that these same musicians had played just a short while earlier. "Life is like that," Dick thought, acknowledging his own opinion that no person is perfect--at least all the time.

Spickler promptly sat in the vehicle's front row, a position that had been reserved for him and Dick. The politician put his hat on his lap and promptly lighted a cigar.

The chief of staff knew their three-hour ride south to Centralia would be boring, unless he could engage his boss and the many others on board in lively conversation.

All but a handful of the seats were taken, primarily by men who worked in management and mid-level bureaucratic positions at federal agencies. Dick counted only five women on board. Three of them were secretaries; one was a stenographer needed to chronicle the proceedings; and the fifth worked as a biologist for the Food & Drug Administration.

Upon arrival in Centralia, scheduled for around 4:45 in the afternoon, the bus was to take them to the new Alexander County Fairgrounds. There, the various politicians and bureaucrats would have slightly more than one hour to rest and have a meal. Then at 6 o'clock that evening the first scheduled public hearing would begin at the complex's indoor arena, the first public gathering in the new $1.3 million facility.

While on the bus, shortly after departing Elko, Spickler had already fallen fast asleep. The senator's neck arched backward, with his mouth wide open. His snoring bellowed in a predictable and methodical cadence, the noise making Dick think of what a beached whale must sound like as the tide recedes.

Light chuckles emitted here and there from the various bureaucrats on board. Dick realized that everyone here realized and respected the need for all of them to refrain from any behavior that might seem to ridicule or degrade the politician.

"These people realize that they are here for only one reason," Dick thought, while standing in the bus aisle at the front of the vehicle and facing the many passengers. Using both of his hands, the crony made downward motions--which he considered an obvious signal for the few remaining chucklers to quiet down.

To Dick's dismay, however, his attempts to keep the noise level to a minimum had a completely opposite effect. Rather than treating this chief of staff as their leader, he suddenly realized that lots of them viewed his physical motions as part of a comic routine. This became evident to him when lots of them burst out in uproarious laughter.

The senator suddenly awakened and sat at attention. The chuckles died down.

But the damage had been done, at least as far as Dick was concerned. This brief event signaled to him that most of these passengers--if not all--essentially considered Spickler as just another powerless or phony Washington politician.

On the bright side, though, at least from Dick's

perspective, virtually all of these so-called "pencil-pushers" here were merely "little Indians"--a term commonly used at the time as a description for people who will do or say whatever they are told.

And, he knew this meant that all of these people were being paid to lie--to tell streams of calculated mistruths--at that evening's scheduled hearings.

"All of these people are the scum of the earth, but we need them," Dick thought as he promptly sat beside his boss, who by this point had fallen back asleep. "The sad fact is that we need them, just as much as they need us. When working efficiently together, we are like the spokes of a wheel."

While still sitting beside the senator, Dick felt increasingly disappointed with his boss. Instead of sleeping like an over-fed alligator on the edge of a swamp, as far as this crony was concerned Spickler should have spent those precious moments meandering up and down the bus aisle--glad-handing these bureaucrats.

"Sir." Dick gently prodded the senator's stomach and whispered into his ear. "Senator, you should wake up and mingle with these passengers. You know, we need..."

"To hell with that, you handle it ... Can't you see that I am busy sleeping."

Although still seated, the senator managed to turn on his right side--now facing the opposite direction from Dick.

Like this or not, the crony realized that he needed to do exactly as the senator commanded. These various federal officials and administrators needed personal reassurances that the senator and his staff were on their side as well--willing and eager to back them up politically if necessary.

During the previous few weeks, the senator--and primarily Dick--had interacted with almost every one of these individuals, either in person or by phone.

Each of them realized the essential need to bring, display and say--only the most positive documents and statements--setting aside and keeping the damning information about the truth under "lock and key" in government files back in Washington, D.C.

The public, they agreed, should never know the "true and irrefutable" details, namely the fact that government scientists had confirmed: many more thousands, or perhaps even tens of thousands, of people throughout Eastern Nevada, Western Utah and Northern Arizona would perish from cancer during the next 25 years; prior to conducting the above-ground nuclear bomb explosions, the government had full knowledge that these deaths would occur; during his eight-year administration of the 1950s, President Dwight David Eisenhower had signed top-secret documents designating the isolated, rural communities within the nuclear fallout zone as an "expendable population;" well aware of the fatal nature of these experiments, insider bureaucrats had ordered their relatives to avoid areas downwind of the Nevada Test Site--while simultaneously issuing press releases to the affected communities, informing everyone living there that "there is nothing to worry about;" and steadily intensifying the nuclear explosions, although realizing that doing so would significantly increase the entire region's long-term cancer death rate.

Along with his boss, and several other U.S. senators who knew these truths, Dick realized that voters would revolt if they discovered these disturbing details.

Dick had frequently advised Senator Spickler that the political upheaval sparked by the Watergate scandal during the previous year during 1974, likely would spark a nationwide voter revolt--particularly in Nevada, Utah and Arizona.

In advising Spickler and some of his closest senatorial allies, Dick repeatedly stressed the need for secrecy. American voters had made their anger clear during the previous 14 months, signifying a groundswell of distain for back-room trickery in the nation's capitol.

Complicating matters multi-fold, many of the bureaucrats now on this bus were the same individuals who had orchestrated the start of nuclear testing in the 1950s. Others among them helped carry out the government's devilish orders during the last half of that decade well into the 1960s. Because of this, when and if the public learned the truth about these shenanigans, streams of federal personnel likely would lose their jobs--adversely impacting a significant number of government agencies.

Under such a scenario, Dick knew that the likely defense--particularly if criminal charges were brought--would be that "I didn't know" and "I was merely following orders from my superiors."

Such wimpy excuses, at least in Dick's mind, would mirror the lame criminal defense strategies of former Nazi death camp guards. Besides beating, shooting, hanging, starving and overworking their Jewish prisoners to death, some of these low-level German army personnel had administered deadly gas that killed their prisoners.

Many millions of Jews perished in these concentration camps throughout much of Germany and Poland. Many German soldiers who grew up as honest, loving and kind young people became mass murderers when allowing themselves to follow orders.

By comparison, Dick knew, many of the "insider" U.S. government bureaucrats had been doing essentially the same thing since the end of World War II. As far as he was concerned the primary difference was that America threatened the lives and health of "a mere" tens of thousands of people, far less than the atrocities inflicted by the Germans.

Even so, while on the bus--going from row-to-row to chat casually with his fellow passengers, Dick tried to hold back a deep inner sense of shame.

A big part of him felt that what he and these bureaucrats were doing seemed morally and ethically "wrong," to the point that the devil would applaud them. At the same time, though, a conflicting emotion emerged. Above all, Dick concluded that the worst immediate dangers had passed. This struck him as logical, because--after all--the U.S. government had suspended its above-ground nuclear explosion tests several years earlier. Any current or future cancers within the nuclear fallout zone region would be the result of actions that had been completed during the 1950s and 1960s.

Nonetheless, the urgency of successfully carrying out this "cover-up" remained as politically and logically necessary as ever before. In the wake of the Vietnam war and the recent Washington scandals, the federal bureaucracy seemed to him as if far more fragile than ever--perhaps at least as vulnerable as during the height of the American Civil War.

On the positive side, Dick personally liked and truly yearned for the well being of his fellow bureaucrats. The senator's crony empathized with them and believed that he fully understood their focused mindset, primarily because he had been one of them for several years.

So, naturally Dick smiled often and laughed occasionally while sharing colorful "insider stories" with many of them there on the bus. From his perspective, their shared time on this road trip seemed to pass by in a flash.

While at the back of the bus while chatting with several officials from the nuclear regulatory agency, he glanced toward the front of the vehicle and spotted the town of Centralia about 10 miles up ahead. His mood improved markedly in those same moments, upon noticing Senator Spickler wandering the aisle; the politician cajoled with many of the same bureaucrats that Dick had been sweet-talking.

When the vehicle finally slowed and turned onto Main Street, without warning Dick got hit by the notion that this surely would emerge as "do or die" time for the Senator's political career.

"Will the people fall for this ruse?" Dick wondered as the bus went through the entrance to new rodeo ground, right on schedule. "Unless our crafty maneuver works, which I hope it will, we literally could experience an intense political revolt--perhaps maybe even riots in the streets."

*

While in her new Food & Drug Administration office

just outside the nation's capitol, Mossad agent Shira Levy read a four-paragraph story buried at the bottom of page A-14 in that morning's "Washington Post."

The article described that day's scheduled start of eight public hearings in isolated Nevada and Utah communities. The item quoted Senator Spickler as saying that he remained determined to "get at the truth" regarding possible radiation-caused cancers.

Well aware that this statement was a bold-faced lie, thanks to the clandestine recording she had made of the politician at the Salt Lake City airport, she emitted a brief smile while alone-- before summarily plopping the newspaper onto her desktop.

"Those creeps will soon get a taste of justice," Shira thought, while pulling out her bottom desk drawer, retrieving her purse from there and then applying dark red lipstick. "I have no doubt that those scallawags have left plenty of damaging evidence within this agency, and at plenty of other bureaucracies as well. ... They're slithery and slimy, for sure, I'll get enough goods on them to help ensure that they fry."

*

Despite his hectic schedule, Doctor James Robbins managed to arrive right on time that day for his noon lunch at Reno's most prestigious restaurant of that era.

Already seated in a private booth at the rear of Harrah's Steakhouse, Sierra Crest Hospital President Gregory Crowley watched the physician approach his table.

The Vietnam War vet walked beside the restaurant's widely acclaimed maître d' Nicholas Sattgart. Although Crowley felt jealous of Robbins, he respected that doctor's calm demeanor and smart appearance--today wearing a crisp white shirt, a yellow tie and dark blue, wrinkle-free slacks. These seemed lavish and yet simple, at least in Crowley's mind.

Well aware that Robbins lacked any inkling of what their ensuing discussion would be about, Crowley had chosen this establishment primarily due to its elegant ambiance and tranquil atmosphere.

In keeping with the hotel's strict policies, the restaurant staff had already adorned each dining table with at least five fresh red roses. These filled the entire dining area with a fragrant and refreshing aura, which Crowley always felt enhanced the sense of smell for every diner. The dark wood walls, the plush red leather booth cushions and framed high-end ink drawings helped contribute to the mystery and aura of wealth.

Still looking at Robbins as he approached, the hospital president stood to shake his guest's hand. Crowley realized that he detested this oncologist because he seemed too perfect--the right appearance, demeanor, candor and intelligence for any given moment. The administrator had never met anyone quite like this before, and realized that--at least in his opinion--the oncologist needed to show his own human frailties. Crowley felt that everyone has many imperfections; the process of acknowledging one's own flaws can emerge as mentally and spiritually cleansing and thought provoking--leading to possible self-improvement.

"Welcome, so glad that you could make it on such short notice." The administrator shook the oncologist's hands as firmly as possible, conveyed as a sign of equal or even superior manliness--intermixed with an appropriate degree of cordiality.

"The pleasure is mine." Doctor Robbins shook hands with equal fervor, a signal to Crowley that the oncologist might have even more class and sophistication than some of Reno's other doctors believed.

As the men sat on opposite sides of the horseshoe-shaped booth, Crowley wondered whether Robbins had ever dined in a worldly and charming place such as this. At least judging from the oncologist's personal history, on file at the hospital's human resources department, Crowley believed that this physician came from humble beginnings--a personal background that never could afford such top-class culture.

"Right off the bat, Doctor Crowley, I can honestly tell you that this is certainly my kind of place." The oncologist summarily took his napkin from the tabletop, placed it on his lap and lifted his water glass--as if, at least in the administrator's mind--to inspect its cleanliness and clarity. "There is almost nothing better than an elegant meal, in a fine establishment such as this, although I must admit that I have never been here before."

Eager to display power and sophistication, Crowley commenced telling Doctor Robbins about some of the "insider" ins-and-outs of this well-to-do venue.

The administrator explained that streams of movie stars and particularly world-renowned entertainers frequently dined here. Those who showed up unexpected often included world famous singers and musicians that appeared in the Harrah's Hotel Showroom or at entertainment venues of other casinos throughout the region. Crowley admitted that in recent years; celebrities that he had spotted included: "Ol' Blue Eyes," Frank Sinatra and his buddy, Sammy Davis Jr.; British crooner Anthony Newley: American rocker Paul Revere; comedienne Totie Fields; country great Glenn Campbell; composer, songwriter and record producer Burt Bacharach, and many others.

Confident that he had Doctor Robbins full attention, without letup Crowley went on to explain that widely renowned multi-millionaire Bill Harrah--the owner of this hotel--was known to use a secret or little-known back door to access this restaurant.

Hidden within the expertly crafted dark wood carpentry on the walls, this doorway gave the casino magnate access from a back-of-the house underground hallway--unseen by the public; this gave exclusive access to a small private dining room at the back of the restaurant. On rare occasions, Crowley told Robbins, top-level executives from the region were allowed to reserve that back room for their own private meetings or quaint parties.

"Jim, can I call you that--by your first name, rather than calling you 'doctor?'"

"By all means."

"Well, Jim, I had unsuccessfully tried to book that back room for us today, but to my regret it was already reserved."

"No one needs to impress me, Gregory--can I call you

that? ... I've been all around the world and experienced my fair share of poverty and supreme elegance."

Careful to avoid showing any facial expressions, Crowley felt an unexpected knot in his stomach upon hearing this. The last thing that he wanted to hear at this moment was that Robbins had become a worldly man, highly experienced in the complex and often conflicting interactions of people from all levels of society-- let alone in many cultures.

"Jim, the attempt at privacy was not an effort to impress you. Instead, it was necessary to help ensure that our conversation remains between us--and us alone."

"I can understand that ... It's obvious that you want to rip into me about something, some huge issue or other ... But before we get into that, can we order first?"

Crowley instantly felt irked by the oncologist's ability to casually and artfully mention, and to predict a critical issue; the administrator had to admit, if only to himself that Robbins possessed an innate and unique ability to simultaneously delve into hot-button issues, all while somehow managing to avoid intense one-on-one conflict.

Both men summarily quieted down, speaking only to tell the waiter their orders. Robbins ordered Italian onion soup, followed by salmon and vegetables. Crowley requested only one thing, a "Snoopy salad."

As the waiter walked away, Robbins told the administrator that "I didn't see that listed ... A Snoopy salad? ... What is that?"

"Of course, it's never on the menu." Crowley took pride in realizing that he was among the handful of diners who had this insider knowledge. "People in-the-know, like me, have learned about this. Only insiders have this knowledge."

"Well, thank you, Gregory--now I can consider myself an insider." Robbins lifted his glass of cabernet as if to propose a toast. "Here is to becoming special."

Once again, that knot tightened in Crowley's stomach. He detested the oncologist's kindness, and particularly his ability to schmooze without seeming even a bit combative.

"I'll drink to that." Crowley reciprocated as their crystal glasses clanked. "As each of us must know, knowledge is power."

Upon saying this, the administrator unexpectedly felt somewhat better, both mentally and physically. Sitting there across from Doctor Robbins, Doctor Crowley realized for the first time that he merely had been jealous of this man from Detroit and San Francisco--envious of his rugged good looks, unhappy that he seemed far more worldly, and even fearful or at least jealous that he might excel much further in the medical industry.

"I know that you're not jealous of me, Gregory," Doctor Robbins said while gently putting his wine glass back on the table. "I know you are not that petty."

This sudden and unexpected statement startled the administrator, who wondered how in the world the oncologist knew what he had been thinking. To Crowley, emotionally stunned and left speechless by Robbins comment, the situation seemed bizarre and other-worldly--almost as if science fiction.

"Oh, Doctor Crowley, quick--before you say anything--and I know that you are trying to find the right words, just about anything to say--you need to know that I've always been somewhat intuitive. ... I'm not trying to show off here, in any way whatsoever, but you need to know that I've always possessed an innate ability to sense people's motivations. What drives them. What makes them tick. Their fears. Their angers. And their hopes. But most of all, their motivations."

"I have to admit that I'm somewhat at a loss for words."

"There is no need, Doctor Crowley, for you to say anything at the moment. I'll just say what I know in my heart and mind that you were about to tell me. ... You were going to threaten to put me on probation or some nonsense like that, for refusing to grant an interview to that slimy newspaper reporter, Duane Shelton. ... You were going to lecture me about the urgent need for propriety, emphasizing that the hospital is stuck in the middle of a political situation--over which it has no control. ... You want me to talk with that green-faced journalist about the probability of people from Eastern Nevada and Western Utah getting cancer due to nuclear radiation. ... With equal emphasis, you were going to chastise me for standing my ground, for continually insisting to your office that the hospital do a far better job in ordering, receiving and distributing pharmaceuticals ... And because of these issues, you were going to threaten to revoke my ability to practice at the hospital."

"Well, yes ... all of the things that you said are right on the mark, but..."

"Let me just finish, please, so that we can just cut our conversation here down to the bare minimum. ... First off, my answer to the first question is 'No, I am not going to talk with that reporter' ... And, my answer to the second issue is 'No, I refuse to back down in my efforts to encourage the hospital to significantly improve its efficiency.'"

Doctor Robbins' unexpected statements left Crowley feeling stunned. The executive pondered the fact that the oncologist had remained calm, even-tempered and solemn while making his bold statements, rather than seeming angry or defensive.

Besides realizing his own jealousy, suddenly Crowley now felt admiration for the other doctor's superior insight, keen intuitive abilities and perhaps most of all his penchant for cleverly and artfully getting straight to the point.

Every fiber of the executive's being wanted to dislike the cancer physician. But instead Doctor Crowley now felt admiration and increasing respect.

Even so, sensing an overriding need to save face, Crowley took a conciliatory approach in hopes of making peace.

"Jim, from what I'm hearing, I think that we can both say that we've reached an understanding." The executive smiled as a waiter delivered appetizers. "I acknowledge the need for the hospital to significantly improve pharmaceutical services, while you also recognize the obligation that each of us has to remain politically astute. ... Agreed?"

"Since you are not being defensive about the issue, I would have to answer with a resounding 'Yes.' ... And, as far as that slippery journalist Duane Shelton is concerned, okay, I will talk with the guy. ... I hope we both can agree, though--you and I--that this clown is potentially a loose cannon that has to be managed. ... Correct?"

"Now that we have this challenge behind us--much faster than I had previously thought possible--let us relax and enjoy our meal. Life is far too short to get all bent out of shape about differences that can be easily ironed out."

"You know, this food is far better than I had expected. How often did you say that you come here? ... If it's at least once a week, I can see why."

Crowley started telling his opinions of the Reno and Lake Tahoe area's best dining establishments and social life. He sensed that Robbins was sucking up his every word, perhaps truly interested in generating and solidifying powerful business relationships.

Yet through the remainder of their leisurely 90-minute meal, the executive refrained from revealing the intense political pressure that he had started to receive from the Food & Drug Administration, the office of Nevada Senator Larry Spickler and the pharmaceutical industry. Collectively and individually, each of these essential participants in the Nevada and nationwide economic landscape had demanded that the Reno hospital--and particularly Doctor Robbins--refrain from acknowledging the possibility of a Silver State cancer cluster caused by nuclear radiation fallout.

"Oh, and Jim, on that nuclear fallout issue, I think that you would probably agree that on that there is no conclusive evidence of a cancer cluster?" Crowley tried to say this casually as they each put on their overcoats, while exiting the steakhouse. "That is what you would tell the reporter, if he asks"

"We each know that is the politically acceptable, line--so,

yes." Robbins slowly fastened the top button on his overcoat, having just quickly snapped the others together. "I will tell that creepy, snot-nosed reporter that there simply are no facts to prove such a disaster. But I will refrain from revealing my honest opinion. ... Although there is no scientific evidence to prove such a conspiracy, I would not trust the feds further than I can hold their feet to the fire."

*

Sheriff Jonathan Peters felt both confident and well-rested as the bus full of politicians and federal officials arrived at the new County Fairgrounds.

The past few days had been hectic for the lawman, as he managed the expansive arena's set-up. This was to mark the facility's first major event since its grand opening four months earlier in early October, as the slow autumn and winter seasons began.

Although Peters' primary duties entailed policing matters, the small community's mega-tight governmental budget also forced him to perform other essential obligations--such as handling the arena's necessary preparations for public events.

Unlike the state's other rodeo facilities within rural areas, this complex featured an enclosed structure. To most of the town's residents, Peters knew, the facility seemed ideal for major gatherings, particularly during nasty winter weather that often brought bone-crunching cold.

Just about everyone in Centralia knew that the metal structure covering nine acres had been built only because the region had garnered $1.4 million in essential federal funds. The so-called "pork-barrel" allotment got approved thanks to Washington sweetheart back-room deals struck by Nevada's freshman Senator Spickler.

While the bus was still en route, Peter had spent the afternoon napping at his modest home on a hillside four miles outside of town. Growing inner tension and frayed nerves motivated the sheriff to take this brief escape, unusual for this lawman who normally considered himself calm and not easily fazed.

Most of all, he dreaded the mere thought of interacting with Senator Spickler, whom the sheriff considered as no better than typical road-kill that rots on isolated Nevada highways. Besides the fact, at least from Peters' view, that the politician "stinks to high heaven," the sheriff also felt both shame and dread due to the fact that Senator Spickler "owned him"--treating the lawman no better than a robin interacts with a worm.

The fact that the sheriff's re-election campaigns depended on back-door funds from Spickler only served to intensify Peters' contempt for the man. From his perspective, to be treated with blatant disrespect was no better than a blatant slap in the face.

To be sure, the sheriff realized that if any fellow other than this politician were involved, the lawman likely would have given this pompous senator an unforgettable beating via a trusty baseball bat--perhaps capped off by a gun butt sharply applied to the middle of the forehead. The sheriff felt a tiny bit of pride for having dispatched more than a few detestable people, using similar methods during the previous five years.

Continually mindful of these possibilities, Peters had convinced his only two deputies to help with set-up for the public hearing--and also to handle that evening's security. Deputies Bernie Tucker, an overweight, pimple-faced oaf in his mid-20s, and David Osborne, a thin and sleepy-eyed law enforcement rookie in his early 60s, had each insisted to the sheriff that they were far too tired to attend--not to mention the inescapable fact that they each disliked Spickler enough to "run over his toes--and that's not all."

"I hope you two baboons realize that the senator can easily have each of us exterminated, if we fail to please him." Peters suddenly took off his own hat while confronting these subordinates in the sheriff's office, on the say before the scheduled hearings. "I wouldn't put murder past that guy. As far as I'm concerned, he is fully capable of the worst kind of slime imaginable. So, if I were you guys--if you don't want to end up in a shallow grave way out in the middle of nowhere sometime this weekend, killed at the hands of Spickler's cronies--I would simply work at the event, while keeping my mouth shut."

Despite his own sense of shame for being one of the senator's lackeys, Peters felt at least a smidgen of pride when noticing his deputies at the arena a half hour before the scheduled arrival of the school bus. Thank heavens their survival instincts had clicked into overdrive, for the sheriff had meant what he said about the senator's apparent propensity to "knock off" any low-level adversary or underlings who defied him.

In fact, with his own eyes, slightly more than three years earlier in 1972, Peters had seen two gunmen--apparent soldiers of the increasingly powerful politician--blow the head off of a rancher who had refused to obey the senator's commands. Jed Stapleton, a crusty old guy who always smoked a corncob pipe and wore dusty-looking overalls, had refused to move from his 327-acre spread about 36 miles east of town.

As far as Peters could tell, Stapleton's fatal mistake had been a failure--or flat-out refusal--to accept the fact that Spickler's political soldiers meant what they said when demanding that the rancher leave his property. Through an "insider" contact, the sheriff had learned that federal officials wanted the rancher's land--where tons of remaining remnants from nuclear fallout could have been used as conclusive evidence proving the government conspiracy. Peters' informant had revealed that although nuclear contaminated ash remained from the bomb explosions, the radiation would not necessarily cause immediate cancers--but instead take a few years or even decades to generate the illness.

Worsening matters multi-fold, Peters had been told, due to prevailing wind currents the fallout landing on Stapleton's ranch had been at least five times greater than elsewhere in the region. The resulting dangers were so severe that Stapleton's beloved wife, Irene, and his three adult children--who had all lived on the ranch--each perished from cancer during the 1960s.

Worried about suffering a similar fate as Stapleton, the sheriff steadily became increasingly wary of the senator--and especially the planned public forum at the rodeo stadium. All along, however, he realized that--although serving as the region's top lawman--the creepy Capitol Hill crowd thought of him as a "mere bug." As a 30-year law enforcement veteran, Peters knew that the mega-powerful United States government would proverbially step on him as if an insect, rather than risk having this conspiracy revealed. To Peters, this conclusion seemed logical because, after all, the feds already had slaughtered thousands of innocent American souls in Nevada, Utah and Arizona.

With his own self-preservation in mind, Peters eagerly greeted the 37 bus passengers, particularly Senator Spickler and Dick Cooper. He feared that to ignore them would emerge as the equivalent of signing his own death warrant. The sheriff briefly shook many of their hands, while signaling for them to go straight to the chow line.

Although cash-strapped, the county hosted this private meal for the officials, beginning as scheduled at 4:30 that afternoon in the rodeo pavilion. Following this 90-minute eating and rest period, the public was to arrive starting at 6 o'clock--giving everyone ample time to get seated before the 6:30 scheduled start of the hearing.

Thanks largely to the arduous work during the previous four days by deputies Bernie Tucker and David Osborne, all the chairs, tables and microphones had been arranged in an effort to bring an aura of professionalism to the proceedings.

At the insistence of Reverend Martin "Scout" Middleton, the special events set-up crew also had placed 14 large speakers at strategic places throughout the large indoor facility. His church and five other Eastern Nevada congregations had collectively loaned these devices in hopes of giving the event a top-class atmosphere.

Following the officials' private meal of ribs, beans, corn on the cob and chocolate cake for desert, 623 residents from throughout the region crowded into the facility as scheduled in the early evening. The sheriff knew this marked the area's highest attendance by far for any public gathering since 1963, when mourners gathered to pray for the soul of the 33rd president of the United States, John F. Kennedy--one day after his assassination.

*

Sheriff Peters breathed a long, deep sign of relief when the nuclear fallout hearings began right on schedule. Sitting at the head table, with public officials on both sides of him, Senator Spickler pounded a gavel--while loudly pronouncing to everyone that "these hearings will now come to order."

While the politician told the crowd of his deep concern for the region and of his own effort to organize these hearings, Peters spotted the chief-of-staff--Dick Cooper--sitting in the front row of the audience. The lawman began grinding his teeth at the sight of this Washington crony, whom he considered as "the scum of the earth ... The very worst about American culture." As far as Peters was concerned, guys like Dick represented everything immoral and wrong about the USA's form of government.

Vile, greedy, sneaky and devilish buffoons like Dick and the senator deserve to get a quick one-way ticket straight into the bowels of hell as far as the sheriff was concerned.

Yet on the positive side, at least from Peters' view, these proceedings would conclude within a few hours--before all of these Washington jerks finally went on their merry way, to the next rural community for another proverbial "dog and pony show."

Sure enough, from the sheriff's perspective, the first hour of the hearing went rather predictable in pretty much the way he had hoped.

Several residents made brief announcements at a microphone, telling of their worries, heartache and concerns. They told of the many cancer deaths of relatives and friends, coupled with their own worries that nuclear fallout might have caused these debilitating or fatal illnesses.

Right on script, dishing out the propaganda that Peters

knew that they would spout, a continual parade of bureaucrats and various federal agency administrators testified that they had been unable to find any scientific evidence to back up such claims.

In each specific instance, the public was essentially told that there essentially was no basis or legitimate reason whatsoever for their claims. Hearing this hogwash, Peters started getting a giant knot in his stomach--because he knew otherwise.

Then at precisely 7:28 that evening, everything suddenly changed.

The microphones in the entire room went dead.

The indoor lights dimmed.

Initially stunned, the sheriff marched quick-step to the back of the room. He ordered deputies Bernie Tucker and David Osborne to immediately fix the problem.

"This is Rebel Radio, broadcasting throughout the great and expansive American West." These words echoed throughout the entire arena, blared from the giant speakers the Reverend Middleton and the various churches had donated.

Upon hearing this, Senator Spickler and the various bureaucrats stood at the head table. Still in disbelief about what was currently happening, Peters saw expressions on all of their faces, looks that he considered signals of disbelief and even fright.

"Hello, this is your announcer Coyote Pete." The voice echoed throughout the room, where Peters saw equally startled expressions throughout the crowd. "We are broadcasting at this moment into the bogus hearings being conducted by perhaps one of the most corrupt senators in American history. ... Right now, ladies and gentlemen, as you hear this, Senator Larry Spickler and his team of corrupt bureaucrats are busy lying to the innocent people of he American West. ... Believe me, we have proof that these people are evil ... The Unites States government cannot be trusted in any way whatsoever...."

As Coyote Pete continued his non-stop diatribe, blasting the officials for being "despicable liars of the worst kind," Dick Cooper quickly stomped up to Sheriff Peters--who at that moment stood at the rear of the arena near the entrance doors.

"Sheriff, if you value your life, you will immediately pull the plug on those speakers." The crony whispered into Peters' right ear. "You have no idea how much power and might is going to come down on you, sir, unless you get this terrible situation under immediate control."

"My deputies are now working on the situation."

"Fix it, or I assure you, sir, you will be a dead man within the next week."

Mortified and lacking any inkling of specifically what to do next, the sheriff suddenly heard the crowd begin to cheer.

While scrambling in an effort to help his deputies locate and unplug the speakers, Peters heard the announcer introduce Paula Davis.

"How in the world did she get onto the airwaves?" the sheriff thought, while running toward the first set of speakers. "How did she pull this off?"

Increasingly desperate to shut off the speakers, Sheriff Peters started working with deputies Tucker and Osborne on the first set of speakers. Wires at the back were stuck, too secure to extract; that unit's main plug to the power line was similarly affixed.

"Holy heavens!" the sheriff shouted at his men. "Fix this blessed thing!"

Even louder cheers accented by applause erupted from the crowd as Paula began her speech via broadcast radio, her voice still heard loud and clear throughout the entire room. She urged the public to impeach Senator Spickler, to seek his criminal conviction and also the immediate imprisonment of virtually every federal official at the arena.

"These are the crooks that killed your family members, your many friends and neighbors." Paula spoke in a strident tone that Peters considered calm, clear and well-reasoned. "The words that I have to describe these people are unmentionable. ... These politicians and bureaucrats are worse than devils ... These are the type of clowns who are willing to kill any of us at random, just to carry out their own evil deeds. Everyone, listen to every word that I have to say ... I can guarantee you that many more of us will be getting deadly cancer during the next few decades--the long-term impact of the nuclear fallout that they cruelly inflicted upon us. ... These creeps know full well that what I'm telling you right now is true, every word of it, and..."

The sheriff became increasingly petrified by the steadily evolving situation as Paula continued her verbal presentation; while assisting his deputies, he saw the senator and all the bureaucrats start to walk away from the front table. The senator tried fruitlessly to speak into several microphones, but all of the them were dead.

Throughout the crowd several groups of spectators intermittently erupted in laughter while seeing this spectacle of obviously rattled and nervous bureaucrats. Paula's voice could still be heard.

At one point Peters looked up from his efforts alongside his deputies to see Dick Cooper. The crony's skin looked bright pink to the lawman, a sharp difference from the chief-of-staff's usual lily-white appearance. Dick continually tried to move a primary electrical power switch to the "off" position, but without success--so increasingly frustrated that he finally yelled: "Shit!"

The sheriff took great delight in seeing and hearing all this. More than ever, he hated these jerks who dared to look down upon him as if he were a mere insect.

As Paula's strident voice continued echoing loud and clear throughout the expansive facility, Peters gazed all around; he noticed that various bureaucrats all were trying without success to disengage the other five huge speakers. At one point six of them simultaneously kicked one of the devices, but to no avail.

This only served to bring more laughter from most spectators, as Paula spoke of the inept and childish behavior of these officials.

"They are like spoiled little babies." Her voice seemed

natural to Peters, who became convinced that she was speaking from the heart--rather than a prepared speech. "These brats, these jerks, these bullies prefer to put all of our lives in danger. They killed my sister, and my niece and they're in process of trying to kill another sister of mine ... Another niece has lost her arm to cancer ... But I'm afraid that the worse is yet to come for all of us, because more cancers are likely to erupt at a steadily increasing pace ... I'm sure many of you have similar stories to tell ... So, we need strength ... So, we need to band together to fight this political corruption ... We need and must do the right thing in... People, we need to increase our valiant fight against these devils!"

Suddenly, the speakers went dead.

Someone from amid the crowd had managed to disengage the speakers.

All electric power went out and the room went pitch black.

A resounding chorus of "oohs" and "ahhs" erupted from the crowd.

The sheriff and his deputies turned on their flashlights, showing the way for the crowd to disperse. As everyone steadily left the building, Peters heard many of them comment to each other that they considered Paula a true hero.

"Mister." Senator Spickler stood at the sheriff's side, whispering into his ear while Dick Cooper also took a place beside them. "What do you have to say for yourself?"

"Sir, I'm sorry ... I'm so very sorry, believe me ... I ..."

The senator leaned closer toward Peters' face.

"Calm down ... Relax ... There is no reason for you to say that you are sorry at this point."

The senator then briefly kissed the sheriff's left front cheek, before saying to the lawman "Goodbye, friend."

Twenty

Mossad agent Shira Levy opened a light brown packet inside her lavish Shyler Street apartment, two blocks from the infamous Watergate Hotel.

At this point just five weeks after accepting the Food & Drug Administration job, she still cherished living alone more than ever. To her great pride, she had already furnished her new residence with high-end furniture fit for a mid-ranking bureaucrat.

Carefully following her intense training, she had only conversed briefly on infrequent occasions with a handful of neighbors. Shire never mentioned her job or family to anyone that she encountered in the five-story building's hallways and elevators.

Upon getting this latest package from underneath a park bench beside the nearby C&O Canal, a popular tourist, jogging and strolling site, she knew right away that the message would be important. The red bold lettering across the package signified this.

As usual, the message was written in a highly complex, impossible-to-crack code that only a handful of operatives including Shira knew how to decipher.

Israeli intelligence officials made a concerted effort to keep her apprised of all significant details involving her overall mission, coupled with essential data regarding the Food and Drug Administration.

The first few items grabbed her attention right away. At an isolated desert 30 miles south of Centralia, Nevada, authorities had found the bodies of three uniformed men--buried in shallow graves a half mile from a little-used highway. Authorities had identified the bodies as Sheriff Jonathan Peters and his two deputies, David Osborne and Bernie Tucker. An autopsy concluded that all three men had suffered blunt force trauma to the head, presumably via four bloody baseball bats found at the scene.

Medical experts surmised that the deputies perished before being buried. The sheriff had suffered a far more excruciating death. Investigators concluded that Peters had been severely beaten, but that he had remained conscious when the killers buried him alive.

The sheriff and his crew had disappeared three days after Senator Spickler's botched attempt at a bogus public hearing in that community. Amazingly, the gathering and its resulting disruption by the interlopers never got reported in the mainstream news media. The only journalist in attendance had been a newspaper intern, Duane Shelton, from the "Reno Globe-Herald" hundreds of miles away. Although only age 19, this University of Nevada student had been labeled as an apparent CIA agent, based on a preliminary investigation by Mossad operatives in the western United States.

The CBS News crew that had filmed the senator's arrival in Nevada at the Elko airport had refrained from attending the Centralia hearing. Those journalists apparently had been told beforehand that the gathering would be boring, unworthy of coverage. Instead, the network had planned to subsequently attend and report on other scheduled hearings planned by Senator Spickler's staff in several larger Eastern Nevada and Eastern Utah towns.

Each attended by several hundred people, those gatherings had been held as scheduled in the communities of Ely, Pahrump, Rhyolite, Elko, Carlin and Eureka. Those sessions were reported in separate small town newspapers; the Centralia community lacked such a reliable publication. Meantime, the CBS Evening News with Walter Cronkite refrained from reporting on any of the gatherings. Top secret intelligence reports indicated that Senator Spickler's staff and other Washington bureaucrats had told mainstream journalists and the TV networks that the Centralia hearings had not been of newsworthy significance on a national scale.

Perhaps most disturbing, according to Shira's insider report from Mossad, the U.S. Federal Bureau of Investigation had declined to investigate the lawmen's deaths. The FBI declared that local and state investigators had failed to find any indication that a federal crime had been committed.

Separately and on their own, Mossad investigators had concluded that the slayings of Sheriff Peters and his crew were carried out by a clandestine group of killers--associated with the Spickler family's massive hotel-casino operations in Las Vegas. Israeli intelligence had deduced this by comparing the lawmen's murders with at least 18 similar, known and verified mob-related killings in Southern Nevada. Like the demise of Peters and his deputies, those victims had been beaten with 34-ounce, Spalding-brand baseball bats that had been haphazardly left at the murder scenes. In each instance, the perpetrators had refrained from leaving fingerprints.

The Israeli government admitted in its clandestine report to Shira that operatives had been unable to find any direct link to the killings and Senator Spickler. Yet Jewish authorities suspected him as the apparent ringleader.

From earlier insider reports that Shira had previously received, she already knew that the Jewish state's overall investigation and interest in Spickler stemmed from his close associations with the mainstream health care industry--primarily the giant pharmaceutical companies. Israel suspected these involved nefarious behind-the-scenes business dealings, plus massive donations from huge drug firms to his election campaigns.

Shira quickly glanced over the remainder of the report. These subsequent details impressed her as equally compelling, just as important as the murders of the lawmen.

Par for the course, the mainstream news media had failed to report this. But according to this document sent by Shira's superiors, the U.S. Federal Communication Commission had started jamming the radio airwaves on the day after the fateful Centralia hearing. This clandestine action blocked Coyote Pete's late-night radio broadcasts that previously had beamed his show from Mexico clear across the vast American west.

Complicating matters multi-fold, the increasingly famous announcer had suddenly disappeared three days after the broadcast--apparently along with Paula, the Centralia woman whom--the report said--had courageously told the truth during their fateful broadcast. Initial intelligence indicated that the couple had quickly fallen in love with each other, apparently hoping to elope at a Las Vegas chapel. Jewish operatives had subsequently confirmed this upon locating a marriage license issued in Southern Nevada's Clark County. The couple eloped one day after Paula's divorce from Hank went through. Her nuptials with Coyote Pete had been performed at the internationally acclaimed Kissing Cupid Drive-Thru Wedding Chapel, followed by a wedding night in the lavish bridal suite at the Las Vegas Hilton--during the same period when famed rocker Elvis Presley performed at the hotel.

From there, as far as Israeli investigators could tell, the trail leading to the newlyweds' whereabouts had gone cold. Jewish officials surmised that the couple apparently went "on the lam," after these lovers learned that a U.S. federal arrest warrant had been issued for the capture of Coyote Pete. When previously blasting his radio show across the American airwaves the announcer had refrained from breaking any federal laws. However, in the wake of the notorious broadcast targeting the Centralia hearing, the U.S. Justice Department had obtained apparent evidence that the announcer--whose real name was Bobby Blair--had broken federal law by shipping massive quantities of marijuana from Mexico into the United States. According to the Mossad report, however, Coyote Pete likely was innocent of those charges, "something that the FBI should have known." Instead, Jewish officials believed, the actually drug smuggler likely was the announcer's adult son, Sean Blair, an inept and potentially murderous criminal who had three separate previous felony convictions in the United States.

Without the Mossad report saying so in specific words,

Shira knew that her homeland tracked these various intricate details--primarily due to Senator Spickler's nefarious ties to the pharmaceutical industry and international organized crime rings.

On the positive side, Shira started smiling as she scoured the final section of this insider, eyes-only report. The final five paragraphs gave a blow-by-blow description of the Nevada freshman senator's attendance to the previous week's Israeli Embassy gala honoring both U.S. President Gerald Ford and Israeli Prime Minister Yitzhak Rabin.

"Senator Spickler is the worst kind of fool imaginable. Thanks to his boundless greed and relentless corruption, we will soon be able to easily use and manipulate him to our best advantage--hopefully for many years to come. Although this politician considers himself as mega-powerful and embossed with wisdom, in all likelihood he is ultra-weak, conniving and eternally foolish. Of course, most politicians across America have just such a reputation, so much so that corruption and persistent lying have made them rather predictable in almost every regard. By contrast, however, Spickler's personal background and his penchant for persistent criminal behavior helps to stand him apart from all the rest.

"Besides being a fat, worthless slob, his most redeeming qualities--at least from the standpoint of a mobster--include his willingness to to use violence to achieve his devilish goals. Far worse than his congressional contemporaries, he is always willing and eager to break the golden rule in an effort to line his own pocket. For instance, in just his first four years in office, the senator has increased his listed net worth from $150,000 to a current level of $4.8 million ... Most of those holdings are in the form of land. This sharp and sudden increase in personal net worth is not too bad for a guy whose relatives officially own and operate the casinos. Instead, while the mainstream liberal U.S. news media essentially "looks the other way," the senator's lucrative land investments are made in conjunction with corporations and individuals who benefit from legislation that he

helps ram through Congress--the best type of 'sweetheart deals' that most congressmen can only dream about.

"Understandably, as a result--just like we previously had predicted--the Senator behaved like a selfish and blatant 'rump-kisser' when interacting with President Ford and our esteemed prime minister. When outside of the presence of those national leaders, while still at our reception in the Embassy Row Hotel, Senator Spickler flat-out admitted to our Israeli ambassador to the United States, Amos Berkovich, that he does and will do anything reasonable to protect the American health care and pharmaceutical industries--while also working hard to protect the international interests of our homeland.

"Truly an amateur in the political arena, at one point after the main course was served and Spickler chatted at his guest table beside our American Embassy's executive assistant--Elijah Horowitz--that on Capitol Hill he can easily make all these things happen 'for a price. We can talk about all this later, in much more detail if you would like.' And as a result, we have a major fish--actually a whale--that we can hook. Once we eventually talk about cash, or confront the senator with details of his many crimes, we can use him as a willing and eager puppet, easily manipulating him for several more decades to our heart's delight."

Although ecstatic that her associates had compiled these compelling details, Shira felt even more energized when reviewing her assignment--described in an addendum at the bottom of the report.

Her superiors ordered her to do whatever possible within the Food and Drug Administration to "get the goods" on Senator Spickler. Shira realized this meant getting irrefutable evidence of this greasy politician's ties to huge pharmaceutical companies and the FDA, plus confirmation that he knew about the nuclear fallout cover-up all along.

"He's the worst kind of killer." She thought about the senator, while placing the file in a metal vault in her bedroom. "Just one slip-up on my part, and I have no doubt whatsoever that Senator Spickler, his creepy crony Dick Cooper, and their many behind-the-scenes thugs will do whatever they possibly can to assassinate me."

*

On July 24 of 1975, slightly more than six months after the woman from Hawaii had entered Sierra Crest Hospital, family and friends planned to gather at Miguel's Mexican Restaurant in Reno to celebrate her survival and her 25th birthday.

Still working as office manager at Doctor Robbins' cancer treatment clinic, Anthony Dunn rushed across town to attend at the last minute.

Anthony's boss, whom he still affectionately called "Son," had been invited, but unexpectedly had to cancel. A sudden onslaught of patients had unexpectedly prevented the physician from attending, so he asked the "General" to go in his place.

Glad that his knee troubles had subsided, Anthony knew that he had not been invited. Nonetheless, Doctor Robbins had insisted that the family would welcome him with open arms, once they learned that he was there as the physician's representative.

Without time to rush home to change clothes, Anthony decided to drive straight from the clinic to the restaurant. While en route, the World War II veteran felt proud of his new 1975 yellow Ford Pinto, which "Son" had bought for him as a bonus.

While driving southbound on Virginia Street through the heart of town, Anthony sang along word-for-word with his radio--belting out the Captain and Tennille tune that had peaked a few weeks earlier on the Billboard charts, "Love Will Keep Us Together."

While stopped at a red light at Virginia and Plumb, four blocks from his destination, Anthony kept thinking what this tune meant to him.

"A little more than year ago today, I felt depressed and hopeless--down in the dumps," Anthony thought, while tapping the steering wheel in rhythm with the beat. "But then I met a man who shows love to all of the world, Doctor Robbins. And because of him, my life has drastically changed for the better and some people are still alive--only because of him."

Without telling anyone that he felt this way, Anthony wished that far more people in the world had as much kindness, integrity and knowledge as Doctor Robbins. Society would be far better off if the world had hundreds of more physicians exactly like his boss.

Anthony felt this far more than ever, although during the previous six months he had learned first-hand that the physician is "merely human"--far from perfect, with the type of occasional quirks and odd behaviors that make each person unique.

Rather than feeling irritated and bothered by the doctor's many distinctive characteristics, Anthony liked the fact that these numerous idiosyncrasies helped make the oncologist seem more like a "regular guy" than an unbelievable real-life Superman.

Some the Doctor's propensities, which Anthony believed might irritate some people, included: jiggling his legs rapid-fire while sitting and talking with patients, an apparent release of nervous tension; an inclination to continually use his left hand to flick his ear, while reading complex medical reports in his office; returning patients' phone calls, sometimes while behaving as if he never had received their messages; and his apparent lack of any effort to generate any sort of personal life for himself--other than his father-and-son type of relationship with Anthony.

Above all, the office receptionist knew first-hand that Doctor Robbins truly and deeply cared for all of his patients, from the very young to those advanced in age. Yet never once to that point had Anthony ever seen his boss cry or show intense emotion after a patient died. Some weeks three or four of the clinic's patients passed away.

Anthony never considered the doctor's failure to display emotion as any sort of sign that he was heartless or uncaring. To the contrary, the receptionist knew of his boss's devotion to these ailing people, primarily due to the oncologist's non-stop, around-the-clock efforts to save them. The doctor's clinic never maintained weekend office hours, while only opening on weekdays. Even so, on Saturdays and Sundays--when many other physicians spent time with their families or enjoyed sporting events with friends--Doctor Robbins always remained at the bedsides of his patients.

To Anthony's great regret and to the disappointment of his boss as well, Northern Nevada still lacked a certified and registered cancer care nurse.

As a result, this University of San Francisco Medical School graduate still had to personally administer chemotherapy regimens to his patients. This contrasted with the general care procedures of virtually all general-care physicians, who each benefited from the assistance of numerous highly trained nurses and other health care industry staffers.

From Anthony's perspective, this challenging situation put Doctor Robbins into a non-stop, 24-hour environment similar to what military doctors must endure amid battle conditions.

The only exception in this physician's current work environment was the fact that he and his Reno-area patients did not currently face the threat of being attacked by soldiers, aircraft and ships armed with guns and bombs.

Anthony knew that Doctor Robbins essentially had been locked into an inescapable situation, similar--at least in some ways--to when military physicians struggle to save lives amid war zones. Like those doctors, the Vietnam War veteran essentially had no escape from his pressing professional responsibilities.

However, most doctors working in war zones are assisted by staffs of highly trained medical experts skilled in treating war wounds. Unlike those physicians, during his initial years practicing in Reno, Doctor Robbins lacked trained assistants who specialized in cancer treatment. He served as the region's only licensed oncologist.

Even college students cramming for final exams get occasional chances to catch at least some sleep. Their most arduous efforts in this regard generally last only a few weeks at most, usually only about twice per year, during the final days before mid-terms and finals. By contrast, Doctor Robbins work schedule had remained non-stop during his previous 14 months of practicing in Reno. The only exception had been in early January of that year--1975--when he had traveled to Eastern Nevada to attend the funeral of Polly Davis.

This was among reasons why Anthony knew that attending Pamela's birthday party and meeting with her relatives there had been extremely important to the doctor. Such devotion to the Davis family had become clear in recent days, when Doctor Robbins occasionally mentioned that he had become increasingly eager to attend.

"Whatever it takes, General, I'm going to be there," the physician had told him while chatting at the clinic, two days before the scheduled gathering. "I'm especially fond of all the Davises, particularly because of what they have had to endure. Collectively and individually, those people are fighters ... As you probably know by now, I appreciate passionate people--and everyone in that family has that fantastic characteristic, especially at times when others in their position would have readily given up all hope."

Fully cognizant of his employer's dogged motivations to remain loyal to his patients, Anthony realized that his boss had wanted to attend Pamela's birthday party. An urgent phone call had come in to the clinic, just as Anthony and the doctor were preparing to close the clinic for the day. The Emergency Room at Sierra Crest reported that one of Doctor Robbins' patients, Byron Neiman, a 36-year-old casino shift manager who had been in a regular patient room, had suddenly become critically ill before being sent to the Emergency Room. The oncologist had been summoned right away in hopes of doing whatever medically possible to save Neiman's life.

Anthony accepted his boss's request without hesitation, agreeing to attend Pamela's birthday party--if only to stay for a few minutes, perhaps to briefly tell everyone that the doctor would like to express his sincere regrets at being unable to show up.

Upon entering the front door of Miguel's Restaurant, across South Virginia Street from the small new Peppermill Diner, Anthony recognized the Davis family right away. He immediately walked straight toward their table, without bothering to wait at the front entrance station.

When making his family approach toward them, from 15 feet away, he noticed the tall man wearing an eye patch, and remembered that everyone called the fellow "Honest." The sight of him stunned Anthony--not because of their confrontation in the hospital lobby on the first night that they met back in September--but because the guy now looked to him as if almost 25 years older than before. Just six months earlier, at least in Anthony's eyes, this once burly fellow had appeared as if a perfect specimen of manliness. Back then, excluding Honest's damaged eye, ear and mouth, from Anthony's perspective Honest had appeared as if in his mid-30s, strong enough to play as a professional football offensive lineman and handsome enough to work as a fancy men's fashion magazine like "GQ." Yet now Anthony viewed the plumber as if a washed-out, wrinkle-faced man of about 60 years old.

As he approached the table, another change became evident to Anthony because by then everyone at the Davis family table was gazing toward him. Before that moment, each time they had met briefly at the clinic, Honest had looked at Anthony straight in the eye, in what the receptionist considered as a manly, confident way. This time, however, the plumber avoided making direct eye contact, instead gazing occasionally at the World War II veteran's upper shoulders and chest. These significant changes in Honest's appearance and demeanor immediately made Anthony feel perplexed and even somewhat sorry for this man.

Had the cancer deaths of Honest's wife, Polly, and his daughter, Peggy, literally wiped out his vigor--literally his reason to live? Had this man become clinically depressed due to the loss of these close relatives?

Just as riveting from Anthony's perspective was the significant change in Pamela's appearance since he last saw her at the clinic a few months earlier. Then she had been as bald as an eagle and almost thin enough--at least from the receptionist's view--to use as a broomstick. Seriously, to him, back then Pamela had looked as gaunt as people photographed in 1945 immediately after being liberated from Nazi concentration camps. Now, Anthony felt joyful on this occasion upon seeing that her body weight remained thin--but almost back up to normal, enough that her rosy cheeks had returned. Equally impressive from Anthony's view, Pamela's hair had grown back at least some--now long enough to cover half of her ears. Her aura of femininity had returned.

"I don't know if all of you remember me?" Anthony stood beside their dining table, although fully realizing that most of them probably would recognize him right away.

They promptly and collectively gave different-worded, yet similar answers: "Sure we do," "How could we forget you?" and "Forgetting you would be impossible, because you have always been super kind to us."

Speaking from his heart, Anthony told them that the doctor wanted to send his sincere regrets at being unable to attend due to an urgent medical emergency. Anthony also said that "I'm so sorry for interrupting. We just wanted to let you know this."

Along with little Penelope and Tommy, everyone already seated then collectively asked Anthony to join them. Careful to avoid offending these diners, he readily agreed.

While taking one of the few unused seats, Anthony began introducing himself to several people that he did not recognize.

Seated at the far end of the table, Pamela--while pointing toward them-- told him the names of several of her close relatives and acquaintances whom he had not met.

"This is my oldest sister, Paula, whom I've become so much closer to--especially during the past several months," Pamela said, before naming the others. Besides Tommy, Penelope and their father Honest, she described Dorothy and Bill McCready and the Reverend Martin "Scout" Middleton and his wife Janelle as longtime family friends.

"I have heard so many positive things about all of you,"

Anthony said, as a chubby waiter of about 5 feet tall handed him a menu. Considering himself skilled at social propriety, Anthony refrained from mentioning Paula's absent husband, the famed radio announcer Coyote Pete. Several days earlier, Anthony had heard a local KOH-AM radio newscast that gave details of the announcer's arrest by federal marshals on the marijuana smuggling charge. Anthony had subsequently mentioned the arrest to Doctor Robbins in a private chat in the physician's clinic office; that is when the "Son" told the "General" that the announcer had recently eloped with Pamela's older sister.

"Pamela, I apologize for failing to bring a present for you." Anthony felt motivated to make this statement, since he always tried to behave in an appropriate gentlemanly manner. "The doctor also wanted me to tell you that he has two unique birthday gifts that he will be giving you."

"Any gift is..." Pamela spoke briefly, before being interrupted by Honest.

"No presents are necessary." The one-eyed man took a long gulp from a Budweiser beer container, before setting it beside two emptied similar bottles on the table near his plate. "Having my sister-in-law still alive here is gift enough."

Left speechless by this declaration, Anthony decided to keep his own mouth shut. The strong, overpowering odor of alcohol permeated from Honest, an odor that the World War II veteran had just finally noticed--while sitting at least 8 feet from the other man. The plumber's inebriated behavior mystified Anthony, because he had heard several people--including the doctor--mention during the past several months that the plumber had been a lifelong teetotaler. Had this widower and Vietnam War veteran become a raging alcoholic within the course of several months? Anthony began to ponder this possibility, surmising that perhaps alcohol abuse had been a primary factor in accelerating this grieving man's aging process. Within the span of just a few minutes, Anthony's overall perspective on this family's situation had drastically changed.

"Everyone, I would like to propose a toast." The Reverend Martin "Scout" Middleton stood, holding his margarita glass high--while the children, Tommy and Penelope, kept playing with a toy Slinky on the tabletop. "Here is to Doctor Robbins, and to Pamela for her courage and determination--and to the Good Lord as well. Without them working collectively together, we would not even be here with our beloved Pamela this evening."

"Here, here!" Honest bellowed, before guzzling all the beer that had remained in his current bottle. Everyone at the table smiled, while drinking whatever beverage that they had, as the preacher sat back down.

"Thank you for saying that, Reverend." Anthony spoke openly from the heart, because he fully agreed with what had just been said. "I think that each one of us is lucky to be here tonight ... It's almost as if this is Thanksgiving Day, and here we are in the middle of summer."

Everyone responded by collectively saying that they agreed, and this topic soon transitioned to what each person thought of Doctor Robbins.

Although using different words and stories, at least from Anthony's perspective, they all had a similar feeling about the physician. This made the "General" increasingly proud of his "son." Starting with Pamela, they all told unique stories about the oncologist. They described: the soothing way Doctor Robbins spoke with them, always eager and ready to listen to whatever thought was on their minds; the admirable way that he worked diligently, non-stop for many hours--as if he had super-human endurance; the exemplary way that he took however much time as necessary to fully explain complex medical challenges in an easy-to-understand description; and also the exhilarating way that he sometimes unexpectedly showed up, telling a quick joke or exhibiting humorous behavior that soothed their nerves and enabled them to feel better.

"I like the doctor." Penelope smiled broadly, before taking another bite of refried beans. "He is nice."

After everyone else had briefly spoken about his boss, Anthony fought back his own inner motivation to begin weeping. He truly loved the physician as a father would a son. Filled with pride, the clinic receptionist used a napkin to cover his face, while trying to behave as if fighting back a sneeze--actually wiping tears from his eyes.

Then, without any warning whatsoever, he realized that everyone else at the table had begun to clap and cheer. Curious as to what was happening, Anthony pulled the cloth away from his face. Right away he realized that all the others were looking past him--their collective gazes affixed toward the restaurant's front door.

Turing his head around 180 degrees, Anthony instantly realized that everyone was applauding the unexpected arrival of Doctor Robbins.

The physician approached their table at a quick pace, as he kept smiling and waving at all of them.

"What's all this cheering about?" The physician stood beside the table, wearing a crisp, light brown suit, accented by a striped red and white satin tie.

"Boss, you..." Anthony found himself at a loss for words.

"Doctor." Pamela held up her wine glass, still seated at the far end of the table. "Your ears must have been burning."

"My ears, burning?" The doctor lightly patted both children on their heads, after they rushed to him and wrapped their arms around his legs. "Why would that be happening?"

Pamela then piped in, "We were all just saying fantastic things about you, doctor. ... You remember me, don't you?"

"You bet I remember you." The physician promptly started strolling confidently around the table, shaking the men's hands and greeting each woman.

From the delightful expressions in everyone's faces, Anthony surmised that these people were truly overjoyed to see his boss. Exceedingly proud of his "Son," he knew that unlike many physicians, Doctor Robbins refrained from behaving "above-it-all."

Within a few minutes after his unexpected arrival, the doctor stood at one side of the long table and spoke casually, his arms moving slowly about in what Anthony considered a friendly and relaxed manner: "Please accept my sincere apologies for being late. ... I had been called to a medical emergency that did not take as long as I had expected ... And, Pamela, I just want to let you know that I have two unique surprises for you ... They are not exactly birthday presents, at least in a technical sense ... But you might choose to consider them that way."

"Okay!" Pamela smiled broadly. "Hand me my presents."

"Well, these gifts are something that I would need to tell you about, rather than hand them over to you."

"Tell me now!" She beamed, and from clear across the long end of the rectangle-shaped table, Anthony noticed that she was blushing--her cheeks rosy red.

"This is something that you might normally want to hear in private, so..."

"I have no secrets to keep from my family and friends. ... You can let everyone know, as far as I am concerned."

Without responding right away, the doctor strolled to the opposite end of the table from Anthony. There, the physician stood beside Pamela, who remained seated.

"Well, the first 'gift,' if you want to call it that, is news that I just received this evening about the results of your recent medical tests. A thorough analysis of your blood and biopsy samples indicates that your body is free of cancer ... This means that your body is in remission."

"My cancer is gone!" Pamela began weeping, and the three other women at the table--Paula, Janelle and Dorothy--summarily did as well. All the men became teary eyed, and the children clapped. "I am cured?"

"Well technically," the doctor gently spoke. "In medical terms, you are considered cured after being in remission for five continuous years. Yet, technically, at this moment we can say with great certainty that your body has no cancer whatsoever."

"Fantastic!" Honest guzzled an entire beer, all at once-- before lightly burping.

Everyone remained quiet for a few moments, as Anthony realized that this had been perhaps one of the most stupendous events that he had personally witnessed.

"Doctor?" Pamela promptly stood and she gave the physician a warm bear hug. "And, you said that you have another birthday surprise for me."

"Well, yes." Doctor Robbins summarily helped Pamela sit back down, before he purloined an unused chair from a nearby table, pulled it next to hers and then sat right beside her. "But that surprise would also come in the form of words, which you also might prefer to hear in private."

"The suspense is killing me!" Pamela said this in such a way that everyone broke out in laughter, except for Honest--who concentrated on another new beer. "Please, doctor, tell me now without delay."

Doctor Robbins explained that he had learned that while she attended the University of Hawaii, Pamela had earned a master's degree in business administration. The physician also said he discovered with delight that right after graduation she had gotten a good job managing a major Honolulu-based auto parts development and distribution business.

"I took the liberty of speaking with the administrators there, and they all told me of your glowing personnel reviews." Doctor Robbins paused momentarily, and Anthony could see that all eyes present remained glued to the physician. "These people swore that their business operations, which previously had been haphazard and off-kilter, became essentially a well-oiled machine under your sensational leadership."

"So, why do you mention this?" Pamela sipped a water, her plate already empty.

"What I'm saying is, that I'm offering you a job--as the manager of my clinic. We need you ... I need you ... Our business is steadily growing, and frankly I lack the time and business acumen to effectively operate the business on my own ... As you can probably very well imagine, Anthony's position at the clinic remains secure ... He has already proven himself as irreplaceable ..."

"But, I..." Pamela stammered.

"Will you take the job?"

"Yes! Yes! Yes ... If I lived, I wondered how I was going to survive ... Well, you know what I mean."

Everyone chuckled softly, a signal to Anthony that these people understood and appreciated what Pamela had been going through.

"Well, fine." The doctor smiled. "We have a deal ... The pay, of course, will not be high right away ... But it could grow significantly in a very short period of time, as we grow and prosper and help more cancer patients."

Unexpectedly, in a flash Anthony realized that Honest had passed out. The plumber's head rested atop his own half-finished plate. Drool oozed from the plumber's wide-open mouth onto the tabletop.

"Doctor, I think that you should know that Honest never drank until this spring." Bill McCready finally spoke, for the first time that evening--as Anthony and Reverend Middleton lifted the inebriated man from the table. "As you might have noticed, he has been going downhill mighty fast. ... As you'll probably learn very soon, plenty of other problems have emerged for us in recent days ... I have little doubt whatsoever that solving these challenges could very well take an act of God."

Twenty-One

Five years later in 1980, Senator Spickler felt as if he had reached near the peak of American political power--several steps below the presidency. Two years earlier he won re-election to a second six-year term, whipping his opponent, Nevada Republican legislator Corky Banfield, by a landslide.

The final tally had Spickler at a near tie in Nevada's rural counties, while a heavy statewide voter turnout got credited by political analysts as a key factor in driving his victory. A political science professor at the state's primary university suggested that the senator had generated luke-warm support in the Silver State's rural areas.

As promised by his many allies in the mainstream medical industry, nine giant pharmaceutical companies gave significant contributions to his campaign. The timing could not possibly have been more ideal from the viewpoint of his chief of staff.

On November 5, the day after that year's general election, when Ronald Reagan won election to his first term as president, Dick Cooper told his boss that having a strong political ally in the White House sharply increased his chances of gaining more power.

Sure enough, although only in his second term, from the view of many political commentators, Senator Spickler "got lucky" because many of his counterparts in Congress were in the process of retiring. This left numerous highly coveted Senate chairmanships up for grabs, most importantly the Ways and Means Committee.

Using several congressional alliances that Spickler had reached during the previous several years, he won an appointment to that post of Senate Minority Whip--just one step below the Democratic Party's top position in that branch of Congress.

"Boss, I'm mega proud of you," Dick told him on the day after the election, with Spickler now entering the third year of his second six-year term. "If all goes as planned, very soon you will be the odds-on favorite as Senate majority leader."

This crony relished his superior's reaction, beaming with a perfect smile so bright and wide that Dick thought of his boss as healthy-looking enough to model for a toothpaste commercial on national TV. Thanks largely to the chief of staff's dogged persistence at "nagging" him, Senator Spickler's appearance had changed dramatically during the previous few years.

This man who had once been so "fat"--a term not yet politically incorrect--that he needed suspenders to hold up his pants, now had a body that Dick considered at least somewhat similar to that of a college athlete. The senator's former round face, which had once resembled that of Santa Claus from his top assistant's view, now was thin and well-defined--showing off a handsomeness that many people previously had failed to notice.

Gone were the days of huge bowls of chocolate pudding at lunch, three servings of heavy cake after dinner, and continual snacking on peanuts throughout the day. From Dick's perspective, this fast-rising political star had evolved into a committed and unstoppable "man on a mission"--fully dedicated to excelling as much as possible in both the physical and political realms.

To the delight of both Dick and his boss, Idaho's third-term Republican Senator Kevin Downing and other top-ranked GOP leaders on Capital Hill had gradually stopped their endless teasing of Spickler in the Senate Dining Room. Dick thought that perhaps the Nevadan's significant change in his own personal and political style had launched this significant transition.

By this point on the infrequent occasions when Spickler dined in the Senate's primary cafeteria, he primarily chose salads laced with plenty of protein like turkey or chicken--always avoiding his previous favorites of starchy and sugary foods. Just as impressive from Dick's perspective, without fail this Lighthouse, Nevada, native arrived for workouts at 5:30 each morning in the

Senate Gym. The exercise regimen consisted of rotating daily between 90-minute runs on treadmills, and lifting weights to bulk up and significantly reduce overall body fat.

Of even more importance, in Dick's view, was the senator's significant improvement in his political skills--particularly during the previous five years. Unlike those days, when the senator often tried to bully his elected opponents and even on occasion to strongarm his counterparts from the same party, by this point Spickler had become highly skilled in the art of what the chief of staff called "give-and-take compromise." This new-found "you-scratch-my-back, and I'll-scratch-yours" philosophy had gone a long way in advancing this politician's fast-rising career.

On the negative side, during the previous half decade Dick had steadily gained 15 pounds, his once-flat belly now featuring a slight paunch over the belt-line. This change resulted in constant needling from the senator, whose only significant health challenge to this point had remained the fact that he refused to give up smoking cigars. Almost every time the boss taunted him as being the "newest fatso on our team," the crony emitted a mild chuckle as if laughing off the criticism. Yet deep inside, Dick--who normally considered himself "as tough as nails"--felt an emotional pain. Rather than showing complete loyalty to his chief of staff, who had never once wavered in fully supporting his superior--at least from Dick's view---the boss became overly cruel in provoking these unnecessary taunts.

Indeed, Dick considered the many growing revisions between the two of them as overly divisive and increasingly alienating. Just five years earlier, at least as far as Dick could tell, the two of them had worked together as if a well-oiled, efficient and seemingly unstoppable machine. By contrast, as the holiday season of 1980 began, the two were almost at odds on almost every political issue and strategy. This transition in their relationship had occurred so slowly over a period of years that Dick had barely noticed the change, until--from his standpoint--it had become too late to reverse their differences.

To this longtime Capitol Hill bureaucrat, the only "saving grace" remained the many secrets that the two of them shared. As far as Dick knew, he was the only person with in-depth and first-hand knowledge of Spickler's many shady dealings--some of them felonious in nature. Although never seriously worrying about his own personal safety, this right-hand-man realized--or at least suspected--that his boss likely would prefer to fire him as soon as possible. Yet all along, the senator refrained from doing so, perhaps out of the politician's own apparent worries that Dick might reveal these many shocking truths.

With these many conflicts in mind, perhaps more than ever, Dick tried to avoid any conflict with his superior at 5:30 in the afternoon on Monday, December 1, 1980, as they stood together at the bottom of the Capitol steps. The pair awaited a limousine, sent by the Israeli Embassy to take them to a lavish pre-Hanukkah gala at the Ritz-Carlton in Georgetown. The senator's alliance with the Jewish people and with Israel had remained strong since they had entered a pact of mutual power five years earlier. This essential connection helped generate massive campaign contributions for the senator.

Unlike several years earlier when the two of them chatted non-stop while traveling to and from major events, this time the men refrained from speaking to each other during the 17-minute drive to the party site. Dick sensed that this was not out of hate, but rather because they felt little need to communicate--while having little use for each other. While en route, the senator kept his eyes glued to his favorite newspaper, the liberal "Washington Post," while Dick chatted with the chauffeur about Washington's emerging hectic holiday season.

Once they arrived, and entered the main party room, Dick immediately recognized powerful Jewish American senators of the time. From his view, the most notable among them included: Republicans Rudy Boschwitz of Minnesota, Jacob J. Javits of New York, and newly elected Warren Rudman of New Hampshire;

and Democrats Howard Metzenbaum of Ohio, Edward Zorinski of Nebraska, Carl Levin of Minnesota, and departing Senator Abraham A. Ribicoff of Connecticut, who had decided to retire. By Dick's count, more than a dozen Jewish congressmen also were in attendance.

To Dick's delight, and he felt that Spickler felt the same, at first glance the Nevada senator seemed to be the only non-Jewish politician at the gala. The chief of staff considered this an honor, an inescapable signal of Spickler's growing power.

In keeping with the usual strategy when encountering other top politicians, the pair went straight to the sprawling kosher hors d'oeuvre table near the center of the room. Like their male counterparts, the Nevadans wore tuxedos--identical to each other, except that unlike Dick, who wore a black bow tie and a cummerbund of similar color, his boss's were red--contrasted by shiny white shoes.

Along with Dick, Senator Spickler struck up a conversation with three Republican senators. The trio seemed respectful and jovial from the crony's perspective, although from a different political party from his superior. Their good-natured banter focused on the newly elected president, Ronald Reagan. The GOP members collectively predicted that the former California governor would emerge as a fantastic commander-in-chief, while Spickler proclaimed that he disagreed--while all the rest of them erupted in good-natured laughter.

Dick initially enjoyed this lively word play, but all that changed in a heartbeat. Momentarily, Dick felt a light tap on his right shoulder and turned around to see Elijah Horowitz--who remained the Israeli Embassy's executive assistant.

The Jewish state official whispered into his ear, saying: "Hello, Dick ... Hope that you are doing great. ... I was just wondering ... Could you and Senator Spickler please follow me ... We, the Israeli embassy officials that is... We have a tremendous holiday gift for the two of you, which we would like to present in private."

Sensing a need for this to remain a private matter, Dick whispered into Horowitz ear: "Can't you just give the present to us now, whatever it is?"

Horowitz gently nudged Dick away from the group of senators, at a respectable distance and obviously out of earshot.

"Dick, this will only take a few minutes. We have something fantastic for you and Senator Spickler, that each of you would want to receive in private ... Believe me, it'll blow your mind."

Careful to avoid offending these super-powerful hosts, Dick told Horowitz "sounds fun ... Let me see," and then promptly went to the group of senators, where he whispered into his boss's ear.

"Sir, we do not want to piss off these people ... They want to take the two of us to a private room now, and present us personally with a spectacular gift."

"Now? ... Does it have to be now?"

"Senator, I get a sense that they want to make this happen as soon as possible. We need to avoid offending them."

Dick considered their current situation as strange and even somewhat abhorrent, as he and Senator Spickler walked with Horowitz down a long hallway from the party room. Within seconds the embassy's assistant director opened a door for them, before the trio entered a small meeting room filled with Edwardian furniture.

"Welcome!" Israeli Ambassador Amos Berkovich motioned for the Americans to sit in adjoining leather-covered chairs. "Please make yourselves comfortable, gentlemen."

"You have presents?" Senator Spickler lighted a large Cigar as he sat, while Dick sat beside him. "What makes us so special?"

"You'll find out in a moment." Berkovich got in a chair on the opposite side of a coffee table from where Dick and the politician sat. "As our first 'gift,' we just have a slide presentation to show you, along with a simultaneous tape recording ... Elijah, you can turn out the lights and start the show."

All lights in the room simultaneously clicked off, as an image appeared on a large viewing screen beside a wall.

Dick immediately recognized the image as a color slide of himself and the senator, sitting beside each other at a small table. The chief of staff immediately realized that this image must have been taken several years earlier, because his own face in the photo looked void of wrinkles. Also in the image, the Senator's huge stomach seemed massive, a sharp contrast to his current flat waistline. The location captured in the photo seemed vaguely familiar, but he failed to remember specifics.

"Hey, guys?" Ambassador Berkovich momentarily smiled while occasionally sipping his cocktail. "Does this location look familiar to either of you?"

"Sure does." Senator Spickler spoke while blowing out cigar smoke. "That is a VIP waiting room at the airport in Salt Lake City."

Hearing this, Dick suddenly realized that his boss was right.

"An amazing memory you have, senator." Berkovich lighted a pipe, before taking a long initial puff. "Indeed, this is the two of you in that very location, nearly six years ago way back in January of 1975. ... Look how each of you have changed in appearance ... Isn't it strange how people evolve over a short period of time?"

"Hey, but I fail to remember the details." Dick interjected, which he knew was out of character for himself because he normally let the boss do all the talking in meetings. "I fail to recall letting anybody snap our photo in such a private setting ... It's interesting how our memory fades."

"Oh, surveillance, of course." The ambassador sucked on his pipe, emitting a sweet odor that Dick considered much more pleasant than the senator's cigar.

"Surveillance?" The senator put his still-burning smoke into an ashtray. "You mean that you people--you Israelis--have been spying on us?"

"Senator, please refrain from offending us by using such offensive terms... Elijah, go ahead now and start playing the recorded tape."

Dick's heartbeat immediately started accelerating, steadily faster as he and the senator could be clearly heard on the recording. Their voices were captured while discussing the nuclear fallout issue. Among the challenges that they could be heard discussing: an overriding need to fool the gullible public; withholding information that the U.S. government had known all along that the radiation would kill tens of thousand of people in Eastern Nevada and Western Utah; organizing phony public hearings to convince the public otherwise; reviewing top secret federal documents on the projected dangers to the public; and the strategy of using these potentially explosive issues to advance the senator's political career.

As the eight-minute tape progressed, Elijah Horowitz handed Dick and his boss copies of the same deplorable documents that the Nevadans had been discussing.

Even in the room's dim light, illuminated only by reflections from the slide projector's viewing screen, Dick could see Senator Spickler's facial skin color change from its usual snowy white to a crimson red.

"This is outrageous!" The politician bolted to a stand, biting his cigar so hard that front half of the smoke fell to the floor. "Dick, hurry, let's get the hell out of here! ... These creeps are attempting to blackmail us!"

Mortified and emotionally numb, Dick remained seated.

The chief of staff watched as two uniformed and armed guards suddenly appeared. Dressed in military garb, each man took a different side of the senator and pulled him back into the same seat where he had just been.

"Shame on you, Senator." Ambassador Berkovich remained calm, his sober demeanor strangely impressive to Dick despite his current predicament. "How dare you accuse us of something as cheap as mere blackmail ... Please have more respect for us than that ... We would never stoop as low as you do."

Dick decided to stay in his own seat, while watching the senator struggle fruitlessly to escape the grips of the two guards. The crony decided that any attempts to free himself would emerge as equally ineffective. Sure enough, Dick briefly turned around in his seat, only to see that four other guards were behind him as well.

"Look, senator." The ambassador pointed toward the viewing screen. "As the old saying goes, 'The show must go on.'"

The next 10 photographs, shown for about 15 seconds each, featured compelling images that made Dick's stomach begin to churn. The three hors d'oeuvres that he had eaten a short time earlier began to shoot up his esophagus. The only thing that prevented him from barfing was to swallow hard and tighten his throat muscles.

He realized that these were color photographs of a murder scene, the site where Sheriff Jonathan Peters and his deputies had been beaten with baseball bats and buried.

The photos captured the dirt-caked and bloody bodies after being unearthed. Until this moment, while viewing this devilish scene, Dick had never had the opportunity--or desired to--personally see the results of murders that he and his boss had personally ordered.

Adding salt to Dick's sudden new emotional wounds, as the slaying site photos were shown, Elijah Horowitz played a tape recording of his boss chatting with Herbert Blitzstein, a Jewish loanshark and bookmaker who had originally worked for the Chicago mob back in the '50s and '60s. Dick knew that Senator Spickler had close political ties with Blitzstein through the casino industry in Las Vegas, where the former Windy City mobster had moved when serving as a top lieutenant for mafia king Anthony Spilotro.

In the tape recording, Senator Spickler could be heard demanding that Blitzstein "eliminate" the sheriff and his deputies as soon as possible, "and in the process, be sure to make them suffer in the worst ways imaginable." The same audio also captured the voice of Dick, clearly heard demanding that "these idiots need to become horrified, knowing that their ultimate end on this earth will soon arrive. ... Then, as they're finished off, we want them to suffer as much physical pain as humanly possible. ... Each needs to be tortured slowly, their limbs broken one by one--until the final blows to the head. First, make the sheriff witness the first and second murders. This way he will know without any doubt whatsoever what he will soon have coming to him ... If there is a God, I hope that he will send the sheriff straight to hell, for allowing that radio broadcast."

    Upon hearing the recording of his own voice, coupled with viewing the gut-wrenching images of the murder scene, Dick could no longer hold back the foods that he had eaten a short while earlier. The chief of staff, now well into his third decade as a Washington bureaucrat, summarily barfed on floor in front of his chair.

    Momentarily oblivious to the others in this private meeting room deep in the heart of the Georgetown hotel, Dick briefly thought of what it would be like to be escorted into Nevada's gas chamber. Until these moments he had never seriously envisioned getting caught. From the current drawn expression on Senator Spickler's trembling face, Dick sensed that his boss felt the same way.

    Instead of struggling to break free like he had been doing a few minutes earlier, by this point the senator remained motionless--keeping his mouth shut.

    Then Ambassador Amos Berkovich stood and proclaimed: "Gentlemen, I am so glad that each of you has enjoyed the first part of this extraordinary show."

    Four men wearing waiter uniforms appeared. Collectively, they rolled up a thin sheet of clear plastic that had previously been put atop the carpet, in the area in front of the chairs where Dick and Senator Spickler had been seating. These servants' collectively worked to remove the crony's puke with little effort. They sprayed a clear fluid from bottles to instantly remove offensive odors.

Berkovich stepped around the table, closer to the Nevadans. The host slightly adjusted his bow tie.

"Okay, guys." The ambassador quickly winked at each of them. "Before we get right into Act Two, I want each of you to know that we have amassed lots more damning details about your stupendous criminal activities."

For the next 15 minutes, the slide show and accompanying audio recordings covered a litany of criminal activities that had been carried out jointly by Dick and Senator Spickler during the previous five years: photos of them accepting cash bribes totaling more than $100,000 each, in most instances the currency given by representatives of executives from huge pharmaceutical companies; the politician's aggressive and eventually successful push for federal legislation--rules requiring that doctors prescribe manmade drugs rather than harmless--but also while outlawing natural remedies; the passage of laws that gave the Food and Drug Administration the authority to carry out these efforts; the introduction of legislation that indirectly lined the senator's pockets, the passage of a controversial nationwide highway construction bill, in exchange a "sweetheart" land purchase deal that instantly made the senator a multi-millionaire; and revealing photos of orgies held at Spickler's 324-acre ranch just outside Lighthouse, Nevada.

As the presentation ended, Dick glanced to his right and saw the senator grip the arms of his chair. The site made the politician's adviser think of what a condemned Nevada prisoner must look like immediately before cyanide pellets are dopped inside the Silver State's infamous gas chamber.

"Okay, you guys." Senator Spickler spoke in a soft, meek voice that Dick considered almost as if that of a child amid mischievous activity--rather than one of the nation's most powerful politicians. "What on earth do you want from us?"

"We do not want anything from you, actually." Ambassador Berkovich strolled to the side of the viewing screen, which still showed an image of Senator Spickler with a giant pile of bribe money. "We're not nearly as greedy as you two morons."

"For heaven's sake, just tell us why you have produced this ungodly entertainment." Dick could hold back no longer, sensing that he felt just as angry as his superior. "Either cut to the chase, or let us go."

Ambassador Berkovich proclaimed that "we do not want anything whatsoever from you idiots." All that Dick and the senator had to do--first and foremost--he said, was to avoid telling all this to U.S. national security administrators. The Jewish official assured them that his nation had numerous informants within the bowels of the USA's national government. Any leak regarding details of that evening's "show" surely would result in the "untimely and painful deaths of the two of you, in precisely the way that you had slaughtered that sheriff and his deputies. ... I pray that you do not allow this same fate to happen to you."

"Please be specific." Senator Spickler sat at attention. "What precisely do you guys want."

"Oh, nothing special, really. ... Just go about your everyday business as you normally would. You two must remain a solid team, and never split apart. We know that you haven't been getting along with each other lately, but you're going to have to mend fences--so to speak--right away."

"Is that all?" Dick yearned for more specifics.

"Just wait for more detailed instructions from us ... Those directives might take us another five, ten or even 20 years to give to you. ... Be patient ... Know that we are on your side, because now--whether you like this or not--you have become our allies for life. ... To be blunt, we own each of you--but we're going to let you roam free until we need your political services. Any attempt to flee on your part will have dire consequences."

*

Shortly after beginning the third trimester of her

pregnancy, Pamela drove westbound on West Seventh Street in northwest Reno.

Feeling happier than she had ever been in her entire life, Pamela felt grateful that she had officially been listed as "cured." Her employer, Doctor Robbins, had given her the tremendous news nearly a half year earlier in July.

Blood tests and body tissue samples confirmed that her body had continuously remained "cancer-free" for five years since her surgery and chemotherapy regimen way back in 1975. To her, those arduous treatments seemed like almost a century ago.

Still employed as manager of the oncologist's clinic, Pamela's life had been blessed by a whirlwind of transitions and challenges since her 25th birthday celebration at Miguel's Mexican Restaurant in Reno.

Now age 30, she had been married since June 8, 1977, to widely acclaimed Reno lawyer Bradley Clausen. The couple had met for the first time in mid-1976 when the lawyer brought his ailing 83-year-old mother, Marilyn, to the clinic for treatment.

Ten years older than Pamela, Bradley had recently been named an "Outstanding Young Lawyer in the USA" by the American Bar Association. He had earned the distinction of partner in one of Nevada's most prestigious law firms. Hooper, Carter and Clausen had offices in Reno, Las Vegas and at Stateline on the shore of Lake Tahoe.

Bradley's substantial annual income of more than $300,000 gave her the option of quitting her cancer clinic managerial job any time she wanted. Since their marriage in downtown Reno's Trinity Episcopal Church near the banks of the Truckee River through the heart of town, Pamela resisted her husband's frequent requests that she quit her job.

Thanks partly to her own salary of $50,000, a highly respectable sum at the time, Pamela felt independent and responsible for her own well being. More than ever, this office manager felt great loyalty to Doctor Robbins, whom she considered as a "man of great integrity, honor and supreme intelligence.

On this particular day, Saturday, December 6, 1980, Pamela was on the latest phase of a mission that had had taken her much of the past year to achieve.

Due to her innate skill at managing the clinic, coupled with her boss's burgeoning and positive reputation, the business had been steadily surging without letup. A thorough analysis of the firm's data indicated that the operation would outgrow the capacity of its rented facility by 1981 or 1982 at the latest.

Sensing a need to seize this as an "great opportunity" rather than a difficult challenge, Pamela had commenced an in-depth analysis. Her research concluded that even if the clinic's steady growth continued as projected through the 1980s, leasing expenses at any other facility would have chewed up the major chunk of revenues.

Armed with this extensive data, on a Tuesday morning shortly after the previous holiday season, in a one-on-one business meeting with the doctor she had argued that he needed to become the "master of his own domain."

Still single and without a girlfriend as far as Pamela knew, the doctor initially balked at her suggestion. She managed to keep her temper in check and to remain professional when the physician kept insisting that he never would go into any debt whatsoever. As a child born in the waning years of the Great Depression, the oncologist explained, he had learned the value of "penny pinching" and never wasting a penny.

Despite Doctor Robbins' continual objections, Pamela persisted in pressing the issue during each of their regular Tuesday morning meetings for eight consecutive weeks.

Well beforehand, aware that her boss likely would remain reluctant, she decided to filibuster the issue. This strategy had eventually paid off--at least somewhat--when the doctor finally relented, giving Pamela the go-ahead to research the possibility of purchasing an existing structure or even constructing a new clinic facility.

After six months of subsequent and extensive research,

Pamela concluded that buying an existing structure was cost prohibitive; the Reno economy was currently undergoing a significant boom. As a result, the handful of office building owners who entertained the possibility of selling their properties demanded purchase costs that she considered unreasonable and even downright offensive in some instances.

Unwilling herself to cave in to the demands of these potential sellers, and well aware that her boss would feel the same, she worked with real estate agent Hugh Reagan in hunting for reasonably priced undeveloped land.

The inner core of Reno's current boundaries already had been "fully built out," leaving no feasible properties within the city--at least from what Pamela and Reagan had found. Finally, on August 23 of that year, on a whim she suggested to the real estate agent that "we should think out of box--go outside of the city's boundaries. There might be treasure to be found where we least expect such riches."

Sure enough, just one week later on the afternoon of Saturday, August 30, with Reagan's help she found an undeveloped four-acre property near the terminus of West Seventh Street. At the time these were merely sprawling hills covered in sagebrush, near the base of Peavine Peak.

A review of the region's long-term Master Development Plan revealed that a major new thoroughfare or expressway-- called North McCarran Boulevard--was to be built during the next few years. Pamela had chosen an undeveloped four-acre property several hundred yards west of this planned major road.

At an asking price of just $150,000, which she considered a "steal" considering Reno's current real estate market, the land afforded expansive views--high above the entire Truckee Meadows. On this brisk, cool and slightly breezy early December day, Doctor Robbins had agreed to meet her at what then was the extreme western end of Seventh Street--at a site that many locals affectionately called "the Seventh Street pits." On fair-weather days, usually from the spring through late summer, off-road motorcycle enthusiasts frequently rumbled around through the sagebrush--their bikes' tires invariably carving huge ruts in the soil.

Finally at that December morning's destination, she parked at the current end of the street, got out of her new light blue Ford Fiesta and held a mug of fresh warm coffee. Arriving ten minutes before her scheduled 9 o'clock morning rendezvous with Doctor Robbins, she sat alone on the hood and poured herself a large cup.

She seized this opportunity to ponder their overall situation, coupled with the many transformations that her family had undergone since her 1975 illness. Her short-term priority remained to convince Doctor Robbins to purchase the property, which he was scheduled to see for the first time that morning.

After taking a long, deep breath of the cool air, Pamela slowly sipped her coffee while savoring the expansive view of downtown Reno far below from six miles away. This community, aptly named the "Biggest Little City in the World" had become what she considered the best and friendliest home to her since leaving Centralia.

By this point, Pamela rarely thought about the three years during her early 20s in Honolulu, a supposed "paradise" that she considered far less friendly and accommodating than northwest Nevada--despite the Aloha State's reputation a the most glorious tropical wonderland on earth.

Back in early 1976, nearly a half year before Pamela met her current husband Bradley, she had wept profusely non-stop for three days after learning that her first husband Jeffrey had been killed in a military jet crash--into the Pacific Ocean, three miles from the west shore of the Hawaiian island of Maui. Pamela had never once stopped loving or being committed to that man, whom just about everyone except her had condemned--not merely due to the fact that they considered him a typical jerk, but primarily because of the cruel, uncaring and selfish way that the pilot had ignored and divorced Pamela at the height of her illness. She acknowledged that this was her own primary character flaw, that she loved people deeply, fully and openly--often in instances where "common sense" would have motivated most other people in her circumstances to feel otherwise.

The many other challenging transitions in her family also left Pamela feeling devastated, her heart and soul feeling crushed--primarily because of her inability to help them, either financially, emotionally or simply by "being there."

Among the most devastating and tragic outcomes, from her view, was the sudden onset of alcoholism that had ravaged her brother-in-law, Abraham "Honest" Davis. Now unemployed and refusing to hunt for any gainful work, Honest had been jailed at least 10 times in recent years for public drunkenness--particularly shocking to her senses because he never drank alcohol until after the death's of his wife Polly and their daughter, Peggy. Matters worsened after five separate check-ins to rehabilitation facilities failed to reverse Honest's downward course. The last definitive details that Pamela had heard about the former plumber confirmed that he had become homeless--his once-famous physical and mental strength by then in tatters. His "Honest Pirate Plumbing" vehicle, the former milk truck, had long since been found abandoned beside U.S. Highway 395, exactly 17 miles north of Reno near the California border.

As far as Pamela was concerned long-time Davis family friends Dorothy and Bill McCready were truly "saints on earth." Living on their meager retirement incomes, the couple had sold their tiny Centralia home, before using the proceeds to buy a modest Reno house on Yori Avenue, a few blocks from Vaughn Junior High School.

Although the McCreadys had never formally adopted the Davis children--Tommy, now 10 and Penelope, aged 7--the couple had essentially embraced the children as their own. The children were students in the fifth and second grades at Veterans Memorial Elementary School on Vassar Street, five blocks from their new residence. At last report, from what Pamela had heard the children had not seen their father in at least 15 months. Despite the

McCreadys admirable efforts to correct the problem, both children had been receiving poor or mediocre grades in school; each child refused to participate in extra-curricular activities.

The last time Pamela had seen the children and the McCreadys, during the Thanksgiving holiday a few weeks before her scheduled rendezvous with Doctor Robbins at the proposed new clinic site, she learned that Tommy rarely spoke. The boy often locked himself in his room, refused to come out for hours on end, and had recently started swearing at his caregivers. On several occasions during the previous few years Pamela had offered to spend time with the children, wanting to take them to the movies, to parks for recreation or to a variety of other public functions.

Unlike her brother, who rarely spoke with anyone, Penelope spent almost all of her free time in the living room of the McCready home. Usually wearing fluffy dresses, the girl invariably had non-stop conversations while all alone with her five favorite Barbie Dolls. Sadly, Dorothy privately admitted to Pamela, this child had her only in-depth conversations with the dolls--while generally ignoring the elderly couple.

While Pamela and Dorothy were alone together one day in the kitchen of the McCready home, the retired county clerk whispered to her that "we could not possibly get by, without the financial help from your boss. ... I bet you don't know this, honey, but Doctor Robbins has been sending us monthly checks for $250 ... At first, we tried to refuse these gifts .... I'm sure you can understand; we have always been self-supporting people. We have pride, you know ... But that's not saying in any way whatsoever that we do not appreciate his kindness ... Believe me, we need every cent that he gives us ... Our world would be a blessed place, if there were far more people like him ... I think we have all known that for quite some time."

"I agree 1,000 percent," Pamela had responded, before suddenly changing the subject when Bill McCready ambled into the kitchen amid the Thanksgiving celebration.

Now, in early December while still perched atop the hood

of car and awaiting Doctor Robbins, Pamela also pondered the plight of her other living sister--Paula.

When a small child herself, Pamela had paid little attention to her oldest sibling, whom she felt never deserved the ample praise from their parents. Yet in recent years the cancer clinic manager's admiration and love for Paula had sharply spiraled upward.

Back in 1978, three years after Pamela's illness her oldest sister's ex-husband Hank had been pummeled to death by three other inmates in the High Desert Penitentiary, 27 miles off U.S. Highway 95 northwest of Las Vegas. Paula grieved the loss, while remaining faithful and loyal to her current husband, Coyote Pete-- who remained imprisoned at the Federal Correctional Institution in Tucson, Arizona.

The former radio announcer and Paula, who by now had become a card dealer at the famed Harold's Club casino, was reunited with her husband following his release from prison in 1979. A federal appeals court had ruled that authorities should drop Coyote's conviction, due to evidence proving that he never conspired with his adult son, Sean Blair, in smuggling 138 truckloads of marijuana from Mexico to the United States.

Thanks to Paula's meager income, she now was able to support them both, living in a tiny three-bedroom home on Broadway Boulevard near South Wells Avenue in Reno. Working in conjunction with Mexican authorities, the U.S. Government, way back in 1975, had obliterated Coyote's clandestine and rebellious radio station just south of the border in Nogales. Additionally, American officials had seized and eventually razed to the ground the isolated, small home surrounded by saguaro-- which Paula had considered adorable.

Proclaiming his refusal "give up hope," Coyote now spent all of his waking time trying to raise funds to launch a legal and licensed Reno-based "rebel-talk radio" station. With equal fervor, Coyote also amassed an organization dedicated to buying, creating and maintaining a ranch fully dedicated to wild horses--which he urged people to "save from the corrupt and devilish federal government, the Bureau of Land Management--which regularly rounds up these glorious animals, for use as dog meat."

Fully cognizant of these various developments, Pamela felt particularly proud of the many advances at Doctor Robbins' cancer care clinic. Now at age 62, Anthony Dunn--whom the physician still called "General"--amazingly seemed to be getting younger as the years passed, at least from Pamela's perspective. Anthony still worked as the clinic's receptionist, always doing his best to help make each of the many cancer patients feel more at ease--and often alleviating their fears, at least somewhat.

To Pamela's delight, the World War II veteran now had a girlfriend, Elizabeth Russell, a distant cousin of the well-known buxom 1940s and 1950s movie star Jane Russell. Like her famous relative, Elizabeth had large, perfectly formed breasts. Yet the physical similarities seemed to end with the 38-D cup size, at least in Pamela's opinion.

Elizabeth's natural blonde hair, coupled with the fact that she towered 3 inches taller than Jane, surely made her even more attractive to men--or at least that's what Pamela thought. The clinic manager sensed that this lesser-known relative must have magnetized just about every red-blooded American guy lucky enough to lay eyes on her.

Pamela believed that with Elizabeth's stunning looks, youthful demeanor, keen intelligence and unpredictable behavior, she easily could have picked just about any eligible gentleman that she wanted. Yet for "some strange reason," which Pamela could never quite figure out, Elizabeth had become magnetized and fully engrossed with the low-paid Anthony Dunn--who occasionally walked with a crutch. His "bum knee" still flared up on occasion, corrected only by occasional cortisone shots administered by Doctor Robbins.

To hear Anthony tell the story, he had first met Elizabeth when visiting an old, historic dude ranch in Washoe Valley, 20 miles south of Reno. The 57-acre spread on Franktown Road, nestled against the eastern edge of the Sierra range, had been a favorite of women who traveled to Northwest Nevada from the 1930s through the early 1960s to get what most people called "a quickie Reno divorce." Boasting the nation's most liberal divorce laws at the time, the Silver State required only that people filing court documents seeking the end of their marriages fulfill a residency requirement of only six weeks.

Elizabeth's famed Dancing Bull Ranch hosted some of the world's most famous celebrities of that era. They included boxer Jack Dempsey, financier Cornelius Vanderbilt Jr., and film star Mary Pickford and Rita Hayworth. The continual influx of the rich and famous eager for a divorce had screeched to a halt in the early 1960s, when many other states nationwide finally "caught on" and loosened their regulations on this process.

In Pamela's opinion, Elizabeth's only serious "flaws"--if they could be called that--were her habit of regularly commenting on her own breast size. The former Hawaiian considered such talk crass, exceptionally gross and in poor taste. The ranch owner, who hailed from Bozeman, Montana, also had what Pamela considered a strange and "spooky" penchant for eating huge sausages--at least in some form--with just about every meal.

Within three months after Anthony first met Elizabeth, he moved from his ant-sized South Reno apartment to her sprawling ranch-style home. According to the receptionist, his new "squeeze" had insisted to him that "you should just quit your stinking job ... Honey, spend all of your time with me."

To his credit, as far as Pamela was concerned, Anthony had balked at the suggestion; he had revealed to the clinic manager late on a Friday after closing time that "quitting is impossible for me, because I have a strong work ethic. And, as quirky as this might sound, it's true--I remain extremely loyal to my boss, whom I consider as if a son."

During the few years since Anthony moved into Elizabeth's home, Pamela had become increasingly mystified--curious as to exactly why and how the dude ranch owner had quickly become magnetized by the aging World War II veteran.

As far as Pamela could tell, Anthony looked like a typical "regular guy," with nothing particularly special at all about his appearance. At 5 feet 7 inches tall, he had a receding hairline, wore thick horn-rimmed glasses seemingly big enough to use as fly swatters, and had a paunch over the waistline that--from Pamela's view--signaled to the world that his apparent days that he might have enjoyed as a virulent lover had long since passed.

Even so, in an effort to keep their office banter at a jovial and light-hearted level, during the past year Pamela had always greeted Anthony in the office setting by asking in a cheery tone: "Anthony, how is your special Dancing Bull doing today?" This double-en tendre always lightened the mood, partly because the receptionist almost always had a different answer to these inquiries. Pamela's favorites by far had been along the lines of "Oh, the bull has been rocking quite a bit lately," or "The bull cannot possibly get enough of his dancing routine," and even "The bull might be naughty, but you'll never know for sure, will you?"

Never in a romantic sense, of course, but Pamela truly loved, cherished and appreciated all of her clinic co-workers--particularly Anthony. During her first five years at the clinic, she only had to fire one person, Emerine Ricardo, a bossy and loud-mouthed registered cancer care nurse who refused to listen to suggestions and always behaved in a repulsive manner that Pamela considered "that of a bitchy, unlovable know-it-all."

Most of all Pamela admired, appreciated and respected her boss, Doctor Robbins. When alone together on rare occasions, without making fun of their superior, Anthony and Pamela joked about how the physician's jittery behavior grated on their nerves. The oncologist invariably tapped pencils against his desktop, used his hands to flick his ears, and shook his legs up and down rapid-fire while sitting. Secretly together, Anthony and Pamela had blamed the doctor's irritating habit on some sort of strange and mystifying nervous condition, or perhaps even pent-up and unreleased sexual tension.

As far as either of them knew, their boss had never dated any women since his arrival in Reno more than six years earlier. These two employees, while acknowledging their shared mutual admiration for the doctor, both admitted that for him to ignore female companionship was "against everything that Mother Nature has intended."

An increasingly wealthy, handsome and charismatic man of Doctor Robbin's superior caliber and positive reputation could easily lure almost any eligible woman that he wanted--or at least that's what Anthony and Pamela occasionally told each other. More than merely a joking matter, this lack of an apparent loving, sexual relationship for the doctor worried each of them greatly--to the point that they wondered whether a lack of female companionship could adversely impact his health.

Among the many questions in this regard that these co-workers had, but never dared to ask their employer, were: was the physician so lonely, perhaps still grieving the tragic loss of his wife in a plane crash, that he could not possibly motivate himself to spend time with a woman; did the fact that a huge percentage of his patients died, make him want to avoid close relationships--always deep-down fearing a potential loss; had the non-stop deaths of his patients--several passing away on a weekly basis--somehow numbed or blocked his ability to get emotionally close to anyone; had the many autopsies that he performed on his buddies and fellow soldiers in Vietnam caused him to forget how to form close bonds with other people; and, more likely--they supposed--had the doctor's own childhood, having to essentially raise his own mother, somehow forced him to "lose out" on learning the vital and essential natural processes of forming intimate relations during his teens with youngsters of his own age?

Lacking any definitive specifics, the pair agreed that broaching the subject with Doctor Robbins would seem inappropriate and definitely "out of bounds." Although Anthony thought of himself as perhaps the closest living person in the whole world to the physician, even with his friendship with this man, he sensed that pushing the topic would seem overly intrusive and perhaps even an attempt to delve into a subject that is "none of my business, or anyone else's business for that matter."

Still proclaiming that he considered himself the best of pals with the doctor, Anthony told Pamela that he and their boss went out to dinner on occasion--perhaps once every month or so. Most of the time, the buddies shared war stories, and tales of their adventures with the opposite sex as young and single men. They often exchanged lively tales about their numerous dalliances while in their late teens and early 20s, details that confirmed to Anthony and Pamela that at least at one time during his life their boss had craved and enjoyed female companionship.

By the early summer of 1980, nearly six months before that fateful December morning when Pamela awaited Doctor Robbins at the top of West Seventh Street, the receptionist and the office manager mutually agreed that they would work together to try to "set the doctor up with a suitable and worthy woman."

Twenty-Two

From her position on the hood of her Ford Fiesta at the top of West Seventh Street, Pamela finally spotted Doctor Robbins' blue Willy's Jeep CJ approaching from a half mile away. Even at that distance, the clinic manager could tell that her boss was traveling with someone in the front passenger seat.

Within a few moments as the vehicle continued uphill, Pamela realized that this was the flowing, long and curly strawberry blonde hair of a woman.

"Good morning, Pamela!" the physician hollered to her in a cheery voice, stopped in the middle of the road beside her parked car. "We're ready to do some exploring."

The sight of this eye-catching woman filled Pamela with excitement, her soul exhilarated by this revelation that the physician was with a stunningly beautiful lady.

Left speechless at this sight and unable to think of anything appropriate to say, Pamela finally realized that she had intended to offer the doctor coffee upon his arrival.

Before another word was spoken, Pamela feasted her eyes upon this mystery gal. For many years the clinic manager had been accustomed to being by far the most beautiful woman in just about any situation.

Yet right away she sensed that this other lady was top-class. To Pamela, the woman's face, complexion and make-up appeared phenomenal--as if she were a cover girl model or a pinup gal for a high-end women's fashion magazine. Far more compelling than these attributes, however, at least from Pamela's view, was this woman's welcoming smile and her reflective eyes.

Without even giving this any thought whatsoever, before

even learning this lady's name Pamela's female intuition gave her a sense that she and this other person already knew each other. The woman wore light tan gloves, similarly colored tight-fitting pants, the type of fur coat that easily made many other women envious, and fashionable boots that looked cozy and warm enough to wear at the North Pole.

"Pamela, this is my friend Marie Rossi?" With his Jeep engine still running, turning up the volume of that week's Number One song on the Billboard Magazine Music charts, "Lady," a Liberty Records album featuring popular crooner Kenny Rogers.

Before answering, the thought kept racing through Pamela's mind--could this actually be true, that the doctor finally has a real-live girlfriend? If this is true, what in the world has taken him so long? Where did they meet? Are they in love, or is this situation merely a passing fancy--a fling?

Mesmerized by these possibilities, Pamela noticed that Marie had her gloved left hand cozily tucked through his right arm.

Even more exhilarating to Pamela, she finally realized that the doctor was smiling in a magical way that she had never seen from him before. As usual and par for the course, from this manager's view the physician was dressed perfect for the occasion--a light brown leather coat, black gloves, tattered and well-worn blue jeans, the type of boots that only "real" rodeo guys use, a cowboy hat that impressed Pamela as being authentic enough to use in an old-West movie, and something else that she had never seen on her boss before--dark sunglasses that hid his eyes from view.

"I'm sorry." Pamela fumbled with her Thermos, still at a loss for words. "I couldn't hear ... What was that you said, doctor?"

"This is Marie Rossi."

Still perplexed and increasingly invigorated by this unexpected revelation, Pamela walked up to the Jeep and smiled as broadly as she could: "So pleased to meet you."

When she heard for the first time, Marie's soft--yet low and husky--Italian accent added to the sense of mystery that continued to swell in Pamela's mind, body and soul.

"Pamela, the feeling is mutual ... I have a hunch that we are going to become great friends very soon, although I'm afraid you might find that I'm difficult to get to know."

Taking long, deep and slow breaths in an effort to calm down, Pamela finally remembered to offer each of them some coffee.

"No thank you." Marie adjusted the buttons of her fur coat. "We just enjoyed a long, leisurely three-hour breakfast in bed together ... We had enough to drink, and ..."

"Marie!" The doctor used what Pamela considered a stern voice, although his tone was far too congenial to be considered a yell. The clinic manager took this as being her boss's way of striving to maintain privacy, specifically his apparent desire to prevent anyone from knowing that he and this attractive woman were lovers. "I mean, yes--thank you, Pamela, but we just had a good breakfast with plenty of beverages."

Pamela then told them that the three of them had the option of hiking about a half mile uphill to the proposed clinic site--or that perhaps they could ride up there in the doctor's four-wheel drive.

"Hop in!" The doctor kept moving the stick-shift, his fingers flipping atop the wooden knob. Upon seeing this, Pamela sensed that in all likelihood by this point Marie realized or had witnessed the physician's propensity to jiggle his fingers, toes and limbs. Only an imbecile would fail to notice.

"Doctor, I'm afraid there is only one passenger seat." Pamela decided to get right to the point, while also striving to sound accommodating--eager to get into the Jeep.

"Oh, there is plenty of room." The physician continued fiddling with the stick shift knob. "I am confident that you fine ladies can figure this out somehow."

Marie lifted her own left leg, which she positioned on the

doctor's side of the stick shift, while her right leg remained on the right side of the device. While doing this, she simultaneously slid closer to him--until only the right side of her own rump remained on the passenger seat. This, in turn, left a space for Pamela to sit.

"I see that you're pregnant," Marie said, patting the available portion of the seat. "Just entering your final trimester? ... It looks to me like you will have plenty of room."

Sure enough, Pamela easily eased into that position, finding herself nuzzled up to the right side of this woman whom she had just met. The mere touch of Marie's fluffy fur coat made her feel unexpected warmth.

"Doctor, I can imagine that the ride will be just a bit rough." Pamela pointed straight, past the spot where the pavement ended about 25 yards ahead of them. "My guess is that we'll be rocking and rolling a little bit, from side to side ... If that's okay with you two, my guess is that we'll get there just fine."

"Let's go for it." Doctor Robbins shifted to first gear, and then promptly to second. "I'm game, if you two are?"

Momentarily, they drove deeper into the sagebrush-covered wilderness. The doctor steered along smoothe white, snowy ruts that had been carved out earlier by other off-road vehicles. The rocking motions back and forth failed to bother Pamela, who sensed that this rough terrain could do no harm to the baby in her womb. She and her husband, Bradley, had already decided to name the child Pollyanna, in honor of Pamela's late sister.

Increasingly excited about showing Doctor Robbins the undeveloped property, Pamela pointed straight, toward the snowy tracks that continued west. She marveled at the expansive skyline. On this cool and invigorating, perfect from her perspective except for the slight but bothersome breeze.

The extreme eastern edge of the great Sierra range could be seen about seven miles to the west. Wisps of clouds from remnants of the overnight storm seemed to her as if a heavenly mist, accenting the snow-covered mountains. The sharp contrast between the terrain everywhere and the blue sky helped make her feel increasingly invigorated, optimistic that hopefully her boss would like and want to purchase the site that she had recently chosen.

"In a strange way, this reminds me of the Alps--at least a bit." Marie snuggled closer to Doctor Robbins as he continued to drive. "Nothing could be better than the great outdoors, far from the everyday madness of civilization."

Pamela continued pointing forward in giving her boss driving directions, while she also commented: "I could not possibly agree with you more, Marie, although millions of people worldwide probably would disagree with us. The mere idea of leaving city life terrifies them, perhaps because solitude such as this forces--or at least enables--us to look deep into our own souls."

The doctor accelerated, thereby increasing the force of their bumpy ride.

Pamela urged him to slow down. She emphasized the need to prepare to turn left off the highly traveled track that they were on. The physician soon turned in the direction that she had suggested. After another three-eights of a mile, Pamela asked him to stop. The three of them hopped from the Jeep. Pamela immediately regretted having forgotten her own thick snow boots. Slushy mud caked onto her normally comfortable shoes, which now seemed to her as if out of place and inappropriate.

Striving to appear professional, rather than a common klutz who fails to plan properly for challenging situations, Pamela marched up a slight incline as the doctor and his lady-friend followed her from close behind.

The clinic manager marched to the middle of 27 wood stakes that previously had been pounded into the ground, each topped off by a red ribbon along the edges of the site. While in the middle of the marked-off property, Pamela gazed toward downtown Reno--clearly visible about 10 miles away and at an elevation averaging about 1,000 feet below where they stood.

"Wow!" Marie said, curling her left arm around Doctor

Robbins' right, as they stood facing the city.

This mysterious woman seemed to purr this from Pamela's perspective.

Pamela explained that they were now on the possible future cancer clinic site, adjacent to a planned street that would be called Sierra Highlands Drive. One mile further to the west of where they were would eventually become the future McQueen High School, at the time the only building under construction in this area. Wanting to give them all the basic details fast, rather than wasting time, she described this untamed region's master plan.

Within 10 years, she said, by 1980 at least 8,000 new homes would surround this entire region. Massive shopping centers would be immediately to the east and south of their current location. The asking price for this undeveloped site was $265,000, a tremendous sum at the time.

"Holy moley!" Doctor Robbins raised his left hand straight up, his right still embracing Marie's arm. Pamela felt thankful that his voice sounded to her as if somewhat positive, without any hint of anger or frustration. "A price like that could be a game-changer."

Pamela responded by proclaiming that they needed to plan for a super-busy future. The doctor's daily patient totals had steadily climbed in recent years. A small percentage of those people were from eastern Nevada's alleged nuclear fallout zone, yet the numbers of those patients kept increasing as well. The Silver State's northwest population was projected to surge considerably during the subsequent 20 or 30 years. Although a few other oncologists had started practicing in this region during the previous few years, Doctor Robbins' clinic still remained the most popular by far among new cancer patients.

"That's true, doctor, as you probably know." Pamela motioned toward the city far below them. "But as you are well aware, location and function are the key to the continued growth and success of your business. ... Even cancer patients want convenience, plus ultra-modern treatment facilities that enable them to feel as comfortable as possible."

Striving to filibuster in order to prevent her boss from seizing any opportunity to interject, Pamela said that this site was by far her preferred and most recommended location. As a stop-gap measure, the clinic manager also told the physician and the Italian woman that she had identified a "second choice," a 3-acre site nearly six miles south of Reno. Also on undeveloped sagebrush-covered land, that less-preferred location was adjacent to a planned future street tentatively designated as Hammill Lane.

"To me, it's all about price--more than just convenience." Doctor Robbins cradled his right arm around Marie's shoulders; the Italian woman reciprocated by moving her left arm around his waist.

When Pamela responded that the south Reno asking price was $200,000, at least $65,000 less than the site where they now stood, he proclaimed: "Now we're talking!"

Pushed to the limit, and sensing a need to argue in favor of her preferred site as much as possible, Pamela immediately started telling him about her thorough "cost-benefit analysis." She insisted that in the long term, spending more now--early on in the process for this high-ground location--would reap the greatest financial rewards by far. She pleaded for him to understand, and to give the matter far more serious thought.

Right away, a full-scale argument erupted that Pamela had failed to anticipate.

Without yelling or acting like a baby, at least from Pamela's perspective, the doctor proclaimed that throughout life he had learned the value of a dollar. He had discovered first-hand that overspending can lead to financial ruin.

"But far more than that, Pamela, this is the time for me to tell you. ... As you know, the welfare of my patients always has been--and always will--remain at the forefront of virtually everything that I do on a professional basis. ... Please keep that in mind, as I tell you a secret that only a handful of people know about."

"A secret?" Pamela suddenly realized that she still held the Thermos, which she had intended to leave in the vehicle. She accidentally dropped the container; it landed with a thud at her feet--splashing slush across Marie's tight tan pants. "Oh, I am so sorry ... I can..."

Pamela immediately bent down, picked up the container and started wiping Marie's legs with her muddy gloves. This only served to worsen the mess on the Italian woman's pants.

"Normally, I would yell at a thing like this." Marie smiled, standing at attention without moving. "But for you, everything is OK ... I admire any lady who shows plenty of spunk. That's the kind of woman that I am, and I always will be."

"Marie, whose side are you on, honey." Doctor Robbins kept his right arm around her shoulders.

"I'm on the side of logic." Marie summarily planted a quick kiss on the physician's right cheek. The site of the Italian woman's hot-pink lipstick embossed on her employer's face made Pamela want to blush--but only for a moment.

"Doctor?" The clinic manager tried to focus on the issue at hand. "What secret were you about to tell me? ... As the business leader of your enterprise, it's critical for me to always have the most pertinent information."

"Okay." The doctor moved his arm from around Marie, and took a few steps away from the two women. "But this is highly sensitive information ... You are not to tell anyone, not a single soul ... Not even the General, whom you know that I admire."

"Sir, I'm all ears." Pamela meant what she said. "I swear that I will never tell."

"Me too!" Marie quickly stepped to the doctor's side, and summarily planted another kiss on his cheek--this time on the opposite side from the original.

"There have been serious threats on my life ... I'm a marked man."

This statement at first numbed Pamela's mind. Precisely what this all might mean initially seemed foreign to her psyche.

The seriousness of the matter became far more clear to her upon hearing his subsequent statement, issued loud and clear.

"I'm supposed to expect a bullet between my eyes, within any day now."

"A bullet? ... Between the eyes?" Pamela immediately went into emotional overdrive, although striving to remain clear-minded. "Who would want to do that?"

Marie immediately hugged him tight, while she proclaimed: "Baby, why didn't you tell me about this? ... What on earth is..."

"This is super-serious." Doctor Robbins gazed toward downtown Reno far below, taking off his sunglasses before he continued speaking. "In fact, if the truth be told--this has literally become a federal case. ... Pamela, due to the extreme danger, you have a right to know these details ... And Marie, I need to level with you here and now as well ... That is why I had decided to tell each of you together, at this time--and in this isolated place--far away from prying eyes and spying ears."

The doctor explained that throughout the previous month, he had been getting persistent phone calls and written messages-- to just about anywhere he went at any given moment.

Each threat specified that Doctor Robbins would die a horrible death before the beginning of the new year--1981--unless he closed his practice and retired.

"The male voice sounds as creepy as you could possibly imagine. The guy keeps speaking in a whisper. He only talks for a sentence or two. ... His specific underlying motives remain unclear to me, and to the FBI as well ... Yes, the feds have entered this investigation ... After conducting a thorough personality analysis on the guy, the bureau's agents have surmised that the guy is most likely not a current or former patient of mine, nor--they say--is he related to any such people. ... This has been going on straight, daily without letup for about three solid months. ... On the negative side, investigators have been unable to trace the source of the phone calls. Today's limited technology is not sophisticated enough for officials to track down the caller; the guy always hangs up fast and worsening matters he somehow--mysteriously--knows the phone numbers of where I am at just about any given time. ... The case became a federal crime when this jerk called and started leaving notes at the Nevada Army National Guard headquarters, where I still serve at least one weekend per month."

"Good God in heaven." Pamela blurted, making no attempt to cover up her fright and concern, her eyes filled with tears. "Why haven't you told me until now?"

The doctor then made an expression that Pamela considered a signal of brave, manly and unwavering strength. Tears flowed down Marie's cheeks; the Italian woman refrained from making a sound--not even a whimper--while hugging her man.

"I'm not afraid, so much for myself--as I am for my staff and my patients, and for the people that I love." Doctor Robbins put his sunglasses back on, his voice sounding increasingly confident to Pamela. "So, no, we do not need to argue about the location of the new clinic. This is not something that we need to get into a war with each other about ... My goal for the long-term, is to bring happiness to you, Pamela, and to your entire family, and to you Marie, and to all of my patients--extending life, and also the quality of life, for people that I treat and for others that I deeply care about."

"Doctor, you know that I'm with you--and I support you--every step of the way." Pamela spoke from the heart. "There is always a solution for..."

"Look!" Marie interrupted, hollering loud. She pointed to the north, toward the snowy tracks that they had recently followed to reach this location. "Is that someone looking at us through binoculars? ... Could that be a sniper!"

Pamela instantly looked in that direction, and she immediately noticed a person who appeared to be standing atop a vehicle--and looking toward the three of them.

"Quick! Ladies!" Doctor Robbins quickly grabbed Pamela

and Marie by their arms, before he hustled the women to the south side of his Jeep--where the three of them hunkered down. The physician summarily pulled handguns from each of his coat pockets, holding one firearm in each of his hands. "We need to take decisive action right away. Believe me, I'm going to do whatever it takes--whatever necessary to save each of you."

Twenty-Three

Eager to make her first direct contact with an Israeli official in three years, agent Shira Levy told her secretary at the Food and Drug Administration: "Diana, I'm feeling ill today ... I'm going straight home to rest. Cancel all my appointments, and tell all callers that I will get back with them tomorrow morning."

Right on schedule on Monday, July 8, 1985, this marked the first sick day that this Mossad agent had taken at the FDA so far in her ten-year tenure at the agency.

Shira's life had evolved far differently than she had planned. Just a decade earlier while on the run from the attempt to assassinate her in Salt Lake City. Back then, she had envisioned spending her entire adult life working for the Israeli spy agency, intermittently moving to new assignments at different locations.

Instead, both she and her superiors within the Israeli government had mutually decided that her post within the U.S. drug regulation agency was far too valuable to leave.

As lead administrator for a critical American government division that considers and decides whether to approve painkillers, she had unfettered access to highly sensitive information on why, how and when officials granted such approvals.

With increased intensity, her homeland maintained at least 100 spies at essential locations across the United States. While some observers might call this "ludicrous," the mere notion that Israel would spy on its closest and strongest ally, Shira knew otherwise.

Judging from the latest insider accounts that Shira had obtained, she knew that at least 150 U.S. government operatives employed by the CIA were embedded deep with Israel's culture and its own leadership infrastructure.

In doing so, she realized, both nations were merely

embracing the 1,000-year-old "The Art of War," the famed Chinese treatise on military strategy. One of its most famous dictates had been: "Keep your friends close, but your enemies closer."

Now in her early 30s and engaged to be married to a non-Jew, a U.S. Defense Department bureaucrat named Ken Miller, Shira had stunned and surprised herself by falling deeply in love with an American--let alone a guy from a different religion.

Thinking of herself as still blessed with what she considered a stunning and magnetic appearance, she realized that this mutual spying between the USA and Israel was done as if via an "unspoken, mutual agreement." Each nation trusted the other, but only somewhat. Both countries felt an essential need to "remain on their toes," just in case the other might venture to cheat. An urgent need amid nuclear proliferation made survival a top priority for each nation. As far as Shira knew, the Americans worried that Israel's nuclear armaments might become compromised, while the Israelis became increasingly concerned about steadily growing corruption deep within the bowels of the U.S. government.

Two weeks before this particular day, in the early summer of 1985, Shira received a coded message requesting her to attend a vital in-person, one-on-one session with a top official representing her homeland. That scheduled meeting was to be outside in broad daylight at precisely 10:48 in the morning at the Jefferson Memorial.

After leaving the Food and Drug Administration's headquarters in Silver Spring, Maryland, in her super-charged, gold-colored 1985 Chevrolet IROC-Z, from the Food and Drug Administration's Silver Spring, Maryland, headquarters, she listened to an increasingly popular tune by Duran Duran--"A View to a Kill." This theme song, made famous largely due to that week's current James Bond spy movie, made her break out in laughter while behind the wheel amid the 37-minute drive.

Spy novels and films were filled with sexy, spectacular

looking people who performed phenomenal fetes that would boggle the minds and bodies of mere humans. By contrast, Shira knew from tedious, first-hand experience during the past 13 years that such clandestine information gathering often takes a long time--with little fanfare.

Another crazy theme about those films involved going to bed with other people, seemingly on a whim--without any consideration whatsoever regarding possible consequences. If that was the case in so-called "real life"--and Shira knew otherwise--she would have had intimate physical relations with many men. Instead, to this point she had bedded down with only one fellow, her fiance--and achieving that significant milestone had taken him two years of continual coaxing and cajoling.

Despite her many years living in the Washington, D.C., area, Shira had never taken the time and energy to visit the Jefferson Memorial. Nonetheless, since early childhood she had adored the iconic third president, author of the Declaration of Independence, first governor of the Commonwealth of Virginia, and as a "founding father" of the USA, an original member of the Continental Congress in the late 1700s.

"That guy would be spinning in his grave at this very moment, if he knew how corrupt and evil the Untied States Congress and its government has become," Shira thought as another recent hit song came on her car radio, "Don't You Forget About Me," by the musical group Simple Minds. Sadly, upon hearing this, she thought that the vast majority of Americans had either forgotten or ignored the essential values upon which their nation was founded--namely honesty, freedom and independence.

So far during her 10-year stint at the FDA, Shira had learned first-hand that political payoffs, back-slapping and a tight-knit good-old-boy system favored giant, multi-billion-dollar pharmaceutical companies.

Her consistent reports to Mossad had confirmed the worst attributes of this demented and corrupt political process. Among those that made Shira angry, despite her training to remain calm and unemotional amid heated conflicts: bureaucrats appointed officials to the agency who had close ties to the large drug companies; the "buddy" system enabled the drug makers to get approval for their most dangerous, addictive and expensive products; partly at the urging of this agency, health care experts with close ties to the companies--nicknamed Big Pharma--got lucrative appointments to professorships at every major medical school in the United States; students studying to become doctors were taught that prescribing these dangerous, hard-to-kick substances "are the only way to go;" in conjunction with various medical associations, the FDA rubber-stamped "required protocol" mandating that doctors prescribe dangerous or even deadly drugs in order to treat specific symptoms; and in most instances, the prescribed pharmaceuticals failed to treat, to lessen or to eliminate the underlying physical conditions that caused specific illnesses or adverse health conditions.

Worsening matters multi-fold and adversely impacting all of American society, Shira's many reports to Mossad detailed how the American medical community had become corrupt and inefficient as well. Among some of what she considered her "most shocking" conclusions within the health care sector: an unknown number of Americans, perhaps hundreds of thousands or even millions of people, became addicted to drugs that had been prescribed by their doctors; many of these people died from overdoses, often before even becoming hooked; the "legal, sanctioned and licensed" medical industry became--by far-- the Biggest and Most Powerful Drug Cartel in the World; with the blessing of the federal government, made possible by huge political campaign contributions to senators and congressmen, the FDA "turned a blind eye" away from these issues; and her reports to Mossad often concluded that "this overall situation is likely to become progressively worse in future decades."

From her view, as if these many dangers and political pitfalls were not enough to worry about--adding insult to injury-- the mainstream American news media virtually ignored the issue.

All along, her carefully researched reports said, these "secrets"-- the clandestine and corrupt methods used in managing the FDA-- had remained secretive within the halls and offices of the agency. People unlucky enough to break this so-called "unwritten Code of Honor" invariably found themselves fired, while immediately black-balled from the entire professional medical industry-- ranging from medical schools and hospitals, to drug companies and even firms that developed new pharmaceuticals.

As a result, Shira had written to Mossad in an in-depth report on August 14, 1983, concluding that: "The U.S. Food and Drug organization has quietly and efficiently--with the blessing of top elected officials--blossomed into the largest legalized Mob Organization that the world has ever known. Along with politicians, the nation's doctors, hospital companies and drug firms are lining their pockets with piles of cash--while the general public suffers greatly as a result. Without any question whatsoever, if this evil trend continues as expected, within several decades Congress likely will enact a unified national health care system. When that happens, in all probability within 30 years from now, the corruption and the damage to the public will have become irreversible. Due to the ongoing "shady, back-room deals," which have become unstoppable, the entire medical industry will begin to disintegrate from its center core. Frustrated consumers essentially will find themselves on a destructive treadmill, unable to find reliable doctors. By then, all physicians will be trained to essentially dish out these poisonous drugs in almost every instance."

Adding insult to injury, from Shira's view, the FDA's unwritten and clandestine mission remained to degrade and obliterate the Homeopathic medical industry. Such health care professionals, at the time a rarity within the United States, posed a considerable threat to the "mainstream" or allopathic medical profession. From the viewpoint of the agency's bureaucrats, Homeopaths "must be stopped at any and all costs." The primary reason stemmed from the fact that Homeopaths administer inexpensive, effective and natural remedies such as plants and herbs. Studies cited by these health care professionals consistently proved that in most instances such inexpensive cures were "far more effective" than Big Pharma products--without causing addictions or overdoses.

From the viewpoint of the FDA's administrators, the essential problem here stemmed from the fact that under national and international law, no company or government can patent or "hold the rights to" any plant that grows in nature.

As a result, Shira's reports said, the huge and corrupt drug companies could not seize or create a monopoly on the types of natural, harmless cures that Homeopaths administered and prescribed. Thus, determined to block the inexpensive natural substances from becoming popular among the general public, the FDA launched propaganda campaigns that included: bogus reports concluding that natural vitamins never help humans--while actually harming people; in-depth yet "phony" research, always concluding that scientists had been "unable to find any conclusive evidence" that specific types of natural remedies administered by Homeopaths were effective; and so-called "independent scientific reports" that universally concluded that each type of natural remedy is "actually harmful to the human body."

In the meantime, increasingly determined to squash the potential competition facing "mainstream" doctors, the FDA also started distributing--or accepting--documents and reports that portrayed Homeopaths as "quacks." Sadly, at least from Shira's view, as documented by 17 of her reports, "for the most part this propaganda system designed to degrade and ruin the reputations of intelligent, hard-working and effective Homeopaths seems to have been working." Adding additional firepower to the FDA's ill-intended public relations campaign, aspiring new doctors at American medical schools were taught to "degrade and put down" any suggestion by patients that they try natural remedies. As a result, amid their required internships and after launching their own medical practices, new physicians invariably told every patient who dared broach the subject things like: "I wouldn't try that if I were you;" "beware of quacks who dish out dangerous substances that have never been fully studied;" or "you're taking your life into your own hands if you dare to follow such advice. Many people may have died when taking the type of natural substance that you are talking about. Much more study is needed."

At an accelerated pace, particularly during the previous few years, Shira had become increasingly aware that documenting and continually tracking these issues had emerged as a top priority for Israel's primary spy agency.

Due to the atrocities suffered by the Jewish people during the Nazi-led Holocaust, which slaughtered many millions of souls of that faith during the 1930s and 1940s, Israel had become increasingly wary of any nation that intentionally endangers its general population. Shira realized that, of course, at least on the surface the American bureaucrats were not openly engaging in the equivalent of cramming live people into ovens and gas chambers the way the Germans' Third Reich had done many years before.

Nonetheless, as specified in her October 18, 1984, report to Mossad, key concerns for Israel in monitoring the FDA should persist, namely: what kind of government would intentionally endanger hundreds of millions of its own citizens?; considering the fact that the bureaucrats who are truly running the USA's government have been willing to go this--far beyond the point of sensible morality--what is to keep them from "going over the top, and actually beginning to openly and intentionally kill its own citizens?;" why, how and can Israel trust such a nation, even if that country happens to be its strongest and closest ally?;" and "considering the proven fact the United States has been willing to go this far, what is to prevent its many other powerful agencies from endangering the American citizenry as well?"

Still fully mindful of all these many critical factors, while still en route in her Camero to the Jefferson Memorial, Shira began wondering why her superiors had requested that she attend what they described as this "critical, one-on-one meeting."

At that point ten years had passed since her rendezvous at the Noah Hebrew Cafe on K Street with Elijah Horowitz--at the time the executive assistant in Israel's embassy to the United States in Washington, D.C.

Shira thought that this was somewhat ironic or perhaps strange, the notion that she had been ordered to meet this same official. By this point she had learned first-hand that such high-ranking administrators rarely last for more than a few years in any position.

Such careers attracted an exceedingly ambitious type of person, at least judging from her experience. The vast majority of such individuals always crave "another spot, even more power"--no matter what position they hold at any given time.

Still proud of her keen memory, Shira recalled that Elijah had been a fairly good looking guy who had seemed to have at least a fair degree of intelligence. Until this morning, she had only met him in person that one time a decade earlier. In her mind, any fellow who manages to hold on to such a pivotal position for that long must be "playing his politics in the right and perfect way."

*

Five minutes before her scheduled rendezvous, Shira found a parking space on Ohio Street one block from the Jefferson Memorial. After parking, she used the mirror at the back of her sun visor to check for one final time, ensuring that her make-up remained perfect. Shira still prided herself in looking great and highly professional at all times, just as she had done since joining Mossad.

For this day, she had chosen a crisp, light brown woman's pantsuit, accented by a fluffy white collar--plus shiny dark brown shoes lined with the same creamy white accents that permeated her medium-size purse. Shira felt confident that her light brown lipstick, accented by a dark liner at the edges, would give the desired appearances of an alluring woman who happened to be highly efficient.

While walking brisk-paced toward the memorial,

she instantly spotted Elijah from 75 yards away. Even from that distance she realized that he no longer wore clothes that distinctively marked him as a man of devout Jewish heritage. Instead, he wore a pure white business suit, accented by a soothing tan tie and similarly colored shiny slip-on shoes. He already started waving toward Shira, and she waved back--smiling broadly.

Soon much closer to Elijah, now just 25 yards away as he stood still, the thought unexpectedly struck Shira that he looked precisely like the "fantasy vision" of the mystery man that she had always hoped since childhood to someday marry. Unlike her fiance, Ken Miller, a thin, wiry fellow with a receding hairline and lacking any hint of athleticism, Elijah had baby-like unblemished skin, a muscular body similar to that of a well-trained soldier, and collar-length, curly hair.

The sight of this official had instantly and unexpectedly made Shira's heart skip faster, and when just 10 yards away she realized that a small film of perspiration had quickly covered her brow. Her breathing rate intensified.

The site of his masculine mouth and perfectly aligned, sparkly white teeth instantly made her think--if only briefly--what a kiss would be like.

Disturbed with herself for thinking this, she said "Hello, Elijah," while striving to avoid pondering the unthinkable. The possibility of being exhilarated by the sight of him had been the furthest thing from this agent's mind when preparing for this day.

The embassy official greeted Shira by holding both of his hands outward toward her, his palms upward. She briefly placed her hands in his, before they embraced each other in a long, tight, and friendly hug. The agent realized that such closeness and intimacy was frowned upon in professional circles, particularly within Mossad and any Israeli governmental organization. Yet Shira's intuition told her that their close interaction was perfectly okay; she realized that the two of them instinctively knew that they shared a close personal and professional bond--excluding the fact that they had met only once before.

Up this close, only about two feet apart and gazing at each other eye-to-eye, she realized that Elijah's once boyish facial features had turned manly and simultaneously soft--as if, at least in her mind, an ideal mixture of independent masculinity and gentle sharing.

"Shira, we could not possibly have wished for a more glorious day, could we?"

"As long as we're going to talk serious business, we might as well enjoy the surroundings." From her purse, Shira pulled a feathery light, fluffy and tan umbrella, which she promptly unfolded as a shield from the sun. "How about a stroll along the edge of the tidal basin?"

"Sounds sensational." Elijah held out his right arm in a "V" shape, and she promptly cradled her left hand through the bend in his elbow. As the pair began their leisurely stroll, she briefly wondered whether this exquisite gentleman had noticed the slight creases that had developed under her eyes; Shira considered these her only physical "flaws" or challenges while still in her mid-30s.

At the slight touch of his bulging biceps, she realized that her nipples had become erect underneath her tan pants-suit. Although eager to concentrate fully on the business at hand, she began wondering whether he might notice this unwanted and unexpected biological signal. Within seconds she decided that she did not care whether he detected these obvious protrusions, and so she turned her head briefly toward Elijah's, and smiled as broadly as she possibly could.

"Shira, I can imagine that you probably have been wondering why I summoned you here, especially on such short notice." He gazed out toward the basin's placid waters as he spoke, the two of them strolling under the branches of cherry trees.

"Whatever I might have thought makes no difference." She casually pointed across the water toward the Washington Monument. "The mystery will soon end, once you tell me ... You must know by now that I enjoy intrigue."

Without saying a word, Elijah slowly and gently edged her toward a park bench on grass beside the walkway, underneath a large and shady tree. Shira unfurled her umbrella as they sat close to one another--not so near that they might appear as if lovers, yet intimate enough to tantalize her imagination. To her, the possibilities seemed endless.

After turning his head in various directions, behavior that she considered an attempt to ensure that no one was close enough to listen to them, Elijah told her: "The danger has increased far more than we might possibly have envisioned. That is why I will quickly and efficiently discuss all the pertinent details. ... Please commit them to memory, and I'll also have a pile of documents to give you."

Shira appreciated his blunt approach, for she had always disliked the type of subtle nuances that--at least in her mind-- tended to waste the time of everyone involved.

Elijah started out by explaining that during the previous three years the Israeli Embassy in Washington had gone through a rapid-fire succession of five different ambassadors. His first and favorite boss there, Amos Berkovich, had been transferred back to their homeland at age 50. Before then, Elijah admitted, he had considered Berkovich's penchant for continual efficiency as a bit overboard--almost as if that boss had been overly paranoid about such matters.

Within three months after Berkovich's departure, Elijah's opinion on this had changed 180 degrees. Before long he had yearned for "the good old days," primarily because--in his mind--the former ambassador's successors were universally inept and inefficient. Thus, at least from Elijah's view, the embassy's operations--which once had been the equivalent of a well-oiled, highly efficient machine--had quickly evolved into chaos.

"I'm afraid that the big losers here are the people of Israel." Upon hearing this, Shira's ears perked up; by this point all her motivations were business oriented. "I'm going to tell you the specific reasons why I summoned you here today ... I have got to be open and honest with you, in order to develop trust.

"Shira, as you probably know, and none of your well-written and valuable reports say this in such specific terms, throughout Israel and across most of Europe, most people expect--and, in fact, in many cases they demand--the option of using and benefiting from natural remedies, particularly those recommended by Homeopathic physicians. Well, you might not realize this, but the long and greedy arm of the USA has reached across the pond--across the Atlantic Ocean--in trying to dictate how the Europeans and even our homeland, administer their own health care systems. The Americans are despicable this way ... They dole out many billions of dollars to individual nations throughout these regions, and across the globe as well. As a caveat, however--a so-called 'special condition' if you will--the United States is beginning to demand that other nations concentrate or focus their own health care and scientific research programs on what we call 'mainstream medicine"--the type of warped ideology that results in unnatural, expansive, addictive and extremely dangerous manmade drugs.

"Of course, you know this is already happening within the United States, far more than the regular and unsuspecting citizens of this land might possibly know. Anyway, the short and even the long-term future of humanity is at stake. ... Specifically, Shira, this is why I have you here today ... Right away, you need to know that this meeting here between us has not been sanctioned by my superiors. If you tell them all about me, that's perfectly okay. But you need to know, there now are those among us--the Israelis and the Jewish people--who are beginning to get tricked by this hogwash--this propaganda--spewed out by the Americans, their nonsense that contends that 'mainstream' doctors know what is best for people. So, as a result of this nonsense, we are expected to never question such authority ... But I say the opposite is true."

Shira's respect for Elijah suddenly soared. She had always appreciated and felt most attracted to what she considered a 'man's-man,' guys like him who are willing to stand their ground for righteous and worthy causes--doing so for the betterment of all humanity. As Shira's admiration for this man steadily increased, she decided to remain quiet, in order to let him get these urgent details off of his chest. While he continued speaking, she took the handkerchief from her purse and wiped another mist of perspiration from her forehead.

"Shira, I want you to know that I have become increasingly frustrated, upon realizing that some of the officials within our embassy here are actually beginning to spout this nonsense--the garbage about the need for so-called 'modern medicine.' These morons insist that our nation, working with successful business leaders in the United States, significantly boost scholarship funds--so that increasing numbers of young Jewish students can attend top-notch medical schools here in the USA.

"These dangers are increasing at an alarming rate. Either blind to the problem or greedy themselves, most of the numerous U.S. Senators of the Jewish faith are beginning to accept sizable political campaign donations from giant pharmaceutical companies and from America's mainstream health care industry. As a result, I'm afraid, rather than standing tall as champions for 'natural cures,' we are becoming at least somewhat wimpy and even corrupt, just like the American political system.

"Thankfully, on the positive side, within Israel our infrastructure and political system remains adamant--strong in retaining processes that continue to allow, and even to encourage, the use and benefits of Homeopathic medicine throughout our society. ... Also, I have not given up hope that we can reverse this terrible trend within the United States.

"That is another reason, Shira, why I have summoned you here today. ... So, please let me explain in further, more in-depth detail. ... And I want to tell you from the start that I am not asking you to work against the official wishes and directives of our homeland ... To do so likely could be perceived as flat-out treason, and I think that you would agree that neither of us would want to do that.

"But let me just say that at this critical juncture in the

ongoing evolution of medical care, here during 1985, together we can achieve great things. ... If we work smart and think smart, working efficiently as a team--you and I--we can covertly do our share to put health care worldwide on the right and natural track ... Precisely how and when we are going to achieve this--if you agree to work with me--remains a huge puzzle. Together, we need to see the so-called Big Picture, how all of the many pieces of this massive challenge would or could fit together, in a nice, tight and efficient package.

"With this proverbial playing field as the basis for our future progress, Shira, let me quickly fill you in on the basics ... Later on today, or whenever you get time, you will be able to review a microchip that I have for you, containing many essential details.

"Suffice it to say that I have identified serious weaknesses within the American infrastructure that we can seize to our advantage ... Our biggest weaponry in this regard, in a non-military sense, stems from the corruption--and even murders-- carried out by numerous current U.S. congressmen and senators. Individually, each of them have been informed that we 'have the goods' on them, evidence of their evil misdeeds. As you can imagine, Shira, perhaps the worst by far is Nevada Senator Larry Spickler--elected to his third term last year by a hare's breath. ... That creep ... You remember the guy that you recorded a decade ago at Salt Lake City airport, proving his corruption?"

"Of course."

"Well, as you will soon see from our file on this wild animal, he is truly the worst kind of skunk imaginable. ... We have refrained from directly contacting Senator Spickler since slamming him with these details five years ago, the unexpected revelation that we know the God-awful truth about his murderous behavior. ... Needless to say, he knows that we are not blackmailing him in the predictable sense. ... Instead, as one of the Devil's most powerful soldiers now walking on this earth, he knows that someday--one day--we will unexpectedly call on him for his political services. ... Believe me, we have plenty of other clowns in Congress who are ready to join these future efforts ... I hope all this helps to put the overall situation into clear perspective."

Shira felt a bit disappointed when Elijah finally stopped speaking. She had latched on to his every word, fully agreeing with everything that this official had to say. For several years, this woman had a mindset similar to his. Yet this marked the first time that she ever had heard anyone with enough gumption to voice these concerns, especially with such free-flowing eloquence. Until these past several minutes, everyone else that she had heard attempting to broach the subject had seemed--in her mind--to tippie-toe around the most critical and controversial aspects of this vital issue. Rather than communicating in sweeping generalities as they had done, Elijah had a tell-it-like-it-is approach that she appreciated and even adored.

"Elijah, what I am about to say might seem odd to you."

"What might that be?"

"I don't even need to put any thought into this ... I'm with you 100 percent, although you probably will lose respect for me for coming to such a hasty decision."

"To the contrary, my admiration for you has burst wide open, upon hearing this."

Without missing a beat, Elijah went on to explain that partly through his directives, some of Mossad's many operatives had been maintaining a close watch on several of the United States' most intelligent medical researchers and physicians. While reviewing streams of reports on these individuals, one of these documents had caught Elijah's attention five years earlier back in 1980. That file chronicled a little-known oncologist in the mid-size town of Reno, Nevada. According to the report, Doctor James Robbins was perhaps the most intelligent, hard-working and industrious oncologist in the United States. At least that was the conclusion of four separate Mossad agents who had quietly observed this physician and dug deeply into his background.

"Unbeknownst to us at the time, Shira, the CIA had begun focusing on this doctor as well. ... As you undoubtedly know, the Central Intelligence Agency is directed or operated to focus solely on international matters outside of the United States. Yet their focus on the health care industry changed to a domestic level, eventually putting this Reno physician into their cross-hairs. ... You see, from their view, we believe, Doctor Robbins posed a threat. Perhaps more than any other physician within the USA, he had direct personal knowledge--based on data from his medical practice--that the cancer rate definitely had increased sharply in the Nevada Test Site's nuclear fallout zone.

"Any public exposure on his part about these damning details would have destroyed the confidence of typical Americans in their government ... From what we have been able to learn, we believe that this physician had the good sense to keep his mouth shut on the issue ... Like any reasonable man should, the doctor knew that essentially "the damage had already been done.' ... No public revelation on his part could possibly have reversed the course of these cancers, which in some instances take many years to emerge.

"Yes, in my eyes Doctor Robbins is the ultimate American hero, although the general public knows little or nothing about him. ... In the meantime, Shira, thanks to the admirable efforts of your counterparts in Mossad, we discovered that five years ago CIA operatives were harassing the physician ... As you might probably guess, those jerks are closely allied to Congress--the same elected leaders who cozy up to Big Pharma.

"They perceived this man as a significant threat to their wicked infrastructure, particularly when he aggressively started complaining about the inefficiency of the American pharmaceutical industry. Even amid his burgeoning medical practice, Doctor Robbins issued regular and frequent complaints to the CEO of Reno's primary hospital, Doctor Crowley. Angered by the unstoppable greed of the drug companies, he began writing and calling those firms--demanding that they improve their products.

"While virtually all other oncologists nationwide kowtowed to the directives of medical industry officials and Big Pharma, this physician became a real dog-fighter, literally a 'raging bull' who happened to remain sensible and level-headed. A true maverick, a proven leader and precisely the kind of rebel that all of us need, he also became the first U.S. physician that we know of to take issue with the deadly Stage IV cancer treatment protocol--as mandated by medical industry officials, in conjunction with Big Pharma.

"Shockingly, our operatives confirmed that the CIA actually considered murdering Doctor Robbins. Such a murder would have set a precedence, the first known and verifiable slaughter of a law-abiding U.S. citizen by his own government. Naturally, we used diplomatic channels to let the Americans know that we had become fully aware of this stupid personal harassment campaign of theirs.

"The jerks who run the USA pulled the plug on that stinky stuff right away, well apparently aware that we were willing and able to blow the lid on their war against this innocent man--using our back channels, if necessary, to bring this to the news media.

"The closest the doctor came to getting shot between the eyes happened about five years ago on a cold, breezy and somewhat snowy December morning--in a wilderness area just outside that city--Reno, Nevada. To his credit, the doctor proved to be such an excellent shot--firing simultaneously from two handguns at long range--so amazingly accurate of a shot that he blew out the tires of a CIA pursuit vehicle. ... We suspect that a sniper had intended to take out the physician and two women that were with him.

"Luckily, Doctor Robbins and his companions escaped without injury. ... Our intervention efforts came just in time. Later that same afternoon we contacted CIA administrators through back channels.

"Since then, the doctor has remained just as much of a maverick as ever. To this day, we are sure, he remains unaware of who precisely was hunting him or why. He remains just as aggressive and dedicated to his many patients as ever. Although a widower, still unmarried, he has had a steady girlfriend for the past five years--supposedly a gal from Italy. ... The precise details of her background remain elusive to us.

"In any event, Doctor Robbins now remains on our radar screen. Those who have monitored him, and throughly chronicled his movements and job performance, universally praise him as having the brilliance and personal qualities that the entire U.S. health care industry desperately needs."

Shira remained quiet when Elijah finally stopped speaking. This embassy official and the Reno oncologist were the type of men that she admired most. She adored brave guys who did "the right thing," while detesting cowards that refused to take any sort of position on the most heated political issues of the day.

"So, where do I come into this picture?" Shira realized that she was no longer perspiring, perhaps thanks to a light cloud cover that had grown overhead.

Elijah wasted no time in telling this under-cover Mossad agent that he needed any and all details that the FDA had on Doctor Robbins--particularly information within the corrupt agency's closed and secret files.

"Of course, he personally has no idea about this now--but that Reno physician might emerge as our best hope. ... If my hunches play out, in the long-term--perhaps even 10 or 20 or even 30 years from now--he could very well emerge as the most logical and best person to save the practice of natural medicine from total destruction ... And with luck and persistence, with us far in the background--but on his side--maybe, just maybe, he will become the one man who finally exposes the truth about the monstrous mainstream medical industry ... Without him, or someone else of his superior caliber, I am afraid that all of society in this country and worldwide will become essentially 'doomed and enslaved' by the corrupt and ineffective conventional medical industry."

Twenty-Four

At age 15, Tommy Davis hated the entire world.

He loathed his mother Polly for dying and leaving him a decade earlier.

The youth's abhorrence toward his father, Honest, had become increasingly intense. With each passing day Tommy became increasingly mad that his alcoholic dad still failed to hold a steady job.

As a pimple-faced sophomore at Reno's Earl Wooster High School, Tommy skipped school far more days than he attended.

The principal, Lyle Shields, had given this young man a stern warning on the final school day before the summer break of 1980: "You will be permanently expelled if you skip school one more time or continue to earn abhorrent grades averaging a dismal D ... Young man, you are far too intelligent to waste your life."

By mid-June of 1985, Tommy contemplated running away forever. He considered hitchhiking all the way to Los Angeles, where he figured that life as a "beach bum" would be far better than living with people that he despised.

Although realizing that Dorothy McCready, the retired county clerk, had been kind to him--his anger toward the entire world had increased when she had died of a sudden heart attack at age 69 a year earlier in 1984.

"If Dorothy loved me, she would not have left me," Tommy had thought at the time, locking himself in his bedroom for three days straight. "Why do all the women that I want to care about end up leaving me? ... To heck with the flowery positive attitudes that people keep talking about all the time, because the entire world sucks."

Tommy could not possible have cared less for his 12-year-old sister, Penelope, who had moved in with their Aunt Paula--the casino card dealer--and her husband Bobby "Cactus Pete" Blair shortly after Dorothy died.

"Nobody cares about me--they've all stuck me with this old man," Tommy often thought, upset that he lived alone with Bill McCready--now in his late 70s.

Although this retired senior gentlemen had always been kind to Tommy and never mistreated him in any way, the youth disliked "Old Bill" the most. The boy had become increasingly frustrated with this fellow's many stories about "how great it is to go fishing--to enjoy solitude and sportsmanship in the great outdoors."

As far as Tommy could tell, the crusty, disheveled looking old guy had failed to catch a single fish for at least the past decade. Throughout that period when this youth had lived with the McCreadys, Bill had gone on numerous fishing excursions with several of his retired buddies--never once returning with a single catch.

"All talk, and no action--that's pretty much what all the adults in my life are pretty much about," Tommy often thought. "They always act high-and-mighty, supposedly God-fearing people, but as far as I'm concerned they're all full of crap."

Even worse, from Tommy's perspective, was the inescapable fact that for the past several years, all of the adults around him--those from his immediate and extended family--frequently kept telling him that "I love you."

"Well, if they love me, if they truly cared about me--they would just leave me alone," Tommy often thought. "They claim that they have my welfare and future in mind, but why do they have to keep nagging me about going to school, insisting that I drop my friends who like to drink alcohol and smoke dope with me, and getting better grades. ... As far as I am concerned, that is all a bunch of bull."

Tommy's contempt for these people remained as intense as ever on August 3, 1985--a cool and unusually balmy Saturday across Northwest Nevada. That time of year is usually blazing hot throughout the Reno area, but this day's weather emerged as similar to mid-spring. August highs throughout the region averaged in the mid-90s, a sharp contrast to this particular day's forecast of only 73, with a slight breeze.

Rain threatened to fall while in the mid-50s under cloudy skies at 6 o'clock that morning as Tommy rode in the back of Cactus Pete's dented blue 1960s pickup truck. This had been heralded to the lad as a "guy's getaway--a male bonding time," an entire morning fishing at Pyramid Lake and enjoying the great outdoors.

Tommy disliked the mere thought of being with all these guys. Besides Cactus Pete and Bill McCready, that doctor that Tommy always heard people saying great things about--James Robbins and his old buddy, Anthony "The General" Dunn--had come along for the ride. The youth would have preferred that his father be there instead of them, although the teen disliked Honest just as much as all of these old farts combined. At the present time, as far as anyone knew, the former plumber was again homeless, away on another one of his many drunken binges.

Tommy still vividly remembered having adored and wanting to emulate his father as a small child, always behaving as obedient and well-mannered as possible. But such polite behavior had stopped by age 10, when the lad had begun thinking that "my dad doesn't give a poop about me. ... As far as I'm concerned, he died mentally and physically way back when mom died."

While sitting in the bed of the pickup with Cactus Pete's miniature schnauzer, Chip, Tommy could hear what he considered an old "fuddy-duddy" tune blaring from the vehicle's radio--"Chattanooga Choo Choo." The announcer on the radio described the song as a 1943 Glenn Miller tune, popular during World War II more than 40 years earlier. All four men riding inside the truck began singing the lyrics, the sound of which made the teenager want to puke. Yet that became impossible, since the young man had refused to eat breakfast before their departure--despite the insistence of Cactus Pete and Bill.

When Cactus Pete finally parked the vehicle near Pyramid Lake's west shore just before 7 o'clock that morning, all four men hopped out of the vehicle. Working together, the guys carried two large folding metal ladders from the truck bed, all 30 yards to the shoreline.

Despite the men's collective urgings for Tommy to "help and join the fun," the teen remained in the bed of the pickup-- where he kept trying to hug the receptionist's dog, holding the animal for as long as possible. Finally, Chip bounded from the vehicle and high-tailed it toward the men, barking in a tone that the teenager considered much too lively and happy-go-lucky. As far as Tommy was concerned, any decent full-grown dog should have a low, husky bark rather than the pesky yips of a mere puppy.

"Heck, not even the dog likes me." Tommy thought. "I wish that I could get as far away as possible from all these jerks. If I could, I would walk 100 miles to get away from all these morons, but that would be a waste of my time and energy. ... I think that tonight, long after we get back to town, that would be a perfect time for me to sneak out and start making my way to LA."

From his position at the back of the truck, Tommy watched intently as each of the four men put on waders. Then, the guys walked far out into the lake--carrying the metal ladders. Finally, using a flotation device to help guide them, the guys erected the ladders about 30 feet out from the shoreline. Only the tops of the ladders remained visible, while the bottoms of these contraptions remains submerged.

In keeping with the process that Bill McCready had explained to him on the previous day, the guys began sharing positions atop the ladders. From those spots, holding their rods with relaxed-looking hands, the men cast their lines into the lake. The most prevalent fish here were considered prized delicacies, particularly the Cui-ui lakesuckers and the tui chub. Another extremely rare breed, the Lahontan cutthroat trout was listed as an endangered species at the time; while en route to the lake, Tommy had heard the men agree that they would immediately release any trout that they might catch.

"These creeps are behaving like morons," Tommy though, while digging through an ice cooler in the pickup truck's bed. "Why do these guys behave as if they're a bunch of boys, instead of grown men."

As Tommy pushed his hands through soda cans at the top inside of the cooler, out the corner of his left eye, he noticed the men lifting their arms in celebration--their automatic reaction as Cactus Pete reeled in a sizable tui chub. Tommy recognized this species thanks to pictures that Bill had shown him from a "Sierra Fisherman" magazine.

Thinking of them as fools, Tommy lifted a six-pack of Budweiser beer from the bottom of the cooler. Without any hesitation, the teenager then jumped from the pickup bed and hustled through the sagebrush-covered wilderness--heading to isolated hills about 150 yards away, the the opposite direction from the shoreline.

"Those old imbeciles will never even know that I am away," Tommy thought about three minutes after his departure. Momentarily, still carrying the purloined brew, he hustled to the opposite side of the small hill; he promptly sat, out of view from the fisherman. "Hopefully, this will be enough for me to get drunk ... That will teach them for failing to keep a good eye on me. They talk about responsibility, but as far as I'm concerned they're guilty of child neglect for failing to watch after me."

Wearing only tattered blue jeans, worn-out tennis shoes and a faded T-shirt emblazoned with an image of his favorite rock band--Queen--Tommy cracked open his first beer of the day and promptly began guzzling.

Just then a light rainfall began. He barely noticed the precipitation, sitting and facing another hillside.

Within a minute, the storm had transitioned into an all-out cloudburst. Until that moment, he had never felt a downpour this heavy, relentless and threatening.

"Tommy, where are you!" he kept hearing the men holler,

the evident worry in their voices making the teenager feel more delighted than he had been in years--maybe even happier than they had ever been before.

"I hope they never find me," Tommy thought. "I hope that they think that I have drowned, and that they then just drive home and forget all about me."

The men's hollering for Tommy continued for the next five minutes, their collective voices as if stupendous music to his ears. The teenager hoped that these men felt as much emotional pain and anguish as he had been experiencing, for just about as long as he could remember.

Rather than begin to subside, the downpour intensified. The relentless rain made Tommy increasingly optimistic that a catastrophic flash flood would suddenly occur.

Instead, without any warning whatsoever, Doctor Robbins stood five feet in front of the teenager. With his face emitting what Tommy considered a sign of genuine concern, the physician took off his own eyeglasses and tucked them into one of the many pockets of his fishing vest.

"Tommy? ... Are you okay?"

"What do you care?"

"I care ... I care a lot."

"Go away, mister."

"I don't think you really want me to go away, do you?"

"Stop trying to tell me how I feel." Tommy opened another beer and began guzzling, the raging downpour still as relentless as ever. "Get the heck out of here, and leave me alone."

"Sorry to tell you this, young man, but I'm not leaving you under any circumstances." The doctor took one of the four remaining beers, opened the can and took a tiny sip, as the first thunder erupted and at least three lightning bolts briefly whitened the skies. "Hey, what a wonderful day for a getaway. ... Maybe we will even catch pneumonia ... Wouldn't that be fun?"

"Quit acting like such a wise guy, doctor, and get your butt out of here and just leave me alone. Leave me here in peace."

"Tommy, you're mighty pissed, aren't you ... You're mad at the entire world."

"How did you know?"

"You are telling me that right now, and you don't even know that you're saying this. ... Tommy, I would say that you're a tremendous communicator, and--to me--the sad thing is that you don't even realize this."

"Stop criticizing me ... I'm tired of people criticizing me all the time."

For the next two minutes, Tommy and Doctor Robbins sat side-by-side without saying a word. The heavy rainfall persisted, amid increasingly loud thunder and the quick buildup of at least eight continually flowing streams that had emerged on the mountainside in front of them.

"Listen, Tommy ... I haven't criticized you, even once. Just tell me why you're so angry, upset with all the world?"

"What difference to you does it make how I feel?"

The physician took a long, slow and deep breath. Tommy worried that this might be a signal that this doctor lacked any interest in him whatsoever, almost as if making a half-hearted yawn.

"How I feel makes no difference, doctor. You don't give a hoot about me, and none of those other guys do either."

"Tell me, Tommy. ... How do you know what we think about you?"

"I just know. Everybody hates me."

"Oh, do they? ... Tell me why you think that way."

"Because, well, I am just angry."

"So, why?"

"You know ... Or, at least you should know, doctor."

"Well, I might make some guess as to what has irritated you so much, but those would only be guesses ... If you want people to know why you're upset, just tell them."

By this point oblivious to the extreme rainfall, Tommy commenced describing a lengthy list of his complaints--suddenly realizing that he had been pent-up with emotion, glad to fully tell someone precisely how he felt. The teenager described his anger toward his family, his mother for leaving him--for dying.

The youth erupted in tears while describing his intense feelings of being abandoned. Tommy confessed that his anger toward his father had been just as emotionally painful as the death of Dorothy McCready. The fact that Aunt Paula had then taken his little sister Penelope away without letting the two of them say goodbye to each other worsened his emotional pain. Tommy admitted that he didn't like saying this out loud, but he actually loved and cared about his little sister.

"Doctor, I don't even know what phone number to reach Penelope at, and I don't have any idea where she lives. Whenever I happen to ask, Bill--the old man--simply says that 'everything has been taken care of' and that 'everything will be okay."

After five continuous minutes of getting these details off his chest, Tommy began realizing that he had finally gotten up enough courage to tell someone how he truly felt. All along, while continuing to speak, the teenager began thinking of how appreciative he felt--primarily the fact that in those crucial moments the doctor made no attempt to interrupt him.

Instead, without being judgmental, at least as far as Tommy could tell, the doctor was simply enabling him to speak his mind without any fear of reprisal.

Feeling as if glad that the proverbial floodgates into his own soul had been fully opened, for the subsequent 10 minutes Tommy told of numerous other issues: the fact that he never cared much for school and never tried to study, primarily because he felt that doing so would be pointless anyway; the fact that none of his Wooster High School friends had been allowed to visit the McCready home; the fact that his father, Honest, had never made a single attempt to contact him during the previous decade; the disturbing truth that no one in his family or his caregivers ever spoke about "anything that truly matters"--as if everyone was dysfunctional, continually walking on eggshells; and Tommy's deep-down feeling that no one had truly loved him other than his late mother.

Still sitting in the same place beside the doctor, Tommy stopped crying at this point--just as the rainfall ceased. The teen paid little attention to the fact that the clouds had already quickly started breaking up overhead.

"Tommy, I can fully understand why you feel the way that you do."

"Really?"

"And I am not judging you at all for what you have just said."

Lacking facial tissue, Tommy used the bottom of his own T-shirt to briefly wipe his nose--also seizing this opportunity to remove the rain and tears from his own face.

"Doctor, you are the first person--the first adult, that is-- who has ever taken the time and effort to ever listen to me."

"Well, that sounds like we might be off to a pretty good start, especially considering the situation that things for us all could be a lot worse than they are."

"What do you mean by that, doctor, when you say 'for all of us.'"

"This is just my guess, Tommy ... I'm not trying to lecture here ... But if you ask me, I think that maybe everyone around you has been going through emotional pain as well. ... Maybe everyone is simply trying to do the best that they know how ... Everyone copes with emotional pain in different ways, or at least so I have been told by the so-called experts who supposedly know far more than I do about these things. ... Your father certainly has had difficulty coping; he tries to handle his problems with booze ... Dorothy and Bill McCready, the best kind of friends that any family could possibly want, tried to cope by doing the best that they possibly knew how ... I don't need to rattle off any more about this ... You get my drift, I'm sure."

"I think that I understand."

"The good thing Tommy, is the fact that there is no 'rule'

that you need to understand all these things ... I guess that old saying is true, that life is confusing."

Tommy finally stood, while the physician remained seated. With his hands posted on each of his own hips, the boy looked down at the medical professional.

"What I fail to understand is, doctor, why some people are liked so much more than others; why some people seem to have lots of good, reliable friends and I don't have any; and why I don't really seem to have anything to feel great about."

"Tommy, I could give you an answer, but the last thing you want is for me to lecture you--and I'm sure that you would not want me to do that."

"Yeah, I guess."

"So, you just want us to drop the issue, and stop talking about the whole thing."

Tommy retrieved another unopened beer from the ground, and tossed the can to Doctor Robbins. The doctor smiled, opened the container and took a sip.

"Well, I do have another question for you, doctor, if you don't mind."

"Fire away."

"Everybody likes you, and I guess that's one of the things that pisses me off, too. Everybody always talks about how fantastic you are, supposedly the greatest guy that they have ever met ... That you always work, trying to save the lives of people ... They always talk about how fantastic you are, and about your supposedly tremendous personality ... Is that the reason why people like you so much, and they dislike me? ... Could it be that I lack any redeeming qualities, while you have all the characteristics that people want and appreciate? ... I know you never try to brag, doctor, but what makes you special? And why do you work so much? You don't need to do that, do you?"

The doctor finally stood.

With his own head visible above the top of the small mound, he waved down toward the other three men, and hollered:

"Hey, guys! Everything is okay!"

Tommy glanced toward the lake shore, where he saw the trio smiling and waving back at the two of them.

"Since you asked, Tommy, do you mind if I tell you my story ... You probably do not know this but I had a pretty rough time as a child, except in a different way than you."

"You did? Really?"

Doctor Robbins told Tommy about his own father abandoning him and his mother when he was a child in Detroit; of living in an orphanage for several years, and of essentially spending his teenage years raising his own mother, Jane.

"There was no one around--no adults anyway--and I even essentially became my mother's caregiver. She was weak, and I decided to be strong--probably because that's the way that I felt I had to be."

The physician explained that as a teenager himself in Southern California, the father of one of his girlfriends--a doctor--became his first mentor.

"Tommy, the one thing that sticks with me the most is that the physician--his name was Doctor Franklin Monroe--that by giving to others, we essentially receive. ... If we give the world hate, he had told me, we will get only hate in return. The key to happiness, that doctor explained, was to learn as much as possible, and then eventually to give to the world as much as you can--and that way, everything usually turns out pretty much all right, at least most of the time ... Believe me, I have lived with that philosophy to this day."

"Wow." Tommy drank more beer, this time sipping rather than chugging. "It was all that simple?"

"Quite the opposite, if you want me to tell you the truth. Going through college, and then medical school, and then..."

"Can I interrupt?"

"By all means. As you've probably guessed by now, I'm not the holier-than-thou type ... Say any thing, or ask any question that you would like."

"Doctor, do you think there is still a chance for me to change my life around? ... Could I start learning and helping, and becoming more like you?"

"Now, remember, I'm not lecturing ... Tommy, I'm just saying what I feel. ... But since you asked, here is what I think. Sure, you can learn more and help other people, and that probably would enable you to feel better emotionally--quite a bit, in fact. But I would hope that you would not strive to become exactly like me or like anyone else for that matter. ... It's just my personal belief, but in my view the world would be a better place if young people grew up to stand on their own two feet--appreciating their own uniqueness."

"What do you mean by that?"

"I'm saying that you will instinctively know what is best for you. And, I think that any guy is far better off in the long run if he becomes his own man."

"But how can I do that now? ... Doctor, I'm living with a guy in his late 70s, a fellow who doesn't seem to know how to catch a single fish."

Tommy and Doctor Robbins each broke out in laughter as soon as the teenager said this. Strangely, the youth felt as if he had just quickly developed a special bond with the physician, who actually had taken the time to listen to him--without being judgmental, and then making suggestions based on life experience, rather than trying to seem superior.

Side by side, the physician and the teenager slowly started walking through the thick sagebrush, toward their three companions.

"Well, Tommy, that is something that I've been meaning to chat with you about, the fact that you live with an ancient person who seems to you as if out of touch with reality ... I've been talking with your Aunt Paula, and with Bill McCready, and I even spoke with your dad about it--briefly--about six months ago during one of his sober periods. I made a proposal to them..."

"A proposal? ... What about? My future?"

"Yep."

"In what way?"

"About the possibility of me adopting you."

"You've got to be kidding me?"

"Not in the least."

"But why would you want to do that?"

"Because I care about people ... Because I care about you ... And because everyone around you, in their own way--whether you realize this or not, Tommy, they all truly love you and want the very best for you."

"Do you already have other children? Are you married?"

"No kids, yet ... My girlfriend, er--my wife, Marie and I, we just got married a few months ago. And she whole-heartedly agrees with this proposal--that is, if you want to, Tommy ... I'm sure this is something you would want to think about."

"I'm thinking right away that my answer is going to be 'yes.'"

"Well, if that's the case--if that is what you eventually decide, Tommy--keep in mind the fact that I'm going to listen to you, whenever you want to talk about anything. But I'm also not going to put up with any bull, and there would be rules."

"What if I decide that I want to become a doctor, just like you someday ... Or, a lawyer ... Or a firefighter, or whatever?"

"You make those decisions ... All that I can promise is that I'll help guide you. Some people insist that life is merely a continual quest for happiness. ... Who can say for sure how things will turn out ... But what I can say for sure is that life always ends up posing challenges for us all. The trick often is to avoid the danger, or--reacting in the way that I usually prefer--facing the worst difficulties head-on."

Twenty-Five

The phone rang in Tommy's dorm room in Nye Hall at the University of Nevada, awakening him from a late-afternoon nap.

"Hello?"

"Tommy, is that you?"

"Maybe." Now a 20-year-old junior majoring in pre-med, he remained clear-minded enough to protect his own privacy. "Who is calling?"

The caller quickly identified himself as Anthony Dunn, the senior receptionist at Doctor Robbins' medical clinic. The World War II veteran quickly explained that there had been a sudden emergency at the facility five miles south of downtown Reno.

"What type of emergency?" Tommy wiped his eyes as he spoke, striving to get a mental grasp on the situation. "Why would you call me? I am not a doctor."

"Please come down here as soon as you can--right away."

"But why would I be needed there? ... I'm busy studying for mid-terms, and..."

"Sorry ... We don't have any time to explain ... Something horrible has happened to the doctor, and he desperately needs you."

"Give me details. I cannot just leave here at the drop of a hat. I've got..."

"This is urgent ... The doctor desperately needs you ... Please hurry."

"Well, okay. ... But there better be a mighty good reason. ... It should take me about 15 minutes to get there."

"Travel safe ... Time is of the essence."

Tommy needed just 33 seconds to whip on his clothes: tight blue jeans that accented his muscular lower body; a well-pressed, collared white shirt; and a spiffy blue blazer that enhanced the outline of his broad shoulders and bulging biceps.

While heading toward his dorm room door, he briefly stopped in front of a mirror and moved his separated fingers through his long, curly brown hair. He paid little attention to his smooth, blemish-free facial skin, which had been riddled with pimples just five years earlier--back when he as a 15-year-old Wooster High School "nobody."

Rather than wait for the elevator, Tommy zipped down the stairway three stories to the main lobby. As he rushed to the building's main door, three young women walking together each smiled at him. He reciprocated but rushed past when one of them exclaimed "Hi, Tommy!" This was the same blonde that he had kissed the previous week at a Sigma Alpha Epsilon fraternity party. Unsure of her name while still in the lobby, he quickly waved and responded by saying, "Howdy."

Unlike just five years earlier, back when Tommy had felt depressed, now in 1990 he felt confident, self-assured and as if he had a bright future ahead.

Soon at the front seat of his new light blue Volkswagen Golf, Tommy turned from the dorm parking lot, heading south on North Sierra Street. Momentarily, he entered the eastbound on-ramp to U.S. Interstate 80, while flipping on the radio. That March's top tune, "Black Velvet" by Alannah Myles inspired Tommy to think of how smooth his life had been since being adopted by Doctor Robbins just five years earlier.

Under the physician's careful guidance and mentorship, Tommy's high school grades had quickly catapulted to the B+ range--a level maintained during his first two years at the university. The young man began feeling self-assured and as if he had a positive life ahead of himself, unlike before when everything had seemed gloomy.

While zipping from I-80 to the southbound lanes of U.S. Interstate 580, Tommy finally realized that this impromptu excursion to the clinic would make him late for work at his part-time evening job shelving books at the Washoe County Library downtown. This would mark his first tardiness at the popular facility, then in his third year working there. That meager income covered his food and lodging expenses, while the doctor paid his tuition as agreed--as long as Tommy maintained at least a B average.

By this point half-way to his destination, Tommy began thinking about his biological father, who had been faithfully attending Alcoholics Anonymous for the previous three years.

Even more impressive, from this university student's perspective, the former plumber had started holding down a good job at the Whispering Wind Wild Horse Ranch. Located 22 miles north of Reno off U.S.Highway 395, the 237-acre spread had been purchased in 1987 by Doctor Robbins.

The physician designated the property as a sanctuary for wild mustangs, declaring that the horses needed to be saved from destructive policies of the U.S. government's federal Bureau of Land Management.

As if to thumb his nose at the bureaucrats, at least from Tommy's perspective, Doctor Robbins hired as the ranch's boss a guy who had been despised and vilified by those morons based in Washington, D.C. Old-time, real-country Nevadans seemed to agree that Cactus Pete was the perfect man for the job.

Although still struggling to start and operate a new low-power talk radio station in the Reno area, the new ranch boss still found time to track down and recruit Honest for the operation. By then in his late 50s, this Vietnam veteran and former Centralia resident quickly seized the opportunity to work as one of three full-time cowboys at the operation.

To Tommy, the most exciting part of this transition had been the off-and-on resumption of his relationship with the man he had once known as his one-and-only dad. After a 12-year estrangement that had begun in 1975 upon his mother's death, in 1987 the elder Davis and Tommy began chatting with each other on a sporadic basis.

At first Honest had admitted his own resentment that

Doctor Robbins and Tommy had agreed to the adoption, quickly approved by the courts amid the former plumber's absence-- which Judge Frederick Bowen had declared as a simple case of abandonment.

Now more than half-way through his undergraduate pre-med studies, Tommy had recently begun to ponder what he previously would have considered as "the unthinkable." This young man felt proud of himself for essentially "burying the hatchet," dropping his hate and revulsion toward Honest--those emotions replaced by forgiveness and love.

Thinking of himself as far more mature and level-minded than he had been just a few years earlier, Tommy developed what he considered a much different type of intellectual and emotional bond with Doctor Robbins. Far more than merely a typical father-son relationship, in this student's mind their interaction was tantamount to the intellectual exchanges between the ancient Greek intellectual Plato and his teacher, Socrates.

From Tommy's perspective, he and Doctor Robbins always communicated on that type of higher level--sharing the mutual goal of increasing their knowledge, while striving to continually devise effective ways for improving society.

Instead of chatting about what Tommy considered the "mundane and boring" everyday lifestyle topics that engrossed the minds of most people, he and his adoptive father often spoke of philosophy, mathematics, health care and governmental ideologies.

Like Socrates had done for Plato, at least in Tommy's mind, Doctor Robbins had taught him how to use his own superior mind to think--rather than merely allowing unfettered emotions to rule and dictate his every action.

Making this self-improvement strategy a cornerstone of his own life, while driving from the freeway onto Kietzke Lane, Tommy began to ponder the reason for this sudden and unexpected summons to the oncologist's clinic.

Turning from Kietzke onto Hammill Lane, he began guessing about the possible reasons for Anthony Dunn's sense of urgency--when on the phone just 10 minutes earlier. Had Doctor Robbins suddenly become seriously ill? Or, perhaps there had been a catastrophic accident of some sort at the clinic.

At exactly 4:13 in the afternoon, Tommy zipped into one of the few open parking spaces into the clinic's parking lot. Momentarily, he ran 25 yards to the clinic's "employees only" back entrance and rapped on the locked metal door.

"Tommy, thank heavens you have arrived," Anthony said right away upon letting this young man inside. "The doctor has been asking for you, pleading for you to get here as quickly as possible."

At this receptionist's side, Tommy saw his Aunt Pamela, who still worked as the clinic's manager after 15 years in that position. She promptly hugged the young man tight as soon as he entered the hallway, with no one there except her, Anthony and Tommy.

"Tommy, the doctor has intentionally locked himself in his own office," Pamela whispered. The university student paid little attention to the fact that his aunt here no longer had the body and hair reflective of an alluring Hollywood movie star. By this point, a mother of three at age 40, she had a slightly pudgy frame and kept her tight hair tied up in a bun--unlike the mid-70s when she kept her flowing, curly blonde mane at chest length. Nonetheless, at least in her nephew's eyes, she remained as attractive as ever.

"Has the doctor cracked?" Tommy tried to get right to the point. "Has he lost his mind somehow, or inadvertently taken some kind of horrible drug?"

"Tommy, we cannot say for sure." Now in his early 70s, Anthony gently rested his right hand on the student's left shoulder. "You, of course, know by now that I love the doctor as if he were my own son. ... You need to realize that..."

"I can hear the doctor crying in his office." Tommy took a step closer to the physician's door, which remained closed. "Please get to the point, so that I can get in there as fast as possible--like he wants. You might not know for sure, but please tell me what you think has occurred, so that I can get an idea of what to say when I go in there."

Pamela held a clipboard that she occasionally glanced at, perhaps--Tommy thought--to check statistics or maybe the list of remaining patients for the afternoon.

"Tommy, five of the doctor's cancer patients died earlier today." Pamela kept staring at the charts. "Since I have been here, that is the highest numbers of his patients who have passed away on a single day--at least as far as I can remember."

Anthony interrupted, a sense of urgency in his voice that Tommy had never heard before. The receptionist finally summarized the apparent heart of the matter: "Think of this, before you go inside and see him. The doctor has always managed to maintain a solemn and dignified demeanor, hiding his emotions from all of us--day in and day out for years on end--even after the deaths of patients whom he truly and deeply cared about ... Knowing this, how much grief can one man stand, before he finally breaks down?"

"Thanks, you two." Tommy stepped up to the doctor's closed office door, keeping his voice at a whisper. "Pray that I say the right and perfect things to help him."

The young man then knocked hard.

"Who is it?"

"Doctor, it's me--Tommy ... I understand that you wanted to see me."

The door quickly opened.

Right away Tommy felt stunned and mesmerized by the sight of his mentor and adoptive father. The physician, who typically stood erect with his shoulders sharply back in a professional, military-style manner, was slumped forward as if lacking energy.

"Doctor, are you okay?" Tommy felt deep concern.

"Come right inside." Doctor Robbins motioned for him to sit in one of the three chairs for patients and their relatives when consulting with the physician. "You are the only person that I feel like talking with this afternoon."

Tommy quickly tried to get as comfortable as possible. As the doctor moved to sit behind his desk, the young man marveled at color photographs on every well, considered by the student as magnetic images of mustangs in the wilderness. Gone were the flimsy black-and-white photos, snapped by a photographer that Tommy considered much less talented than whoever captured these colorful scenes.

Although usually highly observant, Tommy needed at least a half minute before realizing that tears remained on Doctor Robbins' cheeks. Used facial tissue was strewn across one side the desktop, the trashcan to the side of the table also filled.

"Doctor, it looks like you have been crying up a storm."

"Yep." The doctor blew his nose, the noise so loud and corny that it sounded to Tommy as if a train whistle. "As you can see, I finally let loose with my emotions."

"Fantastic."

More tears streamed from the doctor's eyes, which he quickly swept away with tissue. His nose appeared to Tommy as nearly half as red as Rudolph the Red-Nosed Reindeer, not a joking matter considering the fact that this physician had many years earlier earned a reputation as genuinely caring for all of his patients--without becoming overly emotional.

"Tommy, I have not cried since my mother's funeral in 1971, and several years before that when four of my buddies got blown to pieces in Vietnam."

"Doctor, I'm surprised that it took you this long ... I cannot even begin to imagine how many of your patients have died from cancer through the years, due to absolutely no fault of your own."

The doctor fished a comb out of his own pants pocket, and starting combing back his disheveled hair--just a bit thinner from when Tommy had first met him at age 4, more than 16 years earlier.

"I guess my emotions got built up for much too long, without me giving myself any chance for release--to let my grief known to the world."

"Doctor, I cannot even begin to imagine how you can possibly cope with so much death, all around you--everywhere you go in your professional life. You have been nothing less than amazing--and, of course, you still are that way."

"Even if I am what you say, 'amazing,' that has not helped much--hardly at all."

"How can you possibly say that? You are so dedicated, so fully committed to the well being and welfare--the potential survival--of each and every one of your patients."

"Being dedicated and having integrity on my part has little to do with their survival. ... I'm sorry to admit this to you here, but it's true."

"How could you possibly even say that? ... How could you think that way?"

The doctor then explained that this was precisely the reason why he had summoned Tommy and no one else. The physician assured the young man that as a highly intelligent student he was among the few people who would understand.

"Tommy, can you remember way back when you broke down and cried near the shores of Pyramid Lake--five years ago. It seems like almost yesterday, doesn't it."

"I sure do. I've got to admit that I was a smart-mouthed punk."

"But you learned something that day, didn't you? ... You learned that holding our emotions inside for a long time is no good at all. And then you felt good, or at least somewhat better after venting your anger."

"I sure do remember."

"Well, I need to admit that I am a prime example of failing to practice what I preach ... You see, like I've told you a few times before, 'I'm only human. I'm merely a pretty darned good guy, simply trying to do my best at my profession."

"Not a single person who knows the actual facts could deny that what you just said is true. ... You have integrity, and..."

"But I haven't done enough. ... I have only been doing what is required."

"What do you mean by that? Doctor, you work harder than..."

"It's not a matter of how hard I work, or how diligent that I am."

"Sounds to me like you're putting too much blame on yourself. You have got to stop beating yourself up about this situation."

"If you want to know the truth, Tommy, my hands are tied--my hands are literally all tied up, and that is indirectly why so many of these people are passing away."

"I'm perplexed. None of what you're saying makes any sense to me at all. ... I hope that we can assume that you have not lost your mind when saying these things. You seem to still have all of your mental faculties ... I mean, in layman's terms, 'You have not lost your marbles.'"

The physician and the student summarily erupted in laughter. Tommy felt glad to have lightened the mood, at least somewhat.

Once their chuckles subsided, Doctor Robbins said that he had calculated that during the first 15 years of his oncology practice, at least 7,000 of his advanced Stage IV cancer patients had died.

"That's enough people to fill a good-sized graveyard." The doctor paused briefly to blow his nose again. "Only about 140 patients of my patients with that level of the disease survived. ... Now, what do you think of that?"

"Doctor, are you telling me that only about just more than 2 percent--about two out of every 100 Stage IV cancer patients that you have treated survived?"

"You are right on the money in saying that."

"Wow! ... I had no idea."

More tears began to stream down Doctor Robbins' cheeks.

"Tommy, forgive me for behaving this way ... You know

that I'm not a baby ... I'm a professional, a level-headed adult ... I just needed to vent, and you are the person I chose for that. ... Are you still okay with it?"

"I'm all ears ... You have taught me how to be a good listener--a better listener anyway--and I believe that I am doing that now, for me and for you as well."

"Good." The doctor used his entire left arm to gently swipe against his desktop, sweeping away the many discarded tissues--so that they fell into the trashcan. "Please keep listening, because there is much more that I need to tell you."

"This is fascinating. ... Please tell me more."

The physician explained that his results in treating advanced Stage IV cancers mirrored the nationwide statistics. In recent years, medical experts nationwide had finally begun compiling and analyzing comprehensive data on the results. Authorities had failed to compile such data way back in the mid-1970s, when cancer killed Tommy's mother.

Yet tragically, the mainstream American medical industry had done absolutely nothing significant since then to increase the effectiveness of cancer treatment--especially the deadliest forms of the disease.

Doctor Robbins further explained that just like they had done several decades earlier, physicians still had the same basic treatment for advanced cancers.

"Basically, Tommy, if you can remember at all way back when you were just five years old, your 'real father'--Honest--was essentially right. Remember how he always complained that I was poisoning your mother. At the time he became increasingly angry, upset that I was treating your mom with something that was actually killing her?"

"Doctor, my memory has faded somewhat. But, yes, I vaguely recall that Honest kept taking about poisons and that he was angry with you."

"Well, I've got to tell you that--at least in a very specific sense--your father was right on the money ... I am not going to deny that ... In fact, like I say, my hands were tied--and they still are tied ... Understand?"

"This might sound weird for me to say, but I might be getting the big picture."

The physician then explained that all oncologists nationwide were required to follow the same, specific, pre-set treatment protocol--without any deviation whatsoever from these stringent rules. In all Stage IV cancer cases, oncologists were--and still are--required to administer specific dosing levels of extremely poisonous chemotherapy drugs. ... These pharmaceuticals are indeed poisonous ... When intravenously administered into the human body, these deadly substances attack both the healthy cells and the "bad or diseased" cells. The poisons make no exceptions whatsoever, since these drugs lack the ability to differentiate between healthy tissue and the cancers that destroy essential bodily functions.

"As a result of this, Tommy, in many instances the chemo drugs actually kill the patients much faster than the cancer would on its own."

"Then, it's true, what Honest has said ... Those stupid pharmaceuticals might have killed my mother?"

"Even if I were under oath, in a court of law at this very moment, I would have no option other than to say that, 'Yes, in all likelihood, the drugs might have killed your mom, rather than the cancer she suffered from. And that was not even my fault, because all that I did was precisely what the medical industry required me to do."

"This is a tragedy, doctor. This sounds like you might be saying that the mainstream medical industry knows exactly that this is happening, and yet the big drug companies and regular doctors are doing nothing significant to improve treatments?"

"You are correct."

"This is ludicrous. Everyone should be mad at this crazy situation, marching in the streets to protest this asinine situation ... The drug companies are intentionally killing people, at least in a round-about way."

"Once again, you have hit the nail right on the head."

Right away, Tommy heard a light knock on Doctor Robbins' office door.

"Should I open it, doctor?" Tommy tried to be helpful, while also sensing that by giving this open and honest explanation the doctor seemed to have improved.

"Sure."

Tommy summarily opened the door. Anthony and Pamela each stood there, both inquiring whether everything was okay.

"Everything is fine." Doctor Robbins dropped the empty tissue box into the trashcan. "Thank you both for your genuine concern. I'm feeling a little better ... If you could just please give Tommy and me a few more minutes to talk."

The pair smiled, each saying "thank-you" as they closed the door.

"So, doctor, the pharmaceutical keeps killing people?" Tommy became increasingly fascinated. "And, they're not doing anything of any significance to develop a much better, far more effective treatment? ... Why is nothing significant happening?"

"Your guess is as good as mine, son. ... Politics maybe."

"And my Aunt Pamela, who works here for you? She had suffered from advanced Stage IV cancer, just like my mom had? ... And, the mere fact that she is still alive makes her among the two out of every 100 people who had advance-stage cancer before becoming lucky enough to have survived?"

"Technically, yes. The mere fact that she is here, still with us, is a miracle. All that I did was follow the protocol in treating her ... The person who deserves most of the credit besides your aunt for being a head-strong and determined fighter, I suppose--and it's true--is Honest ... Remember, he was the person who convinced her to get treatment."

"Super interesting. And, now, my Aunt Pamela is here--working in your office--striving to maximize efficiency in order to help others. Yet all the while, no matter what she does and what you do, doctor, nearly 98 percent of the advanced stage cancer patients treated in this office--and elsewhere nationwide--are going to die from the disease. ... If the general public realized the truth, they would get angrier than a rodeo bull ... To me, the whole thing stinks to high heaven."

"You are right on target. ... The companies are playing Russian roulette with cancer patients ... To them, I believe, everyday people are about as worthless as rats."

"That's a mighty harsh thing to say."

"Tommy, my analysis might sound cold and calculated. But the facts speak for themselves. ... To me, at least from my perspective, it's almost as if the pharmaceutical companies care far more about profit, than for the welfare of patients."

"But why doesn't somebody do something?"

"Listen carefully, please, to what I am about to say. ... Why would the medical industry and the drug companies want to cure cancer? ... Imagine how much money they would lose, if this wretched disease were suddenly cured--literally wiped off the face of the earth. Think of how many countless billions of dollars in annual revenues that would be lost by hospitals, drug companies and oncologists like myself. ... Sadly, the big losers in this greedy system are the patients--people just like your late mother, and just like five of my patients who died earlier today. ... Yes, greed has taken over the medical industry. Greed has filled the federal regulatory system that approves drugs. ... And greed, either directly or indirectly, has spilled over into our nation's medical schools--where prospective doctors are taught that they must administer dangerous pharmaceuticals, each time that a specific type of prognosis occurs."

"So, does this mean, doctor, what no one will seriously try to cure cancer?"

"Well, I am going to play a huge part in doing that!"

"You are? How?" Tommy sensed that the excitement in this physician's voice was real, almost to the point of being infectious.

"I do not know precisely how I am going to do it ... But I guarantee you, Tommy, that I am going to sharply improve the survival rate for patients suffering the most deadly cancers."

"I keep wanting to ask you how ... It seems like you still have no specific answer."

"Tommy, if I have learned anything in life, it is that the old saying is often true, 'If there is a will, there is a way.' ... I have the will to make this happen, and I have the curiosity and the knowledge to move forward with my goal ... Believe me, I will never, ever give up in this quest, for as long as I am healthy ... I am angry at the medical industry, and I'm equally upset with the drug companies ... But I refuse to let my anger just fester ... I am going to remain more focused on this task than anyone could possibly imagine ... Far too many lives are at stake for me to waste time in this effort ... You are the only person that I am ever going to tell this to, at least in this early stage ... That's largely why I summoned you here today ... I need someone to share my goal with, and I've chosen just one person to do that with--and it's you, Tommy ... You know that I adore your aunt, and my wife, and Anthony--whom I call 'The General.'' ... Perhaps cancer can never be fully cured. ... But I can guarantee you, and mark my words here today--please remember them---I am going to significantly improve the cancer survival rate. And when that happens, the whole world will take notice."

"Wow!"

"My future invention is going to save lives--many hundreds of thousands, or perhaps even millions of people, who all will escape the ravages of cancer, even if the big drug companies start hating me for doing so."

Twenty-Six

Feeling energized and more confident than she had been for the previous several years, Mossad agent Shira Levy knew that this would be a pivotal day, instrumental to the future of health care worldwide.

Amazingly, from her perspective, her associates at the U.S. Food and Drug Administration and the Israeli had been indirectly working toward the same goal.

Officials from the Jewish state and the American agency that regulates pharmaceuticals each had worked diligently to amass funding for a significant international scientific effort.

These mutual endeavors reached a fever pitch on July 23, 1990, slightly more than 15 years after Shira had joined the American agency--while shielding her true identity.

On this historical day, Congress was set to vote on whether to fund a significant research project that scientists had been hoping to launch for the previous several years.

In the final months leading up to that pivotal day, medical experts had vowed that the Human Genome Project would lead to significant developments in medicine.

Researchers explained that in layman's terms, the effort would take 15 years to "unlock the secret to DNA," the essential structure of every cell in the human body.

Over time, these officials promised, this pivotal knowledge would give biologists a clear understanding of virtually every disease and physical affliction plaguing humans.

These scientists also predicted that much later, within perhaps 20 or 30 years after "cracking the code," sometime in the 2020s and beyond--researchers would use the essential data in developing "cures" for everything from heart ailments to cancer.

Yet for all this to happen, the United States Congress

would need to approve a minimum of $3 billion to fund the Human Genome Project.

Sadly, from the perspective of Shira and streams of scientists worldwide, scores of elected leaders in the U.S. House of Representatives and the Senate initially balked at the idea. These opponents insisted that government should refrain from getting involved.

Determined to "win at any cost," Shira and officials at other federal agencies--along with leaders of several nations including Israel--banded together; individually and collectively, these bureaucrats worked behind the scenes to push for full passage of the measure. Every cent was needed if the research were to be a success.

As the leader of their drive in the halls of Congress, working outside the public limelight, these bureaucrats had chosen U.S. Senator Larry Spickler--at that juncture in his fourth term as a Democrat representing Nevada.

Shira felt proud to be among a handful of people who knew the truth.

As that year began, a full decade after Israeli officials had confronted Spickler about his murders and mob-backed behavior, the Jewish nation essentially began "calling in the chips from him for the first time."

From 1980 clear until 1990, the Israeli officials had intentionally refrained from contacting Spickler or confronting him about: the murders of the Nevada sheriff and his deputies; the senator's shady back-door land deals; and his underworld connections.

Yet finally, just as Shira and other officials had secretly hoped for, as 1990 began trusted personnel from the Israeli Embassy in Washington met with Senator Spickler and his longtime chief of staff, Dick Cooper. Without even mentioning the Nevadan's despicable past, embassy staffers Ashar Sandler and Eli Yossef told him: "If you know what is good for you, and for your future, you will ensure that this bill gets passed. The Human

Genome Project must get full funding ... You know what we mean. Any failure, senator, will result in dire consequences for you."

Fully apprised of these developments every step of the way, Shira felt increasingly proud that her homeland had played a pivotal role in putting Spickler on the necessary and predictable political path.

Right out of the starting gate, as President George H.W. Bush approached the midway point in his first and only term as a Republican in the White House, the Silver State Democrat became a standard-bearer for the international scientific effort.

From January through late July of that pivotal year, Shira closely followed news reports on Spickler's aggressive and dogged efforts--in pushing for passage of $3 billion in essential funding for the Human Genome Project.

As a result, in the mindset of many voters, Spickler emerged as somewhat of a hero, a courageous champion doggedly fighting for significant advancements in medical technology. Yet Shira remained among those who knew otherwise; she still considered him as if The Devil's Personal Representative here on earth.

Sadly, at least from Shira's perspective, creeps like this senator and his slimy crony were "necessary evils ... We do not want to live with them, but at the same time--regrettably--we cannot live without them."

Remaining fully mindful of this, at mid-morning on that late July day, Shira sat in the Third Floor break lounge of the Food and Drug Administration's headquarters in Silver Spring, Maryland. Along with several personnel on her immediate staff, she watched a television, featuring live C-Span coverage of the United States Senate.

Shira and the others watched intently while Spickler, appearing in the Senate chambers, gave what she considered as perhaps the most fiery, passionate and heart-felt speech of his entire political career. Moving his arms all about and speaking in a cadence and tone reminiscent of an old-time Southern preacher, the politician spoke of the essential need to pass the bill "for the betterment of all mankind."

Many of Spickler's fellow senators cheered as if he were the greatest champion in fighting for essential research that eventually might enable doctors to save millions of lives. In reality, though, Shira knew of this jerk's murderous past; that thought remained prevalent in her mind every time he mentioned the need to save people.

Exactly 34 minutes after Senator Spickler concluded his historical speech, while still in the agency's break room, Shira broke out in cheers and applause along with her associates-- as they watched the Senate's vote tally. The bill, which many political analysts had previously predicted would fail, passed by an overwhelming majority.

"That clown," Shira thought about the politician, as she and her associates left the break room to return to their various offices. "From now on, we're going to use that skunk to our own advantage, as much as possible ... And, hopefully, with God's grace and guidance, the world's best and most intelligent physicians--the rare people like Doctor James Robbins of Reno, Nevada--will someday develop a cure for cancer."

Twenty-Seven

In mid-1995, more than half way through U.S. President Bill Clinton's first term, and 20 years after launching his oncology practice in Reno, Doctor James Robbins began making a significant change in his career.

Increasingly determined to boost the survival rates among people suffering from advanced Stage IV cancers, the physician began studying for a degree in Homeopathic medicine. While still at the helm of his burgeoning "mainstream" oncology practice, and by then in his late 50s, the doctor started taking correspondence courses--learning everything that he possibly could about natural remedies.

Doctor Robbins had never revealed his goal to his wife, Marie, and his closest associates including his office manager, Pamela, and receptionist, Anthony. The physician had simply told them, "I am doing this, because there has to be a better way."

All along, he had only told the full truth to his adopted son Tommy, by that point entering his third year at the University of Nevada School of Medicine in Reno.

Besides wanting to find a natural pathway toward more effective cancer treatments, on the infrequent occasions that he saw Tommy, Doctor Robbins privately revealed even more compelling details.

"What I am discovering is that natural remedies are generally harmless, while far more effective than expensive, manmade and dangerous drugs," the physician told the young man. "What you are learning now in medical school is only a part of the many available treatments, for a wide variety of ailments and physical afflictions."

Tommy realized that--if he had not known better--he likely would have argued with the doctor about this; at the time as a medical school student earning high grades he was being taught in medical school that drugs produced by huge pharmaceutical companies were "the only way."

Just like Plato was when being taught by Socrates in ancient Greek society thousands of years ago, Tommy tried to remain open-minded about any topic broached--while also aggressively asking plenty of logical and thoughtful questions.

On a unusually cool Saturday in late July, one week after Congress voted to fund the Human Genome Project, Doctor Robbins and Tommy spent the entire afternoon in the physician's study of his exclusive estate inside Reno's luxury Sunnyville Shores development. Tommy liked the fact that he and the doctor made "serious play" out of such incisive, imaginative and penetrating conversations.

The student appreciated the fact that Doctor Robbins had worked hard and with great efficiency for many years, boosting himself up from a low-income lifestyle to what they agreed was a "comfortable income"--thanks to his reputation, skills and a supreme dedication to the welfare of his patients.

All along, from Tommy's perspective the oncologist deserved his undying admiration and respect for serving as a full-bird Colonel--heading the medical branch of the Nevada Army National Guard. If all went as planned, while still only in his late 50s, within two years the physician could retire with a pension of at least $2,500 per month.

At that point, as far as Tommy knew, such an amount was merely "chump change" to a top-notch health care professional of the doctor's supreme reputation and superior caliber. In fact, while still a standard "mainstream" oncologist, the physician had earned at least 15 awards from his counterparts from around the country.

Yet little did those physicians know, at least as far as Tommy could tell, that Doctor Robbins was then in the process of pulling an "end-run"--positioning himself to essentially change the entire playing field within the humongous U.S. health care industry.

Tommy thought of the doctor's quest for more knowledge--far outside the mainstream of American health care--as the equivalent of the famed "flea-flicker" play used by fast-moving and often-effective offenses in football.

As if a typical, low-level defensive line--at least from Tommy's view--just about everyone significant in the American health care industry thought that Doctor Robbins would continue operating his medical practice in the required direction.

Instead, however, as far as Tommy could tell, his mentor was quietly and methodically in the process of making an "end-around." In this way, the student believed, Doctor Robbins essentially had become a "maverick within the medical industry." Instead of following the typical and required career pathway demanded of American oncologists, by studying Homeopathy the physician had begun to set his own course.

"Doctor, I obviously lack your expertise." Tommy sat in a visitor's chair in Doctor Robbin's expansive home office, featuring a giant open window. This afforded an expansive view of the back yard, dotted with fountains, ponds and well-situated plants of many sizes and varieties. "But if you ask me for my prediction, the so-called mainstream medical industry is very likely going to label you as an adversary of theirs--or even perhaps as if an enemy. ... Does it sound to you like I am off track in saying that?"

"Sure, Tommy, you're probably right on target with your analysis, but please understand that I don't care what they--the medical establishment--thinks of me," the doctor sipped a tall, ice-filled glass of an Arnold Palmer. This remained his favorite drink, prepared by mixing lemonade with iced tea.

While Tommy, at age 25, sipped ice water and nibbled corn chips, the two men began playing a verbal game that they invented on the spot. As a committed, dedicated and highly ambitious student, the young man steadily announced a variety of specific ailments. One by one, the medical school pupil listed a different illness--plus the mainstream health care industry's primary drugs required or recommended for addressing each specific problem.

In every instance, however, just as quickly as Tommy mentioned another specific drug, Doctor Robbins instantly told of the many adverse reactions caused by that particular pharmaceutical. Just as impressive from this student's perspective, rather than manmade drugs, the physician spoke of a natural substance that Homeopaths worldwide had proven effective for the same ailment--all without causing adverse side effects.

"Wow!" Tommy exclaimed after 17 straight minutes of this back-and-forth banter. "Doctor, you're really getting all of this down pat. ... You really are a wiz, aren't you?"

"I wouldn't go so far as to say that."

"But how can you be sure that all of this isn't just a bunch of quackery? That seems like a logical question, because you know what the mainstream doctors say."

"Belive me, Tommy, I've read tons of scientific reports on these things, literally piles and piles of in-depth papers, all concluding that well-chosen and specific natural substances can serve as effective remedies. Mother nature has provided humanity with miracle substances, which those of us in the west--tragically-- choose to ignore."

"Once again, though, what about the mainstream doctors?"

"Well, first off, within the realm of Homeopathy, we generally refrain from using the term 'mainstream.' Instead, we often refer to those practitioners dispersing "unnatural, manmade drugs" as allopathic or conventional physicians."

"Doctor, I never knew any of these many specifics until now ... So, that brings up another obvious question. When in the world are you getting enough time to learn all this, especially since your oncology practice seems to remain super-busy?"

"Sometimes I stay up all night studying, even though I work helping patients from the wee morning hours into the evenings--what I've always done."

"Holy-Moly! ... You are now in your late 50s, and you're telling me that you are doing all this ... Heck, what you are currently achieving is a lot more than most of my fellow medical school students. ... I must say that you are amazing."

"I don't know why it is, but people have kept saying those kinds of things about me for the past several decades ... I always respond that 'I am just a regular guy, simply doing what I know that I need to achieve--in an effort to provide each and every one of my patients with the best possible care imaginable."

Mesmerized by the doctor's can-do attitude, and equally captivated by his youthful demeanor, Tommy decided to remain quiet for awhile. Still in medical school, he wondered whether he could maintain the continuous commitment and personal energy that the doctor had maintained without letup for the previous several decades. At this juncture, this native of Centralia, Nevada, had not yet chosen his future medical specialty.

"Doctor, this is a correspondence course that you're taking? Where is it from, and how did you learn about special instruction?"

The physician responded by saying that he had seen a barely noticeable 2-inch-tall advertisement on a rear inside page of a respected U.S. medical journal. On a whim, while increasingly curious, this graduate of the "mainstream" University of California at San Francisco Medical School, researched the little-known school.

"The classes are offered out of an official, certified and prestigious School of Homeopathy--based in Haifa, Israel." The doctor briefly sipped his Arnold Palmer, while gazing through his expansive home office window toward the lavish back yard garden. "I applied and they quickly accepted me as a student, saying to me--flat out--that they were highly impressed. Interestingly, at least from my perspective, they told me that they had already heard many good things about me. And, just as interesting, the administrators there told me that I had become their first student living in this hemisphere ... If any other licensed U.S. doctors had seen the advertisement, they either failed to notice--or they purposefully ignored it, perhaps because we are taught that all Homeopaths are greedy, inept quacks."

"Interesting ... But doctor, do you feel that this additional knowledge will somehow--eventually--enable you to develop a much more effective and non-poisonous treatment for the worst, most deadly cancers?"

"I envision nothing but the best possible outcome ... If it takes my last breath, I will personally develop the most significant natural cancer remedies imaginable."

*

The El Al Airlines flight on August 14, 1995, from Geneva, Switzerland to Tel Aviv in Israel had been smoothe and uneventful until 150 miles from the Jewish nation.

At precisely 2:51 p.m. Greenwich time, The Boeing 747-400 hit unexpected turbulence at 29,500 feet above the Mediterranean Sea.

Sitting immediately to Shira Levy's right and left were her only children, the redheaded 8-year-old Eric and 6-year-old Elvis, who had dark brown hair.

"Mommy, are we going to crash?" Eric asked, grabbing tightly to Shira's left arm.

Mindful enough to ensure that his seat belt remained fastened, Shira decided to behave as positively as possible. Although she initially wondered whether this might the the latest terrorist attack, she briefly kissed this boy's forehead.

"No worries, Eric. ... This is just minor turbulence, something that normally happens on airline flights when aircraft enters pockets of warm or cold air."

The boy smiled up at her, energizing this mother's protective instincts as he said, "Wow! That's cool."

Still in rough turbulence, the plane continued to rock from side to side as Shira glanced to her right to check little Elvis, who remained fast asleep.

"Ladies and gentlemen," an airline hostess spoke into a microphone, from the front of the aisle near the cockpit. "Please ensure that your seatbelts are tightly fastened.. The captain informs me that we have hit unexpected turbulence. We will arrive in Tel Aviv slightly behind schedule, and start our final approach in another 13 minutes."

Shira remained confident that the government chauffeur and limousine would be there to pick up her and the boys. This marked the agent's first return to her homeland in 22 years, an unusually long stretch for any Mossad operative.

She and her husband, Ken Miller, who still worked as a U.S. Defense Department official, had been arguing about this trip for the previous six months.

A native of Boston, Massachusetts, Ken had insisted that the trip would be far too dangerous for him and the boys. The Middle East remained a violent hot-spot, riddled with terrorists, bombers and hijackers.

Finally, after frequent heated discussions with her, Ken had finally agreed that he would take the trip with Shira and the boys. He relented in early July in the back yard of their Alexandria, Virginia, home, after Shira erupted into tears.

While sobbing profusely, she spoke about the boys' Jewish heritage, the fact that the children had a right to see their homeland and to visit their grandparents there, and the essential need to give the kids a lifetime memory while they were still young.

Yet in keeping with Shira's intense training, throughout the entire nine years of their marriage so far, this agent had refrained from telling him the truth about her--especially the fact that she remained a top-level agent for Mossad.

Overjoyed when Ken finally agreed, she then had quickly made arrangements to visit family and to have an urgent meeting with her superiors at Mossad.

More than ever, Shira loved her husband with all her heart--even though just about everything about him remained the opposite of what she had yearned for in a man. In her mind, these attributes seemed endless: instead of being muscular and sturdy, in her mind he was mega-tall and as wiry as a rookie high school basketball player; instead of full, curly and flowing long brown hair, he was bald as a bowling ball; and rather than engaging in long, thoughtful and mind-provoking conversations about philosophy and current issues, Ken always refused to engage in such conversations unless sports became the topic--particularly pro football and the Washington Redskins.

Shira could never mentally pin down precisely why she loved Ken. Every fiber of her being wanted the best for this man, reared in a strict, hard-working and devout Catholic family. Ken's many Massachusetts relatives always behaved as if pleasant and cordial in Shira's presence, but she sensed otherwise--intuitively believing that they detested her heritage, classy behavior, good looks and keen intelligence.

For Shira, the proverbial blasting cap that might destroy her relationship with Ken and his family occurred just two days before their scheduled departure. That evening her husband said that he would not be going on the trip to Israel, claiming that he urgently needed to stay due to a sudden eruption in the war in Bosnia. Ken claimed he was the designated Defense Department leader in coordinating and arranging dozens of U.S. Air Force sorties into the European combat zone between the Serbs and the Croats.

"Darn you!" she had yelled at him in the kitchen of their home, while the boys were asleep in their upstairs bedrooms. "Go ahead, and stay, Ken--while we go on ahead without you. ... Let's never talk about this any more, because I'm afraid if we do, we will be headed straight down the railroad track--straight toward an eventual divorce."

As the airliner started its final approach to Tel Aviv, Shira thought about that incident, which she realized marked one of the few times she had ever lost her cool.

Right after the aircraft arrived at the terminal and came to a full stop, Shira stood and retrieved crutches from the overhead bin for her youngest son. Always wearing metal and rubber leg braces, and about to enter the first grade, little Elvis had muscular dystrophy. He had suffered from a long list of ailments, including severe asthma, since infancy; by contrast, always seemingly the picture of good health, Eric had hardly been sick in his entire life--eager to enter the third grade the following month.

To Shira, the only good thing about her husband's absence was the fact that this enabled her to quickly change this trip's itinerary. No longer needing to sneak away from Ken for secretive rendezvous with her associates, now she could handle those matters right away. This would clear up time for her to spend the remainder of the planned 10-day excursion with the boys and their relatives.

Inside the airport terminal, as Elvis hobbled on his crutches at her right side and Eric held her left hand, Shira noticed a black-suited man who held a cardboard sign embossed with her name. Just 15 minutes later this chauffeur started driving them to downtown Tel Aviv, en route to an office complex where she had a scheduled meeting with several high-ranking Mossad officials.

Shira told the driver to wait in the front loading zone, promising that she expected to return within 90 minutes. The chauffeur initially protested, while complaining that guards would keep ordering him away for security reasons.

"No worries," she said, while standing on the sidewalk next to her boys and leaning her head toward the open front passenger window. "Just tell them my name--Shira Levy--and then I am sure that they will let you stay put here."

The driver briefly protested, wearing a black cap that seemed to her as if five sizes too big, but she walked away with her boys hand-in-hand.

As this trio approached the building's entrance, Eric started complaining that he did not want to go to any sort of business meeting. Instead, he yearned to play outside somewhere--outside of the big city and perhaps go for a hike. Meantime, the disabled Elvis remained quiet every step of the way, always a person who preferred to listen rather than to speak.

"Eric, think positive ... I have everything handled, so that you can have plenty of fun ... As soon as we get inside, you and Elvis will be going to a playroom filled with more toys than you might possibly imagine ... That is one thing that you will quickly learn about our shared homeland ... Here, family means everything."

Sure enough, as soon as a receptionist told them where to find the children's recreation area, Eric rushed toward that indoor complex--while the hobbling little Elvis, who tripped only once along the way, went in that direction as well from close behind.

Feeling confident and energized while about to have her first one-on-one meeting with Mossad officials in several years, Shira took an elevator to the Third Floor. There, she went straight into an office where an entrance sign said: "Bobly Boof Industries." From intelligence reports, she knew that this was a code phrase designating the site as a close-knit, behind-the-scenes operation sanctioned and funded by Mossad.

Within two minutes after Shira arrived at this bogus business, a clerk escorted her to a back office. Once inside, Shira exchanged pleasantries with the only person there.

By this point approaching 80 years old, the former Israeli Ambassador to the United States, Amos Berkovich, looked to her as if a man of about 50--still appearing to her as though clean-cut, dapper and mentally focused. This marked the first time they had met in person; yet thanks to internal communications that had started two decades earlier back in the mid-1970s, she had seen many photographs of him.

Perhaps most of all, she recalled that Berkovich had earned a well-deserved reputation as a stickler for efficiency. Since the earliest days of her Mossad career, Shira had always fashioned herself in the same way--always wanting things in their "right and perfect" places, while continually demanding the best possible performance. Yet as far as Shira could tell, she focused most of her own concentration on meeting deadlines--while Berkovich concentrated primarily on getting desired results, no matter how long such efforts might take.

The first phase of this meeting went smoothly as far as Shira could tell. She and Berkovich reviewed the fact that the loony senator from Nevada, Larry Spickler, was still being used by the Jewish nation as a mere pawn within the U.S. Congress.

At the insistence of Israeli officials, the senator had made a mild atonement for some of his many sins by aggressively and successfully leading the way in compensating the people who suffered from cancer--due to fallout from the nuclear bomb tests.

This time, while careful to avoid organizing phony public meetings on the issue, five years earlier Larry Spickler had aggressively pushed for the successful passage of the Radiation Exposure Compensation Act of 1990. In doing so, working as a puppet for the Jewish state, this greasy politician championed the legislation in which the federal government admitted its culpability in causing thousands of cancer-related deaths and similar illnesses that had not progressed to fatal levels.

Despite this success, Shira agreed with Berkovich that the compensation to the victims was far too little--and much too late.

Under strict provisions of the legislation, the people who qualified as "victims," or their surviving family members, received only the maximum $50,000 per case.

Speaking openly, the agent and her superior agreed that this compensation level that Spickler had negotiated was offensively low. Their mutual questions were far more numerous than the scant answers available: how can a human life be valued at such a minuscule amount; how could such a tiny fee even begin to recover the incomes lost by those families; and why were the descendants of these individuals blatantly overlooked.

Shira still vividly recalled learning many years earlier through various Mossad reports and her own research that many of the children of people who lived in the fallout zone suffered cancer at an alarming rate. Many of these youngsters, lots of whom were born after the nuclear bomb test ended, died of cancer; lots of these angry residents theorized that these youngsters had inherited a propensity for the disease, due to the fact that the DNA within cells of their parents' bodies had been damaged.

Even so, discounting such arguments, the legislation

successfully pushed by Senator Spickler specified that authorized compensation could only go to cancer victims who had lived in the nuclear fallout zone; to qualify, they also needed to reside there any time between January 21, 1951, and the end of July in 1962.

"Excuse me please, for being so blunt, but I feel a need to say here and now that Senator Spickler is a jackass ... If this guy had tried harder, he could have done far better for his constituents and for the residents victimized in adjoining states."

"I fully agree, Agent Levy--but the word that I have to describe him cannot even be spoken here. ... We can better serve our mutual objective here to quickly move on to our other vital topics at hand ... But before we do that, just let me say that we have other long-term plans for this corrupt politician ... Let me just say that I guarantee you, even if it takes another 10 or 20 years, the senator will rightfully get what he has coming to him. And, I'm sure that you now what I mean."

The pair then reviewed Shira's latest in-depth reports on developments within the U.S. pharmaceutical industry.

She felt pleased that little discussion seemed necessary, when Berkovich proclaimed that he fully agreed with her in-depth reasoning and conclusions. In summary, her documentation concluded that since Shira's previous full report of 1990, the biggest drug companies had swollen considerably in size, power and influence.

"The general public across America remails oblivious to the dangers that the medical industry is imposing upon them--is that correct, agent Levy?"

Choosing to avoid side-stepping the most challenging factors of this issue, she explained that the gigantic drug companies had quickly become the largest advertisers on U.S. television. The latest official survey indicated that within the previous two years, drug companies had started spending more on advertising than car manufacturers, airlines, food producers and even--in some instances--political campaigns during election years.

"Mister Berkovich, do I have your permission to speak freely on this issue--without fear of reprisal?"

"By all means. Go ahead."

"This is just my personal opinion, but it seems to me that the entire American political system is being swallowed up by corruption. The huge surge in revenues at the drug companies is just one of the most evident symptoms of this continual evolution. I am only mentioning this, of course, because as you know the United States remains our nation's strongest and most powerful ally. Any sudden or unexpected transition of this horrific magnitude in the American culture could put Israel at tremendous risk--but the drug companies are not the only industry that is essentially making all of the most crucial decisions for the American government ... Can I go off topic, and delve into another extreme and somewhat unrelated concern?"

"Sure, but let us be sure to avoid going too far into a much different realm."

"Well, as you probably know I am a ferocious reader, partly because virtually every aspect of the USA's society has something to do with health care, at least in one way or another. With that clearly understood, I feel an urgent need to tell you that the corruption spreads deep into the United States' banking and financial industries. Besides the pharmaceutical companies, those enterprises are among the largest contributors to that nation's congressional and senatorial campaigns. Meantime, many of the same finance industry executives and economists that help run Wall Street are getting high-level appointments within the American government--specifically to all federal agencies that regulate and monitor the finance industry. As a result, I fear, the U.S. economy will suffer a catastrophic meltdown within just 10 or 15 years from now. This will happen because those greedy, selfish businesses are essentially unfettered--self-regulating themselves. The proverbial house of cards likely will collapse as a result."

"Bravo."

"Mister Berkovich, I'm not being flippant in asking this, but please tell me, why do you say that?"

"Shira, our economic analysts within the United States took 15 years to reach the same conclusion that you just summarized for me within only one minute. Believe me, your supreme intelligence is much appreciated here. You have earned all of our respect, including mine--and as you probably realize, I'm not particularly easy to please."

"Well, I will gladly accept the compliment, while careful to remain sufficiently humble. ... With that understood, sir, do you have any updates or assignments to give me now?"

Berkovich clasped both of his hands behind his neck, and leaned back so far in his chair that Shira briefly worried that he might fall. She failed to detect any tension or worry in this administrator's voice as he described an urgent and evolving situation.

Israel's leading instructors in Homeopathy had just confirmed to Mossad that a widely respected cancer doctor in Reno, Nevada, had recently been accepted into a correspondence course; the instruction was offered by that profession's most respected university, based in Tel Aviv.

"His name is Doctor James Robbins, and..."

"I have heard of him." Shira choose to interrupt, although she immediately regretted doing so--aware that doing so had broken this boss's required protocol. "Oh, please forgive me, sir, for interrupting. ... I was out of bounds in saying that."

"No need to apologize. By all means, you can tell me about this man."

Shira responded by speaking openly and honestly. She described learning that Doctor Robbins, at this point in his late 50s, had earned a tremendous reputation for his integrity, supreme intelligence and his willingness to develop new medical technology.

Rather than scold Shira for being so direct, Berkovich told her that this physician had been the only doctor in the entire

United States to respond to an advertisement--the notice seeking students of Homeopathy.

"Not only is this guy creative, he has loads of spunk and chrisma--always downplaying his own considerable achievements. In fact, I've been told that Doctor Robbins is so sharp that he quickly and easily passed his required oral examinations, thereby earning what we in our nation consider a 'prestigious degree in Homeopathy."

"I'm not arguing with you in any way whatsoever, sir, but I feel a need to ask--why are we concentrating on this one doctor?"

"First off, because unlike virtually all other oncologists in the United States, Doctor Robbins is open-minded about the issue. Taking a far different course from virtually all other American oncologists, who have been universally brainwashed by the leaders of their industry, this guy has shown himself as super-creative while also thinking out-of-the-box. This is the type of attitude that will lead to significantly improved and much safer treatments for the deadliest of cancers."

"Are we going to assist him in that regard?"

"Not at all."

"Well, if that is the case, I would like to ask, why are we spending so much time keeping tabs on Doctor Robbins and talking about him? ... Heck, the man is not even Jewish."

"I wish he were a Jew. ... We have got plenty of talent within our ranks, of course, but this man possesses skills, knowledge and tenacity that are far beyond being merely exceptional."

"But that doesn't answer my question, if I may be so bold. Why are we monitoring his career?"

"We suspect that he may be privately--on his own--trying to develop significant harmless, effective and natural treatments for cancer."

"What on earth leads us to believe that?"

"It all makes perfect sense, Shira, when you really think about it. ... This fellow already has a burgeoning cancer treatment business. Patients flock to this guy's clinic thanks to his exceptional reputation and comforting bedside manner. His days of living in near poverty are long gone, replaced by his well-deserved financial comforts--the kind of sizable income that most people can only dream about."

"That's fine. But, sir, you still haven't answered my question."

"Think, Shira. That's what I'm asking you to do--just think. Keep in mind that in his current position, all Doctor Robbins needs to do is keep working on the proverbial treadmill that he has created--continue treating patients with 'mainstream' medicine. But from what we know, of course, he does not seem resigned to doing that for the rest of his life. To the contrary, by learning Homeopathy and eventually--we believe--adopting those natural remedies into his existing medical practice, he is positioning himself to potentially generate effective cancer treatments that most doctors around the world have never even considered."

"I'm an intelligent person myself, sir, but I'm afraid that you have lost me. If you could take a little time to put this into better focus for me, I..."

Without missing a beat, Berkovich described the situation in much more intricate detail. Ultimately, by becoming one of only a handful of doctors in the world--licensed to practice both allopathic medicine and Homeopathy--Doctor Robbins would have the knowledge and talent to press forward in developing far more effective cancer treatments.

"Sir, that's wonderful ... But in my humble opinion, we do not want to put all of our efforts into one basket. ... Sounds like we are just going to monitor this physician's activities from a distance, to see what he is always up to. ... Right?"

"Nope."

"Do you mean that you're going to send one of our personnel clear out to Reno, Nevada--a fairly unassuming community up in the high desert."

"Yes."

"I would be happy, sir, to de-brief whoever you choose for the assignment."

"Thanks for offering, Shira, but that will not be necessary because you are the person that I have chosen for this job."

"But I can't ... I have a life ... I have a husband, and children, and..."

"You know, Shira, how lucky that you have been, to have been assigned to one place--to a single location--for an extended period of time ... We're talking about 20 straight years that you have lived in the Washington, D.C., area."

"Sir, no ... Er ... I have roots there ... I cannot possibly..."

"Shira, you must realize that you're the best, the ideal person for this task..."

"I can imagine that might be true, but..."

"Your country needs you, Shira. ... The world needs you ... Common people everywhere who yearn for safe and effective medicine need you."

"But my husband, he will never go for this."

Berkovich slowly opened a desk drawer and pulled out a folder, which he placed on the desktop and then slid toward her on the other side.

"I'm afraid to tell you this, Shira, but your husband does not love you. In here, you will find photographs--nasty pictures, I'm afraid--clandestine images of Ken Miller having a sexual affair with another woman. ... Forgive yourself, but you could not possibly have known. Even those of us who are professionally trained as agents--the best among us, even you, Shira--we fail to notice or monitor the very people who should love us the most."

Emotionally stunned and mortified, Shira briefly opened the folder. She quickly flipped through the startling photographs of Ken, naked with other women.

Striving to remain mentally strong, Shira managed to fight back tears. This agent even refrained from sniffling, crying out, yelling or shaking from the tense emotion.

"Shira, it's time for you to move on to a different location. I know that you love your husband, but he doesn't deserve you ... We need you more than he does."

"I'll think about it."

Berkovich retrieved a box of tissue from another drawer, and then handed the container across the desk toward her.

"You can cry all that you want. You don't need to act tough, just because you happen to be with me. We know, here, without any question whatsoever, after many years working together that you are made of steel--perhaps even titanium."

"I'm not going to cry. ... I am going to divorce Ken as soon as I return to the states ... Can I wait until then to give you my decision, about the transfer?"

"You have a lot to think about. But just keep in mind that if you refuse, we'll need to choose another person--and no one else is nearly as qualified as you."

Twenty-Eight

Tommy Davis had always disliked country music while growing up in Centralia and later Reno. As a elementary school student, teenager and young adult he had always quickly changed the radio dial whenever a country tune began to play.

Throughout those decades he felt repulsed by such songs, particularly while attending Wooster High and during his first few years at the University of Nevada.

Beginning from early childhood he had considered the country genre's guitars as too twangy, the storyline as ridiculous and the supposed Southern accents as phony.

Far and away while growing up he had always preferred hard rock, particularly Queen and Kiss, and holdovers from the '70s like Judas Priest and Black Sabbath.

During those trying and personally difficult times he had considered wild, hard-driving and rebellious rock 'n' roll as an emotional necessity. Fashioning himself as a loner at the time, Tommy knew that he was "hooked" on these anti-establishment sounds.

He would always lock himself in his room whenever at home, and crank up the volume as high as possible. Feeling as if without a single friend in the entire world, through his late teens Tommy would use pencils, pens and kitchen utensils to slap his bedroom furniture in perfect sync with every tune.

This pattern had quickly changed rapid-fire when he moved in the late 1990s to Nashville, Tennessee, to begin his oncology residency at Vanderbilt University.

Although still considering himself a "bookworm," constantly studying and dedicating himself to being as professional as possible, for the first time in his life he opened up emotionally and began amassing a growing cadre of friends.

Despite his protestations in mid-1999, six of Tommy's fellow residents convinced him to go with them to a Saturday night performance at the Grand Old Opry, in the heart of downtown Nashville. While en route there in a cranky, rattly and noisy 1973 rambler owned by Wisconsin native J Judith Baker, the thought of going to a country show actually made him at least a tiny bit nauseous.

Yet his reluctance disappeared as soon as that night's show started, featuring the odd mix of old-timer Johnny Cash and that's year's most popular country crooner, media sensation Garth Brooks. Tommy danced and hollered in celebration along with his pals in the venue's aisles, and from that moment forward this native Nevadan remained glued to the country genre.

By this point refusing to be called by what he considered the childish name of "Tommy," this future oncologist started using "Thomas" on all of his business cards, medical documents and official Vanderbilt records.

A towering 6 feet 4 inches tall, and muscular with broad, round shoulders and a thin waistline, Thomas had long, curly brown hair--flowing to the bottom edge of his collar and covering the top half of his ears. He had the same manly face as his biological father, Honest, except without the scars of battle.

At age 30 Thomas had never been married, although highly attracted to women--some of them bold enough to tell him to his face things like "you are a dream," and that someday "you are going to be caught and trapped by some lucky gal."

Feeling oblivious to such concerns, Thomas remained focused and dedicated to his lofty goal of someday entering the Reno practice of his adoptive father. Doctor Robbins had told him upon his departure for Tennessee that "there can be no guarantees of such an outcome."

Thomas had assured his mentor while this life-changing transition clicked into gear that he would do everything possible and reasonable to earn such a position.

As the only person aware of Doctor Robbins' goal of

developing the world's most effective cancer treatment, Thomas became exceedingly proud of this Vietnam War veteran. Now in his early 60s, the senior physician had earned a significant and official designation, thanks to his new degree and license as a Homeopath.

Under this unique distinction, Doctor Robbins had become one of only three licensed and fully certified integrative medical oncologists practicing in the United States.

This extremely rare attribute gave him the unique ability to administer either of two radically different health care methods. Taking his patients' wishes into consideration, he could administer "mainstream" medicines, and natural and effective remedies, or a combination of both.

These dual designations helped draw more patients to the clinic, particularly after Doctor Robbins spent $1.7 million to buy an established and popular Reno business specializing in natural medicines, Beijing Lily's Earthly Remedies.

Although delighted with his mentor's continued success, Thomas rarely spoke by phone with the Northern Nevada physician. The younger doctor remained super-busy with his residency duties in Tennessee, frustrated that his adopted father refrained from learning how to use basic emails. This annoyed the new country music fan, who felt perplexed by Doctor Robbins' refusal to easily learn basic Internet skills--while simultaneously remaining a world-renowned expert in medical technologies.

Thomas' growing frustrations in this regard peaked on May 5, 2000, when his adoptive step-mother, Marie Robbins, made an urgent emergency phone call to him. Ensconced with required residency duties, he accepted an incoming phone call at a Third Floor cancer ward nurse's station in Vanderbilt University Medical Center.

"This is Doctor Davis."

"Hi, Tommy," said the adult female voice, embossed with a thick Italian accent. "I mean, er ... Sorry ... Thomas. This is Marie."

"There has been a sudden death in the family."

"Who? ... Not the doctor, I hope."

"No, it was the man that Doctor Robbins always affectionately called 'The General.' ... The old guy in his early 80s died in his sleep last night of a heart attack."

"Oh, no." This news stunned the oncology resident, just more than a few months after the similar death in mid-March of Bill McCready. Thomas had never told anyone, but he had sobbed all night back then while alone in his Nashville apartment. That death had filled Thomas with unexpected guilt, for never having told that senior citizen of his thanks and eternal gratitude for being his caregiver for many years--although not blood related.

"Thomas, as you can imagine, Doctor Robbins is broken-hearted about The General's death--although passing away suddenly is common at that age ... The doctor is hoping that you can come home to Reno right away for the funeral."

Left speechless by this request, Thomas had no idea of how to respond. He wanted to refrain from offending his mentor, who had rarely made any request of him. Yet professional obligations made Thomas feel as tied down to his Tennessee post. Getting permission to leave for even four days would require a special, in-depth written request to the Vanderbilt hospital's administration. And even then there could be no guarantee that such a decision would be made on time, let alone an affirmative answer.

"Marie, you can rest assured that I am going to do everything that I possibly can to make this happen."

"We all know that the doctor is never pushy or demanding of his relatives. But he will be heartbroken if you are unable to attend, Thomas. ... He loves you and cares for you, far more than you probably realize, and he needs you."

*

Playing hooky from school had been the furthest thing from Thomas' mind since at least 15 years earlier, when mid-way through Reno's Wooster High School.

Yet after failing to receive a response to his written request to Vanderbilt's administration for a short-term leave, he decided to zip out of Nashville for this urgent four-day excursion. He felt that calling in sick daily would "do the trick."

Always preferring to travel light, after arriving at Reno-Tahoe International Airport via Southwest airlines, the budding oncologist carried one small suitcase that contained only two changes of clothes.

Without needing to go to baggage-claim, always an unnecessary hassel in his mind, Thomas went straight outside to the front of the terminal. He waited patiently, standing beside the curb for Marie to pick him up.

The latest country music tunes blared through his head-speakers, attached to a Sony walkman cassette player. Thomas looked forward to seeing Marie, whom he had always liked since first meeting her 20 years earlier when she started dating Doctor Robbins. At the time, he realized that most people who met this native of Italyseemed mystified by her personality and appearance. From his perspective, most people either despised or adored Marie, with only a handful on the middle ground.

As far as Thomas was concerned most people who seemed to dislike Marie were either jealous of her drop-dead gorgeous good looks or disliked the fact that she seemed far more intelligent than them. With equal fervor, at least from his view, those who adored Doctor Robbins' wife loved her bubbly personality, adored her passion for maintaining good health, and appreciated her inquisitive demeanor and superior intelligence.

Even all these years later, Thomas felt grateful for the fact that his adoptive mother had always treated him with respect and kindness--particularly during his rebellious teenage years. Looking back from his perspective as a mature adult, he realized that most women in her position would have demanded that her husband throw the youth out of their home.

Through his late teens and early 20s, Thomas had become increasingly mystified and puzzled by this woman--who always looked to Thomas as if several decades younger than her actual age. His insatiable curiosity had motivated him at age 22 to look deep into her personal background. A sense of admiration resulted upon discovering that during the 1970s Marie had hailed as the highest paid woman's fashion model in Italy. Adored and yearned for by perhaps millions of European men, she had latched onto Doctor Robbins right away upon meeting him by chance. The couple first met on a ski lift at the Heavenly Valley Ski Resort overlooking Lake Tahoe, a mere one-hour drive from Reno.

Inseparable from the then-budding physician from that day forward, Marie had instantly dropped her modeling career. At the time she had shocked much of Europe by suddenly, permanently and mysteriously leaving the fashion and modeling scene. Until then she had adorned the covers of virtually every woman's magazine in Italy, Switzerland, Spain, Great Britain and several other nations.

Marie had given up all that fame and her huge income for Doctor Robbins, whom she described to the media as "the sexiest man alive." This unexpected transition had generated a short-lived news sensation across Europe, while virtually all mainstream media outlets in the United States ignored the story.

In private while Thomas was still a teenager, Doctor Robbins had admitted to the youth that this apparent oversight by American journalists suited him just fine. Back then, as far as this young man could tell, his adoptive father had a modest-- yet steadily growing--income, while his professional reputation steadily improved.

Throughout the several decades since then, as a committed husband and wife, Marie and the Vietnam War veteran had just as many similarities as differences: they both gravitated to the Republican party as staunch conservatives, but she despised liberals while he preferred to give them at least some slack on human rights issues; Marie enjoyed entertaining, and going out in the evening with their friends, while the physician would have preferred a much more private personal life; and the doctor enjoyed playing tennis and other outdoor activities well into his

60s, although his devoted wife always balked at any suggestions that she participate in such competitions.

Amid their many similarities and mild differences, one thing between them remained rock-solid, steady and true, at least from Thomas' perspective. Without any wavering or argument whatsoever the couple had always remained fully devoted and dedicated to him--particularly his desire to enter medical school.

Still fully mindful of these numerous transitions and grateful for the many positive things that the couple had done for him, while standing at the Reno airport's curb he waved toward Marie's car--as soon as he saw the vehicle approach from 150 yards away. Even from that distance, through the tinted windows of her luxury 2000 Lincoln Town Car, he saw the outlines of several other people inside the vehicle.

*

As soon as the vehicle stopped directly in front of Thomas, he noticed through the opened passenger-side windows that an attractive woman sat beside Marie in the front seat and two boys were in the back.

"Welcome home, Thomas!" Marie smiled broadly from behind the wheel, as she leaned toward him. "I would like to introduce you to my new best friend. This is Shira Levy, and these boys in the back are her sons--Eric and Elvis."

While still in the front seat and through the open window, Shira grinned, chirped out a brief "hello," and offered her outstretched arm, which Thomas gently held.

He summarily bent down and briefly kissed the back of her hand, telling Shira, "The pleasure is all mine."

From the back seat, the boys each waved at him and they said "hello."

Still standing on the curb, he responded to them with a similar wave, adding that "you each look like fine young men."

Right away Marie exited the vehicle, while the three others remained inside. She walked to the back of the car and popped open the trunk.

While Marie stood beside Thomas, as he put his suitcase into the rear of the vehicle, she whispered into his ear: "Shira moved to Reno from Washington, D.C., three years ago with her boys. She is divorced, and now works as an executive for the local branch of the Republican Party. ... I know that you will adore her--a lot."

*

The Robbins' estate inside the exclusive, gated Sunnyville Terrace community had become a hubbub of activity by the time Thomas arrived there with Marie, Shira and her sons.

The senior physician greeted them as soon as the vehicle stopped near the crest of a small hill, beside the couple's sprawling ranch-style home.

Thomas hopped from the car right away and gave his mentor a tight bear hug, feeling joyful to see this man whom he admired and adored.

At 6 feet 5 inches tall, Thomas towered above the much more seasoned and experienced physician--who stood only 5 feet 9. From the younger doctor's perspective, however, Doctor Robbins and he were of equal height. The Vanderbilt resident continued looking up to his mentor, still an icon in his mind.

"Doctor, I am so very sorry for your loss," Thomas said.

"Thank you so much." The older physician hugged his adoptive son tight once again. "You realize, perhaps more than anyone, that the General was like a father to me."

"Anthony's work ethic was a supreme example for us all. His perseverance persisted through tough times, long past the point when most others might have quit."

*

Forty-five minutes after their arrival at the Robbins' Estate, Thomas sat in a comfy back-yard chair beside Shira. The mere presence of this woman energized the mind and body of this highly ambitious resident physician.

Thomas appreciated the fact that this Republican Party executive asked plenty of questions about him and his life, all without seeming too nosy and judgmental.

Right off the bat he could tell that this woman had a superior intelligence, as if she always remained fully mindful of everything around them.

His first impression was that of a lady eager to listen and to learn, while also humble and displaying the inescapable qualities of bold leadership.

Together, while chatting with each other, they watched the Eric and Elvis as the boys explored pathways that meandered around various ponds, waterfalls and streams.

Thomas paid particular attention to Elvis, who managed to keep up with his brother while wearing leg braces and using crutches.

"My sons do not know this, Thomas." Shira sipped her orange juice. "But they keep teaching me a lesson every day, about the importance of always remaining curious and continually exploring for new and vibrant possibilities."

In that precise moment, as Shira said this, for the first time Thomas sensed an inescapable sparkle in this woman's personality--as if she really were precisely what she had just said, insatiably curious about the facts.

*

At precisely 1:37 the following morning, Thomas lay alone in his bedroom at the back of the Robbins Estate. Doctor Robbins and Marie had kept the room precisely as it had been when he lived there back in his late teens and early 20s, while on summer and interim breaks from his university studies.

Posters glorifying the hard rock group Queen remained embossed to the walls and all across the ceiling from wall to wall. At this point in life the mere thought of these images seemed weird to him; he now felt convinced that images of country music stars would seem more appropriate.

Yet something far more important to Thomas weighed on his mind. He had been unable to sleep a wink since going to bed at 10:30, following a long, multi-course dinner in the home with family, plus Shira Levy and her boys.

Thomas had always been a sound sleeper, even during his rebellious teenage years. Yet on this particular night something kept pecking at his mind.

Unusual, he kept tossing and turning while alone in bed.

He kept thinking about the alluring and magnetic appearance of the woman, while cognizant of the fact that Shira worked as the executive assistant to Marie--who served as local Republican Party's county and state chairman.

With politics the furthest thing from his mind, Thomas kept: hearing the pleasant and high-pitched cadence of Shira's voice; envisioning the woman's generous lips, which she had occasionally allowed her tongue to slowly run across; remembering her sweet aroma, the sense of which had actually made him break out in perspiration; and her continual devotion to her children, which Thomas considered a sign of Shira's unbending commitment to other people that she cherished.

"Am I in love?" Thomas kept tossing and turning in his bed until at least 4 o'clock that morning.

As soon as the wake-up alarm blared at 6:30, this resident oncologist's first thought was that he would soon be seeing her again.

Twenty-Nine

A white stretch limousine arrived right on schedule at precisely 8:30 that morning for the funeral procession.

During a quick breakfast of ham, eggs and coffee at the home's dining room table Thomas began to wonder whether he had failed to bring appropriate clothes; the thought suddenly struck him that perhaps a dark suit would have been best.

Yet half-way through the meal as the funeral home chauffeur waited outside, Marie and Doctor Robbins assured him that genuine, old-style Western cowboy clothes would do just fine. Thomas still had lots of this type of clothing in his bedroom closet, still perfect fits since his body size had remained the same since living here on intermittent occasions five years earlier when he was 25 years old.

The adoptive parents explained that the General's "celebration of life" would be at the couple's sprawling 1,300-acre ranch a half hour drive north of Reno--the site still fully dedicated to the preservation of wild mustangs.

Right after breakfast, Thomas hustled to his bedroom to quickly put on his authentic western garb. He preferred the comfort of well-worn cowboy boots, while regular business-style shoes universally worn by doctors seemed out of place to him. For good measure, he put on his perfectly fitting white cowboy hat, his preferred color by far since--at his muscular width and size--at least in Thomas' mind, black always made him look like a typical Hollywood movie "bad guy."

At the exact pre-designated time, 8:50 sharp that morning, he walked from the Robbins home to the waiting limousine.

Then, an unexpected event took Thomas by surprise.

He had not known that Shira Levy and her sons had already been inside the vehicle, waiting patiently for the three of them.

As soon as the chauffeur opened the far back, passenger-side door for Thomas he spotted this woman sitting in the same leather-covered seat where he was about to go.

Eric and Elvis, each wearing black western regalia, sat on their mother's other side--opposite from the place where Thomas had hoped to sit.

"Well, howdy, ma'am." The tall physician stood next to the opened limo door, bending down slightly and looking inside--smiling broadly while tipping his hat to her. "Do you mind if I plant myself right down here next to you?"

"Okay, pardner," she said, while tipping her own white hat. "I don't mind at all if you saddle up here."

"Thank ye." He promptly did as offered, before the chauffeur closed the limo door behind him. "I am much obliged."

Right then and there, without any doubt whatsoever, Thomas realized that the first time in his life he had fallen deeply and madly in love.

He remained oblivious to the course in life that this burning passion would lead each of them to, his heart now beating steadily with increasing anticipation.

*

Thomas estimated that at least 350 people had converged at the wild horse ranch for this unique commemoration of his adoptive father's late buddy.

Rather than a somber, tear-filled occasion, the gathering had emerged as the most exciting and exhilarating event that he had attended to that point in his adult life.

Along with several dozen other children, Eric and Elvis romped, played kick-ball and chased each other in a fenced-off area, safely away from the wild animals.

At first, about 150 adults in the grandstands cheered as women riding domesticated horses participated in barrel racing. Cowboys riding their own horses demonstrated cattle-driving techniques in "snaffle-bit" contests.

This marked the first time that Thomas had mentally

grasped how much his adoptive parents' health clinic, professional staff and wild horse preserve were truly appreciated by the entire community.

Several people from amid the crowd erupted into tears during a half-hour round of brief speeches that began at 11 o'clock that morning. Speaking for only about two minutes each, individual representatives of several families described how kind and positive that the General had always been as their relatives battled cancer.

Other speakers mentioned the tremendous generosity that Marie and James Robbins had shown to the entire community. Many of these efforts had been made possible by the General, who: took time to visit homes of many cancer patients along with the doctor, despite his own extremely painful knees; his voluntary overnight stays at the hospital bedsides of many patients through the years, taking turns with Doctor Robbins to visit the ill; and of the friendly jokes that this departed man had told during appropriate situations, in efforts to cheer up the mood in the clinic's waiting room.

Following this initial round of speeches, which Thomas considered compelling and heart-felt, short remarks were made by the General's widow, Elizabeth.

Now at age 91, this Bozeman, Montana, native's fiery speech seemed to Thomas as if as passionate and emotional as that of a woman half her age.

Wearing a sombrero and Argentinian-style shoes, Elizabeth told several tales about the General's many escapades at their Dancing Bull Ranch.

Thomas' favorite yarn had been her description of when-- at age 75--her late husband had awakened at 2 a.m. on a Thursday morning, just in time for him to shovel a truckload of fresh bull manure before sunrise that day.

"Little did I know this at the time, but thanks to the General, that day I was in for a doozy," Elizabeth told the chuckling crowd. "He gobbled down ham and eggs, and then rushed out to his pickup truck in hopes of getting to work at the cancer clinic on time. ... He was heading out the driveway when I lit out after 'em on foot, hollering to the fool that he needed to take a shower before going to work ... Well, I'll be darned if he didn't park the truck and jump out, before whipping off all his clothes down to the underwear. ... He asked for it, so without any hesitation I hosed him down as if he were a hog ... Then he raced to put on fresh, clean skivvies and clothes fetched from the barn, jumped back in his truck and hollered, waving his hat--saying goodbye to me, "whoo-eee!" ... That's the kind of man that the General was ... He took everything with a positive attitude. He loved me, he loved his work, he loved his chores and as just about everybody here knows, he also adored Doctor Robbins and his adorable wife, Marie ... Doctor and Mrs., could you please rise now, so that everyone can see you."

Amid the crowd, in the middle of the grandstands, the couple stood and waved at everyone. From several rows away, Thomas watched his adoptive parents as loud cheers erupted everywhere around them.

"Doctor, I feel a need to address you here and now, in front of everyone," Elizabeth spoke into a hand-held microphone, her voice trembling with emotion. "I know that the General considered you as truly his son, and you thought of him as your father. ... Well, sir, you have been a father figure yourself--a guiding light for our entire community, also deserving praise for your service to our country in the National Guard!"

Caught up in the excitement, Thomas clapped along with the rest of the crowd, as Elizabeth thanked the Robbins Family for hosting the celebration.

Right when the doctor and Marie sat back down, Elizabeth made another brief statement: "Before we eat lunch and spend the rest of this afternoon, having loads of fun, I just want to talk real briefly--for just another minute or so--about what the General considered the greatest accomplishment of his life, by far. ... I would like to introduce all of you to his adult daughters, Charlotte,

Karen and Christine, and their children--the General's grandkids ... Charlotte, I know you just want to say a few brief words on behalf your yourself and your sisters."

Chubby and dressed in a large, flowing orange dress, this steady-voiced woman--whom Thomas guessed was in her late 50s--explained that she and her sisters had been estranged from the General for several decades.

"He was the one who reached out to us," Charlotte said, tears streaming down her face as her sisters openly wept on stage as well. "We had shunned him for so long, but we finally learned the truth--that our mother had lied about him so many years earlier ... He forgave us for failing to remain open-minded, and he brought each of us back into his life. As many of you might know, we had bonded with our father--spending lots of time with him during the past 10 years ... None of that would have been possible without his courage, his perseverance, and his undying love--all at the encouragement of the man that we all love and cherish, Doctor Robbins!"

Once again the crowd erupted into tears and cheers.

*

The heavy throng began hollering in unison that they wanted the physician on stage to speak.

"We want Doctor Robbins! We want Doctor Robbins!"

This cheering persisted non-stop for nearly three minutes, until the doctor finally climbed stairs to the stage and stood in front of the microphone. The crowd's good-natured hollering quickly transitioned into a wild applause.

The doctor spoke for several minutes about his late buddy the General.

"Almost everyone here knows that he was a fighter--more specifically, a peaceful warrior, essentially a maverick--standing out in his own field--always helping people as much as possible, even when times got tough for himself.

"Yes, the General was a maverick, someone who established his own way in life while rebelling against injustice--

always trying to persevere and thrive in the face of overwhelming odds."

While his adoptive father continued speaking, Thomas surveyed the crowd and noticed that most of these hearty folks had tears welled up in their eyes.

"These horses here, these wild and untamed mustangs, they are mavericks as well," Doctor Robbins continued. "These blessed, free and glorious animals continually strive to persevere, always struggling to roam free despite a federal government that wants to kill them.

"Well, everyone, let's hear it right here and now for these wild and roaming mustangs, some of our favorite mavericks!"

More cheers erupted, and Thomas watched several dozen of these untamed horses race across nearby hillsides in this high-desert country.

"Listen, everyone, this is why I have done my part--my humble effort--along with my adorable wife--to save these animals, these mavericks. ... Yes, lots of us here are mavericks, particularly the man and woman who played an essential role in making this mustang sancturary possible. ... Please join me in a loud round of applause in welcoming some true American heroes, genuine American mavericks--Bobby Blair and his adorable wife Paula! ... Please, Bobby and Paula, stand up so everyone can see you."

The couple stood, waving their cowboy hats up high as the crowd went wild.

Suddenly and unexpectedly, Thomas realized that at this point tears flowed down his own cheeks. This future doctor made no attempt to hide his emotions.

"Then, of course, there are the many people and families from throughout Nevada and other western states, who have persevered despite the many cancers caused by radioactive fallout caused by above-ground atomic bomb blasts--reckless experiments conducted by the federal government in the 1950s and 1960s.

"Many of these people died as a result of their disease, and lots of their surviving relatives essentially became mavericks in their own right--launching a peaceful and legal battle against the U.S. government ... Many of them were and they still are, my patients. As lots of you already know, lots of these surviving relatives are here with us today at this fantastic celebration ... I would now ask all of you to stand, everyone here from a family in which someone suffered from cancer due to the radioactive contamination from long ago--or who themselves survived from the disease."

Thomas stood and soon realized that perhaps 75 people from among this total throng of perhaps 350 souls did the same. From his front-row position, he noticed that many of them were trembling, crying, smiling and waving.

At this point from Thomas' perspective the cheers and applause became almost deafening. From a distance in these intense emotional moments he noticed a few dozen young mustangs frolicking and playing amid the nearby sagebrush.

As the cheers finally began to subside, the physician began speaking in what Thomas considered an appropriately humble tone.

"For the past several years, people everywhere have begun calling me the 'Maverick M.D.,' a physician who does as much as possible to carve out a new and previously unexplored pathway in cancer treatment. In this process, as lots of you already know, I refuse to fully embrace the destructive medical protocol that requires conventional oncologists to use deadly chemo and harmful radiation to all advanced-level cancer patients. ... My vow to the general public, and to particularly my patients, is that I will continue doing whatever possible to push the proverbial envelope as far as legally possible--doing my utmost to use natural remedies to dramatically improve cancer survival rates.

"Of course, we have not gathered here today to talk about cancer, or horses, or nuclear bombs. But I just have felt an intense burning need and desire to say these things, about the importance of living life as mavericks--because I know without any doubt whatsoever that these are precisely the type of things that the

General would want me to talk about right here and now.

"Yes, these are classic--but real-life--good-and-evil stories that I am talking about here and now. In remembering the General and what he stood for, each of us here today has a lifelong responsibility to fight against injustice--especially in instances where heartless behavior erupts from our federal government, when it endangers wild horses that yearn to roam free, when it endangers many innocent people who want to live free of radioactive fallout; when it endangers cancer patients by allowing greedy conventional doctors to administer worthless and often-deadly chemo and radiation treatments, and when it devilishly endangers free speech by imposing cumbersome regulations on radio broadcasts, the Internet and any media outlets that dare to challenge the federal buraucracy."

Boisterous cheers erupted from the crowd once again, just as energetic as before as far as Thomas could tell.

"Yes, everyone, happiness is worth fighting for; happiness is worth rebelling as a maverick; and happiness requires true Americans to battle peacefully for freedom throughout their lifetimes ... So, let us continue now and enjoy our freedoms. Let us party for the remainder of this glorious afternoon, precisely what the general would want us to do!"

*

Amid the heavy throng, down in the first row, Thomas spotted Shira Levy standing by her sons. He noticed tears flowing down the face of this woman, who to him had seemed so cheery and positive the previous day and earlier that morning.

From a distance of perhaps 15 yards, Thomas realized that these were not tears of sadness, but rather tears of joy and thoughtfulness.

Seeing this, Thomas realized that he had just fallen even more deeply in love with this woman. To him, that seemed almost impossible, because they had only chatted with each other for about three hours the previous afternoon.

This ambitious doctor in residence realized that his own

emotions made little sense. Since arriving at this celebration he had intentionally tried to avoid Shira, hoping to avoid seeming too desperate, clingy and needy.

In that moment, as Shira continued weeping in happiness and Elizabeth concluded her remarks to the crowd, Thomas turned away from the throngs and ambled alone toward what soon would become the chow lines.

At least 30 people from a local company, Glorious Magic Mountain Catering, had been hired to handle food-serving chores. Nonetheless, hoping to keep occupied and to avoid glamming on to Shira, Thomas volunteered to serve chili to people as they went in a line from station to station to get food dished out onto their plates and into bowls.

Among the first that Thomas greeted were his Aunt Paula, by this point a retired casino card dealer and her husband, Bobby "Cactus Pete" Blair, the rebellious radio announcer. Thomas had always adored this woman for her spunk and determination, particularly way back when she had fought viciously against the despicable federal government. With equal esteem, he appreciated the announcer, who by this point had launched a low-power radio station hailed as American Independence Radio. Now with a barrel-sized belly that replaced his former muscular frame, Cactus Pete had recently started a weekly radio show, "The Good Health King," featuring regular commentary and recommendations from Doctor Robbins. The announcer also continued to co-manage this wild horse refuge in his spare time.

About 15 people behind this couple, Thomas greeted and served chili to his other aunt, Pamela, her husband Bradley--the successful lawyer--and their three adult sons, each now in their 20s--Peter, Paul and Percy. These were the young doctor's cousins, who had each pursued medical degrees, their tuitions paid for by the elder Doctor Robbins and Marie. By this point at age 50, Pamela no longer had the voluptuous body that had once apparently made many men dream that they could know her--still working as the elder physician's efficient clinic manager. Thomas felt delighted to serve all five of them, although they lacked time to chat about anything substantive.

After Thomas served chili to the next 27 people in line, while glancing down at the huge food-filled pot he heard a low voice say: "Hi, son."

Momentarily startled, the Vanderbilt resident promptly looked up, straight into the face of his own biological father-- whom he had not spoken with in 15 years, since being a perennial Wooster High School truant.

Now in his early 70s, Abraham "Honest" Davis still wore a black eye patch, had the same crooked smile and blown-off ear. Yet immediately at first glance, at least from Thomas' perspective, this man appeared much healthier, more vibrant and energetic than he had in many years.

"Hi, pop." Thomas heaped a few heaping ladles full of chili into the former plumber's bowl.

"Son, I haven't had a drop to drink for well over a decade. You might know that I work full-time out here at this ranch ... It's great for me."

"Good to hear that."

"Maybe we could get together sometime, for a cup of coffee, or something?"

"Sounds like a possible plan." Thomas intentionally issued a broad grin while saying this, striving to block the fact that he lacked any emotion regarding this man. While flying to Reno the previous morning, this younger physician had thought briefly about the likelihood that this brief meet-up would occur. Thomas felt as if avoiding any issues from long ago would be best for himself and for everyone involved.

Once Honest headed further away down the chow line, after the next few people Thomas dished out chili to a man whom he immediately recognized from newspaper photos. The journalist Duane Shelton, a former reporter for the Globe-Herald, looked much thinner and far more muscular than Thomas had envisioned. At least judging from brief mentions that Doctor Robbins had made about this fellow in recent years, the guy apparently had matured and even become a strong ally of his adoptive father. Shelton, who always wore large, out-of-style horn-rimmed glasses reminiscent of the late 1960s, frequently served as an editor of Doctor Robbins' many scientific medical reports.

"Hey, as far as I know, we've never met," Thomas told the man, while serving him chili. "I'm Thomas Davis, and I'm starting to hear a lot of positive things about you, particularly from Doctor Robbins."

"I've been following your career closely for quite a while," Duane said, tightly gripping his napkin and utensils. "I'm a little jealous, because I wish that I had an adult son like you ... The doctor always keeps saying fantastic things about you."

"Mister Shelton, he tells me a lot of great things about you, too--I wish that I knew how to write the sensational way that you do. I've seen some of your work, and that makes me even more envious than you might be of me. ... Maybe we'll see each other around sometime."

"Sure thing." Shelton dropped his utensils onto the dirt below, and immediately bent down to pick them up, before promptly heading further up the chow line.

Seeing all these people, the joyful expression in their faces and breathing this clean western air, made Thomas realize that he had been far more homesick for the Reno area than he had previously known. The people of Tennessee and the short-term residents there had been making him feel welcome. But to him, especially during that day at the wild horse ranch, there could be no better and friendlier people than those who choose to make the wide-open American west their home.

Although considering himself as physically fit and with exceptional stamina, Thomas began feeling exhausted and mentally drained while serving in the food line.

Yet Thomas' energy and mood suddenly rebounded the moment that Shira Levy and her sons appeared at this serving station.

"None for me, please." She grinned, showing off her perfect white teeth, while holding two empty bowls. "I have never cared for chili at all. But believe me, the boy's would love some."

"Yeah!" Little Elvis chimed in, holding one of his crutches high in what Thomas considered a victory pose. "I'm hungry!"

The older child, Eric, promptly interrupted: "I'm even hungrier. He's just little, and I'm big ... Put a few extra spoonfuls in mine, please."

"Boys will be boys, won't they?" Shira promptly placed the bowls on separate plates, one held by each child.

In doing so, she spilled her own plate upside down onto the ground.

"Oh no!" Shira exclaimed.

"No worries." Thomas said, immediately bending under the serving table, scooping the mess up into a large apron and tossing all of this into a nearby garbage can. "Shira, how about if you just go down and sit over there at the tables with the boys, and save a place for me? ... I'll be over there in about five minutes, with plates for each of us."

*

As promised, within several minutes Thomas took a seat beside Shira while the boys sat across from them on the other side of the table.

They remained outdoors, although underneath a giant overhead steel roof that covered the entire dining area. Supported by 47 wood beams each at least 20 feet tall, the structure had been designed to protect visitors from rain or snow.

"Boy, this event is super-fantastic, isn't it?" Thomas said, while Eric and Elvis gobbled their food and Shira delicately wiped her mouth with a napkin. "I cannot even begin to imagine how much planning and resources were needed to get this together."

"Your mom--that is, er--Marie, she is the genius behind all this." Shira took a ketchup container from the tabletop and put a little on her hamburger. "She is much smarter and fare more efficient than many people might realize--a genius in her own right."

"Oh, I'm sure that she is not perfect; nobody is." Thomas then took mustard and put that on his hamburger, avoiding the ketchup. "If I heard her right when you guys picked me up at the airport yesterday, she said that you two are best friends? ... Is that right?"

"Mom, can we go play?" Elvis interrupted, while turning around in his fold-up chair and grabbing his crutches.

"Me, too!" Eric quickly stood beside his disabled brother, without waiting for an answer from their mother.

Shira then gave the boys what Thomas considered a stern expression, intermixed with the inescapable aura of pure love for them.

"But boys, you haven't even finished half of your lunch." Shira suddenly set her hamburger back on her own plate--while chewing a small bite. "Well, okay ... But just promise me that you will stay on the safe side of these fences ... Wild horses can be mighty unpredictable."

As soon as the boys scurried away, Thomas latched back on to the topic foremost in his mind. This doctor in residence still remained as insatiably curious as he had been way back in his teens, except by this point far more direct and thoughtful in his questions than he had once been. Instead of behaving self-centered and gloomy, by this point he took pride in wondering more about other people than himself.

"So, you and Marie are best friends?"

"We are inseparable girlfriends," Shira said, occasionally sipping ice water. "The two of us, we share everything."

"I cannot possibly think of anything more fantastic than to have a friend that you can trust, someone very close."

Shira smiled so broadly, with such innocence intermixed with fervor that Thomas kept fighting off the thought that he actually might love this woman. He kept thinking that love-at-first-sight only happens in fantasies, like literature or the movies. Yet while sitting beside Shira, he struggled to keep his eyes off of her.

The intensifying urge to reach over and touch Shira's

delicate hand, intertwining his fingers with hers, became the next challenge for Thomas. Natural instinct told him that this would be an exceptional thing to do, but common sense demanded otherwise.

"You and Marie share everything? ... That's cool."

"We talk about our families, our lives, our hopes, our dreams and our loves."

"Oh, so this means that you have a boyfriend?"

"I wish that was the case ... Maybe I'm just too darned busy."

"You've got to be kidding! ... This is unbelievable ... Do you mean to tell me, young woman, that a lady of your looks, personality and intelligence cannot get a guy?"

"You call me a 'young woman?' ... Well, I appreciate the compliment ... From my perspective, you are the one who is extremely young ... Whether you want to believe this or not, I am old enough to have babysat you--changed your diapers--when you were just a little fellow."

"Come on!"

"No, it's true."

"Hey, I'm 30 years old, young woman ... If you are older than me, which I don't believe for even a second, it's probably by only one or two years."

Shira started laughing so hard that she spilled several drops of water on her plate, obviously struggling--from Thomas' perspective--to keep a bite of food in her mouth.

"Young man, you are a total riot."

"It's you who are the funny one, little girl."

"Ha! ... You call me 'little girl.' ... I'll have you know that I'm in my late 40s. To be even more precise, I'm 47 years old."

"Come on." Thomas enjoyed this light-hearted banter more and more with each passing moment. "I might be gullible ... But, believe me, not that much."

"Hold on to your hopes, young fellow ... I've got proof... I'll show you!"

Thomas watched intently as Shira promptly rifled through her own dark-leather, intricately woven, western-style purse. Within seconds, she whipped out her tan-colored wallet, and showed Thomas her Nevada driver's license.

Physically stunned, emotionally mesmerized and left speechless, he looked at the unmistakably vivid snapshot of Shira's face--before glancing at her year of birth.

Thomas eyes became glued to those numbers: 1953

An overwhelming sense of disappointment, intermixed with a sense of intrigue, enveloped his entire psyche. As a guy born in 1970, this meant that Shira was indeed 17 years older than he. Without saying a word, Thomas handed the purse back to her.

"Hey, don't look so darned disappointed, young man. ... You need to know that I am a genuine cougar."

"What in the heck is a cougar? ... You don't seem to me as if anything like a giant cat that prowls in the mountains or hunts wild prey in an isolated farmland."

Without missing a beat, Shira summarily explained that a "cougar" is a maturing woman who is energized, attracted by and magnetized to much younger men. This woman confessed that she failed to understand precisely why she had felt this way. Perhaps these motivations stemmed from the inescapable fact that guys her own age failed to attract her--lacking the ability to keep up with her physically and emotionally.

Right when Thomas began to ponder the meaning of all this, Marie Robbins and her husband--the increasingly popular oncologist--stepped up right beside the pair as they sat beside each other at the dining table.

"You two look like cute lovebirds, totally engrossed with each other," Marie said, while reaching for the back of the chair where little Elvis had sat a short while earlier. "Do you two mind if we sit down with you for awhile?"

Before Thomas could mentally grasp the right words for a response, Doctor Robbins held the chair where Eric had been. The older physician looked down toward them, grinning as he said:

"Son, that startled expression in your eyes makes you appear as if we have caught you in some sort of an embarrassing situation."

Thomas chuckled nervously, still unable to think of what precisely to say. Deep inside, his own conflicting emotions of budding love and disappointment made him feel increasingly confused. He admitted to himself that he had never experienced such uncertainty, perplexed and puzzled with the mere notion of how to proceed.

"Hello, you two!" Shira grinned broadly, as Thomas tried to fight off his emotional and physical attraction toward her. "Plant your little butts down here, and enjoy this fantastic food."

Doctor Robbins reached across the table and shook Thomas' hand.

"Even from a good distance, I spotted the two of you." Doctor Robbins tucked a white cloth napkin into the collar of his own blue cowboy-style shirt. "Don't take this the wrong way, but you looked like love-struck teenagers together."

Hearing this, Thomas did not know whether to feel angry at this comment, or delighted that someone had noticed his attraction to Shira. The younger doctor decided to keep his mouth shut, rather than risk saying something that he might regret. The Vanderbilt resident considered his mentor as a man of little words, so to hear the oncologist speak in such lively and highly personal terms had been a big surprise.

From that point for the next full hour straight the women did most of the talking. The ladies chatted non-stop about the glorious weather, the joyful expressions all around them, and the fact that the General had played an important role in Doctor Robbins' life. For the most part, the older and younger physicians remained tight-lipped. Thomas sensed that like himself, his mentor preferred being a listener rather than a talker.

Lifting her water glass about 15 minutes into the conversation, Shira proposed a toast among the four of them: "Here is to the two of you, Marie and Doctor Robbins--for all that you each do, for so many people: for maintaining this wild horse sanctuary; for helping many needy families with their urgent medical expenses; for being role models for us all, sensational examples of the best way to behave; for your mutual intelligence; for sharing with me the details of your amazing discoveries; and perhaps most of all--for being my good, irreplaceable friends; and also for having such a fantastic son--the young, handsome and charismatic young man sitting right here beside me."

"Here-here!" Doctor Robbins said, as the four of them tipped their glasses together, before sipping various beverages of water, wine, beer and lemonade.

Right then and there, Thomas decided without any hesitation whatsoever that he would always feel tremendous affection for Shira Levy--no matter what might occur between them in the future.

Thirty

A handful of mainstream doctors who typically prescribed dangerous drugs began to shun Doctor Robbins, beginning in progressively more intense phases from 2001 to 2005. He first noticed this trend at various social functions and parties at numerous Reno-area homes. Meantime, some mainstream physicians also chose to remain friendly with this physician and his wife.

Even so, many standard conventional physicians closely affiliated with the huge drug companies began to ignore him and Marie at social gatherings.

The other doctors' change in behavior marked a significant change from the 1990s, when other physicians and their spouses gravitated to the Robbins at social functions. During those early days the couple got frequent mentions in the popular "Globe-Herald" society column--then written by Duane Shelton.

Without telling his new adversaries how he felt, Doctor Robbins privately sensed that everything came down to one word--"jealousy."

From his view, lots of allopathic physicians had become: envious that as an extremely rare integrative medical oncologist, he had become able to provide patients with "the best of what both worlds have to offer;" insecure with the inescapable fact that he now had these powers, which they lacked; anxious that he might use his unique knowledge and talent to develop vastly superior treatments; and suspicion that he might lure away many of their patients.

Amid these many challenges, Doctor Robbins felt increasingly proud of Marie, especially for her emotional strength and courage in supporting his cutting-edge professional endeavors. From his view, she always stood up for him, particularly in instances where most other spouses would have caved in to social pressure.

Within typical health care settings, medical staffers, patients and casual acquaintances typically referred to him as "Doctor Robbins." All along, his relatives and closest friends adopted the habit of calling him "Jim."

As health care industry technologies steadily evolved and improved during the first five years of the 21st Century, he appreciated how Marie had supported and encouraged his efforts to become a licensed Homeopath during the mid-1990s.

Perhaps most of all, Jim appreciated the fact that--just like he had done--in those early years she began recognizing the fact that in the 1990s cancer patients treated with alternative therapies were experiencing impressive results. This data encouraged Doctor Robbins, who--before adding Homeopathy to his licensing--had become increasingly discouraged, concerned and depressed by his patients' long-term results.

Before starting the correspondence course for a Homeopathic degree, he noticed that practitioners of alternative therapies ignored or avoided many of the traditional treatment protocols typically used by mainstream American doctors.

During that early transitional phase, Jim felt intrigued, mystified and magnetized by the fact that practitioners of these promising alternative therapies avoided many of the treatment protocols that the mainstream U.S. medical industry required him to use. Rather than potentially deadly or extremely dangerous surgery, radiation and chemotherapy, non-traditional medical professionals used safe, non-poisonous natural remedies.

*

By phone on weekday evenings, usually at least once a week--often on Mondays, Doctor Robbins discussed these observations with Thomas. Their communications continued through 2003, while the younger physician remained an oncologist in residence at Vanderbilt.

Throughout that period from 2000 to 2003, Marie's best

friend, Shira Levy, traveled frequently from Reno to Nashville. Thomas and Shira always claimed that they were merely good friends; yet Jim and Marie suspected otherwise, sensing that the pair had become passionate lovers despite their 17-year age difference.

    The families had become so close by then that during Shira's frequent absences from Northern Nevada, the Robbins took care of Shira's boys Eric and Elvis at the couple's Sunnyville Shores estate.

    At one point, during the Hanukkah and Christmas seasons of 2003, Shira had erupted into tears while having dinner alone with Marie.

    "I am desperately in love with your son." Shira had confessed. "I cannot stop thinking about him for a single moment, even though he lives so far away. ... I hope this is not a sin. My feelings are all mixed up ... I hope, Marie, that we can always remain the best of friends, no matter what happens ... Please do not judge me, because I am unable to control what my heart feels."

    Later that evening, while with Jim at their home, Marie told him what had happened. In private, the two of them agreed that they both adored Thomas and Shira--each wanting the best for them.

*

    Doctor Robbins chose to avoid mentioning this during his weekly conversations with Thomas. The Reno physician considered his adoptive son as the perfect person to share his medical secrets with, the only person who could be trusted.

    On infrequent occasions Thomas suggested to Jim that they start communicating via email or even with one-on-one video chats that had become increasingly popular on the Internet. Each time the Reno doctor refused, saying "that's not my style."

    Thomas invariably responded to such statements by speaking in what Jim considered a good-natured tone: "Wouldn't it be funny, doctor, if you got hooked on the latest 21st Century Web-based technologies?"

The men occasionally laughed about this, while Jim's ongoing efforts to develop a vastly superior and natural treatment protocol for cancer remained his primary objective.

Rather than discussing personal issues, in these conversations the men always focused their topics on Jim's latest medical efforts.

Only in these private chats, Doctor Robbins admitted that striving to use the best and most effective aspects of conventional and alternative medicines had become challenging. Jim described this as if a "tightrope and sometimes a minefield."

Jim explained that unlike just about every doctor in the United States, he needed to fully comply with his state's "mainstream" medical board--as well as that jurisdiction's board regulating the actions of Homeopaths. Complicating matters, at least from his view, under Nevada state law some treatments that are listed as legal for Homeopaths cannot be used by standard allopathic physicians.

"As you can very well imagine, Thomas, I need to remain vigilant and super-careful in this regard." Doctor Robbins said in one of their most in-depth phone chats on December 17, 2003--the 100th anniversary of the first airplane flight by the Wright Brothers in Kitty Hawk, North Carolina. "As an integrative medical oncologist, I consider myself on the cutting edge of health care technology. Largely for these reasons, in carefully complying with the regulations of both medical boards, I have found a compromise that enables me to accomplish my clinical medical investigations and keep all transparent."

"Doctor, this is sensational!" Thomas exclaimed by phone, his voice seeming to Jim as if unusually emotional and enthusiastic. "Does this mean that you still hope to create a unique, highly effective cancer treatment protocol--used no where else?"

"That remains my goal, son ... Perhaps more than anyone, you know that I will never give up that quest, if doing so takes until my dying day."

*

On March 8 of the following year, 2004, during one of their weekly phone chats, Thomas revealed that he intended to return to Reno, where he hoped to practice oncology.

Now that his required residency, and a follow-up position at an established medical practice in Nashville had ended, Thomas yearned to return to Nevada--"which, in my heart, I will always consider home."

"I do not want to seem overly bold or pushy in asking for this--but do you think that there might be a position for me at your clinic?"

Doctor Robbins initially refrained from giving a response. From what he had been hearing from Marie, Thomas and Shira had become even more madly in love with each other. The Reno physician realized that by saying "no," he would cause heated conflict within his family. This possible outcome seemed logical to him, mainly because Shira and Marie remained best girlfriends.

"Thomas, how about if we start out by having me make a referral to another Reno oncology clinic--owned and operated by one of my competitors. Then, after earning your stripes there--following a period of several years--perhaps we could consider bringing you on board into my clinic? Of course, there are no guarantees ... Does this sound like an acceptable plan?"

"Fantastic! ... Thank you!"

"I suspect that you and Shira are madly in love with each other?"

"I am never going to deny it."

*

By late May of that year Thomas' move to Reno had been completed.

With Doctor Robbins help and encouragement, the younger oncologist got hired by the Sierra Sky Oncology Center on Ryland Avenue--four blocks from Sierra Crest Hospital, where Thomas also qualified to treat patients in that medical center.

Immediately after returning to town, Thomas moved in to Shira's expansive home with her, Eric and Elvis on Juniper Hill

Road near the exclusive, high-end Caughlin Ranch residential community.

With Jim and Marie, the family had monthly dinner celebrations at Shira's home or in the Robbins' residence. By mid-summer the women had bought domesticated horses for each of the boys at their sprawling wild horse refuge.

At one of these dinners in late July, Doctor Robbins felt surprised, delighted and joyful when Shira and Thomas announced their plans to get married.

Right away Marie erupted in tears, which Jim considered as a signal of her boundless happiness for the couple. For the previous few months, Marie had been encouraging Thomas and Shira to "tie the knot--to make it legal."

Exceedingly proud of Thomas, Doctor Robbins walked with this younger physician to the back yard--where they worked together handling clean-up chores.

"Thomas, take a look at this." Jim handed the younger doctor a piece of paper.

While his adoptive son started reading the document, Jim explained that this was a clipping from a recent "Journal of Oncology" article. The in-depth scientific report on a large retrospective study had concluded that any Stage IV cancer patient entering a retrospective chemotherapy program in the United States had only a 2.1 percent chance of surviving longer than five years.

This meant that only about two out of every 100 advance-stage cancer patients were eventually considered "cured" after being treated by traditional oncology methods.

"I'm not surprised," Thomas said. "This is horrible."

"You can be rest assured that I am going to do everything in my power to develop a far more effective treatment ... People deserve much better than this."

*

Thomas and Shira scheduled their wedding for the following June, in the back yard of Jim and Marie's home with the older couple's full blessing.

While also handling their respective duties as chief executive and chairman of the local Republican Party chapter, Shira and Marie spent much of their free time planning every intricate details of the nuptials.

In the interim, whenever their hectic schedules permitted, Thomas and Jim frequently spoke about the elder oncologist's ongoing efforts to improve cancer treatment results. Doctor Robbins admitted his endeavor emerged as far more difficult than he had once suspected.

"Thomas, as standard mainstream or allopathic oncologists, it's much easier than the complicated tasks that I am faced with now," Jim told Thomas while they cooked hamburgers on the back-yard grill on a pleasant August evening--while the women and children watched TV inside. "As a standard oncologist, you just tell the patient to be in the infusion center on Monday and the protocol is recommended."

"Well, doctor, as you know, it's not super-easy." Thomas flipped the burgers. "But I think that I clearly understand what you are talking about."

"I'm sure that you do." Doctor Robbins sat in a patio chair, popping open a few beers for him and his adoptive son. "As standard oncologists, we just give them the dose schedule, without ever deviating. Also, by following these protocols, oncologists never get into trouble--even if the patient dies from treatment."

The barbecue flames momentarily flared up, while Thomas sipped some of his brew and turned several more burgers. He told the older physician that he could "only just begin to imagine the potential problem when adding non-traditional techniques."

"You are right on the money when saying that, Thomas. When you go outside of the box and add medicine and anything alternative, that's when the criticism comes down on you. It's just much easier for oncologists to follow the straight party line."

*

The men's hectic schedules prevented them from

discussing Doctor Robbins' progress; the doctors finally were able to chat in Jim's home office amid that year's Christmas Eve family celebration. Thomas and Shira had decided to expose the boys' to holiday traditions of the Jewish and Christian faiths.

Following the standard turkey meal with the usual fixings and after a round of gift-giving, the doctors seized an opportunity to meet--while Eric and Elvis watched an Ebeneezer Scrooge movie on TV and the ladies chatted in the kitchen.

Finally in private, Jim revealed to Thomas that he had started studying numerous natural supplements; these included "pawpaw," a natural substance distributed by the Nature's Sunshine company. Growing naturally in the wilderness, this substance is found in pawpaw trees that grow in the Southeastern United States.

"Thomas, this is amazing but true." Doctor Robbins paused momentarily to sip eggnog and nibble a holiday cookie. "My microscopic tests indicated--without any doubt whatsoever--that pawpaw affects the energetics of cancer cells. ... This could emerge as one of the most significant and primary initial breakthroughs that I have long been searching for--God willing."

"I never doubted you for a moment, doctor ... I have always tried to put my full faith and trust in you, just as I know that you have for me as well. ... Most experienced physicians that I know lack your drive and ambition. Instead, they just get themselves into a professional rut, usually by the time that they reach about 55 years old."

The men shared a good laugh. Doctor Robbins sensed that like him, Thomas realized that he would never slow down in these efforts until finding a viable solution. The older doctor passed the eggnog container to his adoptive son, who then promptly filled another glass.

While Thomas stretched across the table to grab more cookies, Jim revealed that he had discovered another vital substance that might emerge as promising. He described Poly-MVA as a complex of palladium and lipoic acid. Loaded with numerous vitamins, it is a tightly bound complex of both of these substances--available in liquid form.

Throughout the previous year, Jim had met people at various conferences for professionals in the alterative medicine industry. Lots of these individuals revealed that Poly-MVA had been used on a limited basis. Adding to the sense of urgency, several former cancer patients who had been treated with the substance told him that they had been in remission for more than five years, and "you have got to study this."

Hearing these details for the first time, Thomas lifted his eggnog high to propose a toast between the two of them: "Doctor, here is to doing just that!"

"Right on!"

*

From Doctor Robbins' perspective, the next two years seemed to blast past within the blink of an eye.

Six months after this energetic physician's holiday chat with Thomas, the wedding of the younger oncologist and Shira became a premiere highlight of his life.

Many of her Jewish relatives from Israel traveled all the way to Reno for the nuptials. Several of them privately told Jim and Marie that for many years they had been intrigued by what Shira did for a living. But now, finally seeing this woman in her own work environment, they felt satisfied and proud of her job as an administrator.

The ceremony was performed in part by the 83-year-old Reverend Martin "Scout" Middleton of Centralia, Nevada--the same man of God who had officiated at the funeral of Thomas' mother three decades earlier. The reverend's towering, kind and frail wife, Janelle, had died from a stroke in 2002.

Myra Soifer, leader of the primary Reno synagogue, co-officiated at the wedding, which featured traditional Jewish songs and foods.

Right on cue, the guests all shouted "Mazel Tov" as Shira and Thomas simultaneously broke a glass--in keeping with Jewish tradition. Loud cheers erupted in Jim and Marie's expansive back yard, before almost everyone in attendance began clapping or participating in traditional Jewish dances and songs.

Amid the celebration, Doctor Robbins considered this event as a much-needed break in his hectic everyday life. He realized more than ever that the following three or four years would become a whirlwind of non-stop activity as he continued to develop and fine-tune his unique cancer treatment protocol.

Along with Marie, Jim felt tremendous joy in seeing Thomas reunite at the wedding celebration with relatives and friends that he had not seen for many years.

From their view, perhaps the most shocking and unexpected reunion was between Thomas and his biological father, Abraham "Honest" Davis.

Jim felt completely taken by surprise upon seeing this former plumber and Thomas tightly hug each other. The biological father--now in his late 70s--each smiled broadly while posing for the camera, arms over each other's shoulders.

Doctor Robbins had recently heard via word-of-mouth that the elder Centralia native had not touched a drop of alcohol in more than a decade.

Adding to the excitement, for the first time since she was a small child, Jim spotted Thomas' younger sister Penelope amid the crowd. Now at age 41, this one-armed woman had flown in from Las Vegas, where she worked as a top-level executive at the Mirage Hotel and Casino.

Tears welled up in Doctor Robbins' eyes as he watched Penelope, Thomas and Honest simultaneously hug each other. The elder physician sensed that this marked the first formal and happy reunion for the three of them since Thomas and Penelope were small children. Like Thomas and Honest had done just a few minutes earlier, this time Penelope joined them in posing for photos of just the three of them.

Other guests quickly joined this throng. Those eager to have their pictures taken with Thomas and Shira included: her many Jewish relatives, some in the United States for the first time; his Aunt Paula and her husband Bobby "Cactus Pete" Blair; Aunt Pamela, her husband Bradley and their adults sons; the late General's adult daughters, each in their late 50s, Charlotte, Karen and Christine; and many other longtime friends.

Doctor Robbins, who had served as best man, proposed the first formal toast in proclaiming: "Here is to never giving up hope, to endless and ever-flowing love, and to this fabulous couple's quest for long life, a glorious family, and happiness!"

Thirty-One

Thomas felt happier and more energetic than ever during their three-week honeymoon, while Jim and Marie cared for the boys in Reno.

They spent the first 10 days in a sprawling and old-style home owned by Thomas' adoptive parents in Chandler, Arizona. Then, following a full day for traveling, the newlyweds spent the last half of their romantic getaway at a house that Doctor Robbins and his wife also owned overlooking the Pacific Ocean in the small Northern California community of Seascape.

Shira and Thomas had initially balked at their offer to use these homes, but the older couple insisted--telling them: "For heaven's sake, you are family."

While in Seascape, with just three days remaining in their excursion, in the wee hours of the morning Thomas awakened to visit the restroom.

Still sleepy and somewhat exhausted after spending plenty of quality time with Shira, Thomas heard her distinctive, high-pitched and chattery voice. The sound emitted from the living room, so he walked in there to investigate.

He saw his new wife sitting in front of a laptop. Shira kept speaking Yiddish, a language that this doctor did not understand. On the screen, Thomas saw the video image of a man's face; this guy's mouth moved in sync with his words.

"Honey, what is going on?" Thomas rubbed his eyes, striving to focus better on the image. "Who are you talking with?"

"Oh!" Shira spilled a glass of ice water onto the same tabletop upon which her laptop rested. "You startled me ... I'm sorry."

She immediately stood and used a napkin to wipe up the mess. Meantime, Thomas kept looking at the image on screen of the stranger's face.

"Shira, who is this person that you're talking with?"

"Oh, it's my--umm ... I ..." She sat back down and looked at the face.

"Who did you say this is, honey?"

"Ah... Cousin ... This is my cousin, Hiram. He is in Tel Aviv."

The man on the screen waved and smiled broadly, while saying something in Yiddish. The guy looked goofy to Thomas, almost as if a clown.

"Great." Thomas bent slightly, waved toward the screen and briefly kissed his new wife's left cheek. "I'm going right back to bed, if you don't mind ... Sleepy."

*

Three months later Thomas saw Doctor Robbins in person for the first time since the wedding. The physicians chatted with each other during the family's annual Labor Day Weekend celebration at the historic Bowers Mansion Regional Park, 24 miles south of Reno.

While the women sunbathed and swam with the children at the facility's 50-yard-long pool, the doctors sat together on a bench. Instead of drinking their usual beers, this time they shared Jim's favorite summertime beverage; as he had for several decades, Doctor Robbins still preferred "Arnold Palmer" beverages.

On Thomas' small boom-box radio, the region's most popular hit country radio station played that week's Number One tune--"Live Like You Were Dying," by the relatively new and fast-rising star, Tim McGraw.

The song seemed ideal for the moment as far as Thomas was concerned, as he listened intently to every word that Doctor Robbins said.

For the first time, the older physician revealed to him that his clinic had become the world's first licensed medical facility to study those amazing natural substances, remedies mentioned by Jim in their earlier conversations.

"Thomas, I had not told you these details before, but I didn't want to get your hopes up to much." The older physician, now in his late 60s, stared intently at three women in their late 20s as they walked past--each lady wearing a tiny bikini. "But you're going to be amazed, when I tell you the results."

"I'm amazed already." Thomas grinned, and proposed a toast with Jim--both of their eyes glued toward these women. "Doctor, if the results are anything like we're seeing now, I'm going to be stunned by what you tell me."

Both men momentarily broke out in laughter, before Doctor Robbins summarily described what had been happening. When the Vietnam War veteran first learned about those promising substances, the pawpaw from Nature's Sunshine and the Poly-MVA, limited research on those substance "held no credence."

In fact, Jim said that at the time no conventional medical oncologist would seriously consider any individual case involving these potential treatments.

But Doctor Robbins launched a large-scale study, determined to get definitive data proving that the substances could generate tremendous results in treating cancer.

A Southern California physician, Mark Hernandez, had agreed to supply Poly-MVA for free to 225 of Doctor Robbins' patients--who all suffered from advanced Stage IV cancers.

"Thomas, this might sound unbelievable, but it's true." Jim took off his own sunglasses while saying this, his suntanned and smoothe-skinned face looking to Thomas as if that of a man in his mid-40s.

The older physician explained that after five years, a whopping 35 percent to 40 percent of those "study group" patients remained alive. That compared to the dismal nationwide five-year survival rate of only about 2 percent when treated by conventional oncologists.

"Wow!" Thomas felt so excited upon hearing this that he spilled his beverage, but didn't worry at all about the mess. "Doctor, you did it!"

"This is not the end ... I'm confident that we'll get even better results very soon."

*

Still ecstatic and joyful about his mentor's significant accomplishments, that night after Thomas and Shira put the boys to bed this young stepfather and doctor finally caved in and decided to tell her the good news.

Through the previous several years, Thomas had told Shira what he considered as mere "bits and pieces" of his mentor's admirable efforts.

Yet on this particular night, for the first time ever, he felt an urgent need to tell her as much detail as possible.

"Once the word gets out, this will change the entire health care industry for the better." Thomas sat in their bed, his feet curled yoga-style and his back erect. "People everywhere should be throwing ticker-tape parades in honor of Doctor Robbins."

Thomas' love and appreciation for his wife swelled even more. He felt thankful that Shira latched on to his every word, proclaiming that she felt equally energized and excited; she had also promised him that she would never tell anyone what "could very well be the world's biggest secret."

As a conventional oncologist, Thomas liked the fact that Shira had been a pharmaceutical industry expert for two decades. Many times the two of them had previously discussed the rampant corruption throughout the U.S. Food and Drug Administration, that benefiting the monopolies of Big Pharma and mainstream medicine.

Excited by his mentor's discoveries, Thomas had difficulty falling asleep that night until dozing off at 1:15 the next morning.

Shortly after awakening at 3:25 to visit the restroom, he heard Shira's chattery voice echoing from the living room. Thomas walked in there, noticing right away that his wife as talking via the Internet with her cousin from Israel.

"Hey, Shira." Thomas casually waved toward his wife from the hallway, briefly saying hello to her before heading back to bed.

"Please say 'hi' to Hiram for me."

*

Eager for a full update from Doctor Robbins on a rare afternoon off from work the following spring, Thomas invited his mentor to lunch that day.

They met at 12:45 on an usually warm Saturday in early April at the new Soo Chin's Chinese Restaurant on South Virginia Street in Reno. Although never a fan of foods from the Far East, Thomas had eagerly said "okay" as soon as Doctor Robbins suggested this venue--energized by the prospect of seeing his adoptive father.

Eager to get to what he considered the most urgent topic at hand, after briefly exchanging the usual pleasantries about how various relatives had been doing, Thomas began to ask a maze of questions.

"Doctor, I am so eager for details." Thomas slowly pulled the paper covering off his chopsticks. "Have you discovered any more amazing natural remedies?"

The younger physician sensed that Jim was equally energized, when beginning to explain his many new exceptional discoveries, study results and scientific conclusions.

Within a span of just 15 minutes, Doctor Robbins revealed a lengthy maze of these vital updates.

"Holy cow!" Thomas briefly gagged on his Chinese food, before quickly regaining his composure. "This is beyond merely 'amazing'--it's 'phenomenal.'"

"Like that old Carpenters tune says, we have 'only just begun.' ... I have even more exciting updates to give you."

Jim explained that he had discovered a unique process for administering the natural products, a loading dose process named the Robbins Immune Therapy. This is administered in a careful, step-by-step process: patients initially receive an intravenous cocktail loaded with natural immune-boosting substances; these people are sent home with "supplements;" and the patients ingest these capsules daily until their tumors go into remission.

Adding plenty of reasons for more optimism, Doctor Robbins' intense research indicated that none of the patients had suffered the symptoms toxicity. Meantime, increasing the natural firepower in battling cancer, along with other treatments, Jim sometimes used low-dose chemotherapy treatment or a unique process called "insulin-potentiated" therapies--sometimes called "IPT."

"Keep in mind, Thomas, that this is an extremely low dose, only about 10 percent to 20 percent of the amount usually given by conventional oncologists. So, as you can imagine, it's very non-toxic."

"And this is working?"

"That's right! ... This might seem like some sort of magic trick, but it's all actually science-based."

Doctor Robbins then went on to explain that in a sense this process is similar to a natural "smart bomb," naturally blasting the cancers away. Such exceptional results had become possible because--as one of only a few integrative medical oncologists in the United States--Jim was able to exploit a known, verifiable weakness in cancer cells.

Cancer craves sugars so much that the cells are covered with insulin receptors. These microscopic objects open as wide as they can in an effort to create a broad pathway for sugars to enter; the sugars provide vital and necessary energy to the deadly cells.

"But when the receptors open wide, Thomas, as you very well know, that's the biological equivalent of a castle without a protective moat. My unique process tricks the cancer into readily accepting the natural substances that eventually kill the disease. Wrongly thinking that simple sugars are available, the cancer cells become receptive to the mixture--while also becoming more accessible to the low-dose chemo."

Thomas' sense of amazement intensified, particularly because this all sounded to him as if simple and basic.

"So, the system that you developed tricks the cancer?"

"You have nailed it right on the head, Thomas. Remember

that cancer needs simple sugars to thrive. The disease is unable to thrive on proteins, fats and high-glycemic carbohydrates."

Increasingly more curious as their lunchtime conversation progressed, Thomas then asked about recommended diets and other therapies for these patients.

Thomas became increasingly grateful as Doctor Robbins went into more detail. The older physician described many of the other basics, which included suggesting to patients that they: enjoy a simpler no-sugar diet, because cancers thrive on that substance; eating alkaline rather than acidic foods, because cancer thrives in acid environments; drink alkaline water and green powders that contain algae, barley grass, ryegrass or wheat-grass; and that they consider using various oxidative therapies, possibly such devices as hyperbolic, ozone, or hydrogen chambers.

"Jim, I imagine that all this sounds somewhat complicating to patients at first, but very soon the vast majority of them probably realize the process is simple ... Am I right?"

"Yes, indeed. To make it simple for them to understand, I tell patients that on a biological level cancer is similar to low-voltage outside patio lights. The disease is just like those systems. When the voltage gets turned up too high on the transformers, the entire process gets burned out. ... All this becomes possible because cancer cells produce only 5 percent of the energy levels used by the body's normal and healthy cells. ... Thanks to these factors, coupled with the effective features of the various natural substances used in the Robbins Immune Therapy, the cancer cells become my system's targets for destruction. The Poly-MVA works on energetics.

Admittedly stunned and proud of his adoptive father's accomplishments, Thomas eventually realized that this lunch had lasted nearly two hours--nearly twice as long as he had anticipated.

Shortly before 3 o'clock the men walked to their parked cars near the restaurant's entrance. Thomas seized that opportunity to ask Doctor Robbins something that the younger physician had been meaning to ask for nearly a year.

"Doctor, can I join your practice--become a part of your team?"

"Thomas, I have to be honest and straight-forward with you now. If you had asked me this a year ago, I would have flat-out said 'no,' that you are not ready ... But I have been closely following your career and the time is now--so the answer today is 'yes,' you are hired on the spot ... But with just one caveat."

"Fantastic! ... What is the special condition?"

"Never, under any circumstances whatsoever, never tell anyone the specifics that I have just told you, or over these past few years for that matter."

"Well, I need to admit that I have told Shira bits and pieces since we were married. She is insatiably curious, you know that."

"No worries whatsoever, Thomas ... Shira is family ... I'm sure that she knows how to keep her mouth shut, and that she will never betray us."

Thirty-Two

The next five years, 2006 through 2010, became the equivalent of an emotional roller coaster ride on a professional basis, from Thomas' perspective.

Although more than 30 years younger than his adoptive father, the former Vanderbilt resident realized that he lacked Doctor Robbins' physical and mental stamina.

The older doctor started most weekdays by playing intense rounds of tennis with several buddies about his age at the Sky Box Exercise Complex. While this was underway, Thomas usually slept as late as possible--occasionally complaining to Shira that he always felt exhausted from the intense work load at his adoptive father's clinic.

At first Thomas had thought that working there would be a breeze--but soon found out otherwise. He learned that Doctor Robbins was a health care purist and hard-liner who continually demanded perfection of himself and everyone on his team.

Most workdays for Thomas ended around 4 o'clock. He would drive home, often feeling sleepy and mentally overwhelmed, feeling somewhat guilty that his mentor usually stayed late in the clinic--sometimes until 10 o'clock or even later.

Doctor Robbins' so-called "old-fashioned work ethic" carried over into other facilities as well. Most mornings after playing tennis--while en route to his clinic--the senior physician would visit his patients, making rounds in local hospital rooms.

Jim often repeated this process in the late afternoons and early evenings, occasionally followed by a quick bite to eat-- before returning to the clinic to conduct more research.

After nearly two years of being out-shined this way, Thomas decided "I am going to step up my game ... I am going to do my best to be more like Jim; I need to prove to myself and to others that I am not a lazy bum, merely trying to ride someone's coattails."

Thanks largely to Shira's loyalty and encouragement, by late 2007 she and Thomas began running together almost every morning. This exercise and a significant improvement in his own fitness helped motivate and energize this Centralia native.

"Thomas, you might not realize this." Doctor Robbins told him during a one-on-one meeting in his office, during the second week of January in 2008. "About a year ago, I began considering whether to put you on probation. ... But to your credit, you went ahead and made significant and positive changes on your own. Right now, son, I consider you as irreplaceable--so, keep up the good work."

*

Early that year Thomas became increasingly frustrated, primarily due to the inescapable fact that the mainstream news media ignored Doctor Robbins' significant medical discoveries.

Together, these doctors had written and sent out several press releases, detailing how natural substances used by at their clinic generated five-year remission rates averaging more than 50 percent--significantly better than the 2.1 percent generated by conventional oncologists.

Instead of praising these significant advancements, in the spring of 2008 Reno's primary newspaper--the "Globe-Herald"--launched in intensive series of front-page articles, each critical of Doctor Robbins' medical procedures.

The stories refrained from mentioning this physician's vastly superior five-year remission rates among his patients suffering from the most advanced cancers.

Remaining intensely loyal to his mentor and adoptive father, Thomas became increasingly angry at the newspaper and the nationwide news media in general.

"The American news media is corrupt to the core," Shira told the doctors and Marie during a family dinner in her and Thomas' home on April 5, 2008. "I know this from my personal experience, when working as an administrator for the Food and Drug Administration near Washington, D.C."

As Eric and Elvis watched "Jeopardy" on TV in the living room, Shira explained her negative opinions about the U.S. news media. She briefly described a situation that Thomas realized that each person at the dining room table already knew about. The drug industry remained corrupt, and the liberal American news media essentially served as the obedient hunting dogs--viciously and persistently attacking alternative medicine.

Sure enough, the "Globe-Herald" articles quoted conventional doctors and even patients--all of them critical of Doctor Robbins for: prescribing natural human growth hormones, even though doing so was perfectly legal; recommending vitamins and certain types of supplements, which the FDA claimed were useless and in some cases even harmful; treating cancer patients with natural substances, a process labeled as "quackery" by mainstream medical experts; and for his daring to proclaim that cancer patients should have a right to refuse deadly, high-dose chemotherapy treatments--using natural remedies instead.

"Doctor Robbins, I love you." Shira declared, holding the older physician's hand as he sat on her immediate right. "You are an amazing man---perhaps the most fantastic person that I have ever met, except perhaps for your son here. And, I must say, that your wife is pretty phenomenal, too."

Marie suddenly broke into tears at the dinner table. Amid uncontrollable sobs she spoke of her love for her husband and her sadness that adversaries had begun smearing his hard-earned reputation.

Shira stood, walked around the table and gently cradled her arms around Marie's shoulders, while Doctor Robbins held his wife's left hand.

Feeling speechless, Thomas remained motionless while listening to his wife speak softly to his adoptive mother.

"Marie, you have every reason to spill your tears," Shira said, while still rubbing her girlfriend's shoulders. "You have legitimate reasons for feeling anger and sadness. Some conventional doctors, and almost every congressional politician are far from angels--in fact, as far as I'm concerned they're all devils."

"Everyone, please listen." Doctor Robbins said, just when Eric and Elvis entered the dining room. Upon seeing the children, Thomas realized that this commotion had lured the children away from the TV. "I suspect Senator Larry Spickler is the worst of them all. I have little doubt that he is leading this smear campaign against me."

Shira asked the boys to rush and get tissue paper and a cold wash cloth for their Grandma Marie, who by this point continued crying--but much more softly.

"In my work at the FDA, I determined that Senator Spickler is a mere puppet, just like all the rest of those clowns." Shira spoke without interruption, while handing Marie a glass of ice water. "From what I know of that man, I suspect that he is not involved in this blatant effort to destroy your reputation, Doctor Robbins. Instead, I suspect that the ringleaders are various local conventional doctors--along with streams of other corrupt politicians and government bureaucrats from across the nation."

Hearing this, Thomas felt as if he had quickly become even angrier and more upset than his adoptive mother.

"How dare they smear my mentor!" Thomas finally felt a need to express his emotion, rather than merely behaving level-headed as usual. "This doctor is a good man--the best imaginable! ... Forgive me, everyone, for being so blunt. I realize that none of you have ever seen me behave this way as an adult."

The boys rushed back into the dining room with a facial tissue and a cool wash cloth, immediately giving them to Marie.

While his wife blew her nose and wiped away her tears, Doctor Robbins told everyone his theory: "Those who keep smearing my good name feel threatened. They realize that my discoveries--dramatically increasing five-year remission rates--could quickly destroy their proverbial Cash Cow. ... Imagine the billions of dollars in annual revenues that the allopathic health care industry would lose, if people knew the truth--that standard chemo treatments are killing many people--perhaps by the tens of thousands or even millions worldwide very year. ... Yes, the sad fact has emerged. Those demons would prefer to kill people, rather than save them--because the chemo generates cascades of non-stop cash for these companies."

Shira pulled a chair close beside Marie's position, and started hugging her girlfriend--who had calmed down by this point.

"Sometimes--and you might not yet realize this--everyone," Shira said. "But sometimes I have a good, intuitive sense about things ... When that happens, I am rarely wrong ... And, what I'm sensing right now is undeniable ... Someday, I believe--and I do not yet know for sure precisely when--but I sense that someday the entire world will know the full truth about your amazing discoveries, Doctor Robbins. ... And, when that happens, as they very well should, people everywhere are going to start revolting against the terrors of mainstream medicine."

*

Business steadily worsened at Doctor Robbins medical clinic, due to a sharp decrease in patient totals. Thomas blamed the national recession, coupled with the damage to his mentor's reputation--caused by the "Globe-Herald" propaganda campaign.

Rather than perceiving Doctor Robbins as an amazing health care industry innovator and maverick as they had done before, lots of people wrongly started thinking of him as a "quack" who eagerly put his patients into unnecessary danger.

The business worsened even more from August through September of 2008, when patient totals nosedived as the stock market and national economy fizzled.

This significant downturn in revenue at the clinic took Thomas by surprise, as his feelings of repulsion and anger toward the "establishment" intensified.

A year earlier in 2007, the clinic's waiting room had been

filled to near capacity most weekday mornings.

By mid-spring of 2009, this significant dip in revenues left Jim and Marie with no viable option other than to sell their vacation homes in Seascape, California, and Chandler, Arizona. The couple also had to lay off several of their clinic's nurses.

"I don't think the situation could get much worse than this," Thomas told Shira as they took one of their usual early morning jogs together in mid-summer. "At this rate, I am afraid, we will need to close down the clinic very soon."

*

Doctor Robbins soldiered forward while always keeping a positive attitude and refusing to accept defeat, at least from Thomas' perspective.

Rather than leave the medical profession--as some traditional physicians obviously wanted him to do--this senior doctor tried to make more innovations.

With the blessings of medical laboratories in South Korea, Germany and Greece, he began modifying, developing and suggesting an all-new cancer testing procedure.

Partly under his guidance, and on an independent basis as well, these foreign laboratories developed a "chemosensitivity test" procedure.

Thanks to this technology, made possible by the 13-year Human Genome Project that ended in 2003, Doctor Robbins was able to start recommending this new testing procedure--which he always described as "essential."

Chemo-sensitivity tests enabled biologists to thoroughly analyze blood specimens from cancer patients who paid an average $3,000 for a single procedure.

In return, the laboratories gave Doctor Robbins a complete and thorough analysis. The results determined: whether chemotherapy on specific patients would fail or possibly succeed on the individual; the specific type or brand of chemo drug that had the probability of generating the best results; and identify Stage IV cancer patients who would never benefit at all from chemo.

"Thomas, chemosensitivity testing is the proverbial goldmine," Doctor Robbins said during a one-on-one conference in his office in October 2009. "We can consider this the proverbial icing on the cake, a blessing for our patients."

"Yet, the media will smear this, too." Thomas commented right away, without having to put much thought into the matter. "If the recent past is any signal of a likely future, that smear-job by the 'Globe-Herald' could emerge as just the beginning of our long-term adversaries' effort to permanently wreck our reputation."

"You've known me for many years, so you know how I tick ... Keeping that in mind, Thomas, what is your guess? ... How will I respond to them?"

"The answer is simple. You will never give up, refusing to cave in to their systematic hogwash."

"You are always brilliant, aren't you, young man?"

"Sir, to the contrary, it is you would serve as king. ... This also means that we're going to battle with them--Big Pharma and any conventional doctors who refuses to acknowledge the power of your discoveries."

"Well, said ... And I believe that we will find more than one way to slay this fire-breathing dragon. Like I've always told you for nearly nearly 35 years now--'I am just a regular guy. But all along, I refuse to be taken down without a good fight.'"

Thirty-Three

Doctor Robbins considered 2009 and 2010 as pivotal years in the history of his career and of his groundbreaking research.

From the beginning of that period patient totals at his clinic began to slightly creep up, but only a bit--still much too sluggish for Pamela to refill staff positions that had been vacated.

Undaunted, with Marie's blessing, Doctor Robbins signed a renewable five-year contract to appear once weekly on Bobby Blair's talk radio show.

No longer using his former moniker, "Cactus Pete," the announcer told Doctor Robbins that he rarely thought of his early career. Those had been the days when Bobby broadcast his shows from just south of Mexico-U.S. Border.

All those years later, this Kentucky native who had dodged the draft during the Vietnam War, no longer used a rebellious and scandalous promotional strategy.

Instead, at his Rowdy Rebel Radio station founded in 2005, Bobby vowed to comply with all local, state and federal laws.

Doctor Robbins considered Bobby as an honest man who kept his word, while never betraying a friend. In fact, from this physician's view the announcer had done a fantastic job managing the wild horse ranch.

By this point in his early 70s, Bobby's once muscular, trim body was now saddled down by excessive body fat and continual fatigue. The announcer's belly flopped over his belt so much that suspenders were required to hold up his pants; this contrasted with 30 years earlier when he had used similar straps to emphasize and accentuate his muscular chest. That long, red and curly beard that once reminded the oncologist of a mischievous leprechaun, was now well-trimmed and gray like that of Santa Claus.

Upon starting on Bobby's station in mid-2009, the "Doctor

Robbins Medical Hour" aired on Friday afternoons--rebroadcast several times weekly.

Still married to Aunt Paula, by this point a retired casino card dealer, Bobby always tried to keep the program lively, fun and informative.

The program's ratings started off at a dismal level, with only a handful of regular listeners. By the end of that year, Marie started urging Jim to drop the program--which she considered a waste of time and money.

Yet the physician insisted on continuing this strategy, telling her: "I refuse to allow the establishment to win--to essentially beat me down and shut my voice forever. ... Remember, honey, we are fighters--and we always will be, no matter how many times that they try to knock me down."

*

The program's listener totals finally began to creep slightly upward after several months. Feeling at least somewhat encouraged by this development, the doctor decided to write at least a few dozen books. He wanted each publication to feature a different aspect of his significant medical discoveries.

"They can smear my name all that they want," Doctor Robbins told Marie while the two of them dined together, when celebrating her 55th birthday. "But those creeps who want to shut me down, they can never take away my right to free speech."

"Yeah, you go get them, honey!" She clinked her wine glass against his. "And may I tell you that--honestly, and I hear people say this about you all the time--you look sensational tonight. You look as if about my age, or maybe even younger."

At that point actually in his early 70s, for the previous several years he had been regularly taking vitamins, supplements and natural remedies--all hailed for significant benefits in optimizing good health. Adding zest to their personal life and successfully reinvigorating his physical energy level, Doctor Robbins also self-injected natural and healthy levels of human growth hormones every day.

As far as Thomas could tell, these natural remedies always worked wonders for his adoptive father. Patients occasionally told this younger doctor that "Doctor Robbins actually looks about as young and as healthy as you."

These two doctors briefly mentioned on occasion during their one-on-one meetings that they still remained upset with the news media--particularly for criticizing Doctor Robbins' unique cancer treatment protocol, and also because journalists had lambasted him for legally prescribing human growth hormone to numerous patients.

Still upset by these bogus allegations, beginning in January of 2010 Doctor Robbins began writing what he considered an in-depth and comprehensive book on the hormone--often called "HGH."

For five straight months beginning in April 2010, without fail every day this physician worked into the wee hours of the morning on his manuscript.

Upon completing the first draft, Doctor Robbins told Marie that he planned to submit the document to former "Globe-Herald" reporter Duane Shelton for a review and possibly for editing. Marie balked at this proposal, suggesting that a much more experienced book publishing industry veteran would do a much better job.

Despite his wife's concerns, Doctor Robbins reached an agreement with Shelton to give the attempt a quick read and then to give his honest opinion.

"Doctor, you have done an admirable job, but I see a huge potential problem," Shelton declared as the men had a lunch three weeks later in the coffee shop at the Peppermill Hotel and Casino. "This entire manuscript needs extensive re-working. By the time this gets done, the final product will look nothing like what you have."

Rather than become angry or defensive, the physician decided to take what he considered "the high road" and give Shelton at least one try at refashioning the work.

Ten years earlier the journalist had voluntarily quit the "Globe-Herald" at age 44, shocking his contemporaries who had felt convinced that he would continue working for the newspaper until old age.

In open meetings with his associates before departing the news media, Shelton declared that he was merely "needing a change." Yet through mutual friends at the time, Doctor Robbins learned the truth: The reporter, who then worked as a society and entertainment columnist, had become angry at the mainstream news business.

"The news media, and particularly newspapers like this, have become increasingly corrupt--in the sense that they are one-sided in favor of the establishment," Shelton had privately told friends. "I am afraid that this situation will only go downhill fast from here, particularly within the realms of politics and anything to do with health care."

Dead-set at striking out on his own, leaving the massive newspaper business chain that his late father helped create, Shelton became an independent editor and ghostwriter of books. Based solely on his positive reputation, the writer soon developed a steadily growing list of current or prospective clients.

By the time Doctor Robbins recruited Shelton, the journalist had edited or ghost-written several dozen books--a handful of them selling quite well.

On the negative side, however, the physician noticed that this book publisher had gradually become chubby, looking less youthful and vibrant. Amid his final years at the "Globe-Herald," Shelton had been razor thin and muscular, with a full head of long, flowing brown hair.

"Doctor, the aging process stinks, doesn't it?" Shelton told the physician during their initial lunch at the Peppermill. "I realize that the two of us have had our sharp differences through the years, especially way back in the late 1970s when I was merely a snot-nosed rookie who didn't know my butt from a whole in the ground."

Always considering himself as "old-school, gentlemanly and polite," Doctor Robbins usually scoffed at such gutter-level trash talk. But this time the physician felt that he had no choice other than to agree. After all, when the mainstream news media had been busy ruining Doctor Robbins' reputation a few years earlier, Shelton had been the only experienced journalist to rush to his defense.

Without hesitation, at the height of that controversy Shelton had written a scathing criticism of what he had hailed as the "'Globe-Herald's' blatant and reckless propaganda campaign, the journalist labeled the "Globe-Herald's" anti-Robbins onslaught as a misguided effort to destroy the solid reputation of a good, decent man--who just happens to be perhaps one of the world's most talented and dedicated physicians."

From Doctor Robbins' perspective, this statement went a long way in endearing him to Shelton--his former adversary from more than four decades earlier.

"Duane, I suspect that Senator Spickler is the ringleader, the top guy conspiring to destroy my hard-earned reputation," the physician said during this initial lunch. "If you asked me for my opinion, I would say that the guy is evil to the core."

"Evil is too good of a word for that creep, Doctor ... I can swear on a Bible that this politician serves as the Devil's official representative here on earth. Lots of people say this, as you might know."

Shelton then confessed that way back at the beginning of his journalism career, he had admired and looked up to Senator Spickler. But this admiration soon changed to utter disappointment, beginning when a rural Nevada sheriff and that lawman's two deputies disappeared and were eventually found slain in the late 1970s--when the politician's office refused to look deeply into the matter.

The journalist's respect for the Lighthouse native nosedived even further when the senator refused to acknowledge the many cancers--obviously caused by radioactive fallout from the above-ground nuclear bombs at the Nevada Test Site. Adding insult to injury, in the early 1990s the senator had pushed through the "measly and offensive" federal compensation plan for victims of those ill-fated experiments.

"It's mind-boggling isn't it, how our worst politicians sometimes get rewarded for their corruption?" Doctor Robbins said. "To think that as a Democrat, he is now the world-famous U.S. Senate Majority leader--pushing crappy legislation through Congress such as Obamacare. ... I have little doubt that Spickler played a leadership role in organizing the propaganda conspiracy against me ... You probably realize, of course, Duane, that my wife Marie still serves as chairman of our local and state Republican Party ... That alone makes me a particularly attractive target for him to take down."

"Doctor, I think that you're correct in one regard, but wrong in another. From my view, yes, he does see you as a prime object to put into the middle of his cross-hairs. ... But the guy is just plane stupid with a capital 'S.' ... He is far too much of a numb-skull to have carefully planned and coordinated the propaganda attack on you. ... Instead, everything that I have been able to learn about this guy indicates that he is nothing but a puppet--a person who has a hollow skull. The way I see the situation, anything positive that he might do in Congress is for purely selfish reasons. But even worse than that, I suspect, someone--either an individual or an agency--has the "goods on him," so to speak. Under my line of thinking, whoever this manipulator is, that entity has confronted him with the inescapable details of his devilish past. ... As a result, although Spickler might be perceived as one of today's most powerful politicians, at least as far as I can tell, he is actually extremely weak. So, believe me, and I am usually right about these things, virtually everything that he does involves kowtowing to his superiors."

Until lunch that day, Doctor Robbins had never envisioned the possibility that he and Shelton would someday become close allies. Like the radio announcer Bobby Blair, the journalist and the physician considered themselves as "mavericks"--standing tall and essentially carving out their own pathways in rebelling against the establishment.

"There are no guarantees, doctor, that we will succeed at your first book project. But believe me, I will do my best to help get you the positive recognition that you truly deserve."

*

While Shelton continued editing the HGH book's initial draft in mid-2010, Doctor Robbins got an unexpected and positive boost from a widely respected media personality.

Then in her early 60s, former 1970s TV sitcom star Susie Winters had become a widely respected author whose many best-selling books concentrated on health issues.

A distant cousin five times removed from the late famous film star Shelly Winters, Susie had starred in the hit ABC-TV program "Five Easy Neighbors;" the basic storyline involved the comic escapades of unmarried young adults.

More than 40 years later, Doctor Robbins vaguely recalled having seen the show or at least parts of it, but only once or twice.

All these fuzzy memories suddenly came back in clear view, as soon as Susie Winters made an unexpected phone call to his Reno clinic on May 5, 2010.

Still widely popular among the public, she asked the physician if she could interview him for her upcoming book "Upper-Cut,"--the true stories of how cutting edge physicians around the world were actually curing cancer.

Eager to re-establish his positive reputation, Doctor Robbins promptly agreed to be interviewed. That decision paid off big-time, at least in a financial sense, in November 2010 when Susie Winters book became an instant international bestseller.

Almost overnight, the appointments made by cancer patients at his Reno clinic increased almost four-fold. Well aware that some authors simply "get it all wrong," he became joyful upon seeing that she had accurately described the Robbins Immune Therapy and also her compelling descriptions of his vastly superior five-year remission rates.

Yet par for the course, at least from his view, the mainstream local and national news media still ignored these details, even after these facts came to light thanks to Winters' book. Occasionally joking in a light-hearted way, Doctor Robbins sometimes told his closest friends that like the comedian Rodney Dangerfield, "I don't get no respect."

At their frequent family dinners, Marie, Thomas and Shira often urged Doctor Robbins to "quit saying that." To them, the severe damage to his reputation was far from a joking matter.

"Doctor, your day to shine in front of the whole world will arrive someday soon--I'm sure of that," Shira said at one point. "Please keep writing your own books and doing the radio show with Bobby Blair."

"My wife is right." Thomas smiled broadly. "You are a fighter, doctor. And we're all fighters here. ... We will never give up, not for a single moment--always having faith that your amazing discoveries will someday magnetize the entire world."

Thirty-Four

Working rapid-fire and around the clock, by this point approaching his mid-70s, over a six-year period Doctor Robbins authored 22 cutting-edge and unique medical books. Each involving natural remedies, the topics ranged from cancer treatments to sleep disorders and the rapid rise of robotics throughout the medical industry.

Some of these self-published books sold more rapidly than others, available at all major online sales venues. Yet none of them came even close to approaching the blockbuster status of Winters' "Upper-Cut," which still lured patients to the Reno clinic.

Sticking to his guns, Shelton had insisted on charging Doctor Robbins the standard and widely accepted industry rate of $35,000 for each book's editing, set-up and placement within the technical realm of "just-in-time publishing." This meant that during a seven-year span the clinic had paid the editor more than $800,000.

These totals concerned Thomas' Aunt Pamela, who continued to serve as the clinic's office manager after more than 40 years with the business.

By this point in her late 60s, on a Tuesday afternoon in early 2015, Pamela asked Doctor Robbins if she could have a brief meeting with him in her office.

"I am afraid, doctor, that it looks like this Shelton guy has been ripping you off," Pamela said. "My analysis, using today's standard 'forensic accounting' methods, indicate that you have only earned about $12,000 on your book sales--a loss of at least $788,000 on your investment."

"I appreciate your admirable efforts and your legitimate concerns, Pamela. ... But Frankly, I do not care about the expenses at all; Duane deserves every penny that he earns from me ... My goal has been to create an enduring legacy, to let the public know that I have made significant medical discoveries ... Even though the mainstream news media ignores my press releases, and national TV news programs, they refuse to put me on the air. At least these books will endure long after I am gone. ... The sad fact remains that due to its left-leaning tendencies, coupled with its close ties to our bloated and corrupt federal government, there is absolutely no chance whatsoever that in my lifetime that the media will ever acknowledge and appreciate my earth-shattering discoveries. Saddest of all, just imagine the tremendous number of people who are still dying of cancer--because they have never heard about me or my effective natural remedies."

*

On April 1, 2016, after nearly eight years of working with Shelton on writing projects, during lunch at the Peppermill, Doctor Robbins revealed his latest decision.

While both of them dined on cobb salads and drank Arnold Palmers, the physician asked Shelton to edit what would undoubtedly become the doctor's last book.

Instead of a medical publication, as explained by the physician, this final publication would be fiction--technically a novel loosely inspired the doctor's real-life story. Loosely based on the actual experiences of Doctor Robbins and many people in his life, the book's final climax phase near the end would give compelling details on his significant medical discoveries.

"Go for it!" Doctor Robbins told Shelton. "Use your imagination, and have fun with the plot. All I ask is that in the end, the character based on me dies of a sudden, massive heart attack--before the world learns of his discoveries. Just as compelling, as you know through the past few decades, many people have compared me with Forrest Gump--a fictional character played in the movies by Tom Hanks; like Forrest, throughout life I have found myself in the midst of earth-shattering situations--always eager and willing to help make the world a better, more loving and safer place."

Rather than behaving like a predictable "yes-man," Shelton

argued that the the novel's plot should feature doctor's significant medical discoveries, which the whole world learns about--once a courageous, talented and determined journalist discovers the truth. Then, although under threat from the mainstream media and running from potential assassins hired by Big Pharma, the journalist--using a name similar to his own--would reveal these sensational discoveries to the entire world.

    Doctor Robbins pushed back at this suggestion, insisting that such a scenario would seem unbelievable. Such a criticism seemed logical, the physician argued, because his many real-life attempts to have journalists expose the truth had proven unsuccessful.

    "Duane, maybe you could end the plot by describing the real-life, recent murders of Homeopaths in the Southeastern United States. I imagine that you have probably seen the news reports. According to at least some news outlets, at least eight practitioners of natural medicines have been slain in Florida alone. ... Have you seen the online articles and blogs, where some observers suggest that perhaps the Food and Drug Administration is behind those murders--trying to scare off Homeopaths?"

    "Yeah. Mighty spooky, huh?"

    "An even better word might be 'creepy.' ... But, yes, I suppose that 'spooky' is right on the money, too ... I would never discount the FDA's ability and willingness to carry out wretched activities, and I would not be shocked to learn that those jerks are murdering good, law-abiding practitioners of natural medicine."

    "But what name should I give to the doctor? And what about his wife? Do you want that character to be drop-dread gorgeous and super-intelligent like Marie, or do you want her to be common-place?"

    "Use your own good judgment, Duane. You realize that Marie has never been overly sensitive to criticism and she is a phenomenal listener, unlike some people who insist on behaving quite the opposite."

    "Well, what about your family members, like your adopted

son Thomas? Do you want me to model the character after him, a high-school drop who--thanks to your help and guidance--before the young man eventually becomes a hard-working and respected doctor in his own right?"

"No, forget about that. Make him a lawyer who eagerly wants to represent my business, a successful attorney who made his own way in life--someone that I truly love, just as much as I cherish Thomas today."

"Okay, but what name should I give the physician?"

Doctor Robbins briefly used a napkin to wipe his mouth. He finally came up with an answer after nearly 20 seconds of careful thought.

"Forsythe ... That's a pretty cool-sounding name ... Call him Doctor James Forsythe, but add a middle initial such as 'W' to give him an even greater sense of mystique."

Thirty-Five

Overjoyed that President Barack Obama had recently left office after completing his second four-year term, Doctor Robbins and Marie drove early on the morning of February 15, 2017, to catch their flight at Reno-Tahoe International Airport.

As planned, Thomas and Shira met them at the American Airlines check-in desk. The younger couple, along with Eric and Elvis--each then in their early 20s--were to travel en masse to Shira's homeland.

Doctor Robbins and his wife had finally agreed to go with them, eager to take their first out-of-country vacation since the mid-1970s.

At first, back on his 78th birthday back in August 2016 when Shira and Marie had first suggested this trip to Doctor Robbins, he immediately responded "No."

The doctor explained that his good buddy, the radio announcer Bobby Blair, had been critically injured in a car wreck the previous week. This man formally called "Cactus Pete" had been driving his retro green 1968 Volkswagen van from Reno's Atlantis Hotel and Casino, turning onto South Virginia Street. At that moment an unmarked Reno police car driven by an off-duty detective, Peter Crichton, zipped through a red light and smashed squarely into the driver's side of Bobby's vehicle.

In five separate statements, witnessed reported that the detective jumped from the police car, while hollering: "I am so very sorry. It was my fault."

An ambulance rushed to the scene, before paramedics zipped the unconscious announcer as quickly as possible to the Sierra Crest Hospital Emergency Room.

While Thomas' Aunt Paula maintained a bedside vigil, 10 days after the wreck, Bobby finally awakened. Traditional drugs administered by conventional doctors failed to get any response. The improvements in his vital signs finally came shortly after the hospital staff began allowing Doctor Robbins to begin administering natural remedies.

The previous week, this older physician finally relented and agreed to go on the vacation to Israel early the following year.

"Thank God, Bobby is finally out of the woods," Doctor Robbins told his relatives. "We almost lost him."

Relenting to the continual requests of his relatives, this senior physician finally agreed during the holiday season of 2016 that he would retire on New Year's Day as 2017 began. With his blessing, Thomas took over leadership chores at the clinic. The younger physician had what his adoptive father considered enough "good sense and smarts" to take and pass a high-end correspondence course in Homeopathy.

Thanks to this designation, Thomas had become fully licensed and qualified to serve as a integrative medical oncologist; this is the same distinction that had enabled his mentor to administer both conventional and non-traditional treatments.

Most important, at least from Doctor Robbins perspective, this transition would enable the clinic to continue administering the unique and effective cancer treatments and immune therapy that he had developed.

To this elder physician's great surprise, lots of of family members had already arrived at the Reno airport to say goodbye--a celebration of this new phase of his life.

They carried signs that said: "We love you, Doctor & Mrs. Robbins! ~ Have fun on your well-deserved vacation!"

Those celebrating included: Pamela with her adult sons--each of them now doctors in residence and her husband, Brad; the late General's surviving adult daughters, now in their 60s--Charlotte, Karen and Christine; Thomas' biological father, Honest, now in his late 80s; Aunt Paula and her husband, the radio announcer Bobby Blair, who had recently been released from the hospital after nearly four months of intensive care; the General's widow, Elizabeth, now aged 103 and riding a wheelchair; the writer and editor Duane Shelton, with his wife Patty, a former "Playboy Magazine" model; and the Reverend Scout Middleton, who had driven alone to Reno from Centralia at age 95 just to say "goodbye."

Tears welled up in Doctor Robbins' eyes--realizing, perhaps more than ever before--that he and Marie were truly loved and adored by these many people.

These friends and relatives waved goodbye up toward them from the airport's ground floor. Doctor Robbins smiled and waved back at them, as he went up an escalator with Marie, Shira and Thomas toward the passenger boarding area.

In that moment, he felt only one regret--that the entire world at large would never know about his significant medical discoveries.

*

Paradoxically, Doctor Robbins felt both exhausted and somewhat energized upon their arrival at La Guardia International Airport in New York City.

They would have a pre-scheduled four-hour layover at this facility, waiting to take their non-stop El Al Airlines flight from the Empire State to Tel Aviv Israel.

Instead of having to sit that entire time in the main passenger terminal, Thomas and Shira revealed that they had arranged a surprise. Along with two personnel from the airline, this younger couple went with Doctor Robbins and Marie to an exclusive VIP lounge--usually reserved only for big-name celebrities.

"We arranged this for you both," Thomas said as they entered. "To us, you are the king and the queen of medicine and of family as well. ... And now, we have a fantastic surprise that we are confident both of you will appreciate--guaranteed."

The airline personnel then closed and secured the doors to this VIP room, with only Doctor Robbins, Thomas, Shira and Marie inside.

"Time for the surprise!" Shira quickly turned on six separate televisions, each already pre-selected to a different channel. "I was instrumental in arranging what you are about to see in actual news reports."

Feeling stunned, excited and speechless--along with Marie, Shira and Thomas--Doctor Robbins watched simultaneous news reports on big-name channels like CNN, Fox News, ABC and the other big networks.

Each reported the arrest of Nevada Senator Larry Spickler on first-degree murder charges, stemming from the 1978 slayings of a rural Nevada sheriff and his two deputies. Totally mesmerized and fully affixed to every word of these in-depth reports, the physician listened carefully to the many other felony charges that a federal grand jury had issued against the senator: conspiracy to defraud the American people, knowingly giving bogus statistics on cancer cases caused by nuclear fallout; illegal insider deals that had sharply increased the value of his own land; working in conjunction with IRS administrators to harass, intimidate and audit numerous conservative political organizations across the United States; and lying under oath to Congress when testifying a few years earlier, saying at the time that he had no close ties to the pharmaceutical industry.

Doctor Robbins jumped and clapped along with his three close relatives, once the magnitude of this breaking story finally became obvious. To this older doctor, the capper--the so-called coup de grâce--finally came when an ABC-TV reporter said: "If convicted in the murders, Senator Spickler would face the possibility of execution by lethal injection, at a federal penitentiary."

Using a remote control, Shira quickly muted the volume on each TV.

"For many years, Doctor Robbins, I have known that this day was finally going to occur. ... Praise God that you are still alive to witness this day."

"I do not know exactly how to respond or what to ask."

Doctor Robbins spoke from the heart, feeling as if in a dream--but knowing full well that all this was actually happening.

"Believe me, doctor, for you the best is yet to come. I am now going to tell you all about this in as much detail as I possibly can."

Shira promptly explained that she had already been working as an operative for the Israeli government when she first moved to Reno in 2000. Her assignment was to peacefully and professionally observe him, because by that point the Jewish homeland had become convinced that he likely would emerge as the world's only doctor to develop a unique and effective protocol for significantly improving the cancer remission rate.

At the time, Shira truly had no idea that she would deeply, madly and inescapably fall in love with Thomas. From that time forward, Shira swore, she had nothing but admirable, honorable and good intentions toward the entire Robbins family. Not even her boys had ever been told the truth about her work for Mossad, the Israeli spy agency.

Then, finally in 2003 just a few months before her wedding with Thomas, the Israeli government had given her permission to break the secret to her future husband and also to Marie. At the time, she said, their intention had been to tell the full truth to Doctor Robbins in the autumn of that year.

But more unexpected advancements in the doctor's research during that period, coupled with updates in Senator Spickler's criminal activities, prevented them from going ahead with that plan.

"Each of us wanted to tell you," Marie stood from her chair in the VIP room, walked 10 yards to her husband's side, and sat beside him. "But, you were in danger, honey--perhaps much more than you might ever realize."

Shira went on to explain that those murders of Homeopaths in Florida actually were carried out by the U.S. CIA, under direct orders from officials at the FDA and also from within the heart of the pharmaceutical industry.

Israeli intelligence had intercepted information that the initial murders had been carried out behind the scenes. During a 10-year span from 2003 to 2013, the federal agents had poisoned to death 78 U.S.-based Homeopaths. Officials targeted only those who were deemed as the biggest threats to Big Pharma and to corrupt American health care industry. A fear among them had emerged, worries based on the fact that more consumers might insist on natural remedies--rather than deadly, expensive and addictive drugs.

"Once my homeland's government became fully cognizant of the scope and breadth of this, doctor, I was assigned to also serve as your full-time bodyguard. ... My homeland made protecting you a top priority. ... As you must realize, at the time you were the world's only physician who was making these vital, cutting-edge advancements. Every step of the way, believe me, I kept my husband and Marie as fully informed as possible ... To their great credit, each of them realized that to tell you what actually was happening would cause an emotional upset--perhaps disrupting or even stopping your admirable and noteworthy efforts to significantly improve cancer treatment."

Shira suddenly stopped talking.

Thomas and Marie seized this as an opportunity to tell Doctor Robbins of their sincerity. Each told him that they were sorry, that telling him might inadvertently cause an "informational leak" that could result in the killings of all of them; and that they had each hoped, prayed and believed that this glorious day of revelations would finally come.

"Wow!" Doctor Robbins kept saying, sucking in a long and deep breath each time this happened. "Wow!"

Momentarily, Shira opened the VIP room doors.

Still affixed to his chair, Doctor Robbins watched as she escorted into the room a curly haired, thin and muscular man in his early 60s. She introduced him as Elijah Horowitz, a former official at the Israeli Embassy to the U.S., who now worked as an internal government communications officer in their homeland.

"Hi, Elijah--long time, no see." Thomas stood and shook the hand of this man, whose face the younger doctor first saw, way back more than a decade earlier when Shira had been chatting with him during middle-of-the-night meetings on Skype.

The younger oncologist and Shira then told Doctor Robbins that Thomas first met Elijah in person in 2008--during one of this official's many Reno excursions.

"Doctor, I realize that all of this has come as a significant surprise to you. So, rather than have me do all of the talking, Elijah has been kind enough to agree to fill you in with all the details ... We're going to have a super celebration when we get to Israel ... Just wait, and see!"

*

Right on schedule at precisely 9:30 in the morning of February 18, 2017, journalists from around the world gathered for an announcement that the Israeli government promised would reveal "the greatest medical discovery in international history ... Cancer patients everywhere are guaranteed to get excited."

A non-stop parade of officials representing Israel's medical industry started off the news conference by welcoming journalists from virtually every network, cable channel, newspaper and online news venue from around the world.

At least 72 TV news cameras recorded every word, as these health care professionals proclaimed that a team of expert researchers had verified the effectiveness of cancer treatments exclusively developed by Doctor James Robbins of Reno, Nevada.

Doctor Abraham Belzer declared that "a whopping" 71 percent of advanced Stage IV cancer patients treated under this maverick physician's care remained free of the disease five years after their treatments.

"Technically, from a medical standpoint, this means that these people have been cured," Belzer said. "This means that on average, about 71 out of every 100 people suffering from advance-stage cancer survive, after being treated by Doctor Robbins.

"Yet to their shame, the mainstream U.S. news media

has ignored this significant story--and in fact, at least one newspaper, the "Reno Globe-Herald," had launched a reckless and inflammatory story about Doctor Robbins more than 10 years ago--intentionally seeking to ruin his once-shining professional reputation."

With James Robbins at his side, Doctor Belzer then revealed that the Israeli government had uncovered corruption deep within the FDA, the U.S. medical industry and Congress. Belzer also promised that at the end of the press conference all journalists present would receive handouts, documents proving the corruption within the United States government and particularly among that nation's elected officials.

"Ooohs" and "ahhs" erupted from among the reporters when Belzer also revealed that it had been the Israeli government, which provided the U.S. Department of Justice with the films and documents leading to the criminal indictments of Nevada Senator Larry Spickler.

"The American people can expect a few dozen more indictments against many of their top elected leaders in the coming weeks and months," Belzer said. "And why, you might ask, have the Israeli officials chosen now to disclose these damning details. Well, the answer should seem simple, at least to anyone who puts just a little thought into the matter. ... Since the Nazi era of the 1930s and 1940s, resulting in the Holocaust--we, the Jewish people--have been increasingly wary of any and all governments that essentially permit their own innocent populations to be used as if mere guinea pigs--discarded and put at risk, as if the people are worthless and expandable. ... Well, the time for such evil behavior to stop is right now ... During the past several years, in private meetings, we have told these details to a handful of well-chosen, hand-picked leaders in the American government--individuals whom we are confident can handle the truth. Understandably, the American people should be up in arms about what their government is doing to them. We, the people of Israel, hope and pray that the United States will remain our strongest and most powerful ally. ... So, naturally, the decision to reveal all of this to you here and now did not come lightly. ... And, now, ladies and gentlemen, I am going to introduce you to Doctor James Robbins."

Hand-in-hand with Marie and Thomas on each side of him--grateful that the whole world was finally watching--spoke of his numerous hopes: that many millions of people each year would now be able to survive cancer, thanks to his new remedies; that the FDA would be dismantled and then reformed, eliminating the agency of "insider corruption;" that the pharmaceutical companies would promptly end their despicable campaign to control and manipulate Congress; that the conventional American medical industry would begin to accept and recommend harmless and effective natural remedies; and that Obamacare be summarily dismantled--replaced by a far better system, without any involvement whatsoever by insurance companies.

"People everywhere, particularly those suffering from cancer, can and should consider this as one of the best days of their lives--now that the truth has finally been told for all to hear. ... Let the word go forth, from this time and from this place, that from now on patients everywhere around the world will demand the end of corruption in the medical industry ... God bless you all!"

Epilogue

The following front-page obituary announcing Doctor Robbins' death appeared in the "Reno Globe-Herald" on September 21, 2020, under the headline "Internationally Acclaimed Reno Physician James Robbins Dies."

"Internationally acclaimed Reno physician James Robbins, recipient of the 2017 Nobel Prize in Medicine, and widely praised for significant discoveries leading to dramatically improved cancer survival rates, died of a sudden heart attack Friday evening in his Reno home. He was 82.

"Doctor Robbins, a native of Detroit, Michigan, and a Vietnam War veteran, became an instant worldwide celebrity in February 2017, when the Israeli government announced his medical discoveries at a packed news conference.

"Two weeks after that press conference, Doctor Robbins, and his immediate family were in a ticker-tape parade through the heart of New York City. An estimated 1.5 million people attended, lining the streets or watching from high above in skyscrapers.

"The same Israeli effort that helped bring Doctor Robbins praise from physicians worldwide also led to the downfall of 19 U.S. senators, including former Nevada Senator Larry Spickler, who had once served as Senate Majority Leader as a Democrat.

"On October 31, 2018, the official 'Nevada Day Holiday,' a jury in federal court convicted Spickler of first-degree murder. Sentenced to death, Spickler, is now on Federal Death Row, awaiting execution in Terra Haute, Indiana.

"The crime was considered a federal case because the slayings had occurred in a wilderness area, overseen by the Bureau of Land Management. Spickler's former chief of staff, Dick Cooper, disappeared in 1999 while on a fishing trip to Lake Tahoe, and federal authorities say that no sign of him has been found.

"An estimated 1.7 million people who suffered from advanced-stage cancer worldwide have gone into remission, after being treated with Doctor Robbins' patented immune therapy process and cancer treatment strategies.

"Bowing to increasingly intense worldwide demand after Israeli officials revealed Doctor Robbins' discoveries in February 2017, conventional physicians worldwide quickly started taking correspondence courses in hopes of becoming Homeopaths.

"Many of these doctors traveled to Reno, to receive intense and in-depth instruction from Doctor Robbins adoptive son, Doctor Thomas Davis--a certified and licensed integrative medical oncologist.

"Financial experts and medical industry analysts in recent months have said that these transitions have virtually transformed the entire pharmaceutical industry. Drug company stocks have plummeted, as increasing numbers of consumers seek far safer and less addictive natural alternatives.

"Last night, upon receiving news of Doctor Robbins' death, Charles Hearst Edwards, executive editor of the "Reno Globe-Herald" issued a public apology that many journalists had been urging him to make for the previous two years.

"In making his apology, Edwards proclaimed that the newspaper regretted its blatant failure' to report positive comments about Doctor Robbins in its expose of 2003. Edwards also admitted that the "Globe-Herald" had dismally failed its readers--and the entire world, for that matter--by intentionally refraining from revealing his amazing medical discoveries, while intentionally trying to damage Doctor Robbins' reputation.

"Funeral arrangements are pending. Family spokesman Duane Shelton, a former "Globe-Herald" reporter and columnist, said that Doctor Robbins had requested to be buried in the Centralia Town Cemetery.

"Doctor Robbins chose that burial site as a symbolic gesture, intended as a symbol to all the world that he deeply loved all of his patients. He will be buried near several of them.

"The physician will be interred next to Thomas' mother, Polly Davis, and his sister, Peggy Davis. Polly, who died at age 32 in late 1974, had been buried with a Christmas holiday nutcracker affectionately named 'Love.' Peggy, who died of cancer at age 4 in early 1975, was buried with a nutcracker named 'Hope.

"At Doctor Robbins request, he will be buried with a nutcracker named 'Faith.'"

About The Authors

James W. Forsythe, M.D., H.M.D., has long been considered one of the most respected physicians in the United States, particularly for his treatment of cancer and the legal use of human growth hormone. In the mid-1960s, Dr. Forsythe graduated with honors from University California at Berkeley and earned his Medical Degree from University of California, San Francisco, before spending two years residency in Pathology at Tripler Army Hospital, Honolulu. After a tour of duty in Vietnam, he returned to San Francisco and completed an internal medicine residency and an oncology fellowship. He is also a world-renowned speaker and author. He has co-authored, been mentioned in and/or written chapters in bestsellers. To name a few: "The Human Genome Playbook for Disrupting Cancer;" "An Alternative Medicine Definitive Guide to Cancer;" "Knockout, Interviews with Doctors who are Curing Cancer" Suzanne Somers' number one bestseller; "The Ultimate Guide To Natural Health, Quick Reference A-Z Directory of Natural Remedies for Diseases and Ailments;" "Anti-Aging Cures;" "The Healing Power of Sleep;" and "Compassionate Oncology ~ What Conventional Cancer Specialists Don't Want You To Know;" and "Obaminable Care," "Complete Pain," "Natural Pain Killers," and "Your Secret to the Fountain of Youth ~ What They Don't Want You to Know About HGH Human Growth Hormone," "Take Control of Your Cancer," "Understanding and Surviving Obamacare," "About Death from a Cancer Doctor's Perspective," "Dr. Forsythe's Whey Protein Anti-Aging Formula," "Emergency Radiation Medical Handbook," "The Human Genome Playbook for Disrupting Cancer," "Medical Robots Are Now Accepting Patients," and "Stoned ~ The Truth About Medical Marijuana and Hemp Oil."

Wayne Rollan Melton has ghost-written many dozens of books, including novels, medical books, biographies, autobiographies, and business publications. A former Editor-on-Loan to "USA Today," Melton serves on the board of directors of a publicly traded international corporation.

Contact Information

Dr. James W. Forsythe, M.D., H.M.D.
Century Wellness Clinic
521 Hammill Lane, Reno, NV 89511-1004
775-827-0707
Website: DrForsythe.com
Email: RenoWellnessDr @ yahoo.com